S.S. Huber

The Dragon's Eye Crystal

Bernadine D. Morris

S.S. Huber
The Dragon's Eye Crystal

By Bernadine D. Morris

Copyright © 2015 Bernadine D. Morris
Published in 2016 - Chilliwack, British Columbia.

Library and Archives Canada Cataloguing in Publications
S.S. Huber - The Dragon's Eye Crystal/Bernadine D. Morris

ISBN 978-0-9948237-0-0

Cover design and illustration © Aaron Parrott 2016
Spoon Lake photo © Bernadine D. Morris
Mount Cheam photo © Kevin James Morris collection
Author Photograph © Don R Young

1.   Fantasy   2.   Science Fiction

Printed by CreateSpace, an Amazon.com company
Available on Kindle and other retail outlets

UNITREE

For my family,
Ken,
Kevin, Lindsay and Kimberly

In loving memory of our son Kevin.

Acknowledgments

My sincere appreciation goes to the following people.

To my husband Ken, whose steadfast love and support have encouraged me throughout the years. Thank you for your patience and understanding. Your common sense and steady ways are beyond measure.

To my three fantastic children, Kevin, Lindsay and Kimberly. In your own unique ways you have been, and will continue to be my source of inspiration. Thank you for your strength and support, especially most recently.

For my son Kevin, who lost his battle to brain cancer on September 18, 2016. We miss your bright light and sunshine smile every day. This book is dedicated to you.

To my two grandchildren, Joshua and Venice; your youthful energy embodies the circle of life.

I am extremely grateful to Aaron Parrott for his artistic flair and for his imaginative visualization of the cover design. With my deepest gratitude, thank you Aaron.

My sincere appreciation goes to Rita Gockener of Alstatte, DE for her assistance in editing German phrasing used in the narrative and to Benni, who let me use his name in the story.

Many thanks to Gill Grigor for her editing skills, fine eye for detail and years of friendship. I am most sincerely grateful.

I am deeply indebted to Margaret Evans, at Earthways Media Ltd., whose copyediting skills, invaluable suggestions and experience have helped facilitate this journey of discovery. Thank you Margaret for your candid encouragement and support in birthing this novel. You have my sincere gratitude.

Å

Preface

Spoon Lake, inspired this story. It nestles in the bowl between Mount Cheam and Lady Peak in the Fraser Valley. Information about Mount Cheam can be found on the internet. Visit
the area on-line or in person. You will fall in love with the
beauty of it all!

© Bernadine D. Morris

© Kevin James Morris

Contents

CHAPTER ONE
Spoon Lake

✧

The steel fist of a jackhammer slammed into the pavement at the Thomas Road intersection. Hamish shouted over the deafening roar. "Hey Syb. What are ya' reading?"

Cupping her hand behind her ear, she yelled back, "Can't hear you."

As the vehicle they were riding in accelerated through the green light, he reached across and flipped over the cover of the book she was holding.

"I said, what are you reading? Hmm, Edible Plants of the Pacific Northwest. Hah! You gonna' get lost on the hike?" snorted Hamish, jabbing her in the ribs. He picked up the book lying on the seat beside her and thumbed through it. "A Brief History of Time! Wo-a-ah! Some heavy readin', Syb."

"No, I won't get lost. And yes, I love this space stuff. It's interesting," replied Sybil, closing her book. "You know they're planning to send people to Mars? Imagine that!"

As they passed the shops in Vedder Village, her attention was drawn to the store fronts whizzing by. At the Keith Wilson intersection the war memorial came into view.

"Hey guys, there used to be an old tank here on the corner," cried Hamish.

"A real tank?" asked Marc.

"Yeah. Dad was military. He helped move it. Said it was a WWII tank called Caroline."

"Way before our time!" said Marc.

"Man, I'd love to explore that thing."

"No way! Could be an old ghost in it. Might grab you and haul you inside," teased Sybil.

"Hah! I don't believe in ghosts," he scoffed. "Ever seen one?"

"Just 'cause you can't see it doesn't mean it isn't there," interrupted Marc, who was sitting beside him. "I've heard a lot of strange stories in my family."

"Your family *is* strange," said Hamish, punching him playfully in the arm.

Thinking about the tank, Sybil's mood turned serious. "There'd be a lot of ghosts if you counted the dead in all those wars. Such a waste! Didn't solve anything."

She was an idealist, sensitive to the problems of the world. Disturbing newspaper headlines and gruesome television reports fed into her worries. There were days when Sybil felt overwhelmed by it all. At those times she ventured into the surrounding forests to experience the healing power of the wilderness.

"Well it's not *that* simple," said Hamish. "Read a history book Sybil Huber! There's always been war."

"I know that," shot back Sybil.

She could feel her anxiety level kick up a notch. Life at school was not always easy for her. How was *that* bullying any different than what caused wars? Didn't it always begin with people?

"What about all that conflict resolution and problem solving stuff we learn about at school? I don't see any difference it makes anywhere in the world."

"Oh here we go again, Miss Goody-two-shoes," groaned Hamish, rolling his eyes. "Not another lecture on politics in the playground."

This topic always inflamed her. Now Hamish's name calling got the best of her. "What's wrong with trying to better the world?" she retaliated. "Call a spade, a spade! That's what my dad always says."

"Yeah? Well my dad's been there. Afghanistan you know."

"All right, all right, quit squabbling you guys," interrupted Marc. He could see their conversation going sideways and tried to head it off.

"Problem solve yourselves already!"

His mop of wavy hair fell forward as he doubled over and covered his ears. The three friends had grown up in the same neighbourhood and he'd listened to these arguments so many times. It was driving him crazy.

He wrinkled his freckled nose and glared at Sybil. "Why don't *you* do something about it?" he challenged.

"We could begin by talking about it at least!" snapped Sybil.

"Yeah, what good does all this talk do?" he countered.

"I suppose," ventured Sybil. "But if you're so smart Mr. Know-it-all, maybe you can figure it out." Throwing her hands up in the air, she gave up.

"Okay, okay! I'll drop the subject," said Sybil, visibly an-noyed.

No use in spoiling the trip by getting into a testy discussion they'd had so many times before. Her friends didn't seem to care. Disgruntled, she kept her thoughts to herself. If we can't solve fights in the schoolyard how can we find world peace, or for that matter, differences between friends?

Sybil glanced over at Hamish, still miffed. She liked to weigh things carefully before she jumped in. Hamish, on the other hand, was always in some sort of predicament.

On the last field trip to Cheam Wetlands he was horsing around and fell in the water. It was a soggy ride home and the teacher was some annoyed. He just couldn't seem to be still. He was always on the move. The time before that, he nearly ended up in the feeding pools at the fish hatchery. Luckily, she yanked him to safety just in time.

The worst was his careless use of firecrackers. One Hallowe'en he set fire to his parents' hedge! The fire truck had to come out. Accident or not, it was dangerous. She had to admit, there were times she disliked his reckless ways.

"Crazy fool!" she muttered under her breath.

"What did you say?" asked Hamish. "Did you just call me a crazy fool?"

"You must admit Hamish, you do get into a lot of hot water. You jump in without thinking," she reminded.

"Yeah, well not everybody can be as logical as you, Sybil Huber," Hamish countered. Her words stung because they were partly true.

Seeing the hurt look on his face, she softened her tone. "Sorry Hamish, you know how I feel when we talk about these things and you won't listen. It gets my back up."

"Yeah, I guess."

Silence opened between them while he sat brooding over her comment. His restless fingers fidgeted with the knot on his shoelace. He stole a glance at her, hating the rift that had opened between them. Her friendship was more important than he cared to admit. Tentatively, he extended his fist. "Still friends Syb?"

Hesitating a moment, she relented and lightly tapped it in a conciliatory fist bump as she locked onto his steely blue eyes. Annoying as he could be, she liked his handsome face and the way his mass of curly brown hair hooded his angular, tanned cheekbones. Their common love of the outdoors was the magnet that cemented their friendship. In spite of their differences, these moods didn't last long.

The hurt in his eyes softened and he gave her a forgiving smile. It widened into a grin, the wrinkles deepening permanent laugh lines at the corners of his eyes.

"Friends," she affirmed. "But sometimes we need to talk about things seriously, Hamish."

"Yeah, I know. But we're on a field trip. I just want some fun. No harping on about war and crime rates. Bullies in the schoolyard? What's that got to do with it?" he retorted.

Sorry that she had opened this can of worms again, she held her tongue and let the conversation slide. Hamish McCrory was the boy next door—well two doors over actually. They had played together in their backyards from the time their moms had arranged their first playdate. Marc Leesom's family had moved in across the street the following year. He fit in easily and the three of them spent hours constructing cardboard forts, ploughing through mud puddles and following their wild imaginations into realms of fantasy.

On the first day of kindergarten, the three of them had walked together with their moms and now they were in grade eight at Vedder Middle School. Since their birthdays fell within a few days of each other, there was always a party to attend. Their first teen year was a milestone and July was barbecue weather, so they had decided on a joint birthday bash, held in Sybil's backyard.

As they grew older, the hours spent playing outside in the sunshine led naturally into outdoor sporting activities. Sybil and Hamish became members of the Explorers club. Marc was keenly aware of the fun he was missing when they discussed hiking, kayaking and camping adventures.

After pestering his parents, they finally relented, allowing him to join. Their families soon became good friends, sharing carpool duties and fundraising for the club. Reflecting on all those years, Sybil recalled the numerous times she'd bailed

Hamish out of trouble. Whatever tiffs they had, he was still her best bud. He would always be there if she needed him. It took years to grow a friend like that.

Letting her anger subside, she relaxed against the seat in thought. As she bent over her backpack, she flipped her long dark hair over her shoulder. Pulling out a forestry map, she unfolded it and traced her finger along the Chipmunk Forest Service Road to Mount Cheam. She was eager to identify the many peaks surrounding the Fraser Valley from the top. Marc looked over her shoulder, following her finger along the route.

"I can't wait!" exclaimed Marc, devouring the map. "You and Sybil have been to Mount Cheam before, haven't you?"

"Yeah, two years ago. Before you joined we went with Explorers Club," replied Hamish, craning his neck to look out the window. "Sure glad Mr. Jacques decided to take our class on this trip."

"Me too," grinned Marc. "Best part is camping overnight!"

Arranging the transportation for thirty-five people was a challenge. If the Explorers club hadn't offered the use of their big SUVs, the field trip would not have gone ahead.

"Good thing Mr. Jacques has friends in Explorers club," said Sybil. "They even supplied the drivers."

"Most of 'em are parents of kids in our class anyway," added Hamish. "That valley below Mount Cheam and Lady Peak. Wow! Wait 'til you see it Marc!"

"I'm stoked!" Marc's easygoing nature softened tensions. His quirky grin lit up his whole face, stirring an infectious ripple of laughter in those around him.

"Hey guys, hear the news yesterday?" he said. "Another sighting of Bigfoot near Hope!"

"Come on. You don't actually believe in Sasquatch, do ya?" Hamish snorted.

"Why not? Been lots of sightings over the years. In fact, Dad saw something weird out there when he was hunting," replied Marc.

"Oh yeah? All that malarkey got started when they found gold at Barkerville. Americans stampeded up from California hopin' to strike it rich. Course people from other countries came too."

"What's that got to do with Bigfoot?" retorted Marc.

"Story goes that some guys in the gold rush tried using camels to pack their gear. Hah! Poor horses and mules. Got so spooked they ran off. Some of 'em even ran over the cliffs 'cause they got so scared!"

"That's baloney," said Marc.

"No. Honest. It's true. Camels didn't work though. Feet got torn to ribbons on the rocks. They're used to soft sand in deserts. So, d'ya know what they did? Turned 'em loose in the wilderness. Couldn't bring 'em all the way back now, could they?"

"You're kidding! They actually had camels in our province?"

"Yeah Marc. It's true. Dad thinks the Bigfoot story came from those loose camels wandering in the forests."

"Ha, that's too funny," laughed Marc.

"Not so funny for the camels," interrupted Sybil. "Poor things!"

"Well, all I'm saying is, camels could look like Bigfoot. Smelly, hairy beasts. Don't ya think?"

"Could be," agreed Marc. "But you think someone would 'a caught one by now. No, I still think Bigfoot is really out there."

"Keep an eye out for him Marc. You might run into him up on Mount Cheam!" laughed Hamish.

The convoy of vehicles followed Chilliwack Lake Road, then turned off the pavement onto the gravel of Chipmunk Creek Road, jostling the passengers as they bounced over the rough roadbed. Then they began the slow ascent of the serpentine logging road that would lead them to the parking area at the trail head.

Hamish sat on the edge of his seat, bursting with the energy that powered his restless nature. Determined to be the first one to the top, his lean body, always ready for adventure, resembled that of a runner at the starting line.

Gaining altitude, the 4WD wound its way carefully along the switchbacks. "Hang on guys," cautioned Sybil, as it tilted precariously, maneuvering its way through the deep gouges in the access road.

"Why did they cut the ditches so deep?" groaned Marc, white knuckling the seat in front of him.

"They don't call this rainbow country for nothing!" laughed Hamish.

The British Columbia coast was actually a rainforest. Because Chilliwack was nestled close to the mountains in the Upper Fraser Valley, weather systems stalled overhead. They dumped a lot of rain in the area before lifting and moving on.

"If it wasn't for those drainage ditches, the road would wash out," explained Sybil.

"All this up and down, I'm getting car sick!" moaned Marc, his face turning a pale shade of green.

"We're nearly there. Try looking out the window. Take some deep breaths," advised Sybil.

Halfway through the next ditch Marc gave a dry heave. "I'm gonna be sick!" he groaned, frantically.

"Here, take this," replied Sybil, handing him a plastic bag from her back pack.

Marc opened the bag and buried his face in it. An explosive ejection wrenched through him as he expelled his breakfast.

"E-e-e-w-w-w!" cried one of the students from the seat in front of him. "Gross!"

"Sh-h-h," said Sybil. "It can't be helped." Reassuring her friend, she gave him an understanding smile.

Dry heaving, he wiped his mouth with a tissue she passed him.

"Oh boy! Sorry guys," he said, embarrassed by the situation. Self-consciously, he rolled down the window for some fresh air.

"No worries buddy," reassured Hamish. "Tie that bag in a knot and we'll toss it in the parking lot outhouse."

Marc gave him a grateful look, took a long deep breath and concentrated on the scenery outside. "Feeling better now," he said.

Their excitement began to build as they neared the parking area. Coming to a halt, the driver asked everyone to remain seated until the other vehicles joined them. Once they were assembled, the organizing teacher, Mr. Jacques, gathered the group to give instructions.

"Okay! Listen up everyone. Make sure you take all your belongings. These vehicles are leaving. They'll come back for us tomorrow afternoon, so don't leave anything behind."

"Hey, Syb. Don't forget your map," teased Hamish.

"We're setting up camp in the meadow first. Once that's done, we'll start the hike," Mr. Jacques continued.

After reinforcing instructions concerning camp rules and safety issues, there was a flurry of activity as the occupants unloaded their supplies. Soon, a mountain of equipment was deposited on the gravelled surface of the parking area. Shouldering their packs, each person picked up an item of gear and trudged up the trail toward the meadow ahead.

"What did I tell you Marc? How beautiful is that!" said Hamish, spreading his arms wide, as he scanned the valley nestled below Lady Peak and Mount Cheam.

On this September morning, it was a glorious panorama, filled with the perfume of alpine flowers and verdant sweetness of meadow grasses. The sun had risen above the range of peaks to the east, scattering spirit shadows that hid in the recesses of rock ledges.

"Pretty awesome all right!" agreed Marc.

The well-worn trail invited the eager feet of the three friends as they crossed a narrow foot bridge. A gurgling stream winked brightly in the morning sun. Suddenly, a faint apparition slid under the bridge and the flow of water seemed to hesitate a moment. Sybil had caught the imperceptible difference out of the corner of her eye, or perhaps it was her intuitive sense that warned her of a hidden presence. She had what ancient folklore referred to as the inner eye. A gift, some called it, but to Sybil it was unsettling. She peered intently into the water, shivered, and slowly moved on, trying to dismiss the eerie feeling of being watched.

"Hurry up Sybil," cried Hamish impatiently, turning back to gaze down the path at his two friends who seemed to be suspended in time on the footbridge. "You're holding everyone up."

"We're coming," retorted Sybil. "Don't get your shirt in a knot!"

She adjusted her pack and hoisted the camp stove higher on her shoulder, as she edged around a grassy knoll. Ahead was the beginning of the open field where they intended to set up camp. Mr. Jacques began organizing the students into groups to help with pitching tents, while others erected tarps and set up the cooking area.

Many of the students were members of Explorers club and were pretty efficient when it came to setting up camp. Had the student population been inexperienced in wilderness activities it was doubtful Mr. Jacques would have even considered this trip. Marc was busy helping Hamish peg down tents when Sybil ambled over.

"Hey, aren't you two finished yet?" she called. "Hurry up, let's go."

Marc and Hamish stood up and studied their friend's excited face.

"What's up?" asked Marc.

"When Hamish and I were here two years ago we wondered about it. Tell us what *you* think Marc."

They dropped the rocks they were using as hammers and followed her loping stride. Two hundred metres to the east lay a symmetrical lake about the size of a basketball court. One could hardly call it a lake, but there it was, almost perfectly round. The shimmering sphere reflected the blue glory of the September sky as the friends gazed into its depths.

"What on earth d'ya suppose made that?" Marc wondered aloud. "The ground is all heaped up on one side."

"Hamish thinks a mudslide coming off Lady Peak caused it. What do you think Marc?" asked Sybil, as she knelt to ripple the surface.

"It's like a missile hit here," suggested Marc, excited by the prospect. "Maybe it was a meteorite!"

"Whatever it was, it's strange," agreed Sybil. "Why is it always filled with water? There's no stream feeding it."

"Maybe an underground spring," suggested Marc, peering into the reflective surface.

Beside him appeared a grinning face. "After the hike we'll go for a dip," challenged Hamish. "Say no, and you'll have to carry my pack down the hill tomorrow."

"Good way to cool off," agreed Sybil, as she studied their reflections.

She was fond of her two friends and enjoyed most of their crazy antics. Although she did not always agree, this time she could imagine how good her tired muscles would feel after a swim.

11

A sudden breeze stirred the surface of the water and their reflections disappeared in a maze of dancing ripples. She pulled out her forestry map, anxious to get started on the trail. She let out a whoop.

"It's here on the map! Spoon Lake. Good name! Looks like someone scooped it out with a giant spoon."

Marc glanced at the field behind them. "Looks like camp is ready. Maybe we'll leave soon. Let's go see what's up."

As they rejoined the group, Mr. Jacques called out, "Okay, gather around. Good job on the campsite guys. Before we leave, everyone choose a buddy. Stay together and watch out for each other. Mrs. Abbot will follow at the end to make sure everybody's okay. Anyone have any questions?"

"Yeah, when's lunch?" Hamish asked.

"We'll eat at the top," replied Mr. Jacques. "One more thing. We'll check out the view in the saddle area before we go up Mount Cheam, so stick together."

"What's the saddle he's talking about?" asked Marc.

"Wait 'til you see it!" laughed Hamish. "It'll curl your toes. It's between Lady Peak and Mount Cheam. Where they join. Looks like a saddle between 'em. You get a bird's-eye view!"

"Lady Peak is a sheer cliff on that side. Straight drop over there!" added Sybil.

"Any more questions?" asked Mr. Jacques.

The students looked at each other. "Let's just get started already," mumbled Hamish.

"No?" concluded Mr. Jacques. "Okay, ready then? Grab your daypacks and let's head out."

The group fell in line and started off at a brisk pace. Hamish, true to form, was in the lead, his face opening into a wide grin. He yelled to his friend.

"Beat you to the top, Marc!" The two boys raced ahead.

"Not so fast you two," called Mr. Jacques. "Sorry guys. Everyone needs to stay behind me."

They stopped on the trail grumbling under their breath, waiting until Mr. Jacques pulled ahead.

"We'll get there soon enough guys," he soothed, remembering his own youthful restless energy.

Sybil pressed forward steadily, pacing herself. It was a long way up and she wanted to conserve energy for the final push at the top. Along the way, scrubby, low-growing blueberries provided welcome fuel to the passing hikers. Munching ravenously, their mouths and hands stained a deep purple. Lady Peak loomed to their right as they traversed her skirts. Although it was mid-September, small patches of snow still lay in shady crevices.

Once they had passed the Lady's flanks and explored the saddle area, their ascent of Mount Cheam began. Along the way, boulders offered resting spots for the weary group as they paused to catch their breath. It was at one of these stops that Mr. Jacques cautioned them again.

"Careful when we reach the top. Don't get too close to the edge. If you want pictures please wait for me, Mrs. Abbot or one of the parents."

"Mr. Jacques seems pretty nervous about this hike. Ever heard the story about his friend?" Sybil asked in a subdued voice.

"Heard he didn't hike for over a year after that," whispered Hamish.

"What story?" asked Marc.

"Two years ago. He was with his buddy on Mt. Slesse. Probably trying to get to the cairn area," explained Sybil, quietly.

"Cairn? What are you talking about?"

"Long time ago a plane crashed. Fifty-four people aboard. The crash site was too steep. Couldn't recover anyone, so now it's a memorial site."

"Some of 'em were from a Vancouver football team," added Hamish.

"Pretty awful about his friend. The story I heard was that they were crossing a steep grade. Rocks were still frosted over. Gone in seconds," recounted Sybil.

"Poor Mr. Jacques," said Marc, thinking how terrible it would be to see his best friend fall.

"Both were experienced climbers," added Hamish. "Could have been him, if he'd been in the lead."

"Anything can happen in the mountains," replied Sybil.

"Yeah, step on loose rocks or slippery moss and it is game over." Hamish's voice grew sharp, remembering his own experience.

"Watch yourself at the top this time, Hamish. You got pretty close to the edge two years ago," warned Sybil.

"Nah, I'll be fine, Syb. I never make the same mistake twice."

Sybil recoiled at the thought of it. Mount Cheam dropped away in a steep cliff formation to the valley floor, over two-thousand metres below. Her hair stood on end and the base of her neck prickled, as she imagined the wild fall over the edge. Thinking of all the scrapes he'd been in, she promised herself to keep an eye on him. Sometimes his recklessness scared her.

After endless switch backs, the last grind to the top was over loose shale, barren and windswept. Just above, was the knob of the summit framed against the backdrop of clear blue sky. They approached the final assent with extraordinary caution.

"Wh-h-e-e-w," whistled Marc, creeping forward on all fours to look over the edge. "Long way down!" The dizzying height kept them crouching low on the rocky outcrop that fell away into thin air.

Hamish tossed a pebble over the edge and watched it plunge downward, disappearing in a haze of green. It ricocheted off the rock faces to meet the tree line far below.

"Some drop!" he whistled, then stood up suddenly to get a better look.

"Stay down," warned Sybil. "It's too dangerous to be standing so close."

"Don't worry, Syb. I'm fine," protested Hamish. "Come on, try it. Stand up slowly."

He extended his hand to her. Gathering courage, Sybil reached for it and felt the muscles contract in her thighs, as she unfolded her wobbling legs.

"What a view!" breathed Sybil. "Hey, it's not so bad. Come on Marc."

Slowly, Marc stood up, and joined his two friends scanning the valley. A breathtaking vista spread from horizon to horizon.

"There's Mt. Baker," said Sybil, pointing at the largest snowy peak to the south. "You know it's a dormant volcano?"

"A volcano?" asked Marc.

"Yeah. Don't know how dormant though. I Googled it. Last eruption was 1843 and in 1975 it actually vented steam! You know, small. Nothing big. Still it's a little worrying."

"Awesome! We'd get lots of ash in Chilliwack if it ever blew!" exclaimed Marc.

"I don't want 'a be around for that!" cried Hamish.

"Sun's high. Must be almost noon," said Sybil, shielding her eyes against the brilliant disk overhead. She hauled in a deep breath. "Amazing how pure the air is up here!"

"And look at the smog down there!" replied Hamish, faking a hacking cough. "Gross!"

Far below, a dense murky blanket smudged the view of the city on the valley floor. Chilliwack lay hidden somewhere in the suffocating density.

"We live in that stuff," groaned Marc. "What a mess!"

Sybil studied the scene for a few moments. A prickle of fear rose up her spine and crawled across her scalp. An odd movement in the top of the smoggy roof caught her attention. It seemed to her as if a hand was snaking its way upward. Long wispy fingers wove through the tree line and around rocky bluffs. Skyward it slithered, until it neared the edge.

"Ei-i-e-e-gh!!" shrieked Sybil. She stumbled backward, falling into the loose shale. "Let's get out of here," she wailed.

Her friends were at a loss. What was wrong with her? She looked as though she had seen a ghost!

"Sybil, what happened? Are you hurt?" shouted Hamish.

"No-o-o, I…" Sybil said, forcing a fake smile. She recovered her composure and shook off the attention she had attracted. "It's nothing. Just a wasp," she giggled nervously. "I hate wasps. They give me the heebie-jeebies."

"For Pete's sake, Sybil," scolded Marc. "You scared us half to death. Let's find a place for lunch. I'm starved."

The students scrambled down the slope a few metres and scattered into groups on rocky ledges, diving into their lunches with gusto. The excitement caused by her startling drama was all but forgotten. But Sybil remained deeply concerned and apprehensive by what she had experienced.

After returning to the crest of the summit to snap photos Hamish and Marc walked downhill to where Sybil was standing with a group of classmates. They arrived just in time to hear the taunting voice of Wesley Peters.

"You're a freak Sybil. Loser!" he jeered.

It was during these times that her chest burned angrily, a raw open wound of discomfort. She drew a deep breath and looked him straight in the eye.

"Leave me alone, Wesley."

"Hey! Stop that!" yelled Hamish, coming up to Sybil. "Get lost, Wesley!"

"Stay out'a this McRoar, you wuss. More like McMe-e-ow. Here puss, puss."

Wesley knew how to push his buttons. He hated being called that. His fists hardened into balls and he stood his ground. Wesley advanced with clenched fists and glared into his face. Standing toe to toe, his black wiry hair brushed Hamish's forehead. The group surrounding them stepped back. The angry scowl etched on Wesley's face meant a fight was about to erupt.

"Meee-eowww," goaded Wesley's buddy, Alex. "Hamish has a girlfriend. Hamish has a girlfriend."

Alex enjoyed this feeling of power when he was with Wesley. They were bullies and together they made life miserable for many of the students at school.

"Step back Wesley."

His face distorted into an ugly sneer. "Make me."

Sybil intervened, with a placatory gesture. "No problem Hamish, let it go. It's not worth the trouble."

"Yeah, wimp," Alex needled. "Go on, let your girlfriend fight for you."

"All right!" demanded Mr. Jacques. "What's going on here?"

"Oh, nothing really," replied Sybil. "We're okay."

She did not want any more trouble with Wesley or Alex. If she wanted to live the rest of the school year in peace, the best thing to do was not get them into trouble.

Mr. Jacques eyed them thoughtfully, then said, "All right guys, but it's time we head back to camp. Listen up everyone. Gather up any garbage before we head downhill. Make sure nothing is left behind."

It was sheer relief to run down the slopes after the brush with Wesley. Adrenalin-pumped, Hamish sped on ahead leaving his two friends to a steadier pace. Approaching Wesley and Alex from behind, they caught snatches of their conversation.

"My feet are killing me," whined Alex.

"Oh you big wimp," sneered Wesley.

"But it's a long way down and my knees hurt," he griped.

"Get a grip on it Alex, it's not much farther. Sit down and catch your breath. I'll wait for you."

Alex plunked down on a grassy tuft, puffing hard from the gruelling work out. Propping his feet on a boulder, he wiped the sweat off his forehead with his arm. "Oh man, I'm beat."

"Hey guys, we're nearly there," encouraged Sybil, trying to build a little rapport.

"Get lost you freak!" snarled Wesley, shoving his foot out to trip her.

Anticipating his usual nastiness, she nimbly hopped over.

"No need to be so snarky Wesley," replied Sybil, turning to confront him.

"Forget it Sybil, those two don't listen to reason," muttered Marc. He tugged on her arm and they continued down the trail.

"You're wastin' your time."

Sybil poked him in the back. "You may be right Marc, but wasn't it you on the way up here this morning, who said to do something about it?"

He stopped mid-trail, swung around and studied Sybil's flushed face. "Yeah, you're right. I did. But I don't think being nice to Wesley is going to work. He's too far gone."

"Nonsense," replied Sybil, ever the optimist. "You can't give up on people. Who knows what has happened in his life. Maybe a little kindness will do some good."

"Well, nothing seems to have worked so far," said Marc. "He's a nasty piece of work."

Hamish had slowed his pace, allowing his friends to catch up. "That Wesley Peters sure thinks he's something."

"We were just discussing him," replied Sybil. "Marc here, thinks there's no hope for the guy. Maybe he's right. I've tried being nice to him, but he's so mean."

"I'd like to see him get what he deserves one day," added Marc. "And just what did happen to you at the top Sybil? You're not afraid of wasps!"

"Oh that," whispered Sybil. "I've had this creepy feeling ever since we crossed the stream before we set up camp. You know me, it's not so much seeing, as knowing something's about to happen."

"Yeah," Hamish replied. "You do have a knack for guessing things. It's uncanny. How d'you do that? If we knew, we could bottle it and make a fortune," he laughed.

"It's not funny Hamish. I get really scared sometimes. So quit teasing me. You know about some of the things that have happened."

"Ah-h Syb, don't be mad, I'm only joking," said Hamish, laying his hand on her shoulder and giving it a little squeeze. "Truth is, I wish I could do that."

"Yeah," said Marc. "Imagine knowing something will happen before it actually does. You really have an advantage over us mere mortals," he sighed, looking to the heavens in mock despair. Seeing the concern on her face, he reassured, "Seriously Sybil, we've got your back. You know that, don't you?"

"Sure," replied Sybil. "Thanks guys."

When they were nearing base camp, the three of them broke into a run.

"Last one in has to scrub camp pots tonight!" yelled Hamish.

They dashed to their tents in search of bathing suits. After a frantic scramble, they emerged, squealing with excitement and running headlong over the meadow.

"O-o-w-w-w!" howled Hamish, as he tripped on a root and fell, leaving Sybil and Marc in the lead. Two great splashes signalled triumph over their friend.

"Ha, ha, Hamish, we beat you!" laughed Marc. A moment later, Hamish dove into the lake beside his friends, enjoying their good-natured ribbing.

"Feels great!" cried Hamish. "Don't even mind scrubbing pots after this."

They swam lengths back and forth across the breadth of the lake. While relaxing and floating on their backs, a cold wind swept the surface depositing ice crystals on their hair. Sybil's eyes grew large. The faces of her two companions became obscured by a frosty mist that settled over the water.

"Br-r-r-r. It's cold," shivered Sybil. "Let's get out of here."

Chilled to the bone, they swam quickly to shore and clambered up the bank, wrapping themselves in thick beach towels. Back at the tents they dried off and dressed in warm clothes, dismissing the strange occurrence.

While contributing to dinner preparations, Sybil mulled over the earlier events of the day. She'd had these premonitions before and was determined not to let it ruin the rest of her trip. Seeking out Mr. Jacques, she found him supervising a group and joined in.

"First, you wrap a layer of foil around your dinner. Then cover it in a couple of sheets of wet newsprint. Last, you follow up with an outer layer of foil," instructed Mr. Jacques. "Now they're ready to go in the coals," he said, shovelling a layer over the dinner packets.

Lost in thought, Sybil stood watching the embers, listening to them sizzle and pop. Soon, delicious aromas escaped the steaming bundles hidden under the coals.

"They should be ready," said Mr. Jacques. "Sybil, grab that shovel please and pull 'em out."

He handed out the dinners. Gingerly peeling back the charred foil and blowing on their fingertips, they settled in quietly, too hungry and tired for conversation.

"Ah-h-h-h, man that was s-o-o good," sighed Marc, wiping his mouth on his sleeve. "What's for dessert? Oh boy, I love s'mores!" he cried, when he spied the bag of marshmallows and chocolate bars.

Stuffing marshmallows on roasting sticks they held them over the glowing charcoals. Hamish blew out his flaming fireball as his marshmallow went up in smoke.

"Slowly, Hamish. Hold your stick away from the heat. Let it roast gently," advised Sybil.

"Oh, don't be so bossy," he countered. "A little charring is good, puts hair on my chest."

He sandwiched the blackened goo between two graham crackers, letting the hot marshmallow melt the piece of chocolate. Then he bit off an edge carefully, trying not to burn his tongue. Downing the last morsel he licked his fingers clean with a contented sigh.

"Nothin' better than that to finish a cookout."

Lying back on the grassy knoll, they relaxed in front of the campfire, exhausted after the day's exertion. "I am so-o stuffed," moaned Hamish, gazing up at the stars winking in the inky blackness.

"Me-e too. Oh-h-h—think I'm gonna' be sick," groaned Marc, holding his stomach.

"Serves you right. That's what you get for pigging out," chided Sybil.

"But it was so good! Couldn't help myself," replied Hamish.

"I'm whacked. Come on Hamish, let's hit the sack," yawned Marc. "See you in the morning guys."

The party dwindled as individuals drifted off to their tents. Sybil stayed on to watch the dying embers of the fire, making sure the ashes were cold before she too turned in. Only the stars kept watch, drifting in the black sea above.

A swishing sound rippled the tent where Sybil lay drifting on the edge of sleep. Startled into awareness, her heart raced thunderously in her chest. Again she heard it, this time close to her right ear.

"Hey Syb," an urgent whisper, followed by a giggle, stifled Sybil's nervous alarm. "We're going for a midnight swim, wanna' come?" Hamish's mischievous snort exploded in the still night air.

"Sh-h-h-h, you'll have the whole camp awake, you dope," warned Marc. "Hurry up Sybil. Get your bathing suit on."

As much as Sybil wanted to stay in her warm sleeping bag, she also wanted to join her friends. Throwing caution aside, she slipped quickly into her swimsuit, wrapped herself in a thick terry towel and crept out into the moonlight. Silvery radiance bathed the valley floor.

The moon had risen over the shoulder of Lady Peak and was peering into her slumbering face. Beneath her, the pool of water lay silent. Hurrying over the meadow, the three friends neared the water's edge and in a moment were submerged in the silvery liquid. After crossing the width of the lake a few times, they lay on their backs floating out toward the middle.

Suddenly, a low rumble shook the valley. The water rippled in reply. A warm current tickled their toes and spread upward enveloping their shivering bodies.

"It's like a hot tub," giggled Hamish. "Wow, this feels awesome!"

"Hey you, sink or swim!" teased Marc, ducking Hamish's head under. The two boys played water tag back and forth across the pool until Hamish scuttled out of the water onto the far shore.

"Hey guys, get over here. I want you to see this!" he called in a hoarse whisper.

"It's too cold out there. You go. I'm staying here where it's warm," protested Sybil.

Marc swam to the far side leaving Sybil to enjoy the warmth. Steam rose around her while she relaxed in the soothing liquid.

The moon was hidden in shadow as a lone cloud drifted slowly across its face. Suddenly, a burbling sound broke the night air, accompanied by an eerie hollow moan. A slow, steady tremor spread across the valley, shaking the ground in undulating waves. The rumble grew and the earth rocked in violent spasms. The water began to roil. Foam gathered in the center and hissing spray spun past Sybil's ears.

"E-e-e-a-ah! Help! Help me!" shrieked Sybil. She started to spin in the whirlpool that was gaining speed.

"Sybil! Sybil, hang on!" shouted the boys.

Hamish searched the shore frantically. There, a long tree branch. That would work! He grabbed the thick end and reached out over the tumult engulfing his friend. Round and round she spun.

"Grab the end Syb!" cried Marc, while he helped Hamish steady the branch. Each time she came around, she missed. Waving frantically, her shrieks of terror filled the night.

"Hold on Syb, we'll get you!" cried the boys, trying desperately to reach her. Screams erupted from the tents back at camp, as their classmates tumbled out.

"Help! Over here! At the lake!" yelled Hamish.

Knocked to his knees several times, Mr. Jacques fought his way across the open meadow, yelling a desperate warning.

"Earthquake! It's an earthquake! Hang on, I'm on my way!"

"Hurry! Sybil's in the water!" shouted Hamish, relieved that help was coming.

Mr. Jacques raced up and desperately joined the rescue attempt. Violent tremors shook the earth, rumbling and groaning, as a seismic wave opened a rift in the floor of Spoon Lake. The speed of the whirlpool gathered momentum. Round and round the water boiled and hissed. In an instant Sybil's head disappeared. She fought her way to the surface, gulped a huge lungful of air, fighting against the swift current that finally pulled her under.

The dizzying speed of the centrifuge sucked her down. She disappeared in a labyrinth of mazes carved out of rock in the beginning of time. Moving at warp speed, twisting, turning and gliding through space-time she travelled, first through darkness, then drifting through a space alight with a myriad of stars. Then darkness again at top speed through a tunnel of dazzling colours.

Nearing the edge of what appeared to be a vast void, she was suddenly and inexplicably thrust out into the coolness of a silvery moonlit night, somewhere far below Spoon Lake. Crashing with a thud against the rough moss-laden trunk of a huge Douglas fir tree, she lay terrified, trembling in the soft glow of the moonlight. Lacy shadow patterns traced across her face as the branches swayed in the soft breeze.

Clinging to the mossy trunk Sybil reassured herself, checking for injuries. No broken bones, no cuts, no bruises. Perplexed and shaken, she wondered how she managed to escape without injury. The moon was in the exact spot it had been only moments before.

Shivering from the chill air and wet bathing suit, it dawned on her. She was stranded somewhere far below the peak of Mount Cheam, which stood off to her right. Thoughts skittered across her mind like bubbles on a hot griddle. What happened?

Where am I? How will I get back? Panic gripped her insides as fear rose in her throat, constricting it into a taut rope of terror.

Before she could formulate any answers, Sybil's common sense kicked in. Tonight would be a battle against the cold. She must fight for her life in an attempt to ward off hypothermia. Already, her teeth were rattling in her head like the jackhammer of the road crew they had passed earlier that morning. Sybil catapulted into action.

Gathering soft, feathery branches from nearby cedar trees, she heaped them into a mound under the trailing branches of the Douglas fir. She burrowed down into the comforting bed of aromatic lace, curling up to conserve warmth. Each cedar bough seemed to radiate an incandescent glow, finally quelling her uncontrollable shivers.

Buried beneath the pile of greens, Sybil's mind darted about. Was it only yesterday she was baking cookies in her mom's warm kitchen? They were discussing the trip her family had taken over the summer.

"I want you to know about the women in our family," her mom had said.

Gazing at her daughter, she saw a mirrored reflection of herself. While Sybil had not reached her full height, Franceska Huber felt sure her daughter would grow to be as tall as she was. Most women in her ancestry were at least six feet.

"Well, I'm tired of hearing about it!" Sybil's voice was on the edge of impertinence.

Quietly, her mom walked over and placed her hand gently over Sybil's, stilling the nervous tension. "It's best to accept what we cannot change, Sybil."

"But I hate it, mom! I just want it to be gone!" wailed Sybil, covering the offending spot with her hand. The Huber female ancestors all bore the same birthmark that signified them as healers. Two scarlet-red circles lay side by side, intersecting each other just under the collarbone on her left chest. At times the double rings burned hotly under her shirt and Sybil's face blushed crimson with embarrassment.

"Oh, honey, don't fight against it so," soothed her mother. "One day you will come to appreciate what you have inherited."

"I don't care, I just want to be normal like everyone else!" shouted Sybil. "I don't want to hear any more stories about those old women."

She was fed up with listening to her mom talk about ancient times when her ancestors roamed the continent of Europe, finally settling in the Black Forest. Why did she insist on harping on about it? Those unwanted visions she had were spooky. The unworldly presence coming from their huts where they treated the wounded and sick, scared her. What did that have to do with how she lived now?

"It's important you learn the secrets of the land, where to go for medicinal plants and how to prepare and administer the concoctions Sybil," urged her mom.

"I don't want to learn any of that. Everyone already thinks I'm a freak," groaned Sybil.

Her mom's gaze fell on Sybil's troubled face.

"Surely not everyone…" her voice drifted off, recalling her own coming of age with the *gift*. "You have plenty of good friends at school," she continued. "And they are the only ones that really matter in the long run."

"But what if someone sees it? I'll be sharing a tent."

For seven years at Sardis Elementary she had been able to conceal the mark that set her apart. It became increasingly harder when changing gym strip during her first year at middle school. Now this camping trip in grade eight would be impossible! She resented it bitterly.

"You don't know what it's like," countered Sybil.

"Well you may not think so now, Sybil. But I was young once too and felt exactly as you feel now. I know it isn't easy being different. But one day it will make more sense." Patting her arm reassuringly, she said, "Just give it time, honey pie."

Sybil's mood eased when she heard the name her mom always called her. She turned and gave her a long hug that seemed to warm from the inside out, softening the tension she felt.

"Okay mom," she said, almost in a whisper. "I'll try harder. Honest I will."

Overhearing the conversation, Sybil's dad entered the kitchen, gently placing his arm around her back. "Don't fret, Sybil. Your mom knows what she's talking about. One day, you'll see how much good you can do with this."

Taking heart, she drew a deep breath and leaned against his broad, comforting shoulder. His quiet, steady nature grounded Sybil to reality in a different sense. He led a very ordinary existence, free of the *gift*, yet very much supportive of the two special women in his life.

He lifted her chin and studied her warm brown eyes with pride. As a seasoned runner, he had entered the Vancouver Sun Run many times. The fact that Sybil excelled in her school's cross-country team gave him much pleasure. Most mornings Sybil rose early to join him, running the ten kilometre distance with easy grace, her long legs stretching forward, dark tresses flowing behind.

Changing the subject, he said, "What's for dinner ladies?"

"We're baking your favourite chocolate chip cookies, but they are for dessert only. Hands off James," scolded Franceska, playfully slapping his offending fingers.

"Okay, okay, I'll wait," he grinned. He tried a new tactic and lifted a cooking pot lid. "What's in the pot?"

"Go ahead, you can look," Sybil encouraged. "Mom and I are making vegetarian stir-fry with sticky rice."

"Yum!" her dad responded. "I love stir-fry. Thanks girls!" he beamed.

Sybil and her mom grew most of their own vegetables in gardens and greenhouses in the backyard. This family trait was passed through the generations from those early women, who were extremely well-schooled in husbandry and living off the land. It was this connection to the earth and to all living creatures that allowed them to live in comfort. They were skilled in identifying the edible wild plants of the area as well. Perhaps that accounted for Sybil's interest in the subject.

Drifting in and out of sleep, a fragment of their last conversation surfaced—her mom's final words before she walked the four blocks to school. "Sybil dear, take care and try to have fun on the field trip."

Her mother would be frantic! Maybe her dad was already on his way. Surely by now they would know there has been an earthquake. How did she survive that? Struggling to make sense of the night's events she fell into an exhausted sleep, oblivious to the moon as it stalked through the night sky in search of its daytime resting place.

CHAPTER TWO
Police Alert

Sybil's family had known their share of tragedy in the past. Thirteen years earlier, their story had made headlines for months.

Sybil was born in Chilliwack General Hospital, one of a set of twins. The pregnancy and delivery had gone remarkably well. There was much joy in the delivery room when two wailing infants, born three minutes apart, drew their first breaths. James Galowin was beside himself with pride. He elatedly sailed through the hospital corridors between Franceska's room and the neonate suite where his two offspring slept and gained strength.

"Have we settled on any names dear?" Franceska smiled at her husband. It was a hard decision, knowing they were expecting twins. They were prepared for the event of boys or girls, Simon and Samuel or Sybil and Susan—now there was one of each.

"It's a no brainer," he said with a grin. Since we have a boy and a girl how about Sybil and Simon? Sounds like a matched pair."

"Sybil Huber and Simon Galowin. Or, hmm maybe…" her voice trailed off as she pondered the implication of the tiny rings, the infinity sign on Simon's chest. "You know our women must retain their maiden name, right, but I don't believe there's any reason Simon can't go by your last name."

"Sure, if you think."

He understood the responsibility she carried. An unbroken line of Huber women retained their healing power by being true to the calling, including the name they were born with. He sighed, rubbed his chin and backtracked.

"Maybe we'd better think this through. If Simon has the birthmark, does he have the gift? Has a male child ever inherited these powers?"

"I don't think so. Not to my knowledge. But it is possible. Maybe we should register him as Simon Huber and watch for signs."

"Sounds like a plan."

He was anxious to get his family safely home. Three days ago the twins were in incubators for the first twenty-four hours, as a precautionary measure. The two infants soon thrived on their mother's milk, gaining weight steadily. Their lusty howls resounded off the walls, assuring everyone they were firmly planted on terra firma, healthy and here to stay.

James arrived at the hospital early on the day of discharge, two car seats securely anchored in the back of their four-door Jeep Wrangler. Parking near the entrance, allowing for ease of transporting two squirming bundles, he locked up and walked toward the main doors. At the elevator, he pressed the button and waited impatiently for the next lift. After what seemed an eternity, he stepped inside, waited for the doors to close and rode the elevator to the third floor. Crossing to the maternity suite, he swung open the door and was confronted by a scene rife with chaos. Nurses were scurrying about and a police officer was standing guard at a crime scene blocked by yellow tape, warning: Police Line Do Not Cross.

He stood riveted to one spot, shocked by events unfolding before him. What was all the commotion about? Directly ahead of him was an officer standing at attention, the yellow stripes on his pant legs ramrod straight, his spit-polished boots reflecting the glare of overhead lights. On his upper arm, three yellow chevrons denoted the rank of Sergeant with the Royal Canadian Mounted Police. He advanced toward the official.

"Sorry," warned the uniform. "No one is allowed in this hall."

"Sir, I am taking my wife and newborns home today," protested James Galowin. "I can't leave without them."

The officer's eyes narrowed in concentration. "Did you say newborns?" He paused, then said, "Sir, may I please have your name."

"I'm James Galowin and I am here to collect my wife Franceska."

"Is your wife Franceska Huber?" queried the officer, trying to establish positive identity.

"Yes, sorry officer. My wife goes by her maiden name."

"I'm Sgt. William O'Harah. One of our investigators stopped by your house this morning. No one was home. We've been trying to reach you on your cell phone. There was an 'out of service area' message. We also left messages on your land line."

"Sorry," replied James, rubbing his chin. "Dropped it in a sink full of water shaving this morning. So rushed. Didn't even check my messages." Now alarmed, he quickly added. "Why are you trying to reach me?"

"Please follow me," instructed Sgt. O'Harah. "We have established a command centre down the hall in the lounge area."

"What is this all about?" His voice began to rise in consternation.

The sergeant's attitude softened with empathy. "Sorry, Mr. Galowin, bear with me please. I will explain in a moment."

James was beginning to dread what he was about to hear. The short walk in the medicinal atmosphere seemed to stretch on endlessly.

"Here we are," said the officer, opening a door and ushering him into a room. Franceska was sitting on a lounge chair, tears coursing down her cheeks. She blew her nose, hiccoughed spasmodically, and sobbed into a tissue. Her body convulsed with deep uncontrollable grief.

"Franceska! Are you okay? Wh-a-what's going on?" he stammered, rushing to her side.

She looked up, wailing anew. "Oh James! I-I-I ca-can't be-l-ieve it!" she choked back, dissolving in paroxysmal fits of sobbing.

Sergeant O'Harah intervened. "I'm sorry Mr. Galowin. I'm afraid there is some bad news." There was no way to soften the blow but to tell him straight out. "One of your newborns has been abducted."

"No!" shouted James, the blood draining from his face. "How could that happen?"

He sank to the chair beside Franceska. Now understanding her horror, he gathered her in his arms, clinging to her for his own sake, as much as for hers. He collected his thoughts for the next question, afraid to hear the answer.

"Which one was taken? Who is left?" He steeled himself for the reply, neither of which he wanted to hear.

"It's Simon," rasped Franceska's voice. "They've taken Simon. We have only Sybil left."

James pivoted in the direction of the sergeant. "Do something. Can't you do something?"

He knew it was a thoughtless comment. Of course they were doing something. That's why they were here, but he needed to know the details. "Sorry sir, this has been a terrible blow," he apologized.

"No need to apologize Mr. Galowin. This is truly a difficult time for you and your wife. An Amber Alert was issued as soon as the call came in. We are out in full force across the province. As we speak, a Canada-wide search is underway. A task force has been established to focus solely on this case."

James gulped, nodding with a measure of reassurance.

"I know this is rough, but we do have a few questions we need to ask. Any information you can give us, as to who or why anyone might do this, would be very helpful."

"I have no idea why anyone would wish us harm," Franceska's quavering voice came from behind her tissue.

"Nor do I," said James, scratching his head. "I can't think of anything. We're just an average family living in an ordinary sub-division in Chilliwack. Nothing we do could possibly have any bearing on this."

Franceska grew quiet as she heard his last comments. No, we aren't really an ordinary family, she thought to herself. But I can't very well come out with it can I? So she bit her lip and stifled the urge to reveal all she knew.

"We'll have to wait. There may be a ransom note or a phone call asking for money. It's the usual motive in abduction cases," said the Mountie.

"But we don't have that kind of money!" James retorted. "How are we to pay if we get the call?"

The officer turned to him, understanding the situation. "We don't encourage payment to kidnappers. Do you have any relatives you can turn to?"

"No," said James. "There aren't any relatives. We are the last of our line in Canada."

"The best thing you can do now is to go home and wait for any contact, if it's coming. We'll place a wiretap on your land line. If we can get a trace on the call we'll have a good lead. To be safe, in case it's someone you know, we'll also monitor your cell. Oh! Your cell phone! You dropped it in the water."

"I'll replace it as soon as I leave here," replied James, impatient to get the investigation underway.

"How did they manage to get all the way to the neonate nursery without being seen?" agonized Franceska. "Surely someone must have noticed something!"

"We're taking statements from the night staff right now. And we have the tapes from the security monitors. If there was an unauthorized trespasser it will show up," reassured Sgt. O'Harah.

In a secluded treatment room, Cpl. Doug Stanton sat facing the night nurse in charge. "Your full name please and how long have you worked at Chilliwack General?"

"It's Jessica Foster, and I have been at this hospital for over five years. It is my first night shift of this set."

"Tell me Ms. Foster, were you at your station all night?"

"No sir, I made rounds every hour and distributed meds as required. The remainder of the time I was at the nursing station finishing reports. Except of course for dinner breaks. We relieve each other for those."

"Did you notice anything out of the ordinary Ms. Foster?"

"No, there was nothing unusual. Everything was quiet. If anyone came on the ward, we would have noticed."

"Who else worked the night shift?"

"Wendy Chan was the other R.N. on the ward with me, along with an L.P.N., Andrea de Hahn. Another R.N., Sarah Warrington, was working in the nursery unit. We've all stayed back for questioning. There's no going home until we have this sorted out with you."

In turn, Cpl. Stanton conducted his interrogations with the other two ward staff, resulting in no further information.

"Now, Ms. Warrington," Cpl. Stanton began. He appraised the neonate duty nurse, flipped the page in his notebook and began his questioning. "May I have your full name please?"

"Sarah Jane Warrington," she answered, clenching her hands together, trying to still the nervous twitch.

"When did you first discover the infant Simon Huber was missing?"

"Let me see," she collected her thoughts. "At 2:00 a.m. I did the scheduled changing and feeding. There was nothing out of the ordinary. The newborns were settled in their hospital bassinets by around 4:00 a.m. No one was seen entering or leaving the restricted area."

Her chin began to tremble uncontrollably as she fought to maintain control. "I-I be-gan my hourly check at 5:00 a.m." A sudden tear escaped her left eye, tracing a wet track down her cheek. "When I saw the child was not in his bassinet, I checked the ward clock. It was precisely 5:03 a.m., to be exact."

It was clear to the officer, Ms. Warrington was terribly shaken. "This is dreadful. Most upsetting," she went on. "I am absolutely horrified. I was here in the nursery all night, except when Wendy Chan relieved me for my breaks. I can't imagine how this happened."

"You didn't notice anything unusual Ms. Warrington?"

"N-o-o-o, I don't think so," she said slowly. "Unless," she stopped in mid-sentence. "At the time I thought it rather odd, although I doubt this has anything to do with it. I felt very chilly around 4:00 a.m. It was the strangest thing, as though an iceberg had entered the room. But then again, at that time of the morning, circadian rhythms do slow up a bit. I put it down to weariness and circulatory fluctuations. I just added a cardigan and soon warmed up. Still, it was an odd sensation—cold to the bone."

"All right Miss…er…rather Ms. Warrington. This has been a long night for all of you. I think we're pretty well finished. If we have any further questions, we'll be in touch."

He eyed her with appreciation. This was someone he would like to get to know better. "The Forensics Section will be here shortly to dust for fingerprints. Before you leave, we'll need a sample of prints from all who worked last night. Any other staff working on this ward will need to come to the detachment to provide their prints."

The crime scene was dusted for fingerprints, ruling out the ward staff. No outside matches were found. Video surveillance tapes of pedestrian traffic entering and exiting the hospital were collected and taken to the police station for review.

James and Franceska left the hospital shortly after giving statements to the investigating officers. Upon arrival at home with their remaining newborn, James sat down in his study to think.

"Honey," he called. There was no reply. "Franceska, dear." Again no answer.

He rose slowly and walked into the kitchen. Not there. He crossed the living room and climbed the flight of stairs to the upper floor. The first door to the left was closed. Turning the doorknob, James found it was locked. He knocked lightly.

"Who is it?" Franceska's voice was husky with fear.

"Franceska, honey, it's me. Please let me in." Alarmed by this sudden distrust in their own home, he reassured her. "Everything is okay Franceska. I'm here, there's nothing to worry about. It's safe."

Franceska opened the door a crack and peeped through, breathing a sigh of relief when she saw James standing alone on the other side.

"What if they come to our home?" She dared to speak the unthinkable. "Do they know where we live?"

"We'll keep the doors locked and the alarm system set at all times, even during the day. No one is going to get in. Not with out us knowing."

"Are you sure?" Her reticent fear was palpable, hanging like thick fog obscuring the room, blocking the sunlight of joy that should have ushered them home.

"The police have promised to step up presence in our neighbourhood. In fact, a marked cruiser has been parked across the street since we arrived home," he reassured.

"Oh good," sighed Franceska. Her shoulders relaxed imperceptibly, as she exhaled.

"Sybil will sleep in our room tonight," said James. He moved the bassinet across the hall, settling it next to Franceska's side of the bed.

"Thank you James. I will rest better knowing she is next to me," she sighed, thinking of the sleepless hours that lay ahead.

"Bring Sybil downstairs with us while we decide what to do next. I have some ideas I want to tell you about."

Franceska gently picked up their sleeping daughter and cradled her softly against her breast. She followed James to the lower floor and sat in the padded arm chair in his study while he went to the kitchen to brew some tea. Franceska listened intently, startling with every creak the old home emitted, waiting impatiently for her husband to return.

"Here, try this cup of chamomile tea. It will settle you a little. We've had a horrendous day."

He sat at his desk and shuffled some paper aside making room for the pad on which he had been figuring. A portfolio lay open before him.

"I've been working out some finances. As near as I can estimate, Franceska, we'll be able to raise $10,000 as a reward for information."

"That much? We have that much to spare?" she asked incredulously.

"Yes. I will be able to cash in some savings. Hopefully it will be enough to bring in some leads." He squared his shoulders. "If necessary, we can raise it even higher."

"I'm so thankful for you James. I have been numb all morning. Just can't seem to shake this fog gathered in my brain. So glad you can think and make some logical decisions."

This was no easy task by any means. James Galowin's primary source of income was derived from a privately owned sporting goods store, Nature's Gateway Inc., which provided adequate family support. Secondary income from White Water Rafting Tours, operated as a seasonal business, supplemented the family coffers.

In addition to this, Franceska fashioned jewelry and homemade soap, which she marketed as a cottage industry from their home. Her long term plans were to expand into the dried herb industry once her gardens matured enough to meet the demand. It would set them back financially if a claim was made, but they clung to desperate hope that it would generate the kind of tips needed to solve the abduction of their son.

The doorbell rang, interrupting their discussion. James closed his documents, filed them away in his desk drawer and answered the door.

Cpl. Stanton smiled and said, "Hello Mr. Galowin. Thought I'd stop to see how you and your wife are doing. Turning to the older woman beside him he said, "This is Elsa Hendricks who works with Victims Service & Support. May we come in please?"

"Yes, please do."

"I am sorry this has happened," Elsa began, offering her hand. He shook it, noticing the strength of her grip. She had a kind smile.

"Excuse me, please." The corporal turned aside briefly to take a call. "Sorry for the interruption, been called to the office. I'll leave you with Elsa. If you need anything further, please call me."

"Thank you," said James. As he bid farewell, he was glad to see the police cruiser still parked across the street. Then he turned to the woman.

"Come meet my wife," he said, ushering her down the hall. "We can talk in my study."

Franceska rose to greet Elsa. The kindly handshake and warm smile imparted a measure of calm. "Please sit," said Franceska, indicating an armchair next to her.

Elsa began directly. "I'm a Service Worker with Victims Service." Handing them her card and a brochure outlining services she said, "We provide information on the justice system and can help you with referrals to other agencies and resources. I'm here to help, anything you need—applications, forms, or if you just want to talk. I'll even go with you when you talk to the police."

"Thank you. You're very kind," said Franceska.

"This is all pretty overwhelming for you. I just wanted to make contact for now. We can meet again when you've had more time."

Soft baby sounds came from the cradle as their infant daughter squirmed and stretched.

"Oh, the wee one. Please, may I see?"

Franceska nodded and Elsa leaned across to have a look.

"Has her mother's dark hair. And such a tiny nose. What a sweet babe," she smiled gently.

"Thank you. And thank you for coming today."

"I will stay in touch," said Elsa. She shook Franceska's hand and smiled reassuringly. "Call me any time please, at the number on my card."

James walked her to the door and shook her hand as she said goodbye. "Thank you. We'll call you if we have any questions." Then he returned to his study.

Franceska sipped her tea and gazed at her daughter who lay sleeping in the cradle beside her. She nudged it slightly, setting it swinging in a gentle arcing motion.

"I feel so much better knowing they are watching the house," she whispered to her newborn. "We'll keep you safe."

James, admiring his wife's motherly instincts, snapped to attention. He had things to do. "I'll contact Sgt. O'Harah immediately and set this reward for information in motion. He'll know best how to handle this."

Cpl. Stanton arrived at the detachment and met up with the head of surveillance, Cpl. Steve Siromi.

"Our constables are out making door to door enquiries. They've generated a few leads. Most promising came from a neighbouring subdivision near the hospital."

"What have you got Doug?"

"A man out jogging with his dog around 5 a.m. saw a suspicious vehicle leaving the hospital area."

"Where was it parked?"

"Across the street. Drove away without headlights. Switched 'em on halfway up the block. Rolled right through the stop sign."

"Got a make or model?"

"Tan Dodge Caravan. Personalized plate. GO FIGR."

"Hah! People come up with the darnedest!"

"We ran it. Belongs to one Daniel C. Strang."

"Got a record?"

"Ahuh. Theft, DUI, possession, on probation."

"Good work Doug! We'll stake him out. See what's shakin', maybe we'll get lucky."

Later that afternoon at the Chilliwack Detachment, Sgt. O'Harah entered the room where his corporal and a constable sat viewing the hospital videos. "Find anything guys?"

"Nothing of consequence," replied Cst. Atwal. "But there are a few blips. Puzzling. See here." She backed up the disc and pressed the play button. "This is the view of the main front entrance. Shortly after 4:00 a.m. there's an oddity."

"It's nothing we can substantiate with cold hard evidence," affirmed Cpl. Stanton. "But look," he said, stopping the disc. He pointed out the odd rippling effect that was frozen by the stop button.

"It looks like some sort of apparition," offered Cst. Atwal.

"Nonsense! There's no way a camera can capture an apparition constable," scoffed the sergeant. "You must be seeing things." He squinted at the eerie projection, taking a closer look. "Hmmm…there does appear to be some sort of interference on the screen." His cold, calculating mind refused to be swayed by conjecture.

"Not only that," said Cpl. Stanton, fast-forwarding the disc to 4:13 a.m. "Here is that same odd hazy ripple again."

Sgt. O'Harah's eyebrows shot up in confounded wonder. He rubbed his forehead and pondered the disturbing information. Coincidence? His analytical mind shoved the mounting questions out of the way and returned to the cold-hard-fact corner of his intellect. His common sense told him to disallow such nonsense. He glared at the screen, his attention focused on a second hazy ripple off to the far right. He jabbed his finger toward the anomaly at the edge of the screen.

"See here, another one!" He pressed play. The two ripples met up, hesitated for a minute and slid out of view.

41

"Now, watch this," said Cst. Atwal, switching discs in the DVD player. She pressed the button and let it spin. "This is the video retrieved from the hall leading to the neonate nursery."

Sgt. O'Harah leaned in closer, gripping the back of the chair. He watched as the hazy distortion on the screen swept down the corridor. His probing eyes checked the time on the player. It was 4:08 a.m. The ripple disappeared. With his eyes riveted to the screen, he was astounded to see the same strange phenomena occupy the hall three minutes later, rippling along in the opposite direction.

"By gosh, I think you're right!" acknowledged the sergeant.

"Is this some sort of witchery!" the corporal stared disbelievingly at the screen.

"Witchery? The occult? C'mon Doug!"

"These weird images! You got another theory?"

"Yeah! Camera malfunction. Light. Shadows. Anything! We're not writing up ghosts in the police report. The Crown will laugh us out of the province!"

"What do you suggest then?"

"Don't know. It's a first."

"How about reporting what we see? Call it anomalies, flaws on the video corresponding with times on the DVD. Let Crown Counsel do what they want with it."

"That'd cover our bases. Meet legal requirements," conceded Sgt. O'Harah. "Go ahead Doug. Write it up."

He turned away from the screen, privately wondering about the family he had met earlier that morning. What sort of people were they? Could there be something in their background worth checking? He pulled the corporal aside and was about to issue directives. Then thinking better of it, he changed his tack.

"Never mind Doug, just a thought. I'll catch up with you later."

He had always resisted talk of the wee folk whenever those in his Irish family background raised the subject. Leprechauns and such had no place in three-dimensional society. Good solid proof of existence had always been his standby. But the events of the afternoon left him rattled, questioning his own sanity. The spectre of spirits rising in his imagination preoccupied his thoughts. I'm going to check into this family myself he decided, intrigued by the images on the screen.

That evening he remained at work far into the night, running both the Galowin and Huber names on PRIME, the RCMP provincial database; a tool that would give him the most accurate information available to crime fighting. Nothing came up. No criminal records registered in either name.

Then he tried a different approach and punched the names into CPIC, the Canadian Police Information Centre, which connected Canada-wide information. Again, cross-references produced nothing of value to aid in uncovering any significant background information on the family. Rubbing his bleary eyes, he muttered, "There must be something to account for the strangeness on those DVDs."

The task force worked around the clock, following up leads that came in through tip lines and cold calls to the front desk. James and Franceska waited impatiently for the expected phone call or ransom note that never came. It was devastating. The loss of one so young tugged at everyone's heartstrings. The office was abuzz with a flurry of activity. There was a growing sense of urgency, knowing that the best results occurred in the first forty-eight hours. Beyond that, the trail began to grow stale.

"Those poor parents. What if it was one of our children?" commented Cpl. Stanton.

"Heartbreaking, Doug. It's a strange case. Bizarre clues. Extremely baffling," responded Sgt. O'Harah.

"None of it makes much sense. No ransom calls. What's the motive? Human trafficking?"

"It's especially hard when it involves children," said the sergeant. "All we can do is keep on the case. Something has to crack."

"We need a lucky break. If only someone would come forward. Anything, the least clue."

Cpl. Stanton was getting desperate. Knowing how distressed she was, he'd kept in touch with Sarah Warrington, the neonatal nurse on duty that night. In his heart, he made it a mission on her behalf to find the child and arrest the perpetrator.

Frequent broadcasts over the airwaves offered a reward for information leading to the apprehension of the culprit. The manhunt carried on for months. Eventually, the few tips dwindled. They were running out of leads. As time elapsed, the family grew more desperate, scraping together what they could to increase the reward for any information from the public. The ensuing investigation and massive search revealed nothing. It was as though the little newborn had vanished into thin air.

It was a cold case file.

CHAPTER THREE
The City of Hetopia

✧

The velvet cloak of night gave way to the pearly light of dawn. As the sky lightened, sunlight filtered through the cedar bed sending probing fingers of healing energy, massaging Sybil's aching muscles.

A fragment of memory pried its way into her slumber. Sybil awoke abruptly to the realization that she was stranded somewhere far below the campsite. Fighting off panic, she sat up. Everything seemed quite normal. Perhaps she'd had a nightmare. But no, she should be in a sleeping bag. It must have happened, the moonlight swim, the spinning, the lights, the speed and the rumbling. That horrible rumbling!

Suddenly, a soft fluttering sound caught her attention as the fir bough above her dipped and swayed with the weight of an unknown presence. She stared upward, gulping convulsively. A huge pair of shimmering white wings flexed and folded themselves neatly against a set of muscular shoulders.

As the creature turned, two huge brown eyes ringed with silvery eyelashes swivelled around and fixed her with a mesmerizing stare. Studying the creature, she saw the face was that of a man. The head was crowned by a halo of snowy-white curls. Beneath the luminous eyes a nose jutted out sharply, like the beak of an eagle. A mouthful of even white teeth was shaped in a kindly smile. The lips did not move, yet Sybil heard a voice resonate through her mind like the peal of soft vesper bells.

The being unfurled its enormous wingspan and descended slowly to the forest floor to a spot directly in front of her.

"Good Morning my Lady Sybil. Do not be alarmed. You are welcome here. I mean you no harm. I trust my friends the Cedar Sprites have kept you warm and comfortable throughout the night?"

Astounded by the apparition before her, Sybil managed to stammer an answer, "Ahh, g-good m-morning. Wh-who, who are you?"

"Oh please do forgive me kind Lady. I am Maerwyn, your guide from Hetopia. I have been awaiting your arrival. We have been expecting you for a very long time."

"Y-you, you have?" Sybil stared at Maerwyn in amazement. "Why? How could you possibly know me?"

"Oh dear, I see we do have a lot of explaining to do," pealed Maerwyn in his politest vesper-like tone. *"You're quite sure that you have no idea why you are here? H-m-m-m…they didn't tell me anything about this at the assembly. Well, never you mind Sybil, all is well, nothing to worry about."*

Sybil struggled to control rising panic. "How do you know my name? Where am I?"

"Ahh, well I can only tell you briefly now Sybil. It is of the utmost importance that I get you to our destination as quickly as possible. There may be forces about that threaten your safety. I am to escort you to Hetopia and by all that is in my power, I mean to do so as expeditiously as possible."

"Where? No! I want to go home! Home!"

"Come now my dear, you must not fret," soothed the bells. *"You are in good hands and all will be explained shortly at the Great Hall in Hetopia."*

"The great what?" cried Sybil. "I'm not going anywhere but home!"

"All in good time. Now, you look frightfully cold in that garment. We must do something about that."

Gazing into the depths of the kindly brown eyes, Sybil caught sight of the slightest twinkle, felt a tingling sensation and in an instant she was clad in a robe of the softest fabric. Never before had she seen this colour. It was a hue that was closest to the blue in a rainbow that she could imagine, and yet it was not such a blue. On her feet she wore soft, silvery slippers with wings embossed on the heels. Perched on her forehead, sat a wreath of delicate pale blue petals. Their intoxicating scent made her head giddy with a sense of joy that, for a moment, overwhelmed her fear.

"Come my Lady," Maerwyn bowed with a flourish.

"No! I can't. And how come I can hear you but you aren't speaking?"

"Oh, we Hetopians speak Telepath. It is something you can learn. We will teach you. But if you're more comfortable I will switch to your language."

"Please do!"

"Now, we must leave at once. I must get you to safety!"

With that, he rose from the forest floor, extended his powerful hands to her and lifted her gently into flying position.

"W-w-wait! What did you say your name was?"

"It's Maerwyn."

"Maerwyn, I-I can't fly!" protested Sybil.

"Nonsense, my Lady. You have the gift of flight! These silver-winged slippers have imparted it to you. Come now. Do not be afraid," reassured her guide. "I have been entrusted with this task. Your well-being is my priority. And s-o-o, we are off!" He lifted her gently to treetop level.

"See! There's nothing to fear!" Imperceptibly he let go of her arms and she hovered just above the giant Douglas fir, under which she had spent the night.

An astonished, "Ohhhh!" escaped Sybil's bewildered lips. Her last attempt at protest was completely overwhelmed by the new sensation of hanging suspended in mid-air. She turned and traced a fingertip farewell to the tree. The fir nodded its feathery, green crown and the arm branches expressed its delight by making a sweeping curtsy. The cedar boughs rustled, while pin-points of light danced incandescently throughout. Only then was Sybil made aware of the tiny creatures that had come to her aid in the chill of the long dark night.

"Who are they?" gasped Sybil.

"Those are the Cedar Sprites. They give the cedar tree its special qualities of warmth. They are also responsible for the pungent odour that is unique to the cedar family. We have a wonderful system here in the Fifth dimension."

"The fifth what?"

"You are in the realm of the Fifth dimension, Sybil my dear," chimed Maerwyn with delight, as he appraised her baffled expression.

"What is that? Where is that!?"

"Come now, surely you have some knowledge of it. How do you suppose you have acquired the ability to know things beforehand? And those rings on your chest are a sign that you are connected to the Fifth dimension. You have the gift of healing as well, right?"

"How do you know that!?" Sybil was astounded. Blushing at the thought of the rings on her chest she stammered, "I-I was born with them. I thought I was just different, that's all."

After all those years of uncertainty and rebellion, after all the conversations with her mother, she was finally beginning to understand. Maybe they *were* more than just ordinary birthmarks.

They were well above the valley floor now. Directly ahead loomed the peak of Mount Cheam. Swooping into the bowl below where she had camped the evening before, Spoon Lake's jewel-blue eye winked at her knowingly in the dazzling sunlight. There was no sign of the campsite!

"Where are my friends? They were here just last night at the foot of Mount Cheam and Lady Peak."

"Remember now my dear Sybil, you are in the Fifth dimension. And, I can see that we are going to need geography lessons. That is Chemandor Tower and behind is Ladonisia Pique. I do suppose the names are quite similar really, wouldn't you say?"

Sybil stared at the strange man, her mind grappling with a sudden clarity of time and space. During the descent from Spoon Lake to the valley floor Sybil had entered a warp in the fabric of consciousness. She found herself, not in the future nor the past, but in another dimension of the present. She was in a parallel universe.

"I guess..." Somehow Sybil began to sense a calm. She didn't understand it, but she felt safe in Maerwyn's company.

They left the lush green basin between the peaks and flew along the grey expanse of water winding its way up the delta toward the Fraser Canyon. "Where are we going, Maerwyn?"

"Do you see that massive channel of water directly below us Sybil? We call that Fraezorian Floe."

"In my world that is known as the Fraser River," replied Sybil. "We're heading east toward the city of Hope, right?"

"Yes, but we call it Hetopia. I am a member of the race known as the Zaepharim which inhabits that area. We are an ancient race of magical beings who have existed since the beginning of time. Really quite fitting that your people have named it Hope! It is the expectation of hope that is extended to the human race. For it is written in the ancient manuscripts of Paracleses that Hetopians will succor the One who will preserve Life."

"Will succor what?" Sybil stared at him. "That is too weird."

Maerwyn glanced at her benevolently. A radiant glow illuminated the vista ahead. Drawing nearer, Sybil caught her breath. The beautiful city of Hetopia lay nestled in the mountains past the upper end of the Fraser Valley. Glowing turrets emblazoned with golden light, crowned the tops of the blue crystal palaces that rose before her. Lush vines festooned the archways enclosing the city avenues and displays of multi-hued flora cascaded from window casements. Marble cobbled walkways connected the lush green parks where Zaepharim relaxed, enjoying each other's presence. The scent of an exotic spice wafted toward them on warm currents of air.

"What is that perfume?" Sybil inhaled the intoxicating scent drifting on the wind.

"It is the Pallid Elusive. Rare. Grows only in our valley," replied Maerwyn. "Unique fragrance. It is exceptionally fragile and retiring. Very fortunate if you catch a glimpse of it at all. I, myself, have seen it fleetingly only once. I looked away very quickly for fear of injuring it."

"Why?" Sybil had always been drawn to plants and she was intrigued by the unusual properties Maerwyn was describing.

"They bloom in the undergrowth of the old growth forest. A shade loving plant. As far as we know, the blossom is pale cream in colour, shaped like a trumpet. It has the uncanny ability to know if it is being observed and rapidly retreats. Reserved little soul, closes right up. Perhaps the intrusion of eyesight alone bruises its fragile blossom—puts it at risk."

"Wow, that's cool!"

Maerwyn smiled to himself. Her expressions were indeed strange, as he had been warned. But innocent, which appealed to him greatly.

"The green sword-like leaves surrounding it seem to offer protection. Certainly they bristle menacingly when we inadvertently stumble upon it."

"It's enough just to inhale their fragrance," smiled Sybil.

"Yes, we Hetopians respect the Elusive and leave it be."

Circling the city slowly, Sybil was overwhelmed by the beauty below. Multitudes of mellow flutes, sweet and low, gently caressed her ears as she strained to hear the message they seemed to impart.

"What are the flutes saying Maerwyn?"

"It is our welcome. All of Hetopia has been awaiting your presence. Let us circle the city once more so everyone can catch a glimpse of you."

Seriously, Sybil thought. They are awaiting my presence? So is everyone back at camp! She bit her lip nervously. An uncomfortable shyness slowly creeping up her throat flushed her face with embarrassment.

Soaring toward a structure with blue crystal turrets at city centre, Sybil caught sight of a majestic old Zaepharim standing on the steps leading to the portal of the palace. Presently they landed in front of the ancient one.

Extending her arms in welcome, Ebihinin vespered a greeting in soft bell-tones, *"Welcome to the city of Hetopia, Sybil. You have had quite a journey."*

"Ebihinin, Sybil prefers to use her own language," said Maerwyn.

"Of course. We can communicate in whatever way you find the most comfortable Sybil," replied Ebihinin, switching vernacular seamlessly.

Quietly murmuring her appreciation, Sybil extended both hands in greeting, as was the custom of the Zaepharim. She felt a strange, warm tingling when their fingers touched. Sybil instinctively drew back but Ebihinin just smiled, stroking her guest's hand momentarily before withdrawing the gesture.

The gentleness of Ebihinin's touch put Sybil at ease and she slowly began to relax under her kind gaze.

"Come enter within. A bath has been made ready. When you have rested please join us in the Great Hall. We have prepared a feast in your honour." Turning to a lovely young Zaepharim, she added, "This is Aithne. She will show you to your quarters and render assistance."

Sybil was in awe of the gracious manner of the revered being before her. The kindness in her voice matched the soft appeal of her magnificent eyes as waves of warmth penetrated to the recesses of Sybil's soul. A crowning cascade of silvery locks fell about the sturdy shoulders robed in delicate azure-blue gauze. Silvery eyelashes characteristic to all Zaepharim veiled the warm blue orbs beneath.

Following her refreshing bath, Maerwyn arrived at the door of Sybil's chamber. Together they left her room and proceeded to the Great Hall through a maze of polished glass hallways.

"Are you rested my Lady?"

"After last night, that bath was very energizing, thank you," replied Sybil, astounded by the unique architecture they were passing through.

Sweet-scented breezes wafted through the corridors, while the faint swish of footfalls of those who had passed before, lingered in the air. Ascending a grand staircase of glass, Sybil found herself standing before what appeared to be a vast blue space that seemed to go on forever, reflecting eternity.

"Where are we going?" she asked, looking down at the drop into the clear blue.

"Take my hand," replied Maerwyn.

He grasped her trembling fingers and stepped out into thin air. Sybil found herself stepping through a blue veil that ran off her shoulders like quicksilver. Before her, lay a great transparent hall. Above, on the gleaming vault, a gigantic system of prisms caught the sunlight and separated into wide shafts of rainbow hues, forming the walls of the hexagonal Great Hall.

"Oh my!" Sybil was transfixed by the splendour before her. "This is amazing. How…?"

"Come forward please Sybil," sighed the delicate tones of Ebihinin. She beckoned her nearer the crystal altar stone directly under the huge system of prisms.

Entering the sacred space, Sybil's vision became exquisitely sensitive to details around her. Below her was endless sky, adrift with a sea of white clouds. Suspended in space, her heightened sense of awareness caught a flow of energy and her body tingled in the presence of the love surrounding her.

"We have much to show you Sybil. First, the Red Chamber," said the Ancient One. She escorted Sybil through the veil of red mist into the Valley of Commitment. "This is the first of the colours of the rainbow. It represents passion and knowledge of the heart. Here you will find courage to sustain you on the journey ahead."

Sybil glanced at the Elder, suddenly fearful. What journey? And why was she going to need courage? She just wanted to go home. This was all pretty nice stuff but was it real or was she dreaming?

Before them, a wall of rock sent forth a jewel-red elixir. Ebihinin plunged a crystal goblet into the liquid, brought it forth and held it to Sybil's lips.

"Drink deeply. You will have need of much courage in the time ahead." The heady fragrance of the fruity mixture fortified her as the passionate warmth radiated through her veins.

Passing back through the veil into the Great Hall, Sybil was astonished by the change in herself. She seemed to have grown in stature, but no, she was exactly as before, at eye level with Ebihinin's calm blue gaze. Why did she feel so different?

Ebihinin sighed a soft reassurance, "You have expanded into the limits of the Realm of Courage. You will feel thus until we have entered all of the chambers, whereby you will achieve a balance."

She was guided to her right, through the misty orange hue revealing the splendour of a vast panorama. It was the sunrise in all its glory, heralding the dawn of a new day.

"This colour represents the glory of all that is to come, the promise of the future. Stand forth with your eyes closed. Bask in its warmth. It will fill you with hope. The promise of hope in the future will sustain you."

Obeying her command, Sybil's heart grew lighter as she expanded into the Realm of Hope.

When she entered the yellow mist, a tangy fragrance of citrus assailed her senses. Inhaling the pungent scent, her mouth watered. Row upon row of ancient, gnarled trees towered above her. Nestled in leafy, dark green foliage, star-shaped yellow fruit corkscrewed skyward.

"You must aim for the stars Sybil. Always go beyond what you think is possible. Eat of this fruit and your mind will expand to the Realm of Possibilities."

Gazing into the sky-blue depths of Ebihinin's starry eyes, Sybil took the piece of fruit offered to her by the kindly, old hands. The sharp acidic flavour of the fruit opened Sybil to the Realm of Possibilities.

Upon entering the green veil, Sybil became aware of a refreshingly cold tingle. Giant stocks of mint extending as far as the horizon waved gently in the breeze. Sybil entered the forest of mint, walking through the icy coolness. When she breathed in the sharp aroma, her head cleared. Entering a trance, she centered deep inside herself. Within the recesses of her being, she entered the Realm of Faith, an ever-changing and ever-growing presence.

"You will need a deep and abiding faith in yourself in order to meet the challenges ahead," rang the soothing tones of Ebihinin's bell-like voice.

When Sybil stepped through the misty blue veil of colour, her senses came alive with the delicate jubilations of tinkling bells. A carpet of delicate bluebells waved their greeting at her feet.

"These are the bells of telepathy, Sybil. It is how we Hetopians communicate. This will give you the power to make yourself understood, but more importantly to understand others. This gift is the basis of good communication."

Sybil grew, expanding into the Realm of Truth and Honesty.

When they arrived at the last veil, the violet hue shimmered and danced with excitement.

"Before we enter, I want you to understand one thing." Ebihinin's voice held a deep sense of mystery. "Behind this veil we will be unable to see. Your sight will dim. Your mind will yearn for the knowledge that dwells in the violet chamber. It is not for us to know. This is the Realm of Mystery. It is beyond all knowing."

As they passed through the violet veil of light, Sybil seemed to have stepped into a lavender fog that shrouded her vision.

"You are in the Presence of the Eternal, where mysteries dwell."

The eternal where mysteries dwell? What am I doing here? Mystery? This was all a mystery! She couldn't deny this was pretty cool, but what did it have to do with her? She was just an ordinary school girl, who happened to get caught in an earthquake. But, hey! That didn't make sense either!

Entering the Great Hall once more Ebihinin said, "Now that you have received these gifts, we must proceed to the Book of Wisdom."

She brought forth a key in the shape of a compass rose with eight points, one each for North, South, East, West and the halfway points between the directions. At the centre of the key lay an intricate design of a dragon.

Ebihinin placed the key into the altar stone and turned. A stray beam of light from above focused on a spot directly in front of the altar and a stairway opened into the depths of the sky below.

"Follow me," directed the soft voice.

Sybil strained to see past the filmy blue robes, as they descended. Cool moist air and the sound of rushing water echoing within, told Sybil they were entering an enormous light-filled cavern. Presently they stopped before a glassy pool of water.

Ebihinin turned to Sybil and said, "This is the Great Book of Wisdom. The Book of Paracleses offers comfort and courage." She touched the surface and the water rearranged itself into beautiful script.

"Let me see now. Just a little further." She rippled the water again and the mirrored image settled into place. "Ah, yes here it is." She began to read.

✧

Songs of Hope

Blues hold the secret within, let go of all fear to win
To double your powers seek that which was lost
The past holds the key.
By the water, he weeps, while others pray.
Captive by night, invisible by day
Joined for all eternity, your past holds the key
The journey is long, be strong of heart
Be joined forever, never more to part.

Sybil studied the words with great interest, her brows knitting together in concentration. Maerwyn had told her that she was the one they had been waiting for. Why? What did these words mean? She must think. 'Your past holds the key'. Thoughts flitted through her mind. 'Joined for all eternity'.

What long journey? Why? To where? She knew she had to concentrate but she was feeling increasingly uneasy. When was she going home?

"I'm sorry, Ebihinin. I can't seem to make any sense of this. What does it mean? The blues hold the secret? Here we are, all in blue. Do you suppose it means us?"

"No, my dear Sybil. It is a mystery to us. We had hoped that you could tell us more about this. What is this water the writings speak of? The answer must lie partly in the Third dimension. You must try to remember Sybil. Something to do with water; and the past holds the key. What has happened in your past?"

"H-m-m-m…" Sybil thought, but the more she tried to decipher it, the more confused she became. She was never any good at riddles. "I need some time to think about this," Sybil conceded slowly.

Nervous anxiety was building. She could feel herself beginning to unravel. This was all a lot of nonsense. How could anyone expect her to know anything about this? They must be mistaken. They have the wrong person. She was about to protest but thought better of it. What's the use? They seemed very certain of themselves. And sure, they were very kind. She felt safe here. But it didn't add up. Anything she had tried to say had been ignored or maybe she hadn't tried hard enough to express her feelings. She was beginning to shut down. A sense of defeat overcame her and her shoulders sagged with weariness.

Perceptively, Ebihinin understood the turmoil on Sybil's face. Willing her to calmness, she sent waves of compassion toward the young woman standing before her.

"Perhaps after a good night's sleep it will make more sense," reassured Ebihinin. "You have had a long and unusual day. We can't expect you to solve it all right now. Come, let us surface."

Ebihinin turned on her heels and ascended to the Great Hall once more. Isn't that strange, thought Sybil. She and Maerwyn seemed to float up the stairs. She distinctly remembered Maerwyn's wings. Where are they? And Ebihinin never did have wings. Maerwyn had wings when we met, I thought all Zaepharim would have them. Her bafflement fed the anxiety gnawing at the pit of her stomach. Things sure are strange in the Fifth dimension!

Once more in the Great Hall, Sybil looked around at the veils of colour. This certainly was an unusual place. The blue veil! Maybe it would help her. Telepathy. Perhaps the person she must find would send her a message. But how far did telepathic messages transmit? If the journey was long, maybe she would have to travel before she could use telepathy. But where to?

After dinner that evening Sybil retired to her room. It had been a very long, very strange and tiring day. She crossed the floor to the bed. A coverlet of earthy-green velvet fabric had been turned back in welcome.

Across the foot of the bed lay a soft white gown. She caught hold of it, carried it into the wash chamber to the right of her room and stood before a mirror. Her solemn eyes stared back at her. Leaning in closer, she caught stray locks of hair in her hands and pushed them behind her ears.

"What have you got yourself into?" she whispered. The remnants of repressed fear welled up, closing steel fingers around her throat in a deadly stranglehold. She was far from home, in a land of which she knew nothing. Concern for her parents shattered her calm and the tears she had quashed began to flow unbidden. She gave into them, mourning her loss, not knowing when or if she would ever see them again.

"Why is this happening to me?" she cried, grimacing at her reflection. Overwhelmed by loneliness and fear she hunched down in the corner of the room and wept until she was spent. Stifling her last sobs, she raised her head, blew her nose on a tissue and shook back her hair. Maerwyn has brought me safely here, she thought. He is a guide I can trust. Not that I had much of a choice. At the thought of this, a sudden hot wave of rage flared. "How dare they!" she spat.

Fuelled by anger, pushing with the strength of her thigh muscles, she slowly rose, sliding her back against the wall until she faced her reflection once again. Staring at her puffy eyes, she took a deep breath and held it until her lungs ached. There's no use in crying, she told herself. She let her breath escape in a rush, then hauled in more deep breaths, one after another until she had calmed herself. The anger that had consumed her slowly subsided.

She had to admit this was a fantastical experience, utterly nonsensical. A sparkle of light twinkled in the dark eyes staring back at her from the mirror. Truth be told, it was intriguing and it was beginning to appeal to her sense of adventure and curiosity.

Squaring her shoulders, she vowed to do her best. After all, her mother, her father too, had told her she would understand one day. Maybe they were right. Maybe this was part of what they meant.

Aithne must have been here, Sybil thought, as she considered the gown that had been laid out for her. She quickly washed away the last traces of her tears, undressed and slipped it over her head, pulling her long hair over the frilled collar.

She approached the warm glow from a fire pit in the centre of the room, extending her hands to warm them. Even here in Hetopia, the September evenings held a chill. Pondering the source of heat, she watched the amber glow fade from the pit. I must remember to ask Maerwyn about this, she promised herself.

Plumping the snowy-white pillow, she climbed into bed and let her head sink into the downy softness. Laying in the darkness, doubts began to creep in once more. The day's events churned relentlessly, her mind racing in wild speculation. With her thoughts in turmoil, she turned the ancient writings over and over until exhaustion finally carried her into a deep sleep.

A wispy apparition beckoned her, while deep bells tolled a warning. Sybil found herself drawn down a long dark tunnel, fear twisting a knot in her throat. Ahead, a figure flitted in and out of view. Sybil started to run but the tunnel seemed to grow longer. The faster she ran, the further the figure receded. At last she stumbled and fell headlong into water. Coughing and spluttering, Sybil woke with a jolt.

Heart racing and out of breath, she sat up in bed. Silvery moonbeams spread pools of light on her coverlet. Hauling in deep breaths of cool night air, she calmed herself, realizing it was only a dream. Where had she seen that figure before? Was it familiar? And those bells, she had heard them before! The water? She had fallen into a lake!

Throwing back the covers Sybil bounded out of bed, dressed feverishly and stood at the window scanning the view. She was in the east wing of the Crystal Palace and the scene below her lay slumbering as the moon waned. Faint streaks of light backlit the range of mountains heralding a new day. Birds of every hue, rustled and chirped their greeting to the morning sun. Their fantastic plumage shone in the translucent first light.

Sybil raced out of her chamber and ran down the long gleaming corridors. In full flight, she rounded a corner and—ummph—careened straight into Maerwyn.

"Where are you off to so early my Lady? There is no need to rush. Time here is elastic. You can stretch it out or compress it. One only needs to focus. Watch." Maerwyn stood quietly. His breathing grew long and deep. Centered in himself, he gently laid his hand on Sybil's forehead. She felt herself elongate. Her thoughts slowed and her world expanded, flowing around the fabric of time.

"Now tell me. Why are you running?"

Sybil's thoughts flowed toward Macrwyn in slow motion. She entered his mind-space and felt the peace resonating within, silence amid the sound.

"Oh, Maerwyn! How did you do that?"

His inner space expanded again and Sybil found herself enclosed by the warmth of his mind. Trust and inner calm replaced the flurry of activity that was Sybil's mind.

Maerwyn's hand left her forehead. Sybil found herself once again facing him. "Oh! That was wonderful. Thank you Maerwyn!"

"This is the way it is between all Hetopian's Sybil. It is nothing out of the ordinary. You too can learn how to do this."

"This is amazing Maerwyn! Everything is so different here. I have been meaning to ask. When we first met, you had wings. I thought all Zaepharim had wings, but Ebihinin doesn't and yours have disappeared!"

"Oh that!" chuckled Maerwyn. "Well now, how would you have come to believe that I could fly, or indeed that you could, if you had not seen my wings? I simply took that form to make it easier for you Sybil. Now that you have flown with me, we don't need those anymore do we? Nice touch, wouldn't you say?" Maerwyn exploded with laughter, bell-like tones resounding through the corridor.

The humour of it struck Sybil and she dissolved into laughter, welcoming release from her nervous tension of the last twenty-four hours. With her sides aching, tears streaming down her cheeks, Sybil leaned against Maerwyn shaking uncontrollably. Gasping for air, Sybil spluttered, "The Third dimension does have its limitations!" They collapsed in a heap, bells and laughter ringing throughout the halls.

"Did you sleep well?" asked Maerwyn, when he finally caught his breath.

"The room was very cosy. The fire pit was awesome. How does it work?"

"Pretty simple really," grinned Maerwyn. "It's solar energy. We capture the sun's rays for light and heat. The heat is stored in underground caverns. The lava rocks reach super-hot temperatures, which we then channel to our distributing centres."

"Oh! It's a bit like thermal energy we use in the Third dimension."

Suddenly remembering why she had been in such a hurry she said, "I was coming to find you Maerwyn. Last night I had a dream. I think it's a clue to understanding the writings. I must speak with Ebihinin."

Straightening himself up, Maerwyn lifted Sybil to her feet and smoothed her stray locks back into place. "She is in the Morning Sanctuary. Come, I will show you."

Sybil glided after Maerwyn as he sailed around a corner into a long avenue of mist. When they approached the waterfall entrance, dewdrops had condensed on Sybil's dark tresses.

"Come through the falls." Maerwyn disappeared ahead of her. Sybil was reluctant to get wet. Entering the falls, she felt invigorated, as though she'd had a shower. Emerging on the other side, to her utter surprise, she was completely dry! Sybil turned back and stretched forth her hand to touch the back of the waterfall. Her hand slipped right through. It wasn't water at all! Sybil stared at the dazzling light. The bones in her hand were clearly visible.

"What is that?" exclaimed Sybil.

"This is the Wellness Floe. We come here every day for scanning. It clears our systems, detects disorder and promotes long life," said Maerwyn.

"Now that is my kind of health clinic, no more needles! We could use something like this where I come from."

Further along the path, Ebihinin appeared in the mist ahead. "Good morning, my dear. Did you sleep well? I see you have come by way of the Floe; you look positively radiant."

"Oh yes, I feel so much better this morning. I had the strangest dream last night. I think it has shown me where I must begin the search. But there are so many unanswered questions."

"What is it Sybil? Are you wondering, why it is you who has been called? What it is that you are supposed to do? Over the centuries we have often wondered this too. We must consult the manuscripts again. There is so much more that you need to know, but all in good time my dear." Ebihinin turned and disappeared into the mist. "Come along. First we must take care of ourselves."

Sybil moved down the trail following Ebihinin through an archway of fragrant foliage. The scene before her was awash in vibrant pearly tones. To the left, Ebihinin sat reclining against a mossy embankment, her toes nestled in green softness, luxuriating in the stillness of the morning. Silently, Sybil seated herself beside Ebihinin, closed her eyes and drank in the quiet peacefulness that permeated the Morning Sanctuary.

When she opened her eyes, she saw that Ebihinin's face had taken on a luminous radiance. Energy flowed around and through her. Her body pulsated with radiant light. Sybil looked at her own hand and realized this was also happening to her. The double rings on her chest vibrated and Sybil began to feel completely present, at peace with those rings.

"Let us go now to the Great Hall and consult the ancient writings once again. We will have more insight after our morning preparations." Ebihinin rose, swept down the path and back through the falls. They entered the Great Hall once more and proceeded directly to the altar where Ebihinin focused the prisms. Descending into the sky below, they came to the pool.

Ebihinin grasped Sybil's hand and extended it over the water. She felt waves of power flow outward when she touched the glassy surface. Energy leapt through her fingers, the surface rippled and settled as the Book of Wisdom rearranged itself, presenting a clear script.

✦

Songs of Lament

Deep in the heartland, a force unknown
Gathers in power, all the world will moan.
A battle of the sea, a battle for the earth.
Gives rise to violence, and that of new birth.
Amidst weeping and sighs
Tales of sadness and woe,
One shall appear as guide
Above and in darkness below.
Powers of Ice prevail at last,
Crystal of the Dragon, danger's past.

Sybil turned the words over in her mind, committing them to memory. What did the writings say last night? The past holds the key. By the water he weeps while others pray. H-m-m...I wonder. A fragment of understanding clicked into place.

Her thoughts returned to the previous summer. She and her mother had made a pilgrimage, honouring their family roots. She had heard the story many times, of how her mother's great-great-grandparents, arrived by steamship via New York in the mid-1800s. Their closeness to the earth drew them inland to settle on a farm in Minnesota.

At the turn of the century, they ventured north to Canada to seek out a living in the wilderness of the Northwest Territories. Two years later, in 1905, it became the province of Saskatchewan. It was a harsh existence, especially during the long, bitterly cold winters. Prairie life exacted a tremendous toll on those who braved the frontier in order to find a better way of life for their families.

It was to this life, as a young bride, Franceska's great-great-grandmother, Claire Huber, came with her husband and infant son. They travelled by rail through Montana to the Canadian border. From that point, the remainder of the excursion was made in a sturdy wagon drawn by a team of oxen. The trip was a slow, arduous journey spanning a period of three weeks.

Arriving at their destination, all that greeted them was a barren landscape largely devoid of inhabitants. True, there were people, members of a great nation of Cree, but Claire Huber rarely saw them. Only traces of smoke from wood fires in the distance indicated their presence.

Her only visitors in that first year were the wild animals, waterfowl, songbirds, hordes of magpies and crows whose raucous calls sweetened the hardship of her existence.

Soon, other settlers began to arrive and a lively settlement sprang up near the body of water from which it had taken its name; Lenore Lake. Claire Huber was buried there in a small well-kept cemetery in the town near where she had lived.

Sybil visited the area with her mother a number of times in her early years. Memories of the past summer drew sharply into focus as she relived that day.

Standing at the foot of her ancestor's gravesite, her mother taught her the chants that only the Huber women knew. It was thrilling and surreal, knowing she was part of something mysterious and eternal.

Gazing at the inscription on the granite headstone of her great-great-great-grandmother, she shivered convulsively and tried to shake off the feeling that someone was watching.

CLAIRE ELIZABETH HUBER
March 24, 1880 – Sept. 23, 1946
A GIFTED SOUL

The bell tower in the church beside the graveyard began to toll, a deep resonant sound issuing forth measured peals that broke the silence, sending a flurry of pigeons skyward. The ominous ringing gathered the clouds of the heavens. They watched the birds swoop and shift as one body, ranging northward toward the lake. The strange events sent disturbing waves of fear coursing along Sybil's spine.

Following her mother along the path between the gravestones they approached a black wrought iron gate. Across the way stood a two-storey log cabin.

The two Huber women stood riveted to the spot, mesmerized by the spectacle before them. A thin veil of mist gathered, encircling the old cabin. Shadowy shapes loomed and receded as the mist thickened. Hand in hand they were drawn hypnotically toward the spectre. At the window a beckoning shape wavered, then grew indistinct. A thin sighing whisper sent chills up the nape of Sybil's neck. Her flesh puckered and crawled with apprehension.

"Find it…you must find it…you must find it," pleaded the vaporous voice.

A distant train whistle ruptured the trance as the two women strained to catch the strange message. The mist receded, drawing a veil across the barrier that bridged the threshold separating the two worlds.

Sybil was aware of the warmth created by the throbbing rhythm of the mark over her heart. The usual disgust she felt toward it was replaced by a feeling of peace. Magnetic waves of energy flowed off the ends of her fingertips as the power welled inside her. Claire's arrival had brought the *gift* that Sybil now possessed, passed on through the generations.

Her mind made a leap of intuition. Instinctively she knew! This is where she must begin her search. She must return to Lenore Lake! But what would it look like in the Fifth dimension? How would she find her way? Turning to Ebihinin and Maerwyn, she shared her thoughts.

"Last night I had a dream. Bells were tolling and a strange figure appeared. I tried to follow but fell into the water. I've been there before. I must return to my ancestral home at Lenore Lake. Do you know of this in the Fifth dimension?"

"Where is this located?" asked Maerwyn. Ebihinin tapped a crystal to her left and a holographic image of the Fifth dimension hovered before them.

Studying it for several minutes, Sybil realized that the geography was exactly the same as in the Third. The only difference that she could see was in the names, as she and Maerwyn had discussed earlier. Her eyes followed the direction she had travelled with her mother. Saskanahook must be Saskatchewan! Tracing the route more closely she found Leanora Basine. That must be Lenore Lake in the Third dimension!

Excited by her discovery, Sybil danced around Maerwyn, pulling him with her while he hovered in space, clearly overjoyed by her find. Ebihinin tapped the crystal and the hologram receded.

"Well my dear, you are an amazing young woman," chimed Ebihinin. "We must now gather our resources for the journey ahead. It is imperative we use all means at our disposal. The country you are going into is fraught with peril. A once peaceful population of Leanori Truids lived there. Now it is under the influence of the Graenwolven. Over the years the locals have lived in abject poverty under this regime. Recently, there is a growing fear that all Leanori have perished."

"Oh," sighed Sybil. Her stomach tightened into knots of fear. This did not sound easy. How would she, a mere girl, prevail against these Graenwolven?

"There, there," soothed Ebihinin, noticing the worried frown on Sybil's face. "Remember now, it is written in the Great Book. You will find a way."

"Can you tell me more about these Lea-Leanori Tru-Truids? Who are they?"

"Traditionally they inhabited the area surrounding the Leanora Basine, Sybil. We have had many chilling reports of disturbances in weather patterns and unusual sightings in the area. It's as though someone or something is trying to alter the climate."

"But why would anyone do that?" cried Sybil.

"I tell you, it is all very disturbing to the rest of us," confided Maerwyn. "It has had an effect on our way of life, even here in Hetopia. The magnetic wave energy is a bit off these days. It takes so much longer to regain strength when one has been sharing the same frequency too long."

"Well, I do remember reports in the Third dimension about crop circles. I wonder if they have anything to do with this."

While they were speaking, a large Zaepharim appeared before them. His snowy countenance radiated warmth as he stood facing Ebihinin.

"Good morning," he bell-toned, waving a greeting.

"Greetings Longille. What have you to report?" Ebihinin inquired of the huge Zaepharim. "Before we go on, please do forgive me. Sybil this is Longille. Longille, this is Sybil who has arrived from the Third dimension. This is the One we have been expecting. At long last she has arrived."

Longille fixed his golden eyes on Sybil and gestured in a grand way. *"I'm so very pleased to make your acquaintance."*

Maerwyn intervened, "Sybil prefers to use her language Longille."

"Sorry, of course." He repeated his welcome, "Very pleased to meet you, Sybil."

"And I, you," replied Sybil.

Longille turned his attention back to Ebihinin. "I have just returned from the east. I'm afraid the news is much worse. The land is parched. Nothing is growing. Food is scarce. The inhabitants of the area, if any are left, are suffering terribly. Wells have gone dry and raging fires sweep through the northern forests. It is as though all the forces of the universe have gone awry."

"Indeed, it does appear that the Universal Energy has been altered," observed Ebihinin. "There have been many disturbing accounts of such phenomena elsewhere as well. Tell me, in your opinion Longille, having recently come from Central Caenadria, would it be possible for Sybil to make the journey without being detected? We must get her to Leanora Basine very soon."

"It is not entirely impossible to do that. However, she will need our guidance and protection to be sure of the way. I can be ready by dawn of tomorrow if necessary."

"I knew we could count on you Longille. You are a trusted and reliable courier. Maerwyn will make the journey with you."

At the mention of his name, Maerwyn straightened his shoulders. "I am at your service Ebihinin. It is an honour. We will see that Sybil arrives safely, remaining with her until she is ready to return."

He smiled at Longille, "Let us meet tonight to plan the route we must take. Meanwhile we shall prepare Sybil for the journey. Come Sybil, we must visit the Wellness Floe once more." He turned and glided up the stairway to the Great Hall above and forged ahead on the Sanctuary trail.

As they approached, Sybil was aware of the change in the Floe. The dazzling intensity of the light had concentrated in a wide swath preceding the entrance. Following Maerwyn through the falls, they stopped.

"Herein lies a pool. Once you bathe in it Sybil, you will be charged with super energy, enhancing your powers of concentration. Your eyesight will magnify tenfold."

Continuing along the path they veered to the left onto another trail, which brought them to a shimmering pond. Taking Sybil's hand, Maerwyn guided her to the edge of the pool and motioned for her to proceed.

Sybil immersed herself, ducking her head under the surface. She opened her eyes to behold, as in a dream, beautiful horizons of distant lands. Each vista rose before her with crystalline clarity. Rising out of the liquid she emerged fully aware of minute details, every blade of grass, every leaf, the mist in the distance. She seemed to be part of the landscape.

Maerwyn's voice broke the reverie. "This power must only be used for the common good. Those who would misuse it will recognize it in you. They will attempt to wrest it from you. Guard it well."

While talking, they strolled along another path to where a beautifully plumed bird, perched on a treetop, emitted a series of melodious notes. The way opened into a clearing to where a golden aviary shone in the morning sun. As Longille held the door for Sybil, Maerwyn gestured, "Please enter. You will be given the Gift of Song. Those who hear it will be mesmerized, unable to see or move. The power of the melody will capture attention completely."

Upon entering, the soft click of the door closed behind her, initiating the beginning of a hypnotic melody; a choir of bird-song. Her own voice trilled the ancient scales, ascending and descending in perfect pitch. One of the birds cocked his head at her, and in a flutter of wings the flock took flight, circling Sybil and bestowing the Gift of Song. Amidst a downy shower of feathers, Sybil found her full voice. The departing flock listened while her vocals rose and echoed in the empty chamber, harmonious crescendos reverberating off the golden walls.

Maerwyn, Longille and Sybil wandered along the forests of the Wellness Sanctuary, savouring the peaceful solitude. It was nearly noon before they re-emerged through the falls. A resplendent repast had been prepared in the dining room of the Great Hall. Succulent fruits, delectable vegetables, mountains of saffron rice, pilafs of ancient grains, nuts, and berries were laden on low glass tables. Satin cushions were tossed in inviting arrays. Reclining in comfort, the guests dined amidst low murmurs of appreciation.

Discussion turned to the journey ahead. "Are you nearly ready to depart?" inquired Ebihinin.

"Yes, all is ready. We are planning to leave at dawn tomorrow," replied Maerwyn.

Sybil had been swept along by the preparations in the Sanctuary. Now she held back. Was she ready to embark on this strange journey? It was all so dream-like. Her glance fell on Ebihinin whose serene gaze sent a measure of calmness her way. *You are ready Sybil.* She nodded her head in reply.

CHAPTER FOUR
Graenwolven Territory

Before daybreak Sybil rose to prepare for her journey. Maerwyn and Longille had been up through the night consulting the stars.

"It is indeed a favourable time to travel my Lady," reported Maerwyn. "The alignment of the planets Juno and Mauritia will allow us to proceed with a minimum of disruption in the Plasmic Energy Force. We will be virtually undetected until we re-enter our destination."

Ebihinin had been listening quietly to the conversation. She extended both hands in a gesture of farewell blessing. "Remember to call on the natural strength you have been endowed with Sybil. When in doubt, use the gifts you have received here as a guide. May your Life Energy protect you and speed you on your way."

She stood and watched as the trio rose above the city and flew eastward out of sight.

The first rays of morning sun broke over the horizon, setting the snow-capped mountains ablaze. Dark crags deepened into fiery pinks as the sun chased spirit shadows into the valleys.

"What a glorious morning to be travelling," cried Longille, as they swooped over the jagged peaks. "It won't be long before we reach the Okenagean Basine. Legend says the land mass shifted. The inland sea was diverted. Sea monsters are now trapped in what is left."

"I have seen them myself," said Maerwyn. "What a sight! Two gigantic heads breaking the surface of the waters. Magnificent!"

"Peaceful beings, I hear," added Longille.

"Yes, that is generally understood to be so," agreed Maerwyn. "A number of years ago I was dispatched on a trade mission to Kalenowel City on the Basine," explained Maerwyn. "That is when I first saw them."

"It is where we Hetopians acquired the star fruit you ate in the Yellow Chamber of the Great Hall Sybil," said Longille.

"I thought star fruit only grew in the Yellow Chamber!" said Sybil.

"Same fruit but the Yellow Chamber gives it special qualities," replied Maerwyn.

"Do the Hetopians trade with other cultures?"

"Oh yes. There's an intricate network of mutual support in the west," replied Longille. "Both Maerwyn and I are ambassadors representing the Hetopians on this side of the Roccocian Prominences. We are in safe territory until we enter the flatlands. There we must use extreme caution."

"As far as our Intelligence has uncovered, the territory as far east as the Granitean Sheald has fallen to the Graenwolven," Longille said. "Not much is known about the fierce race that has invaded from the north."

"The peaceable folk known in the Centralian region are now subject to abject poverty and deprivation. Cruel overlords have been exploiting them for nearly a decade," said Maerwyn. He shook his head sadly. "Alas, the soil is exhausted and the country is barren, a virtual desert."

Longille continued, "At first the Graenwolven made great promises to lead the Centralians in production for trade on the World Market. However, this was only a ruse to establish huge conglomerate landholdings to subdue the population. As far as we know, once they had gained control, the Centralians were rounded up and housed in camps patrolled by the Namors Guardia. We think they are Graenwolven enforcers that maintain control in the realm."

"It is a huge worry to us on the coast," added Maerwyn.

"How are we going to enter flatlands territory without being discovered?" asked Sybil. "It is a very long distance to travel before we find Leanora Basine."

"Ah-ha-h-h," cried Maerwyn. "That is where we Hetopians excel my dear." He drew a huge breath. Unable to contain his glee, his laughter rolled forth, resounding over the countryside below. "We have an extraordinary talent for entering the Plasmic Energy Force without even so much as a ripple. We can fly virtually undetected."

"Flying at the speed of light, we enter the Energy Force at an angle of ninety degrees precisely," Longille clarified. "Have done it many times."

"Plasmic Energy Force? Speed of Light? Not possible!" said Sybil. "A right angle turn. Can't be done at that speed! I can't do that!"

"Oh yes you can. Hold both of our hands Sybil," reassured Maerwyn. "We will slip you through with us. You'll see. Nothing to it."

They had been skimming the snowy peaks of the Roccocian Prominences. Gradually the jagged granite gave way to gently rolling hills. Ahead of them lay the flatlands.

"It is time Sybil," whispered Maerwyn. "We must maintain absolute silence now. Are you ready?"

Sybil nodded her head imperceptibly, scrunching her eyes tightly shut.

"Here we go. Hold fast!" Maerwyn and Longille accelerated.

The wind raked icy fingers through Sybil's hair and deposited a frosty rime on her skin as she was propelled forward at warp speed. Abruptly, she felt herself change direction and she was jerked upward through the Energy Force. They levelled off and resumed normal speed.

"That was scary!" cried Sybil.

Remembering Maerwyn's admonition of absolute silence, eyes wide with fear, she clamped her hand over her mouth.

"No need to worry now Sybil," Maerwyn reassured. "We have entered the protective zone in the Plasmic Energy Force. We cannot be heard by outside agencies. When we reach our destination we will exit the zone just before landing. It will be extremely dangerous at that time. The Namors Guardia will detect our re-entry. Once landed, we'll have only normal escape routes open to us. And as a precaution, once we land it might be best if we speak to each other in Telepath if we find others."

"Who are these Namors Guardia?" Sybil asked.

"No one is sure how or why they came to be here, but it seems they are the ruling body in control. The Leanori Truids have all but vanished," replied Maerwyn.

"Let's do a little exploring to find the safest place to land," Longille suggested.

"Do you recall anything about the area when you visited with your mother last summer?" asked Maerwyn. *"Is there anything in the Third dimension that may offer us some protection?"*

"Obviously the lake will still be there. It is far enough from the village. We can move to a safer position before the Namors Guardia are dispatched," Sybil replied.

"Absolutely," Maerwyn grinned at her.

"What? Why are you looking at me like that?" asked Sybil.

"Just admiring your ability to speak Telepath!" chuckled Maerwyn.

"So I am!" Sybil was startled by her newly found ability.

That blue veil, the bells of telepathy, what a valuable gift, she thought. She wasn't sure how it worked. It just seemed to happen.

"How did I do that?"

"Once you have been given the gift, it is easily picked up," explained Maerwyn. *"The only thing you must learn, is how to separate it from your private thoughts."*

"Yes," confirmed Longille. *"That's the complex part. You must set the intention to transmit. All other thoughts are your own, separate and personal."*

"Interesting! What a useful language!"

Resuming the conversation, she went on, "I still prefer my own language, if you don't mind, but I do see the sense in using Telepath if we want to keep our conversation private."

"Yes, that is most agreeable," agreed Longille.

"You said re-entry was dangerous. They will be able to detect where we land. That means they will investigate the point of entry first."

"Yes. Once landed, we must move as quickly as possible," said Longille.

"We can travel undetected on the ground. By the time they reach our landing place, we'll be long gone," replied Sybil.

Circling north of the village they approached the lake shores. When they veered east, Sybil caught sight of an abandoned farmyard. The old house sagged under the years of neglect, its weathered grey siding peeling off in splinters.

"There, let's head for that old yard once we land. It's only a few kilometres from the lake. We can spend the night in the abandoned house," suggested Sybil.

"Capital idea Sybil!" agreed Longille. "I saw a wharf on the lake shore near that end. Good landing spot."

Turning back, they flew over the wharf. "Land near that old fish net. It might be useful," suggested Sybil.

"We'll maintain holding pattern and land after nightfall," agreed Maerwyn. "Meanwhile, shall we have a look at what is happening in Leanora village?"

Heading southward, a desolate landscape spread out beneath them. Dusty farmland, parched from years of drought and mismanagement, begged for rain.

At the north end of the village the towers of a forbidding castle loomed into view. It had once been a grand structure constructed of fieldstone common to the area. Each stone was cut and fashioned to fit snugly, interfacing to achieve a smooth exterior. The surfaces were now discoloured with years of grime, the rock face beginning to crumble with decay.

Ramparts encircled the main walls where two sentries patrolled, eyes roving over the village and outward to the horizons. A sudden hot gust unfurled a black flag, revealing a Graenwolven motif in red, fluttering atop the tallest tower. In the second tower, hung a huge brass gong replacing the bell that had once been the pride of the Leanorian townspeople. Etched on its surface was a ferocious non-descript head, defying interpretation. Its evil eyes glinted through the yellow sheen of the brass, challenging anyone to enter its space. A third tower sheltered a small courtyard.

Flying nearer, the scowling faces of the guards revealed coal-black eyes hooded by an overhanging forehead that rose high, flaring into bony protuberances framing the hideous skull. Elongated noses protruded from the flat facial plane above a slit-like mouth. Sybil cringed in horror at the sentries pacing back and forth in measured determination.

"Ughhh! I don't want to run into those guards on a dark night or anytime for that matter!" Sybil grimaced with disgust. Near the village centre, there was no movement on the streets. More Namors Guardia patrolled what appeared to be a deserted settlement.

"How many Namors, Longille?" asked Maerwyn. "Let's make another pass to check out the numbers so we know what we are up against. Surely this small village wouldn't have a full battalion."

"Besides the two on the towers, I see two at the north end, two covering the main street, and two more on the south end of the village. They seem to work in pairs. The two at the north end will get to the Basine first," calculated Longille. "And by the looks of them, they can move fast. I don't believe the tower guards will leave their posts but they may call for reinforcements."

"Time to head back to the Basine. Nightfall is fast approaching," said Maerwyn.

Searing hues of burnt orange faded to smoky amethyst as dusk fell. Gray tones deepened to sooty black and darkness settled over the land.

"Ready? Hold tight!" warned Longille, as they accelerated north once more. Again, the sudden rush of icy wind and the swift direction change raked her hair. This time Sybil kept her eyes open, fascinated by the blur of dimly lit landscape below. They landed with a soft thud next to the net as planned.

"Grab hold of this net. We'll drag it behind us to cover our tracks," said Sybil.

Swiftly, the trio headed for the shelter of the farmyard about four kilometres south-east of the shore, trailing the net in the dusty soil. Desiccated stubble scratched their shins as they sped across fields of long-ago harvested graen. Powder dry soil sent puffs of dust into the inky blackness of the night sky, as their legs pistoned over the barren landscape. Running hard, they reached the long dry grass of the unkempt farmyard. Sinister straw-like fingers grabbed at their ankles as they slogged their way through the matted grass toward the house.

It was impenetrable; boarded up by dejected hands that had long ago given up eking out existence in a desert that had once yielded rich harvests.

"Run for the barn," said Sybil.

They turned in unison, rasping their way through the long dry grass toward the yawning chasm where the door stood ajar. The sagging roof etched a line of blackness against the night sky.

Gaining entry to the barn, the odour of musty hay assaulted their nostrils as they felt their way cautiously through the bovine cavern. A faint scent of cattle that had once habituated the space hung heavily in the night air. Inching forward, Sybil who was in the lead, felt the rungs of a ladder leading to a loft. Slowly she started to climb, propelling herself upward into the airless interior of the hayloft. Followed closely by Maerwyn and Longille, she reached the loft where they settled at the far end on a mouldering pile of hay. Soft rustling sounds indicated they were not alone, as small creatures settled for the night.

"Do you think Namors Guardia have reached the Basine by now?" Sybil ventured. "Hope they don't search this way. That net should have concealed our tracks enough to buy us time."

"That was ingenious Sybil," replied Longille. "I was in such a hurry to get out of there. Never thought to drag a net to cover tracks. This walking mode is uncommon, hard to get used to. But we don't dare enter the Plasmic Energy Force until we're ready to leave again."

"You wouldn't need to know such things. You fly everywhere," Sybil laughed. "We learned to cover tracks in Explorers Club. Even in the light of day tomorrow, this wind will cover any trace of footprints. We'll be safe for a while."

"Let's get some rest," suggested Maerwyn. He walked toward the window at the south end of the loft and added, "I'll take the first watch."

Sometime in the night, Longille had relieved Maerwyn at his post. He stood gazing out of the window watching the first faint glow of dawn lighten the sky. Long fingers of light seeped through the cracks of the hip roof barn, illuminating dusty particles suspended in the dank air. Sybil stirred, rolled over and snuggled against Maerwyn's shoulder for warmth. He woke with a start and murmured a faint greeting. Sybil cracked open one eye, then sat up stretching and yawning.

"Good morning," she whispered. "Why didn't you wake me to keep watch?" she scolded, looking at Longille standing at the window. "I am perfectly capable of doing sentry duty. If we don't work together, we don't stand a chance here."

"Absolutely right," agreed Maerwyn. "You were so tired last night, we didn't have the heart to wake you. From now on, we will all do our share. You can take the first watch tonight."

"But now we must see to morning needs," said Longille, producing a pouch. "What shall we have for breakfast? Ebihinin provided us with a BanquoeBag which yields all manner of sustenance. It is part of the gear we Hetopians carry on field trips. Quite ingenious wouldn't you say?"

"That's some bag!" said Sybil, as Longille produced thick slices of crusty wheat bread laden with butter. He crouched beside them on the mouldering hay and handed out two cold globes of milk.

"What are our plans for the day?" asked Maerwyn, while they sat munching their breakfast.

Longille folded the BanquoeBag, tucked it back under his tunic and reclined against the soft hay. He was about to answer, when he caught a faint sound. Longille held up two fingers for silence, covering his lips, his eyes alert with caution. He crossed silently to the window and peered into the morning light. Sybil and Maerwyn stole to his side for a peek. From the west, the sound of boots resounded on the dusty road.

"It sounds like a whole army of them!" Maerwyn looked around the loft for an escape, but there was none.

The friends watched from the window, while a squad of ten sentries swung into the driveway, marched to a halt in front of the old house and stood at attention. Surveying the scene below, Sybil's nostrils flared. She tensed for action, her adrenalin-soaked nerve endings preparing for flight.

The scaly brown bodies were clothed in leather skins. Each countenance closely resembled the next. The same bony protuberances she saw the day before gave the squad a ghastly aura, as though they wore a natural helmet. Every guard shouldered a formidable weapon, a huge scythe. Its curved brass blade glittered ominously in the morning sun. Except for a medal in the form of two golden graen sheaves on his chest and a black stripe on his left shoulder, nothing distinguished the leader from the others. Two flashing black eyes scathed the morning air as he barked orders.

"Fan out and search the yard. Check the buildings. Leave not one iota of space unaccounted for. Move! On the double!"

"Yes Sir!" The sentries sprang into action, responding in unison. They began a methodical search using a grid pattern, their long, pointed noses snorkel-sniffing under shrubs, empty graeneries and shops that stood vacant in the yard.

Sybil moved automatically. She felt herself drawn to the north end of the loft. Under the hay in the west corner, Sybil found what she was searching for, a trapdoor, concealed so neatly, she had to hunt for it. Groping with her hand she found the secreted latch and pulled upward. It swung free, opening wide enough for the three of them to slip inside.

"Hurry, get in!" she urged, slipping into Telepath out of fear.

Maerwyn and Longille lay down under the floorboards, while Sybil lowered the door, pulling armfuls of hay over top, scuttling inside at the last minute. With thundering hearts their breath came in short puffing rasps, labouring to quell the suffocating fear. Listening intently, their ears alert to the sentries tramping over the floor, they recoiled in horror as the weight of a Guardia stood directly on the trapdoor. Holding their breath, it seemed the snuffling would never stop as he poked his long inquisitive nose through the mouldering hay.

"Ahh-choo! Ahh-choo!" Great explosive sneezes reverberated through the hayloft. "Ahh-choo! Ahh-choo!"

"Come on, let's get out of here. There's nothing up here. This hay is killing me!" wheezed the gruff voice above Sybil's tightly closed eyes.

The footsteps and harsh voices withdrew, tramping down the ladder of the loft. From a distance, the voices continued to emit guttural outbursts, stabbing the already stifling heat of the morning air.

"We have searched everywhere sir," reported one of the guards. "There's no one here. They did not come this way."

"Well, they've gone somewhere!" growled the commander in frustration. "We have been searching all night. They can't disappear into thin air! We know from the disturbance in the Plasmic Energy Force that three have entered. Form up and we'll search the other side of the Basine."

As soon as the distant thud of boots receded, Sybil, Maerwyn and Longille crept from their hiding place.

"That was a close call! It's a wonder those snouts didn't sniff us out!" Maerwyn exclaimed. "Lethal weapons if you ask me!"

"They look like those brass hooks they carry!" added Longille.

"Yeeiiigh," agreed Sybil. "That mouldy hay sure saved us! If it hadn't been for the mildew…" she shuddered, hating to think about what would have happened next.

"How did you know the trapdoor was there Sybil?" inquired Maerwyn incredulously.

"I can't explain it. I think I've been here before," replied Sybil. "The whole area is familiar. My people did settle and live here long ago. Maybe the Third and Fifth Dimensions aren't so different after all!"

"If that is the case, it will be an advantage," interjected Maerwyn. "Now let's plan our next move. We must figure out the purpose of Sybil's arrival in the Fifth dimension. You said you had a dream about water. How did that reading from the Book of Wisdom go?"

"We must decipher the legends," said Longille, quoting the script from memory.

Songs of Hope

Blues hold the secret within, let go of all fear to win
To double your powers seek that which was lost
The past holds the key.
By the water, he weeps, while others pray.
Captive by night, invisible by day
Joined for all eternity, your past holds the key
The journey is long, be strong of heart
Be joined forever, never more to part.

"I must find something from my past?" sighed Sybil. "Who is weeping by the waters, captive by night and invisible by day? How can one be invisible? It doesn't make any sense."

"Wait a minute," said Longille. 'By the waters he weeps, while others pray. Captive by night.' There must be something to that. I think we should wait until dark and go back to Leanora Basine. We must make a careful search of the shores for some clue."

"But that lake is nearly thirty kilometres long! What can we find in the dark?" asked Sybil. "It could take weeks. Won't be easy with heavy patrols by the lake."

"No, I don't think so," Maerwyn replied. "That is the least likely place they would expect us to go. They'd think we would distance ourselves from the entry point," he reasoned.

"Good point Maerwyn. Best chance is after dark," conceded Sybil. "We'll leave tonight."

It was nearly eleven o'clock when the three figures left the loft. The pale moon had risen in the eastern sky, casting soft shadows over the farmyard. Once they crossed the stubble field, they made steady progress and soon came to the dock near the southern tip of the lake where they had landed.

"I think we should check the eastern shore first," suggested Longille. In agreement, they set off proceeding north along the lake. They had been walking for some time when suddenly Sybil held her hand up in alarm.

"Get down," she warned. They flattened themselves against the dry landscape as a group of Namors Guardia emerged from a clump of shrubs two-hundred metres to their right.

"We have our orders," snapped a guttural voice. "Search this side of the Basine again before morning. You there, Sznog and SzMorg go north along the shore. Eventually you will meet Guardia coming from the other direction."

Gesturing to the guards on his left he barked, "You two go south on the shore until you meet up with the western contingent. SzGark, you come with me. We will begin another search outward from here. If they're still around we'll find them."

Maerwyn signalled Longille and Sybil to move ahead along the shoreline. They were being pushed steadily northward by those pointed proboscises poking here and there, snuffling, snuffling, snuffling!

In haste, they put distance between themselves and the search party, wading through the shallows of the lakeshore to confound the nasal intelligence of the Namors Guardia. Moonlight reflections wavered in the watery depths as the ripples spread outward. They had been pushing hard for nearly an hour when suddenly Sybil was stopped in her tracks.

"Oof! Ouch!" she muttered, scraping her shin on a large boulder in the shallows. She picked her way around it moving forward slowly. Ten metres ahead she saw a shadow looming out of the scrub.

CHAPTER FIVE
The Leanoria Truids

Wading through a tangle of weeds, she whispered, "It's a boat! Wonder if it will float long enough to get us out of here."

"Only one way to find out," Maerwyn replied. He dragged it toward the water and held it steady for his two companions to hop in. Scrambling aboard, he shoved off with one of the oars and began rowing furiously.

"Maerwyn, slow down! You're making too much noise," cautioned Sybil. He let the oars go slack, waiting for the ripples to settle. In the distance they could hear murmured grunts and snuffles south of their location. The boat drifted for a bit. Maerwyn slowly resumed a steady pull on the oars, dipping lightly into the water. His concerted efforts moved them far out onto the lake propelling the boat ever northward.

"Tell me more about the race that lived here before the Graenwolven invasion?" Sybil wanted to know. "If some of them are still around, maybe they can help us."

"It is well documented. Centralians inhabited the flatlands for thousands of years," said Maerwyn. "They lived a peaceful existence as an agrarian society in harmony with the land. According to our Intelligence, that has changed since the invasion. Many areas of Centralia have been destroyed, although we hear there are pockets of resistance attempting to rise up against them."

"Fascinating really," agreed Longille. "Rumour has it the Leanorians nearly disappeared but they discovered a method of duplicating themselves. Of course no one knows for sure. You know how stories go."

"Something is definitely wrong. We saw only Guardia in the village. Are they all in hiding or are they being held as prisoners?" asked Sybil.

"Both possibilities could be true I suppose," answered Maerwyn. "After Graenwolven moved into the area, they placed them in work camps. Now that the area is devastated with drought and the soil is exhausted, we fear many have perished. Some may have escaped. But how could they exist in such terrible conditions as these?"

The eastern sky had lightened considerably while they were talking. The distant shore grew more distinct.

"We need to find cover before daybreak," Sybil's worried frown puckered her forehead.

She looked around in wonder at the parched landscape. The drought had left the lake bed retracted, a dwarf of its former size. The high water mark was up near the tree line. Cracks lacerated a wide mud flat dried to a hard finish. In the distance, she caught a slight movement. The ragged edges of her breath escaped convulsively.

"It's the Namors. They're moving along the shoreline."

"Point the prow toward the centre of the lake Longille," Maerwyn instructed. "If we turn the stern toward them, we'll be less visible."

Longille took over rowing and steered steadily toward the centre. Far out on the water, he pulled up the oars and laid them across the gunnels. Resting his weary arms, he scanned the horizon from where they had come, reassuring himself they were less conspicuous.

A faint lapping caught the attention of the three on board. The boat drifted as they sat in silence, pondering the peculiar sound. The intensity increased, growing into the distinct sound of waves lapping against the shore. Startled, the trio sat gripped in tension. Waves began to circle them, building a wall of water higher, higher, until they lost sight of the distant shore beyond. Inside the wall the surface was smooth as mirrored glass.

"What is happening?" Sybil felt panicky. "I don't like this."

Memories of her wild ride in the tumultuous whirlpool of Spoon Lake, flooded Sybil's mind with terror.

"Steady now my dear," soothed Maerwyn. "At least we are out of sight of the Guardia. It appears as though someone or something has come to our aid."

The glassy surface increased in width and they found themselves on a broad expanse of calm water, enclosed by a protective wall of water.

Peering overboard Maerwyn and Longille both let out an incredulous exhalation.

"Would you look at that!" they pealed in unison, switching instantly to Telepath. *"Down below Sybil."*

Sybil gathered her courage and peeped over the side of the boat. *"Where did that come from? How did they get down there!?"* she exclaimed.

Directly beneath them was a city. Faces smiled up at them and people waved, beckoning them to climb overboard and join them in the depths below. To the starboard, a stairway of water-gel descended to the lake floor.

"Shall we go?" asked Longille.

"What choice do we have? Better this, than heading back to the mud-flats into the arms of the Namors Guardia," said Maerwyn. *"What do you think Sybil?"*

"Beyond weird! Like everything in the Fifth Dimension! Can't turn back now though. Besides, how would we escape this wall of water? Drop anchor Longille."

She stepped over the side of the boat and stood on the landing of the water-gel casement. Maerwyn and Longille followed her onto the landing and the three friends walked down into the city. Water walls towered around the settlement, encased by an invisible protective shield. Above them, the bottom of their boat bobbed gently, casting a shadow on the lake floor below. Sybil reached out to touch the side of the wall. It undulated and shimmered. A school of perch glided past her outstretched hand, their golden fishy eyes examining her curiously.

A delegation from the lake bottom city stood on the landing, waiting to greet them. First one, then another extended his hand, cupping their guests' elbows and shaking the whole forearm in a vigorous welcoming grasp.

"Greetings and welcome to friends from the west. You are the first people we have seen in a very long time." The speaker was beside himself with joyous excitement.

"I am Gergenon. My companion here goes by the name of Gerardo. We have been aware of your arrival ever since you left the Plasmic Energy Force. Concerned for your safety with the Namors Guardia so near, we have kept a vigilant watch over you."

While Maerwyn introduced himself and his two companions, Sybil stared incredulously. The representatives were identical! Two cerulean blue eyes looked out of a face that seemed to be made of velvet. So smooth was the creamy pink skin. Sybil resisted the urge to run her fingertips along the high cheekbones—like quotation marks bracketing a broad smile of pearly teeth. Raised bushy eyebrows gave them a quizzical expression that cast a comical look of merriment in the twinkling orbs beneath. A mop of brown hair framed the face, cascading down the sideburns into a long flowing beard. Each wore a generic suit of navy blue. The only distinguishing feature was a silver badge pinned to the left lapel of the suit bearing their name and serial number. Genuine affection spilled forth as they continued to voice their concerns.

"We are delighted to have you among us. Please do come and make yourselves at home. We have prepared lodging for your comfort. You must be exhausted following last night's ordeal," said Gerardo.

"And hungry," added Gergenon. "We must dine."

Turning on his heels, he led the guests down the walkway toward the centre of the city. Approaching a glass-domed building, Gergenon turned to Sybil appraising her with curious eyes.

"How is it you come to be in these parts young lady? It is much too dangerous for someone of your age to be travelling hereabouts."

Sybil stared at him in amazement. These were peculiar people indeed and she did not altogether trust them. At a loss for words, she did not know how to respond. If she was to achieve the purpose of her visit, she would have to tell them something, would have to go on blind faith.

"Don't really have the answer to that Gergenon. Seems I have been chosen for a task. I'm here to discover what it is. Perhaps your people can help."

Gergenon nodded his understanding and clapped his hands together, rubbing them in anticipation. "Lunch is served," he announced.

They entered a dining hall with long rows of wooden tables flanked by benches. Diners were already seated at the communal tables. Young women rushed hurriedly back and forth with serving dishes. "Please take a seat and help yourselves to food."

Sybil graciously accepted the seat near Gergenon and Gerardo. "Thank you," she answered, gaping in stunned silence at the women of the commune.

The open stares of intense scrutiny cast a microbial pall across her skin. All they need is a microscope, she thought.

Noticing there was no one else her age, really threw her. What happened to the children? She sensed the distrust under their polite façade. Maybe there was even a bit of revulsion. Could she blame them? They hadn't been outside of this commune, at least she didn't think they had. The only two that seemed to be at ease were Gergenon and Gerardo. Curious.

Sybil glanced sideways at Longille and Maerwyn. She'd been with them long enough to recognize the sheen that developed on their faces, when they were working through discomfort.

"This is bizarre," she said. *"But better here than on the lakeshore."*

Longille caught her eye and nodded. He nudged Maerwyn and asked, *"What do you make of this?"*

"Certainly odd. Agreed though, better here than out there."

The three companions watched the women scurrying about. It was astounding how alike they were!

Each of them had round smooth faces with arched eyebrows perched over sky-blue eyes. Cascades of wavy brown hair fell to waist level. A simply cut overdress in a deep shade of blue fell to knee level. Again, the only way of discerning between them was a silver pin with name and serial number fastened at their breast. Row upon row of men and women, all identical, lined the tables engaged in polite conversation.

After they had piled mounds of broiled fish, green vegetables and other lake bottom delicacies on their plates Sybil asked, "Who are you people and how long have you lived here Gerardo?"

Between bites, he replied, "It has been nearly ten years since the Graenwolven invasion. We are the last of the Leanorians, at least of those who fled and succeeded in escaping. Most of our people were caught, placed in camps and forced to work on the big estates. Alas, the land is exhausted. You've seen the devastation out there. As far as we know, all of our people have perished. Hard labour and starvation have taken their toll."

Gergenon picked up where he left off. "We, here, are very fortunate. There are two members still present today who pioneered this method of farming. They set up the first underwater colony, prior to the invasion. Because it was experimental, it wasn't well publicized."

"Thank the Energy Force for that!" interjected Gerardo. "If the Graenwolven ever suspected or discovered us, it would be fatal!"

Gergenon continued, "As it is, I can't see how they will last much longer. There's barely anything left to live on. We're biding our time, hoping they will soon give up the area as useless."

"Please excuse me if I seem rude," ventured Sybil. "I have another question."

"Not at all Sybil," replied Gergenon. "Please ask."

"Well," replied Sybil, hesitantly. "I was wondering why you all look alike. Isn't it confusing? How do you tell each other apart without the pins?"

"That is part of the experiment Sybil. We've discovered a duplicating method. Without that, we would have been lost as a nation. I will explain later, after you have had your dinner. In fact, it will be much easier to understand if we show you."

"I've noticed there are no children here? What has happened to them?" Sybil was curious to know.

"Children? Those awful tales from the olden days! Babies. Messy diapers. Spitting up. Bawling all night. Great Golden Fish Eyes! Why bother? No, no, no," tutted Gergenon. "Too much work!" He laughed suddenly at the very idea.

"We have a much better system," Gerardo joined in. "Besides, once duplicated, there's no need. Messy business that other way. But all in good time. Wait 'til you see. Clever, clever, clever," he grinned broadly.

"These guys are humdingers," said Sybil. *"Who doesn't like babies?"*

"Humdingers?" asked Maerwyn.

"You know, humdingers, nincompoops. Someone who doesn't make much sense. They're cuckoo!"

Longille was turning a shade of blue, stifling the urge to explode in laughter. Maerwyn choked on a fish ball. Sybil had the oddest expressions! His shoulders began to shake and he doubled over to hide his amusement. He coughed up a chunk and dropped it under the table.

Longille thumped his back. "You okay there friend?"

"Yes, yes." Maerwyn straightened up. "Sorry, my apologies. The fish is a bit spicy, very good, but spicy. I'm not used to it." Changing the topic, lest they break out into laughter, he forged ahead.

"There's another matter that we should discuss. We are on a very important mission. This young woman has come to us from the Third dimension. Apparently her ancestors, who first arrived in this area, farmed all these years here as well. In the Third dimension, it is not a coincidence that they are experiencing a blistering drought. Our fates seem intertwined. If we are to see our way through this mess, we must work together."

Sybil sat in silence, contemplating what she had been hearing. With all this mayhem, she'd nearly forgotten her mission. 'Seek that which is lost.' Again she was confronted with this task. What was she to find?

Bollywocks! This is too much to expect of me. I just want to go home. This is absolute rubbish. Hamish where are you when I need you? Marc you said you'd have my back. Midnight swims! Hah! Now look where it's landed me.

She came back to the present conversation with a start.

"Now that is very interesting," replied Gergenon. "How is it that Sybil is among us? Is it not written that the gulf between the Third and Fifth dimensions is insurmountable? This cannot be!"

Gulf my foot, thought Sybil. All you need is a stupid little lake and a midnight swim.

"Ah, but it is. Is it not also written, that one will come seeking that which is lost?" replied Longille.

Written, schmitten! Sybil's patience was wearing thin. What a bunch of hocus pocus. Her sense of normalcy was going under. Reality no longer existed. This is some crazy stuff! I think I'm losing it. She stared at the rows of identical people. A sickening hollow opened up inside and threatened to swallow her. Down the rabbit hole! How do I get out of here!?

Her eyes darted about, then came to rest on Maerwyn's serene face, sitting across from her. He was aware of the agitation beneath her relatively calm exterior. She holds herself together well, he thought. Her eyes sought his and locked for a moment. He sent waves of peace, channelling them to her as he had been taught in training. She inhaled deeply, visibly relaxed and came to rest in the serene flow he had created.

"Thank you, Maerwyn."

"Yes, yes, you are right, come to think of it," Gergenon conceded. "If that is the case, we will be of the utmost assistance wherever possible."

Gerardo cleared his throat. "Since it appears we have finished, shall we retire to the administrative hall? We can continue our discussion in depth. Perhaps we can provide some suggestions."

"Right then," replied Gergenon. He pushed away from the table and stood up, waiting for the others to rise. Then he led them out the door and along back streets toward the administrative building.

Sybil was glad to be out of the dining hall. The place was stifling, oppressive. There was no room for individuality, no freedom of spirit. How long would she have to live here? Her stomach heaved. The thought sickened her. What if they were trapped here?

When they rounded a corner the street opened into a wide courtyard. Directly opposite, stood a huge structure. Double doors opened into a cavernous hall that echoed as their footsteps clattered across the polished floors. Their soft voices magnified, resounding into an unintelligible cacophony, so that Sybil's ears rang painfully. It was impossible to understand any conversation taking place.

After passing through a far door into a section with office spaces, Sybil couldn't help commenting on the experience, "That was a confusing jumble of noise. What is wrong with that hall?"

"Clever thing it is!" replied Gergenon. "Part of our secret coding system, Sybil. You see, no one can decipher what has been said once we pass through the Echo Chamber. It is our safeguard."

"Anyone who comes through it, cannot repeat what is learned here. It comes out encrypted as echoes!" added Gerardo, proudly. "Now let's go on to the Duplicating Chamber."

Leaving the business rooms by a labyrinth of intricate mirror mazes, Gerardo skillfully led the way through a section enclosed by mirrored walls, floor and ceiling. It had a confounding effect on the visitors. No one could discern what or who was real or reflection.

"This is bizarre," Sybil telepathed, gazing at her reflections. As her eyes roved about, Longille and Maerwyn splintered into multiple images. *"We're beginning to look like Leanorian lake bottom dwellers! All the same!"*

"Best be on our guard!" Longille replied.

It took a moment to recognize Sybil's subtle sense of humour. Her grinning face was fractured everywhere, mischievous eyes reflecting back at them a hundredfold. Maerwyn's contorted face checked the impulse to erupt in a fit of giggles.

"Stop, Sybil!" warned Longille. *"You'll have us rolling on the floor and how would we explain that one?"*

"No spicy fish balls here," Maerwyn snickered. Longille grimaced, biting his tongue to keep from laughing.

Watching her companions' faces going through contortions, Sybil succumbed. A snort of laughter exploded, as she tried to hold it back. Then she dissolved into fits of feigned sneezes and coughing interspersed with belly laugh guffaws.

"Bless you my dear," Longille added his support to her ruse.

"Pardon me please! Must have an allergy. I hope I didn't splatter your mirrors."

After the oppressive dining hall, the comic sense of relief restored much of Sybil's aplomb. Laughter always had this effect on her. She rebounded, the levity of the moment restoring much of her self-confidence.

Carrying on, Gergenon dismissed her concern with a wave and led them through the maze to the back of the room, their images bouncing off the reflective surfaces, an endless duplication reaching into infinity. He stopped abruptly inside a mirrored enclosure. Although the difference in the wall was not apparent, he began to inform them of its unique properties.

"This north side is transparent. When we step through it, we enter an energy field which vitalizes our bodies. Our cells begin to divide and duplicate. After twenty-four hours the whole body is ready to split off, emerging as a separate entity. Thus, we have maintained the species, ensuring survival."

"The first prototypes chosen for the experiment were healthy physical specimens, deemed of superior quality. It was those two who were able to withstand the harsh existence necessary to replenish the population," explained Gerardo.

"We may look alike but I assure you we are separate people with our own thoughts, feelings, likes and dislikes. We assign a name and serial number which is recorded in a ledger kept locked in a vault," Gergenon continued.

"No one has access except those of us who have been chosen as recorders," Gerardo indicated his official rank on his badge. It is imperative to keep the genetic files with meticulous accuracy or it would be bureaucratic mayhem."

"No doubt!" Sybil understood more than most, the importance of one's heritage. It was her mother's passion, especially given their unique family background.

Maerwyn and Longille stood beside her, dumbfounded.

"It is time," said Gergernon, turning to exit the room through the system of mazes. "Let us take leave. We shall discuss our course of action. You must try to discover why you are here, Sybil."

Entering a room in the business section off the Chamber, the five seated themselves in comfortable armchairs. The Leanorians seemed a stalwart people. They made every attempt to reassure Sybil that she was a welcomed ally in their struggle against the tyranny of the Graenwolven. Any discussion within these walls was safeguarded by the Echo Chamber, which precluded the entry and exit from the administrative hall. They were free to speak with honesty.

The Hetopians and Sybil sat in stunned silence for a moment. Eventually Maerwyn mustered a semblance of politeness and said, "That is truly remarkable!"

Longille cleared his throat and asked, "Where on earth did you discover this clever technology?"

"Absolutely amazing," added Sybil.

"That's the thing. No one is exactly sure. Those who designed it have passed on," he said with a tinge of sadness. "Our archives were lost in a minor flood when the gel casement sprung a leak."

Noticing the alarm registered on his guests' faces, he hastily reassured them. "Oh, no need for concern. The problem has been rectified with strong fortifications."

"They've passed on? Sorry…" Sybil hesitated, biting her lip. "We shouldn't have asked."

"No need. 'Tis part of life," he replied. Then brightening the mood, he laughed and resumed the conversation.

"Come now," said Gergenon. "Tell us more of your journey," he smiled encouragingly. "How did you come to the Fifth dimension?"

Sybil, who was exhausted by the treacherous events of the last day, gave a sparing tale ending with the morning's discovery of the lake city. For some inward reason, she was reluctant to reveal too many details to these people. True, it was a relief to be away from the probing noses of the Namors Guardia, but her cautious nature had proved reliable in the past.

Gergernon had welcomed them as friends from the west when they first met. How did he know where they were from? Following her instincts, she stifled a yawn and smiled, feigning a relaxed composure. She mulled over the details of the Duplicating Chamber. Not entirely convinced, her intuition told her there was more to the Chamber than they were led to believe.

"Please do forgive us," Gerardo apologized. "I see that you are tired. In our willingness to help, we have forgotten your ordeal of last night. After you've had a rest, you will feel more refreshed. Rooms have been prepared for you. Tonight we shall relax and resume our talks in the morning."

Re-entering the Echo Chamber, the sound reverberated through Sybil's brain. Her thoughts had been clear, well organized, but when she tried to recount what she had seen, her words came out jumbled. And so, the secret of the Duplicating Chamber was never to be repeated.

Following Gergenon, the three friends wound their way past huge aquariums of fish farms, lake-bottom gardens and a variety of greenhouses. Finally, they arrived at a row of low shelters, where they were assigned separate sleeping quarters.

"Dinner is served at six. We will await your presence in the dining hall. Rest well."

Bidding farewell, Gergenon turned on his heel and left.

"What do you think of that?" queried Sybil. "The Echo Chamber has silenced us, so we can't ever discuss it."

"Not so," responded Maerwyn in Telepath. *"The Echo Chamber encodes the spoken word but not our telepathic messages!"*

"Ahh, ha! You are right once again," thought Sybil, in reply. After her visit to the Blue Chamber in the Hetopian Great Hall, her ability to communicate in Telepath grew steadily, when she remembered to practice the art. She was delighted by the thought that she could make herself understood without being overheard by the Leanorians.

"But how do the Leanorians communicate after they go through the Echo Chamber?" Maerwyn asked. *"They must have their own system."*

"I agree entirely," Longille added. *"I get the distinct feeling they are hiding something."*

"I don't think these people are, what they say they are," telepathed Sybil. *"I think there is more to the Duplicating Chamber."*

Maerwyn interrupted her thoughts with a suggestion. *"Why don't we have a closer look when everyone has settled for the night? We might discover more if we can get inside again."*

"Excellent idea! Now let's grab a quick power nap, we'll need it for tonight," suggested Longille, as he disappeared into his sleeping quarters. *"See you for dinner at six."*

CHAPTER SIX
A Shocking Discovery

Long after dinner, when the moon had risen over the transparent dome of the city, casting elongated silvery shafts along the lake floor, Sybil and her two companions slipped out of their sleeping quarters. Edging stealthily along the outside walls of buildings, they crept past the slumbering Leanorians. Before them, loomed an outline of the administrative building. Pacing the outside wall Sybil observed that it was 175 footsteps in length. "That's 25 more than what I counted when we were inside this morning."

"How ever did you manage that in the maze?" asked Longille, his eyebrows arched in wonderment.

"The maze went forward, then made left and right turns. I only counted the forward steps. When it doubled back, I subtracted from the forward steps," grinned Sybil.

"Aren't you a resourceful one!" said Longille. "You have mathematical talent and great deductive reasoning!"

Maerwyn confirmed her figures. "I made my own calculations with similar results. The building must have a concealed compartment at the back."

"If so, we need to find out why." Sybil had barely slipped out her thought, when she wondered how dangerous an exploration might be.

"Say! I think Telepath has circumvented their code system!" interrupted Maerwyn, translating automatically in his head. "We are now conversing freely about this in both languages!"

"Some code system. Guess they never heard of Telepath before," laughed Sybil.

Longille interrupted their thoughts. "I don't think we should investigate tonight. We should spend more time here getting acquainted. If we watch closely we may uncover more information."

Retracing their footsteps, Sybil thought she caught a slight movement in the darkness beyond the square. *"Stop! Listen!"* Sybil warned. *"Is that someone moving along the street?"*

"Where?" asked Longille.

"There, in the shadows. Under the trees," she replied, peering suspiciously in that direction. *"What was that?"* she asked. *"Thought I heard a grunt."*

"I didn't hear anything. Did you Longille?" asked Maerwyn.

"No," he answered, standing quietly. They remained frozen for a few minutes. All was still.

"Must be my imagination. Getting the better of me," she was forced to admit. *"It's creepy here. Let's get back before we're caught."*

Melting into the shadows along the wall, they slid past the building running silently toward the cover of the inky blackness in the trees lining the courtyard. Back in the warmth of her bed, Sybil pondered the events of the day. I am imagining things she thought. Still, she could not shake the uneasy feeling she'd had, when she recalled the prickling fear in the darkness near the courtyard. She resolved that, when the time was right, it would be her task to investigate the mystery of the Duplicating Hall. She must do it alone. Maerwyn and Longille would have to cover for her absence. Once she had devised her plan, she drifted into a deep sleep.

Life at the settlement fell into a semblance of routine. Rising early, feigned camaraderie, probing questions and meals outlined their days.

"While we're here it's best to fit in," suggested Maerwyn. "We'll do our share of work with the crews in the aquariums, green houses and vegetable fields."

"It will be interesting to learn about their farming practices," agreed Sybil. "And pick up information about the colony."

Working alongside the Leanorians, they soon discovered subtle differences in character of the clones. Confusion over who was who, was resolved by a glance at the silver name plate. As time went on, their uneasiness grew.

"I'm beginning to feel more like a captive than a guest," Sybil confided, arching her eyebrows at Longille. "It's been weeks since we arrived."

"Maerwyn and I were just saying that last evening."

"I'm going to check out the Duplicating Chamber tonight." Sybil's revelation produced an immediate response.

"You can't go alone! One of us will come with you Sybil," objected Maerwyn.

"No, that's impossible. Accounting for two missing people? Too hard," she countered. "Alone, that's the best way. You and Longille have to stay and provide a cover story for me."

"You're right," agreed Longille, grudgingly.

"It's too dangerous!" said Maerwyn.

"Two people?" she repeated. "Impossible. One person has the best chance," she said adamantly. "There's no other way!"

"I see the sense of what you're saying," Maerwyn reticently agreed. He knew she was right but it was hard to think of her alone in the Duplicating Chamber.

Although she was quaking inside, she hoped her words would dispel their fears. "I should be gone only a few hours. Back in time for breakfast. No one will suspect."

Reluctantly, they had to agree. They couldn't afford to waste any further time at the colony.

After dinner that evening, Sybil complained of feeling ill. Gergenon offered an infusion of medicinal tea to alleviate her discomfort. She accepted gratefully and retired to her sleeping quarters. When the shadows deepened, she slipped from her room, thankful for the moonless night that concealed her movements. Crossing the courtyard, she silently entered the Echo Chamber; her soft footfalls magnifying into a thousand whispered negatives forbidding her passage. Without the confusing reflections, navigating the mirrored maze in the dark was much easier. Her heightened sense of touch soon led her to the Duplicating Chamber.

She slipped inside and walked the length of the room slowly, reaching out tentatively, until the invisible wall gave way under her hand. Hesitant, fearing the unknown, she retreated and followed the width of the room, probing slowly with each step until abruptly encountering a corner.

Groping in the darkness, a portion of the adjacent wall gave way and swung inward. Cautiously advancing through a hall, Sybil's left foot encountered thin air. She caught herself, nearly tumbling down a flight of stairs. Descending to the bottom, she felt the outline of a doorway. Now what? A momentary pang of panic gripped her.

Feeling along the front edge, her hand encountered a latch. It was unlocked! She lifted it and let the door swing open, recoiling from the stale air within. Recalling her entry into the Red Chamber, the feeling of courage flooded her wavering resolve.

Safely out of the Chamber, she activated an illuminator, part of the field supplies afforded them by Ebihinin, which Longille had concealed in his invisible rucksack. Similar to her penlight back home, the minute taper was no more than a few centimeters in length. When switched off, it hung invisibly on her belt. The slight bumping, as it hung against her thigh, provided a measure of security. Reactivating the switch, the devise threw off a beam, illuminating the whole of the cavern.

Concentrating a shaft of light that penetrated the darkness ahead, she hurried along the tunnel stopping occasionally to catch her breath. Ghastly shadows bounced off the walls, elongating and retreating along the passageway. Reinforcing timbers hung overhead, spaced at intervals to prevent a cave in.

Rounding a curve, a fork in the tunnel loomed ahead. After a moment of indecision, she favoured the right passage and entered it stealthily. Ten minutes along, she arrived at an open cave-like area where supplies were stacked to the ceiling. A huge cache of assorted boxes of dried and canned goods had been stockpiled. To the left, another room carved out of the subterranean cavity, held an enormous supply of weaponry.

She whistled softly under her breath, backed away cautiously and began to retrace her steps. Distant voices halted her progress. She turned in the direction of the food cache and slipped behind some wooden crates in the corner near the back. Trembling with fear, her heart racing wildly, she held her breath in the pitch blackness. Hoping to confuse their olfactory senses she hid among the fragrant boxes of dried herbs. Two burly Namors Guardia entered the room, carrying smoky torches casting grotesque shadows off the walls. Their hideous faces glowered in the dim light.

"The commander is in a foul mood these days," grunted one of the guards.

"Yeah, we've been searching for weeks for those three aliens. It's a real mystery! Where do you think they're holed up?"

"Puzzling. My guess is they've had help. No one can hide that well in this terrain. Maybe there are some pockets of resistant Leanori still out there."

"We have to find them and roust them out. Scum like that need to be eradicated," said the first guard. "Grab those supplies and let's get back to headquarters." They hoisted boxes upon their shoulders, turned and exited the cave, their long shadows weaving distorted images ahead of them.

Once they were out of earshot, Sybil crept from her hiding place. Cautiously she made her way back to the converging fork in the tunnel and slipped silently into the left passage moving at a swift pace to regain lost time.

Sybil had been jogtrotting for over an hour, when the tunnel began to slope upward. Hiking the hills around home had always been her strength and the familiar exhilaration quickened her steps in anticipation. The air grew lighter and the damp, fusty smell was replaced by fresh draughts of oxygen rich air coming from ahead. She rounded a bend and was confronted by an arched, securely bolted wooden door.

Sliding up to it, she pressed her ear tightly against the timbers and listened. There was no movement on the other side. Drawing a deep breath, she shifted the bolt, lifted the latch and warily opened the door a crack. It appeared to be a vacant basement. Sconces in the walls held sputtering torches. She opened the door wider, stepped inside and began to explore.

Closed doorways branched off the main hall. Listening carefully at one of them, she entered, crossed the floor to a window and peeked through. It was facing the inside of a courtyard. Above her, a sentry stood guard on the far parapet. She was inside of the village castle and that was a Namors Guardia!

This is not good, thought Sybil, trying to smother her fears. Realizing the connection, her caution about the Leanorians resurfaced. Swiftly retreating, she crossed the hall to the opposite door, entered and approached another window. Across the street from the castle loomed a huge fortress.

"Looks like a prison," she whispered. Exiting the room she continued down the hall and mounted a set of stairs, working her way in the direction of this building. Quaking with fear in front of a door at the end, she hesitated momentarily. Squelching her inner critic, she braced herself, "You made it this far. You can do this."

Sybil opened the door cautiously and was confronted by a fierce, snarling hound who growled at her menacingly. With ears plastered back, his massive head bobbed warily. The rumble in his throat intensified. Steeling her nerves, she reached into the BanquoeBag and produced a thick juicy steak. The angry snarl faded. His nose twitched with excitement, as the salivating beast cautiously approached. He snatched the steak and gobbled it down ravenously.

"You poor boy. You're starving."

Pulling out another steak, she slid her hand along his flank feeling the frame of gaunt ribs. "There's a good dog, have another."

"Come lad," she patted him on the head. "Follow me. There's plenty more for you." The dog obediently trotted alongside, in hopeful anticipation. He looked up at her, whimpering slightly as if to say thank you. Then he licked her hand.

"Lead the way boy. Where does this go?" she encouraged the hound.

He moved ahead. Turning left, the hound went down a flight of stairs and proceeded through another hall. They were now underground again. Then he loped up another stairwell and emerged in a foyer guarded by two more vicious dogs who backed away snarling.

Sybil produced more steaks, calmly talking to them in hushed tones. These two animals were in worse condition than the first.

"Here you go, this will do you some good," she soothed, throwing them food.

They wolfed it down voraciously, begging for more. Steak after steak was consumed, while Sybil crossed the foyer and entered the door beyond. This hall appeared to be a series of prison cells. She stood still, listening for a hint of sound.

Farther along the way, the unmistakable sob of someone in distress reached her ears. Edging her way down the corridor toward the source, she approached the cell, then stood on tiptoe to peer through the narrow barred window.

"O-h-h-h!" gasped Sybil, almost inaudibly.

In the cell was a thin teenage boy. He hunched against the grey cell wall, sniffling from the cold and pulled a grimy blanket about his shoulders. Shrinking back against the wall, stunned by her discovery, she wondered what to do next. Working up courage, she again looked through the bars.

"Don't be afraid," she whispered. "My name is Sybil."

The boy jerked up in fright and cringed into the dark corner. Leaning forward in fear, his long, grimy hair concealed his face. "Don't be afraid," she quickly reassured him again. "What is your name? How did you come to be in this place? Please, I don't have much time."

The boy's sad eyes met hers. His voice, raspy from disuse and the cool night air wavered, "They call me Simon. I have lived here a very long time."

"Simon!" Sybil was stunned. "S-S-Simon? How old are you?"

Her mind reverberated with shock. Could this be...? A tsunamic wave of realization rolled over her. For a moment her vision greyed. Her legs faltered and she slumped to the floor. Simon, her twin? Impossible! Couldn't be!

She had grown up knowing about Simon's abduction. Her parents lived in hope that he would one day be found. As the years dragged on, their grief turned to despair. Eventually they spoke less and less of him, trying to bury the painful memory.

Each of them had worn a tiny hospital bracelet; Sybil and Simon. She had always known his name and cherished the hope that somewhere another person who had shared her mother's warmth, still lived. Was this why she was in the Fifth dimension? Was this the reason?

"I don't know how old I am," he answered. "First I lived with a family of five. Leanori, the last of a group who survived the Graenwolven invasion. Don't know what's happened to them. I've been locked up here ever since. Maybe two summer seasons."

Sybil scrambled to recover her senses and raised herself to standing position. She looked in again at the boy, this time appraising him from head to toe. Yes. He had the same dark hair as her mother, the same serious brown eyes. Certainly the high cheek bones were present. And the dimple in the chin resembled her father. She wasn't sure how to handle this.

"You can't stay locked up in this place. Let's get you out of there!"

A look of anguish crossed his face. "It's impossible," lamented Simon.

"Nonsense! Nothing is impossible."

Inspired by the tangy remembrance of star fruit corkscrewing toward the skies in the Realm of Possibilities, her will to find a way rose above the doubts threatening to stop her. She must leave this place and find the keys to the cells. No one would suspect her presence, if the dogs were under control. There probably weren't enough Namors Guardia to keep a full complement of staff on the night shift. The hounds were left to do the job, she reasoned.

"I'm going to look for keys," she told Simon. "Be back as soon as I can."

Emerging from the cell block, the dogs trotted up to her, whining in anticipation.

"Down boys," she commanded softly and produced more food, leaving them gnawing vigorously on bones.

Quickly searching a number of rooms, she at last found a set of key rings hanging on a wooden peg. Snatching them off the wall, she fled back to the cells.

"Found keys! Should have you free in no time."

Frantically trying one key after another, the lock finally turned and the door swung open. Simon was on his feet, ready to flee. Running through the maze of corridors, Sybil retraced the route from memory. Somewhere along the way, they took a wrong turn arriving back in the cell block hall.

"Blast it! Let's go! Hurry!"

This time the dogs picked up their bones, wagged their tails and swung in behind them. With the big male in the lead, she got her bearings and found her way to the basement where the tunnel emerged. Glancing at her watch she saw it was nearing three o'clock in the morning. They would have to hurry. The two young people raced down the tunnel with the dogs loping on ahead. Abruptly, the dogs came to a stop and growled a soft warning; muzzles quivering, lips drawn back, they bared their teeth.

"Someone is coming!" cried Sybil. "Quick!"

The sound of boots approaching from the opposite direction, struck terror in their hearts. Spinning on their heels, they retreated through the tunnel. Reaching the basement, Sybil threw open the door, motioned Simon forward and closed it behind them.

Crossing to the window, she pried open the casement and clambered out into the still night air. Leaning over the sash, she grabbed Simon's arms and tugged him through the opening.

The dogs were sniffing and whining fitfully on the other side of the door.

"Oh no! The dogs. They'll lead them to us," she hissed.

Hopping back over the window sill, she flung open the door. The dogs launched themselves through the opening and jumped out the window to Simon's beckoning hand. Following them, she cleared the sash and closed the window behind herself.

"Come boys," she whispered, calling the dogs to her side. Obediently they leaned against her. "You must be silent and heel," she commanded the lead dog.

The big male fell in line at her side. The others followed suit. Simon closed the ranks and they set off in single file hugging the castle wall. Rounding the corner, they crossed the shadowy lea toward the tall, scraggly evergreens skirting the perimeter of the compound.

Once under cover, they set out at a fast pace heading east. Sybil had only one destination in mind. If they could get to the old farmyard, they would have a safe hiding spot.

After flying over the area, she had a pretty good understanding of the lay of the land. If she calculated right, it had to be about four or five kilometres away. The dusty powder of the barren fields rose up, choking them as they pounded hard toward freedom. About halfway there, they stopped to catch their breath, listening for footfalls of pursuing guards. All was quiet.

Sitting slumped over on a stump, Simon gave a dry heave.

"Too much time in that cell. Not used to running," he wheezed.

Sybil pulled a globe from the BanquoeBag and offered him cool sweet water, then took a long drink herself.

Labouring heavily, Simon's breath came in ragged gasps. "Much farther?"

"Maybe halfway. We can make it."

Simon held up his hand. "A minute. Lungs are aching."

Doubled over with his elbows on his knees, his thoughts raced. He had no idea who this strange girl was. This was insane. Where did she come from? Could he trust her?

"Where are we going?" he asked when he'd regained his breath.

"To an old barn. Not far. We can hide there."

Sybil squatted in front of Simon, bursting to find out more about him. Her brother—what was he like? How did he get here? Who brought him here? Why? Her mind spun with a thousand questions.

The big male whined, anxious to move on. Then a low rumble came from deep in his throat. He lifted his nose and sniffed the westerly breeze. Rising to his feet he tensed, the fir bristling on his back.

"Something's out there!" Simon lifted frightened eyes to her.

"We have to go," she said, jumping to her feet and setting off at a frantic pace. Her long strides covered the ground with determination.

The fugitives kept up a steady gait, stopping only to catch their breaths, until they reached the farmyard where Sybil and the Hetopian guides had taken refuge that first night. It all seemed so very long ago. She wondered what was to become of Maerwyn and Longille. There hadn't been any communication with them since she left. How close would they need to be in order to receive her messages? Warning them of the Leanorian involvement was utmost in her mind. Still, she was not sure how they were connected to events at the castle.

"This way," she panted, exhausted from their run.

Sybil led her companions across the yard toward the barn. Scrambling up the ladder, they gained entry to the loft and collapsed on the hay. The dogs circled below, whining softly, missing the two kind people in the loft above. Sybil descended the ladder, cupped her hand and poured cool fresh water for each to drink. When they'd had enough, she gave them each a fresh bone to gnaw on and motioned them to lie down in the hay that had sifted through the cracks above.

"Keep watch," she commanded and climbed the ladder once more.

Simon was fast asleep. She laid on the hay beside him and drifted into an exhausted sleep. When the sun was high over-head, she woke with a start. Why had she slept so long? And where was Simon? Looking into the barn below, she caught sight of him playing with the dogs and relaxed.

"Hey Simon," Sybil called softly. "Come up here. I want to show you something."

Simon bounded up the ladder and stood next to her. He was taller than her by five centimetres. This boy beside me could be my brother, she thought, still astounded by her discovery. Finding the right time to break this news to him would be difficult. It would have to be done gently. Leading him to the far north-west corner, she pulled the hay aside and showed him the trapdoor, where she and the Hetopians had hidden. Shuddering at the close call they'd had, she lifted the door, exposing the space under the floorboards.

"In case we need to hide," she said. "We used it the first day we arrived. It saved us from the Namors Guardia."

"Whe-e-ew," whistled Simon softly. "You'd never know it was here! They sure are hideous brutes, aren't they?" He stared at her realizing what she had just said. "Us?"

"It's a long story. I came with two friends from the west. They are guides from a place called Hetopia."

"Hetopia? Never heard of it. So when did you arrive?" he queried, his curiosity mounting.

"Well now, let me think. I guess it was about a month ago now. I've lost track of time. Maerwyn was keeping count of the days by knotting a piece of twine he found in this loft. He would have that with him."

"Is Maerwyn one of the guides?"

"Yes, and the other is Longille. They are both trusted friends who have seen me through a good deal of danger."

"Where are they now?" asked Simon, looking about the loft.

"Not sure. Back where I left them I guess. I can't contact them."

She paused. Simon stared at her, waiting for her to go on. She took a deep breath.

"I need to explain to you why I am here. Simon, what I am about to tell you may not be easy to understand or believe."

"Go on, I'm listening."

"I am not from this world. I am from the Third dimension, which is a parallel universe to where we are now. We are in the Fifth dimension."

"The Third what?" Simon's eyebrows lifted in disbelief.

"I was crossed over for a reason. And I now believe that reason is you Simon."

"Me? Why? You don't even know me."

Sybil studied Simon's baffled expression before she continued. This was going to be tricky.

"Before I arrived here, I was living in the west in a city called Chilliwack. The province I come from is British Columbia, which is part of the country of Canada."

"That sounds like Caenadria, where we are now."

"Yes, Maerwyn and I compared names as we flew over."

"Flew! How? That's impossible!"

"Entirely possible," replied Sybil. "In the Third dimension we have such things as airplanes, helicopters, jets and space shuttles. We have even landed on the moon."

"Really?" Simon's voice was full of scorn. This girl was touched in the head.

Bernadine D. Morris

"I'm serious. And in the Fifth, the Hetopians fly without machines. Yes, I know. I was as disbelieving as you, but I had no choice. Maerwyn lifted me to treetop level and let go of my arms. I flew Simon!"

"I'll believe that when I see it!" said Simon, doubt firmly etched across his face.

"That is how we got here to the flatlands. Where I live, there are many mountains. Gorgeous; a beautiful land in both the Third and Fifth. And I believe that before the Graenwolven invasion, this once was a lush and beautiful land too."

Simon sat unmoving, saying nothing. Something is definitely wrong with her, he thought. Flying? What nonsense. She must be delusional.

"In the Third dimension, I visited this area with my mother whose people lived here. In fact my great-great-great-grandmother Claire Huber—that's three greats if you lost count, is buried in the cemetery at Lenore Lake. That is the town inhabited by the Graenwolven here in the Fifth dimension. Sounds confusing?" she asked.

"You have to ask?" Simon scoffed.

"I assure you, it is absolutely true. Wait until you meet my friends Maerwyn and Longille."

"That is some fantastic fairy tale! Stop it Sybil or you'll have me believing in angels."

"Well, who is to say otherwise? The Hetopians are as close to what I think of as angels. They are an ancient race of beings living in the west—that is west in the Fifth dimension. They have taught me so much Simon. I am very grateful to them."

He decided to humour her. "Okay, so they can fly. Why don't you fly now Sybil? Show me."

"We flew into this area through the Plasmic Energy Force. When we landed, the Graenwolven were able to detect our point of entry. That is why they've had search parties out looking for us. As long as we remain on the ground, they are not able to locate us, other than by the usual means of tracking. This has been an adventure all right, but a very dangerous one."

"That doesn't explain why you have come looking for me."

"This will come as a shock to you Simon. And I don't know how to tell you any other way, but to come straight out and say it."

He stared at her.

"I believe you are my brother."

"Wh-a-a-at?" His jaw dropped open. Stunned into silence, he glared at her in dazed confusion. Then he managed to stammer, "I-I'm your br-brother?"

"Yes," said Sybil. "It is written in the Book of Wisdom in the Songs of Hope that One would come. Listen to these clues.

Blues hold the secret within, let go of all fear to win
To double your powers seek that which was lost
The past holds the key.
By the water, he weeps, while others pray.
Captive by night, invisible by day
Joined for all eternity, your past holds the key
The journey is long, be strong of heart
Be joined forever, never more to part.

"At birth, I had a twin brother. His name was Simon. The day before we were to go home with our mother, he was abducted. Do you ever remember seeing a hospital bracelet? It would have had your name on it. Perhaps the people you lived with saved it."

"No," Simon replied. "Nothing like that."

"I don't know why you were taken. We need to go back to Hetopia to figure out why I had to find you."

"Are you kidding? You want me to leave here and go back with you and the Hetopians? I scarcely know you. And you are telling me this wild story about the Third dimension and me being your brother! That's crazy!"

He studied her face a long while and was forced to admit she seemed sincere and very sure of herself.

"I have to think."

He strode off and stood with his back to her, face downcast. The bottom had just dropped out of the world he had known. Gathering his courage, he ignored the hollow pit of aching loneliness in his stomach. Interlacing his fingers, he clasped his hands behind his head, took a deep breath and straightened up. He turned and walked back to her.

"Okay, so let's say I am your brother. Got any proof?"

"Do you have any marks on your chest?"

Self-consciously he considered her question, then replied, "Well, if you mean, do I have two sores that never seem to heal? Yes I do," he admitted.

Sybil grew more excited. "Would you mind showing them to me?"

"I suppose you could take a look, but I don't see what it has to do with any of this," he murmured, hesitantly shifting his shirt to expose the two angry red rings above his heart. "They are always sore to touch."

"I have the same marks!"

"You do?" He was skeptical. "What are they?"

"It is the infinity sign. The women in our family are healers. We are bearers of the gift passed through the generations."

"How come I have them? I'm not a woman!" he objected.

"You are the first male to have inherited. This must mean something very special for us Simon. I have a feeling that our fate is linked and together we must heal these wounds."

"How can we do that?" whispered Simon.

"Remember, I said our family has a gift of healing," replied Sybil. "If you don't mind, let me place my hand over them. Please, I think you must do the same for me."

Slowly, tentatively, they both extended their right hands, until their arms drew parallel to each other. Hovering an inch from the surface of the rings, both Sybil and Simon felt a warm glow. The rings tingled as healing energy passed between them.

The unhealed wounds from childhood closed to form a protective shield of energy around their hearts. Together they stood, rapt in the knowledge that they had come home to each other. What had been missing, was now whole. Strength flowed between them. A bond of new understanding began to develop. It was the beginning of a journey that would cement their family connection.

Simon looked steadily at Sybil. Is this really my sister? Is all that she just said, true? What did he have to lose if he went with her? He knew he couldn't stay here. If he was recaptured by the Namors Gardia, his fate would be terminal.

"Well, there's nothing keeping me here. The people I knew are gone. The Namors Guardia are chasing us. Except for those three furry pals in the barn down there, you are my only friend."

Sybil sighed with relief.

"Thank you Simon. I know it's a shock being told you are my twin. I was blown away when you told me your name was Simon. And I have known all along that I had a brother. Thought I was prepared for anything. But you! My brother!? It's monumental!"

"Staggering!" Simon was beginning to warm to the idea.

With new understanding, Simon conceded perhaps she was right. Still, he was not completely convinced. "Suppose we go west. How do we get there and what is your plan once we arrive? Where and how will we live?"

"The first thing we have to do is make contact with Maerwyn and Longille."

"Where are they now?" asked Simon, coming back to the question he had asked earlier.

Sybil quickly told him how they had discovered the lake bottom city and that the people had an ability to duplicate themselves.

"It's really weird. They all look alike!"

"They look alike? You mean like twins?"

"No, not the same as twins, Simon. They discovered a method of duplicating themselves and claim this is what has saved them as a people."

"You got 'a be kidding! That's unreal!"

"Yeah, I know. But I can see it happening. In the Third dimension they've actually produced clones of animals. The first one was Dolly the sheep."

"What the heck's a clone?" asked Simon.

"Well," said Sybil, trying to decide how to best explain. "In the Third dimension scientists have taken cells from animals and have grown them to an exact replica of the original creature!"

"Out of this world!" said Simon, running his hand over his scalp, which had begun to prickle. "That's a little creepy."

"Yeah, I suppose it is, especially when you first hear about it. But you get used to the idea after a while."

"Didn't living with the lake bottom dwellers freak you out?"

"I must admit, it was a bit unnerving, but everything in the Fifth is extremely odd to me."

Her attention again focused on the Leanorian settlement. "The biggest concern I have, is the tunnel I found at their site. It leads to the castle and I saw Namors Gaurdia in that tunnel."

"Does that mean they can access the Leanorian community? Or does it mean that the Leanorians are in charge?"

"Don't know. We need to find out more," declared Sybil. "Why was a boat there for us to find? A little too convenient, don't you think?"

"Coincidences rarely are what they seem."

"I left Maerwyn and Longille at the city so they could provide a cover story for me. I didn't think I would be gone longer than overnight."

"Then we must get back to the city. What is the best way?"

"It's too dangerous to try the tunnel again. That's impossible. I think we should try crossing the water, assuming we can even find a boat. It is risky and we might not locate the entry way again. In spite of the drought, the Basine is still a very large body of water. If we get close enough, I may be able to contact Maerwyn and Longille."

"How do you propose to do that?"

"Telepathy," Sybil kept her voice matter of fact, watching for his reaction. He didn't disappoint her.

"Telepathy?"

"Telepathy, you know. Ohhh! I guess you wouldn't. People communicate without words. They can read or hear each other's thoughts. Well it's more than reading thoughts. The one communicating needs to set the intention before transmitting a message. Sort of like a cell phone radio frequency."

Simon stared at her, lost. Oh boy, Sybil thought. This is going to take a while.

"It's a hand-held device that sends radio signals to the nearest tower, forming non-ionizing radiation. It transmits your voice to other people far away. Only these guys don't need a cell phone, they just transmit."

"No way! Man, I really want to meet these guys! Going west is sounding better by the minute. So, when do we leave for the lake?"

"There's no use waiting around for the Namors to find us. They will have discovered that you're missing by now and will be scouring the countryside. It has always been best to travel at night, so we'll leave as soon as it gets dark."

"The sooner the better. After a bite to eat, we should get some rest."

"Should we take the dogs with us? With any luck we might find another boat. I wonder how they will react to being on the water."

"Good question. We can't just leave them here. Besides, we would have to lock them up. They wouldn't stay. That's not safe for them and they would howl to be set free. If they were discovered that would indicate we were here. After all, they were guard dogs."

"Some guard dogs! A little kindness and a lot of food can do wonders!" laughed Sybil. "All right, let's take them with us. They've warned us about the Namors Guardia before. Maybe they can help in other ways."

Later that evening they set off across the familiar stubble field once more. The lapping of water against the shore indicated they had reached the Basine. Continuing northward along the lake, they travelled swiftly and silently. The dogs, happy to be on the trail, stayed close to Sybil who was in the lead. Simon closed the rear flank. At regular intervals, Sybil stopped for a brief rest, trying to make contact with Maerwyn.

They had been skirting the shore for over an hour when she tried again.

"Surely we must be coming within range soon!" The desperation mounting in her voice, sent a chill up Simon's spine.

This time, to her relief, she heard Maerwyn's anxious communication.

"Where are you my Lady? We are frantic about you! What has happened? Can't cover for you much longer! The Leanorians are becoming suspicious."

Sybil let out a long, slow sigh of relief. *"Thank goodness! There's so much to tell you!"*

"Sybil! You're safe! Thank the Universal Fates!"

"Listen Maerwyn. There's a tunnel leading from the Duplicating Chamber to Graenwolven castle in Leanoria. We can't trust the Leanorians."

"They must be allies then!" replied Maerwyn.

"I found someone locked in the dungeon. We couldn't get back through the tunnel, so we spent last night and today at the old farm."

"Where are you now?" asked Maerwyn.

"Right now, we're heading north along the lake. Hoped to get in range to make contact. Can you get away and join up with us? We need to leave here as soon as possible!"

Suddenly the dogs stiffened, the ruffs on their necks stood on end, and a low warning rumble issued from their throats. The hair on the nape of Sybil's neck rose. A prickle of fear crawled across her scalp.

Approaching swiftly from the north, the sound of a contingent of Namors, boots running double time, resounded through the night air. Simon spun on his heels, loping across the dried mud flats, the dogs and Sybil close behind. They fled southward, while Sybil alerted Maerwyn of the peril they were in.

Without warning, two fierce Guardia jumped from a thicket of shrubs shouting, "Halt, who goes there!"

Simon's legs wobbled and he collapsed to his knees.

"Oh no," he groaned in despair, thinking of the hideous Graenwolven and the jail cell awaiting him.

Backing away, the dogs growled softly, retreating from the memory of their cruel masters. The contingent from the north came up behind them, cutting off any hope of escape. Sybil's heart leapt convulsively, stifling the terror lodged in her throat. Fighting waves of nausea, she sent a cry of distress.

"We've been caught! Help us Maerwyn!"

The two Guardia from the south shouted triumphantly. "Ah, ha! Now we have you! You're goin' back to Leanoria. It's the dungeon for you boy!"

The Guardia from the north pulled up to the group.

"And who is this with you? You are part of that invasion force that came in a few weeks back, aren't you?"

Sybil bit her lip and kept silent. Her mind was reeling summersaults as she fought the sickening revulsion, her gorge rising into her throat.

"You don't look like much. A mere slip of a girl," sneered their burly leader.

He yanked Simon up off his knees and shoved him forward. "Thought you could escape did you? You! Fall in line!" He glared at Sybil. "You, behind him."

They set off, heading southward toward Graenwolven castle. Sybil and Simon had no choice but to march between the columns of Namors.

"Maerwyn, they're taking us to the dungeon at Leanoria!" Sybil managed to get the message out before they were out of range. The dogs trailed at a safe distance, slinking cautiously behind the weary captives.

"Get in there!" shouted a burly Namor, banging the cell door shut on Simon. Then he turned to Sybil. "And you!" he bellowed, towering over her. "On your knees!"

Sybil obeyed, cowering in terror.

"You will tell me! Who are the other two?" he roared.

Sybil was tongue-tied. Struck mute by the terror in her throat.

"No? We know there were three. Where are they?" He pummeled the cell wall.

Sybil slumped to the floor, out cold.

"Harummph!!" he snorted. "Not so brave now!" he laughed, then grabbed her arm and dragged her into the adjoining cell, slamming the door shut and turning the key.

"We'll deal with you tomorrow!" he huffed, glaring at Simon through the cell window.

His heavy boots clumped down the hall. The resounding slam of the door echoed the death knell of their freedom throughout the corridor.

"Sybil, Sybil. Are you all right?" Simon's anxious whisper floated through the damp air to the cell beside him.

Sybil lay against the wall, unmoving. "Sybil, please, please be okay," he pleaded.

A soft moan came from the adjacent cell as Sybil regained consciousness. Dim yellow light filtered through the veil of fear. She rolled onto her side and sat up slowly, rubbing her chafed knees.

"Oh-h Simon..." A long moment passed. "Simon, I thought I was going to die," her subdued voice seeped through the crack under the door.

"Thank the Fifth!" Simon's relieved sigh filtered out of his cell. Trying to comfort her, he reached through the small window and gestured feebly. "I am so sorry Sybil." His guilt was palpable. "It's my fault. All this. You're here because of me." A stifled sob escaped his lips.

Hearing the care in his voice, the remorse he felt, stiffened her spine. "No! I'm here because I want to be." Hope flooded back in, as she recalled her mission. Her terror began to subside. "I refuse to accept this!"

"What can we do? No escape for us now." Simon's years of hopelessness flooded over him pinning him to the cell floor.

"I kept the keys!" Sybil whispered. "But we have to wait for Maerwyn and Longille. They will try to come through the tunnel."

The horror she'd experienced at the hands of the burly Guardia, had brought her to her lowest ebb. Through fear, she'd forgotten the Hetopian gifts and her own strength.

"We push back!" seethed Sybil, a hot rush of anger empowering her. "We can do this Simon."

Maerwyn, who had been up most of the night pacing with worry, headed out the door to raise the alarm with Longille. He woke with a start as Maerwyn's voice invaded his sleep. "Sybil has been caught! Get up!"

Longille became fully alert in an instant, fixing Maerwyn with an alarmed stare. "What's happened?"

"The Guardia have caught Sybil. They're being taken to the dungeon at Graenwolven castle," Maerwyn related. We must leave as soon as we can! This could get complicated!"

"Don't worry, I'll handle Gergenon in the morning," replied Longille. Then realizing what Maerwyn had just said, he asked, "They?" His eyes grew round in surprise and the long silvery eyelashes fluttered with excitement. "Did you say, they?" he repeated.

"Yes Longille. Sybil found someone locked in the dungeon at Graenwolven castle."

"Who?"

"No time to say. All I know is someone is with her and they're being taken back."

At dinner Longille made his best excuses for Sybil, saying that she was able to eat the bit of food he had taken to her earlier. She would be up for breakfast the next morning and would resume her work in the greenhouses along with them. They visited well into the evening with their hosts, then turned in for the night.

Under the cover of darkness they made their way to the Duplicating Chamber. Exploring the interior, they came to the wall at the back and found the tunnel opening. Stealthily they crept along the passages until arriving at a fork that divided the way.

"Which way should we go?" chimed Longille, reverting to Telepath. *"Right or left?"*

"We'll split up and explore, then meet back here," replied Maerwyn. *"You take the right tunnel and I will go left."*

Departing on a run, Longille soon found the stash of stockpiled food goods and weaponry. Rushing back along the passage he turned the corner into the left tunnel and ran straight into Maerwyn who was running at top speed.

"There's a large troop of Graenwolven coming down this tunnel. Quick! Up the other one! We have to find another way to the castle."

"I found a cache of stored goods and weaponry up that way. Might be another way out past that!"

Running silently, they made their way to the storage caverns. Pushing deeper into the tunnel system, they found a door bearing a large Graenwolven emblem. Hesitating momentarily, Maerwyn lifted the latch, cautiously opened the door and peered through the opening to see an enormous Namors Guardia standing at attention. His fierce scowl glowered to alertness.

"You there! Stop!" he barked.

Maerwyn and Longille turned and fled along the way they had come, outdistancing the heavy footsteps behind them. There was no choice. They must follow the left passage and hope the troop had already passed. Turning up the left tunnel they fled the pursuing Namor. Sybil was in peril, they must get to her. When the way grew steeper and the stale air freshened they sensed hope of finding her.

Rounding a bend, they encountered the arched wooden door Sybil had entered. Maerwyn moved the bolt, lifted the latch and stepped into the hall. Entering the nearest door, he crossed to the window and surveyed the scene. Estimating the fortress across the road, to be a prison block, they scurried along the corridor, down a flight of steps and through another passageway.

"Sybil, are you here? We're in the hall moving toward what looks to be a fortress."

The reply came immediately. *"Longille! Thank the Fifth dimension! I was so worried about you and Maerwyn! We're in the cell block, straight up the hall to the end cell. It is safe to come through. The Namors Guardia have left."*

"Thank the Universal Stars!" sighed Longille.

"They've left guard dogs on watch," Sybil warned. *"Don't worry they won't hurt you. I'll keep them busy."* She drew forth more treats and called the hounds to the cell door.

In a moment Maerwyn and Longille arrived breathlessly. "Oh, I do miss the Hetopian way of travel! This bipedal mode of getting around is archaic!" jangled Longille. "Now how do we get you out of there?"

"No problem!" replied Sybil. "I have a set of keys safely stowed in the BanquoeBag. We were waiting. Hoping you would get here before we had to go."

Sybil brandished the keys, handed them to Longille and in a moment the cell doors jarred open. The dogs were on their feet inspecting the newcomers, sniffing warily around their feet.

"It's okay boys. They are friends. Here, give them a treat Maerwyn and they'll be lifelong pals. Poor things are badly neglected."

Having quieted the hounds, she turned to Simon and introduced her two companions from Hetopia. "Maerwyn and Longille, this is Simon. I'll explain on the way. Quick, follow the hounds."

The lead dog set off on a fast trot moving down the hall, retracing the route to the room through which they had escaped the night before. Rushing to the window, Sybil undid the latch and pried it open. The hounds sailed over the sash and the others followed behind. Pressing themselves close to the exterior wall, they regrouped at the corner, crossed to the evergreens and escaped into the darkness. Once more, they sprinted hard toward the old farm in the distance, the hounds eager for the freedom of the fields. Halfway there, Simon's energy was flagging. Longille bent down, hoisted him onto his back and the pace quickened.

"Maerwyn and I have been so worried! We couldn't hold the Leanorians off much longer. Our suspicions about them are well-founded. But how do they fit into what is happening in Graenwolven territory?"

"We need to find out," replied Sybil.

Unsure how to break the news about Simon she blurted out, "Simon is my twin brother. It is Simon I was meant to find."

Longille gaped, while Merwyn managed to splutter, "Your brother! Sybil, are you sure? How can this be your brother?"

"Yes, positive. It's referred to in the Book of Wisdom. Simon was abducted from the hospital before our parents could bring us home," explained Sybil.

"How did he come to be in the Fifth dimension?" queried Longille.

"Must be another way to cross over," Sybil speculated, then went on to explain. "He's been in that prison for two years. He lived with a family of Leanori Truids for seven years. Before that, he remembers nothing."

"So that is why you're here?" asked Maerwyn. "But what now?"

"I don't know," replied Sybil. "We'll take shelter in the old barn until we can plan our next move. I feel safe there, as though I am connected to it in some way."

Hurrying on, they approached the farm, crossed the yard and entered the sheltering stillness of the barn. After scaling the ladder to the loft, they sat on the soft hay mound grateful to relax for a moment following their gruelling flight. The morning sun began to peep over the horizon, sending long shafts of golden-orange fingers through the cracks in the roof.

Sybil, who had been carrying the BanquoeBag, distributed much needed nourishment and took care of the hounds in the barn below. "Keep watch boys!" she commanded and rejoined her friends in the loft.

Maerwyn and Longille turned to Simon. "Pleased to make your acquaintance. How are you feeling Simon? You must be surprised by all this!"

Simon, who was in awe of the formidable beings, glanced shyly in their direction and hesitated before speaking. "Well enough, I guess. It's a big shock to learn of my connection to Sybil. Not sure about this Third Dimension she talks about…" his voice faltered.

"Yes, Simon. Sybil is from the Third dimension," Maerwyn nodded. "It is I who brought her to the Fifth."

Accepting this, Simon went on, "I had no hope left. Never thought I'd see freedom again. Can't tell you how grateful I feel."

"We are here to assist Sybil on her mission," replied Longille. "Seems you are somehow connected to it."

Simon's voice quavered with emotion, "Thank y-you Sybil, Maer-wyn, Lon-gille."

His raw feelings surfaced and spilled over. Tears of relief coursed unabashedly down his cheeks. His shoulders shook convulsively as he tried to hold back the anguish erupting from deep within. Uncontrollable sobs forced through his fierce determination of control. It was no use. A long, low wail escaped, as the years of deprivation washed away, released by the pent up flood of emotion no longer holding him bound. The hounds in the barn below began to howl, instinctively joining Simon in his release.

Sybil covered the distance between them and drew Simon into a long consoling embrace. She held him until his shoulders stopped quaking and there were no tears left. No words were needed.

CHAPTER SEVEN
Flight

✧

Sybil stood gazing out the window of the loft. Shimmering waves of heat rose from the land toward the south. This is insane, she thought. I wish I was back home. She could feel her anger rising. Spoon Lake! Hah! Wish I'd never seen it. This place is nuts! Everyone here is crazy! Absolutely bonkers.

Maerwyn placed his hand gently on her shoulder. "What's wrong Sybil?"

"What's wrong?" Her patience was coming to an end. "I hate this place. We found Simon. Mission accomplished, now let's get out of here."

"Right, Sybil. What about Simon?"

Turning toward Simon, who was sitting on the hay beside Longille, she noted his gaunt features, his thin arms, and the dark hollows under his eyes. He needed rest and good food. He needed time to recover.

She walked over and sat beside him. "Simon," she began gently. "Do you want to leave here?"

Longille placed a reassuring hand on his shoulder. "How do you feel about coming to Hetopia with us?"

Simon looked at them a long time. In a daze, he stood up and walked to the window. Looking at the scorched land and wavering heat, he shook his head.

He was torn. "The people I lived with?" It was a half question. "Can't just leave them."

"We'll be back. I promise somehow, some way, we'll find them," said Sybil.

He returned to Sybil and joined her on the hay pile, sitting hunched over with his head in his hands.

"It's not safe here," said Maerwyn, crouching on the floor in front of him. "Come with us. You need to get well."

Simon wavered, "I don't know."

"There's nothing left here," Sybil said more urgently. "We can't stay much longer."

He nodded slowly, "I guess."

At the thought of having to face the Namors, he cringed. To be alone again? With a heavy heart, he agreed.

"Okay, I will go. But my people?"

"Promise," said Sybil, squeezing his arm.

Longille prepared Simon, explaining how they would accelerate speed and gain entrance to the Plasmic Energy Force.

"I'm afraid. I don't think I can…"

"It's okay," Sybil quickly reassured him. "I felt the same way. Nothing to it."

"What about the hounds?" he asked, concern etched across his forehead. "Can they come?"

"The conveniences of this realm are open to all creatures. But it's different for them. We need a mind net to carry them," replied Maerwyn.

He climbed down the ladder and called the hounds. Placing his hands one by one on each of their heads, reassurance flowed off his palms, communicating the plan so they would understand what was expected.

"They will travel well," he called up to the loft.

"If the dogs can go, then I'm ready," said Simon. He had fallen in love with the big male who seemed to sense his needs.

After a last look around the loft, they joined Maerwyn on the floor of the barn.

"Eyes closed now. Concentrate. Imagine a strong net connecting us. Its strength will support all that is held within."

Once the mind net had been fully formed, it wasn't necessary to maintain concentration. The hounds were brought on board as the four friends grasped hands. Once again came a swift rush of air and coldness settled on their foreheads. With a sudden jerk, they hit warp speed and re-entered the Plasmic Energy Force.

After levelling off, Simon let out a burst of excitement. "Whoaa! Monumental!" He looked over at Sybil, a slow grin spreading across his face. "Right, nothing to it!"

Flying? Never in his life had it ever occurred to him. His family, just maybe…it could be possible. For the first time, hope, a tiny seed in his chest, began to sprout.

Circling the farm below for a final look, they each said a grateful farewell. Accelerating north-west, they made a pass over the lake, catching a glimpse of the Leanorian lake bottom settlement in the depths below.

"It's huge!" exclaimed Sybil. "Never would have guessed."

Simon's eyes bulged. "That's unbelievable!"

Once more, they flew south toward Graenwolven castle and the prison that had held Simon captive. Mixed feelings of fear and revulsion fought with his desire to stay and find the only family he had known.

As the fortress loomed before him, he thought of the long hours spent studying light patterns. Angles, created by shadows from the barred windows intersecting with lines on the stone block walls, fascinated him. Watching the shifting play of shadow and light cast by the sun and moon had eased the monotony of the long hours in captivity.

Accelerating toward the west, they left the flatlands behind. Sybil breathed a sigh of relief. Third Realm seemed a distant memory, but the mountains meant she was closer to home at least.

"What are those?" asked Simon.

"Those are the Roccocian Prominences," replied Longille. "We're entering home territory."

"Prominences?"

"Mountains," said Sybil. "Back home in Third we call them mountains."

"They're spectacular!"

"I miss them," sighed Sybil.

Longille gave Maerwyn a nod. "We're setting down on one of those meadows. The hounds need a stretch."

Spying a grassy meadow ahead, they landed on a slope carpeted with wild alpine flowers. The mind net dissolved and the dogs found themselves chest deep in colourful blooms.

Simon picked up a stick and threw it. "Go get it boy!"

The big male bounded after it, springing over the tall grass in huge leaps. He retrieved the stick and brought it to Simon, who threw it again. This time all three hounds raced for it. Again the big male brought it back, dropping it at Simon's feet.

Sybil found another stick and threw it for the other dogs. Maerwyn and Longille settled back to watch the excitement, their snowy heads protruding above the blooms, as they lounged in the meadow. Breaking out the BanquoeBag, Longille pulled forth globes of cool water. The dogs loped over, tongues lolling and lapped it from his hand.

Simon and Sybil plopped down in the long grass, inhaling the sweet scent of the alpine meadow. Lying on their backs, they studied lazy clouds drifting in the blue vault above.

"Look at that one," Simon called. "It looks like a dragon!"

"And there's a butterfly," added Sybil.

They were lost in the healing energy of youthful play. The Hetopians were content to stay for as long as the two young people were engaged. The sun was descending the afternoon sky when Longille made the first move.

"Best be going. We want to reach Hetopia before dinner."

"Ahhh, a decent meal. BanquoeBag rations are wonderful but there's nothing like a hot home-cooked meal," added Maerwyn.

The hounds scrambled aboard and they set off once more. Before the sun had reached the four o'clock position Hetopia came into view.

"Incredible!" exclaimed Simon, catching sight of the blue crystal turrets of the Hetopian palace.

The hours spent with the dogs in the meadow had lifted his spirits. And Sybil was becoming more fun, he had to admit. Still, she was a strange girl. He didn't quite know what to think of her.

Amazed by the splendour of the city nestled on the valley floor, he thought of the parched and withered land they had left. He inhaled the fragrant air and for the second time his hope buoyed on the updraft of the sweet scent that drifted on the breeze.

"That's the Pallid Elusive," explained Sybil.

"The what?"

"It's a shy flower. Hardly anyone has seen it. Maerwyn caught a small glimpse once. It retreats inside its leaves, as though it is painful to be seen. That's the heavenly scent you smell."

"A shy flower?" Strange concept, he thought. He took another deep breath, visibly relaxing, excited by the thought of the new land he was entering.

While Maerwyn and Longille had lounged in the meadow watching them at play, they had discussed how to introduce Simon to Hetopia. Deciding he would be best served by a gradual entry to community life, they planned to approach the palace by way of a secluded rear entry. Seldom used, it provided a quiet access to ground floor level. They had purposefully maintained silence, not transmitting their whereabouts. Ebihinin alone was aware of their imminent arrival and had made the necessary arrangements. Maneuvering to their planned approach, they set down outside the portal.

"We're here," Longille beamed. "This is the back entry Simon. There is a set of apartments we can use, so we have some privacy."

"Thank you," replied Simon. "I appreciate that."

Longille made note of Simon's polite responses. After what he had experienced at the hands of the Graenwolven, he wondered about the seven years Simon had spent with the Leanori. There had been a proper upbringing, of that he was sure.

Happy to be free, the dogs capered around them and followed them through to the set of apartments. Sybil walked next to Simon, curious about his responses. Not long ago, she had experienced the same overwhelming newness of this foreign land.

"What do you think Simon?"

"Beautiful! Strange. So much colour! Leanoria is grey and lifeless."

"It is pretty awesome," she agreed.

"This is your room Simon," said Maerwyn, opening an ornately carved door. Within, was a freshly made bed with the same earthy-green velvet coverlet that had been on Sybil's bed the first night she had arrived in Hetopia. The cover was folded back invitingly. A night shirt of softly woven fabric lay on the foot of the bed. The same type of brazier in the centre of the room, gave off a warm glow against the chill of the evening to come.

"Thank you!" Simon's appreciative voice warmed the Hetopian's hearts. This young man was a genuine soul.

He entered and sat in front of the brazier, basking in the warmth after the coldness of re-entry. Longille came to stand beside him, while Maerwynn took Sybil to her room.

"Over there on the left is a washroom. Come, I'll show you how to run a bath." He led the way with Simon in tow.

Turning on a spigot, the large oval tub filled with warm water. Sudsy bubbles grew on the surface.

"There are towels on the rack. When you have finished, there's a set of clean clothes for you on the chair. Enjoy your bath," smiled Longille. He turned and left the room.

Simon looked around in wonder. He undressed and lowered himself into the froth. It smelled heavenly, clean, like the meadows he had played in that afternoon. Lifting a handful of the foam to eye level, he held it up to the sunlight streaming through the window. Peering through the bubbles, he was fascinated by the rainbow hues arching across the surface of each one. Watching the colours shift and dance, he blew gently and some of them broke free and sailed into the air. They drifted lazily on a small current of air coming from the window, ephemeral wisps, disappearing as quickly as dreams upon waking.

This was luxury. He relaxed in the soothing warmth of the tub soaking away the grime, the fear, the years of deprivation. Ducking his head under water, he gave his long hair a good scrub. It had been a long time since he'd had it cut, and a wash in Graenwolven prison didn't happen often.

He lifted his toes out of the bathwater and laughed at the funny little wrinkles forming on them. Then he pulled the plug and watched the water disappear down the drain. When there was nothing but a remnant of froth on the bottom of the tub, he refilled it and rinsed away the residue of soap from his hair and skin.

Climbing out of the tub he wrapped himself in a thick towel and dried off. He turned and rinsed the soap film from the tub, whisking it away with a cloth from the towel rack.

After donning the soft blue tunic left on the chair, he pulled on the loose leggings. Odd sort of pants, he thought. But they were comfortable enough. Putting on the soft footwear, he turned to gaze in the mirror over the wash basin. Startled by the reflection, he jerked back in dismay.

An odd wobbling sensation in the pit of his stomach made him light-headed. He sat down on the chair and lowered his head between his knees until the sensation passed. It's been two years since I looked in a mirror. I can't expect to look the same. But I am the same. Just the outside has changed, he reassured himself.

Gathering courage, he stood up again to have another look. Yeah, same brown eyes. My hair is long but the colour is the same. I'm two years older. My face has changed. He puffed out his upper lip to examine the dark shadow of fine down developing there. Hmm, I'll need to shave soon. Watching his pa back at the farm scrape away his whiskers was always fun. He noticed the hollows in his cheeks. My face is more angular. But I think it's because I have lost weight more than anything else. The Namors didn't spare much food my way.

When Sybil and Simon emerged from their rooms, they stared at each other. Simon had transformed. Under the layers of grime was a decent looking young man. His hair was tied back in a tail at the nape of his neck. If she didn't know better, she would have wondered if it was even the same boy.

She smiled shyly at him as he approached her. "How was your bath?"

"Miraculous! Can't believe I would ever feel so good again!"

"You look nice," she said

"I look different!" he told her, relating the fact he had not seen himself in a mirror for two years.

"Are you hungry?" she asked. "Longille and Maerwyn said to come to the kitchen. It's that way," she indicated, pointing to a wide hall leading deeper into the apartment.

"I'm famished!" he admitted, leading the way.

Sybil followed him, noticing he was a bit taller than she was. She liked the way his tunic hung on his shoulders. Same broad frame as dad, she thought. He needs good wholesome food and he will fill out. He'll be back on his feet in no time. Still, Sybil worried about him. Had his experience left permanent scars? Would he be able to rise above it? A story she had read about a phoenix came to mind. It rose out of the ashes. He was no bird, but he was a strong Huber man.

"Hello Simon!" Longille tipped his head to one side. "You look transformed!"

"No, not transformed. But certainly a lot cleaner!" Simon smiled broadly.

Maerwyn beckoned them to the long, low table and they reclined on soft cushions, feet tucked in cross-legged fashion, as though they were at a campfire. Steaming bowls of grains and nuts, vegetables grilled to perfection and fish fillets were laid out. A plate of fruit stood on the sideboard. He offered the first bowl to Simon who accepted it gratefully. Taking a generous portion of each dish, he loaded his plate to capacity. Settling back, he enjoyed the first decent meal he'd had in a very long time. Sybil and the Hetopians watched him savour every mouthful, enjoying their meal all the more by seeing his obvious pleasure.

After the meal had been cleared away, they relaxed in front of the main brazier in the common living area, chatting about plans for the next day.

"I would like to have my hair cut," Simon said. "It's so matted. Hard to care for."

"We'll have the city cosmetic come by tomorrow," assured Maerwyn. "He does a great job."

"Will he do mine too?" asked Sybil.

"Surely. And we'll have the coatier take measurements. He'll do up some serviceable clothing for both of you," added Longille.

Stifling a yawn, Sybil stretched her arms. "Excuse me. I can't stay awake any longer." She stood and walked across the room. "Goodnight. See you in the morning."

Simon fought back the urge, but in the end a yawn forced his jaws open. Soon all three were yawning. They gave in and followed Sybil, retiring for the night.

Simon undressed, pulled on the soft nightshirt and climbed into the luxurious comfort of the bed. He undid the pony tail and spread his hair across the pillow, letting his head sink into the downy softness. Lying on his back, he smiled over his good fortune. Just this morning he was in enemy territory. Now he was floating in a sea of feather down. For the first time in a very long time, he felt safe. He closed his eyes and drifted into sleep.

He was running, fear clutching his innards. His legs were going nowhere while his fists pumped up and down. Knee-deep in sand he was being sucked down a funnel shape. He grabbed a root but it broke. He was falling endlessly. A loud scream curdled the air.

"What?" cried Sybil, leaping out of bed. She threw open her door and stood in the hall, heart pounding wildly.

The hounds set up a frenzy of barking. Maerwyn and Longille bounded through their doors.

"What is it?"

Another scream came from the end of the hall.

The dogs surged ahead, barking wildly. Sybil raced after them with the Hetopians close behind. She flung open Simon's door and crossed the room.

"Simon, wake up. You're safe," softly reassuring, she caught his flailing arms in her hands, stilling his thrashing movements.

"You're having a nightmare. Wake up."

Maerwyn and Longille skirted the foot of the bed and knelt beside him. Chiming softly, the bells of telepathy broke through the fog of bad dreams. Simon roused and woke, panting as though he had run a foot race.

"Wha...where am I?" his groggy sleep-filled voice was fraught with terror.

"You're in Hetopia. It's me Sybil. I'm here. Maerwyn and Longille are here too, right beside you."

Simon struggled to sit up. A bed sheet wrapped around his torso. "Get off me!" he yelled, panicky.

"Simon, you're safe. It's me Sybil. It's a bad dream."

Simon continued to struggle while Longille freed him from the strangling stricture of the sheet. At last, he broke loose and gasped. Free of the tortuous ligature, he drew a long deep breath and swung his legs over the side of the bed.

Maerwyn continued sending soothing chimes in Telepath, while Sybil rubbed his shoulder, reassuring him that it was only a dream. His breathing slowed, returning to normal, as he came to full awareness of his surroundings.

Moonlight spilled into the room illuminating his face. It had a moist sheen and his night shirt was soaked in sweat. Longille crossed to a closet and returned with a dry one.

"Here Simon, let's get you out of that shirt."

Simon rose and crossed to the washroom. He doused his face with cool water, dried himself off and changed. Then he returned to sit on the side of his bed.

"That one's a dooser," he admitted. "Can't get away no matter how hard I run."

"It's over now," said Sybil.

"It's the same dream. Always the same."

"Have a drink," said Longille, holding out a glass of cool water.

"We'll sit with you until you drift off to sleep again," Sybil's calming voice comforted him.

Late next morning, the big male came looking for Simon. He sniffed at the crack under his door, whined, then let out a soft woof. Shortly, the door opened and Simon knelt to greet the hound with a playful tussle of his ruff.

"Come in boy."

The dog bounded into the room and careened around the brazier with excitement.

"Hey, slow down!" called Simon. "You'll knock something over. Come."

He sidled up to Simon and wriggled in glee.

"Let's go find Sybil."

They headed into the hallway and found her in the living area with Maerwyn and Longille.

"Hey, sleepyhead," teased Sybil. "Thought you'd never wake up."

"You missed breakfast!" Longille said. "No problem. We saved you some on the counter in the kitchen." He left the room and returned shortly, carrying a tray decked out with an array of fruit, toasted rolls, honey and grain cereal. "You must have been some tired after that nightmare," he added. "Slept right through."

"I hate that dream. It comes often."

"Once you've finished breakfast, we'll see what we can do about it," Maerwyn's soft voice reassured. "A visit to the Wellness Floe will set things in order."

"I love that place!" cried Sybil.

"Wellness what?" asked Simon, tugging at the pony tail he had tied. It never stayed tight and it was bugging him.

"You have to see it," Sybil couldn't resist adding to the mystery. "Hard to explain."

141

"Let's just say that you will feel a whole lot better once you are finished," Maerwyn grinned.

"Don't tease," scolded Longille. "What they mean is we have a wellness sanctuary. A place of peace and healing. You will enjoy it."

"Like a spa," added Sybil.

"A spa?"

"Like I said. You have to see it."

She rose and stood looking out the window. She was anxious to be off to the sanctuary. When she turned back, Simon had finished and the Hetopians were preparing to leave.

"Can the dogs come?" Simon asked.

"Yes, they'll benefit too," replied Maerwyn. He led the group out the door, taking the short cut through the forest.

Arriving at the Wellness Floe, Simon stopped, staring in wonder at the sheen of the falls. The path led directly under them. The hounds stopped, whimpering uneasily. The big male approached, sniffed and warily backed away.

"Are we going through that?" Simon asked hesitantly.

"You won't get wet," smiled Sybil.

"You sure?"

"Yes. Been through it a few times."

The Hetopians disappeared through the falls.

"Go ahead Simon," Sybil encouraged. "I'll be right behind you."

Simon took a deep breath, then plunged forward. Taking the big male by the ruff, Sybil guided him through the falls and the other dogs followed.

On the other side, Simon had stopped to marvel. He turned back, just as Sybil had done on her first time and stuck his hand through the cascading floe. He marvelled at the radiance of his hand through the light spilling downward and couldn't resist plunging it back and forth through the falls. His long held interest in the play of light beams captured his imagination.

"What is it?"

"Not sure. They haven't told me. Radiant light of some sort," Sybil explained.

"We come every morning," Maerwyn said. "The Floe detects and clears disorders. Spending time in the sanctuary heals us."

"Hetopians live a very long time," added Longille.

"Cool!" Simon was in awe. His face had already begun to take on a glow. Extraordinary, thought Simon. Sure glad I decided to come. Then a sudden thought occurred to him. If he had decided to stay in Leanoria, would they have left him there? He didn't think so.

"Let's carry on. Ebihinin is waiting for us," advised Maerwyn. He turned and set off down the path.

Rounding a bend in the trail, Ebihinin stood transposed against the backdrop of greenery. She turned at their approach and extended her arms.

"Welcome Sybil. Wonderful to see you safe among us," she embraced her gently.

"Ebihinin! It is great to be back in Hetopia."

Turning to face Simon, Ebihinin said, "Please introduce us Sybil." Although she had been alerted about the discovery of her brother, Ebihinin allowed Sybil the pleasure of introductions.

"This is Simon. My brother from the Third. Simon this is Ebihinin," she beamed with pride.

Ebihinin smiled gently at Simon and extended both arms in a hospitable clasp.

"Welcome to Hetopia Simon. Sybil has done well by finding you!"

"I am grateful Ebihinin. Thank you for my stay in Hetopia."

He turned to look at Sybil, realizing more fully that she had begun the search. She had found him. His feelings of strangeness around her began to dissolve. If she was his sister, and he wasn't entirely used to this idea—perhaps it might be all right after all.

His fine manners impressed Ebihinin further and she smiled broadly, extending an invitation to follow her. Simon was overawed by the newness, the strangeness of all he was seeing and feeling. The big hound brushed his legs, sensing his need. He reached down and ran his hand along the soothing fur of his back.

Passing through the archway of fragrant foliage, the vibrant pearly tones of the sanctuary opened to greet them. Ebihinin was already seated on the mossy bank and her face had begun to transform. A luminous radiance of healing energy flowed around and through her.

Simon's first thought was that she was on fire. He crossed the clearing and stood before her, fascinated.

"Come Simon, sit here beside me," Ebihinin patted the moss next to her and Simon took his place on the bank. The hound settled at his feet.

"Sybil come sit with me," he whispered, glad of her nearness in the unfamiliar surroundings.

The two Hetopians reclined with the other dogs on the embankment facing them.

Simon touched his sister's hand for reassurance. A bright glow of energy began to develop between them. She looked at Simon in wonder, returning his steadfast gaze. Her family had seen a video on Kirlian photography. Was this what she was seeing?

Steeping in the moment, taking in energy, they became relaxed and refreshed, completely present. The inherited double rings vibrated with the same frequency.

Every morning, following their sojourn in the Sanctuary they took the dogs on long rambles through the woods. Sybil's rumpled spirits of the past months had smoothed to a pleasant glow of satisfaction. Simon's night terrors had receded and she was confident he was making headway. They continued to rest and heal in Hetopia. Growing more comfortable together, they began to appreciate the strengths unique to themselves and to each other.

Simon took note of Sybil's quirky little ways, the way she flipped her hair back, chatted amiably with the Hetopians and laughed easily. At first, he thought her an odd girl but she seemed to be changing. He noticed her calmness whenever they entered the forests surrounding the palace. She was peaceful and easy to be with during those times.

Best of all, he liked the way she stayed near when he asked about the Third dimension. It was a scary prospect. While she was nothing like the older sister he knew in Leanoria, she did seem to care and to understand his uneasiness. At the thought of his other family, a penetrating loneliness wrapped him in a shroud of misery.

"You okay Simon?" Sybil had sensed the shift in his mood.

"I guess. Just thinking of my other family back there," he jerked his chin toward the east.

Other family. He had said other. She dared to hope. Does that mean he's beginning to think of me as family? What were they like? She wanted to know but was afraid to go on.

"Do you want to talk about it?"

"Not right now. Maybe sometime…"

Accepting that, she changed the subject.

"Race you to the river!"

She was on her feet running before he could gather his thoughts and his legs under himself.

She is one fast runner he noted, as he sped after her. Wonder what she was like in the Third. What sorts of things did she like to do? His curiosity grew and he began to ply her with questions. Over the days they spent together, a bond of trust began to form. He warmed to her, learning more about her life in the Third.

She, in turn, admired his ability to catch on easily to concepts of the Third realm. Her hope grew, thinking that one day soon he would be ready to go with her. His politeness toward her and the Hetopians impressed her and she made a note to work on her own manners. Sometimes she felt her impatience led her to speak too hastily.

Whenever a strange awkwardness developed, the dogs were the bridge that smoothed the way between them, providing a playful backdrop to their growing relationship. They were forging a bond of trust, a trust that was as easy and connected as family.

He seldom spoke of his life back in Leanoria anymore, but she knew. His concern was a hot ember smouldering just below his calm exterior. She listened quietly, as one day a tidbit of his past was revealed.

"I had an older sister and two brothers."

The distress beginning to form on his brow and a crack in his voice told her the feelings were very raw.

Covering his hand, she reassured him, "I made a promise. We'll go back one day Simon."

It was after this line of communication had begun to open, when Sybil recognized that an urgent need to return to her own home was gnawing at her. She had repressed such thoughts while she was in Graenwolven territory. Now the swell of yearning cast a restless pall around her. The dogs sensed it and whimpered their understanding. The big male laid his head in her lap and gazed deeply into her eyes. Every time she sat in the woods or on the floor near the brazier, he came to her.

When it had festered long enough, she approached Longille and Maerwyn.

"I need to go home," she said. "My parents. It's not fair to them. How am I going to explain where I've been? How am I going to tell them about Simon?"

Maerwyn patted her arm softly. "Perhaps the time is right. However, Longille and I both feel that Simon is not ready to go."

"I agree. Best I go first."

"Yes, alone is best. Our use of elastic time will ease your transition," Longille suggested.

"Elastic time?"

"Remember when we stood in the hall after you came sailing around the corner and bumped into me?" asked Maerwyn.

"Yes, I was sure in a hurry. You showed me how to slow time. That was cool!"

"It is even possible to slow it so that it flows backwards."

"Backwards!"

"Yes, backwards."

"You mean like time travel?"

"You could call it that."

Longille was enjoying the exchange between the two, watching Sybil's expression change from incredulity to one of possibility.

"We'll begin this afternoon," he said resolutely. "With the two of us teaching you, it won't be long before you are ready."

All that week the two Hetopians practiced with Sybil. First Maerwyn with his laid-back style of teaching, prompted her in the fine art of growing present, slowing time, then to experiencing the moment before.

"Feels like déjà vu!" she laughed, telling them about the uneasiness of her premonitions. "It isn't too much different."

"It is rather along the same line. But it requires more to take you a leap beyond," said Maerwyn.

Longille's intense method of relaying information carried her further. Within two weeks, Sybil had begun to grasp the principles of time travel and was able to go back to when she had first arrived in Hetopia. She didn't dare cross over into Third, to the day of the field trip, until she was ready. Time travel required a lot of practice. One couldn't just travel willy-nilly. It took precise concentration.

With training Sybil grew stronger, until one day Longille and Maerwyn felt confident she was ready to do some short forays into the past.

"While you are away, we'll teach Simon. He needs to know this too," said Longille. "We'll break the news tonight after dinner."

"I hate to leave Simon." She now had an idea of how Simon had felt leaving family in Centralia.

"Come back when the time is right," said Maerwyn.

Lounging before the brazier that evening, Sybil broached the subject. "Maerwyn and Longille have been teaching me the art of time travel Simon.

"Time travel?" He looked up in surprise.

"Yes. It will be useful in the times ahead."

"Do you think you could teach me?" he asked, excited by the idea.

"Certainly. It isn't that hard really," assured Longille. "Sybil has already made good progress."

"She has?" Wow, he thought, she's pretty clever.

"She misses home, wants to go back to Third. Besides, it would be good for her to prepare the way for your return."

"You do want to go back with me some day, don't you?" she asked hopefully, afraid to hear his answer.

Watching her out of the corner of his eye, he rubbed his chin in thought. His hesitation made her fidget and he realized he was enjoying this. He couldn't resist teasing her a little.

"Hmm, I am quite enjoying Hetopia. Couldn't be anywhere better."

Sybil's crest-fallen face told the story. He had wanted to know. Did she care? Did she really want him to come?

"Let me think about it," he tightened the tension a bit more. When her chin developed a slight quiver, he relented.

"Of course I want to go with you Sybil," he laughed. "Wondered if you really wanted me. Thought maybe you were just being polite."

"Simon, you devil," she scolded. Remembering all those stories about brothers teasing their sisters, she threatened, "Just you wait Simon Huber."

"When are you planning to leave?"

"Not sure. Maybe tomorrow or maybe in a few days. I could use a little more practice."

Tomorrow or a few days? His mind began to race. What was he going to do here in Hetopia without her? He wasn't prepared for that. He began to feel a bit panicky. How long would she be gone? What if she couldn't get back? That same hollow ache opened up whenever he remembered his family back in Leanoria. He had to admit he was beginning to grow quite fond of Sybil. The long days spent with her in the forests and countryside of Hetopia had become a time of healing. A bond of trust had developed between them. Still, he needed to know, to hear it from her.

"When will you be coming back?" he asked. A slight quaver in his voice alerted Sybil.

"I need to prepare the way Simon. We can't just bring you home to Third without letting Mom and Dad know first. I need to break this gently to them."

"Will they even believe you?"

"What can I say? It won't be easy. I'm not sure how that will go at first."

"I'm afraid. What if they don't believe you? Or me?" His doubts began to crowd in on him.

"I thought of telling Mom first because she will find it easier to believe. But the shock. It might be too much for her. Dad on the other hand—well, I think he might find it harder. It will be a huge blow for both of them. They will need each other for support. That's why I think I need to tell them both at the same time."

Now that she was working out the details, she realized there was a feeling of reticence within. The truth of it was, she could not bear the thought of parting. Hetopia was a good place to live. She would miss Maerwyn and Longille. But mostly, she would miss Simon. If he had planned to stay, she would have had to think about it.

She prolonged her departure, hoping to give Simon more time to adjust to the idea of her going. She spent every day reinforcing the bond of trust, reassuring him that she would be back as soon as she could.

"Simon, you know I must go soon. Are you going to be okay with this?"

"I'm getting used to the idea. I think so."

"Just know that I will be back soon."

"Yes, it's best to go now. I have the dogs. And Maerwyn and Longille will be here."

"Then I will leave tomorrow."

He nodded silently.

"Not sure where I should re-enter," Sybil bit her lip. "If I go back to the day I disappeared, maybe I can change that. But then I wouldn't have come to the Fifth. Or maybe the day after the quake."

The ingenuity of the solution struck her. It was simple logic. "I can make up a story for the day after. That's what I'll do!"

It would be easy. Now that she had it all figured out, she was chomping at the bit to go.

"Oh! I need my bathing suit! Can't go back in these clothes!"

"Nothing to it," chuckled Maerwyn. "I recall perfectly well what you were wearing."

The same twinkle in his eye caught hers and she found herself standing dripping wet in the swimsuit she had worn that night.

Simon let out a howl of laughter, "Sybil you look like a drowned rat!"

"Don't tease me! You just remember when it's your turn, I'll be the one who decides where we will land!" Giving it back to Simon felt good!

She has been too shocked to ask at the time. Now, remembering the blue gown and silver-embossed slippers, when she had first met Maerwyn, she asked, "How do you do that?"

"Think Sybil. Simon?"

"It's magic?" Simon's half-question revealed that he didn't entirely think this was a possibility at all.

"Stretch your minds," Longille dropped a subtle hint. He watched their baffled expressions slowly change. When the 'ah ha!' happened, that precise moment of revelation when the answer pops into awareness, he grinned broadly.

"Time travel!" they both cried.

"Of course!" A deep satisfying belly laugh rolled out of Maerwyn. They had caught on quickly. These two had a chance. They would make the most of situations.

When it came time to leave, Sybil began to have second thoughts. What if she didn't get it right and she landed somewhere unknown? Or worse still, wasn't able to get back to Hetopia. The thought of leaving Simon and not seeing him again hung in mid-air.

"Maerwyn, I…" The look on her face warned him.

"Don't even think it Sybil. Longille and I have prepared you for this. You are ready. You are capable."

"But what if I can't get back again?"

"It's just the reverse. You've practiced this many times without fail. You can do this. Believe! Besides there's always the portal at Spoon Lake."

Bolstered by his vote of confidence, she suppressed her misgivings, gave them all a final hug and said, "Okay, here goes."

She focused on her breathing, cleared her mind and found the small quiet place within. There was a slight tingling as time slowed, reversed and flowed in a dream-like layer. She left Hetopia and travelled backward in time. The transition was seamless.

She found herself standing on the forest service road that led to Mount Cheam. Evidence of an earthquake lay in front of her. Rocks had tumbled off the slope above and lay haphazardly across the road. This means they must still be up there, she reasoned.

Stooping to clear the rocks, she made headway but the heavier ones foiled her efforts. She grabbed a thick branch to lever the large rocks, leaning her full weight into it. Still they wouldn't budge. She sat down on a log to catch her breath. The morning air was chilly and the sweat she had worked up, evaporated, making her even colder.

"Back to work or freeze," she muttered.

It wasn't long before she heard the grind of an engine making its way up the mountain. Good, she thought, help is coming. She was still working when it rounded the bend. Glancing up, she saw the familiar shape of their Jeep Wrangler making its way toward her.

When it stopped, her dad jumped out and shouted, "Sybil, honey are you all right? What are you doing down here? Where is everybody?" The concern in his voice was bordering on frantic.

"Hi Dad!" She ran to meet him and jumped into his arms, clinging to him like she did as a young child.

"What are you doing in a bathing suit?" he asked, astonished.

"Long story Dad," she sighed. "When we get home, okay?"

"You're mother and I have been up all night worrying. This earthquake! Figured you guys might need help up here. You must be cold!"

He walked back to the vehicle and retrieved a coat her mother had packed along 'just in case.'

"Here put this on, Sybil."

Gratefully accepting the warmth of the coat, she muttered, "These rocks are too heavy."

"Let me tackle that big one. Good thinking with the lever." He leaned his full weight on it. The rock shifted slightly but didn't budge.

"Maybe both of us," Sybil suggested, adding her weight to the branch. This time the rock moved, tipped over and rolled down the ravine, crashing thunderously through the underbrush.

"That was the worst of 'em," said her father, as they continued clearing.

Completing the job, they jumped into the jeep and made their way up the grade to the parking area. The camp was packed up and everyone was huddled around, waiting anxiously for the SUVs to pick them up.

"Hello," called James. "Everyone okay up here?" They got out of the jeep and stood in front of the grill.

"Sybil! H-how!?" Mr. Jacques shrieked. He rushed over to where they were standing. "H-ow, how did you...?" He looked like he was about to keel over.

"Sybil!" Hamish and Marc broke from the group and tore across the road. They swarmed her. "Thought you were a goner!" Their red puffy eyes indicated they had been crying through the night.

"It's okay, everyone. I'm fine. Really I am. Found my way out of a cave system. When Spoon Lake let go, I rode the water down. Emptied into an underground stream. Eventually it led out. Sure was glad to see open sky again!"

"Where was that?" Mr. Jacques asked, incredulously. Colour was slowly returning to his face. "You sure you're okay?"

It had been a nightmare. Trying to comfort a class of 30 students after Sybil's disappearance was almost more than he could handle. Small aftershocks set everyone's nerves on edge. Regretting the field trip, he chastised himself for ever having considered it.

"Where did you come out?" he repeated, dumbfounded by the possibility.

"Oh, a ways down the hill," she said vaguely. "I'm fine. Got turned around out there. Probably couldn't find it again. Lucky I found the road!" she lied.

Her dad could tell she was uncomfortable.

"The SUVs are on their way up," he said, to change the subject. "Had to shift a few rocks, but the road is clear now. I can take Sybil with me. Hamish and Marc, you want to ride with us? Talked to your folks before I left. They're pretty worried."

"Glad of the help," replied Mr. Jacques, relieved Sybil was going home with her dad. He wasn't sure how to respond to her needs.

"Do you have your gear ready to go?"

"We'll get our stuff Dad."

She followed Hamish and Marc to where they had piled their equipment.

"We got yours here too," Marc's subdued voice came out in a low ebb.

"Gosh, we're so sorry Sybil," said Hamish, his voice cracking with emotion. "Thought I'd never see you again." A tear escaped his right eye and slid down his cheek.

Man, he's really upset. But I can't tell him what really happened, at least not now, if ever. She gave him a grin and held out her balled fist for a bump.

"Lighten up you two! You can't get rid of me that easy!"

Soon the whole group was packed up and headed downhill. There didn't appear to be too much damage from the quake. A few downed hydro lines around town were restored within a day. Fallen trees were cleared from roads by the city crews. Many of the older buildings in the area had sustained some damage. Mt. Baker to the south had let out a puff and continued to steam.

When they pulled up in front of their house, Sybil's mom jumped off the front porch and ran to the jeep. She flung open the door and wrapped her arms around Sybil in a crushing hug.

"I was so worried! Glad you're home safe and sound! Goodness child what are you dressed in?"

"Long story," said James. "Later, okay?"

The McCrorys and Leesoms were rushing toward them. "Landsakes! Glad you guys are back," cried Hamish's mom, overcome with emotion. Tears of relief were gushing down her cheeks. "Let's get you home."

155

"We had no idea what went on up on that mountain," said Marc's mom. "Could 'a been a rock slide." The relief in her voice broke the tension of the homecoming. "Time for a good hot breakfast. Thanks James, for bringing them home."

"No problem. Catch you later, okay?"

After they departed, Franceska drew her arm around Sybil's shoulders and walked her up the steps to their front door. Her dad carried her gear into the house and deposited it in the sunroom for sorting out later.

The relief of seeing her parents and her home again caught up with Sybil and she slumped to the floor with her back against the sofa.

"You need a hot bath girl. Then you can tell us all about it," said her mom. She led her upstairs and ran a tub of hot water.

Sybil lowered herself into it and soaked away the cares of the past months. Time travel was certainly mystifying. How long had she been away? Four, five months…maybe less?

CHAPTER EIGHT
Bridging the Gap

✧

After she had dressed, Sybil went downstairs to the kitchen.

"Sit here honey," said her mom. "Have a bite to eat."

Her dad sat in his usual place, while her mom drew up a chair beside her. "Okay. Tell us what happened up there on the mountain?" her mom began.

"I told Dad it was a long story."

"We're listening," he encouraged.

"It all started on the hike. Had these premonitions. You know Mom."

"Yes I do."

"That first night Hamish and Marc asked me to go for a midnight swim."

"Maybe a bit dangerous in the dark?" her dad half-queried.

"The quake struck when I was in Spoon Lake."

While she was talking, it occurred to her that perhaps it would be better to wait a day or two before she told them what really happened. She weighed the situation. It wouldn't be right to lie to them even by omission. She couldn't very well let them believe the story she had told at the parking lot, about riding the water down to an underground cave and finding her way out. And she would have to tell them sooner or later. Then what? Lying? Would they ever trust her again? No, the best was to come clean right away. Besides, her mom had some experience with paranormal stuff. She could not risk losing their trust by lying. And she trusted her parents enough to know they would at least listen.

Taking a deep breath, she ploughed forward, relating all that had happened. She told them about her arrival at Hetopia in the Fifth dimension. She told them about Maerwyn, Longille and Ebihinin, about her travels to Graenwolven territory, the Leanorians in the lake bottom, and learning time travel. The only thing she held back was Simon. That would be too much for them right now.

"That's some story!" Sybil's dad said. He half wondered if the quake had affected her. But the *gift* was part of their lives and he had learned better than to take things lightly. Still, this was a wild story. Hetopia, lake bottom settlements? He didn't know what to make of it all. And time travel? He sat unspeaking, digesting what he had heard.

Sybil went on, peripherally aware of her dad's silence. The look on his face, was it one of skepticism, horror? Was there some contempt playing at the corners of his mouth? But her dad had always been there for her, for them. Now a sliver of doubt wedged its way into her awareness. She was unsure, maybe even a little scared of losing her dad's support. She turned to her mother.

"Mom. All this was at Lenore Lake. You can imagine how I felt!"

"Yes, we just visited there this summer."

"Remember that eerie voice? We both heard it. Telling us to find it."

"Ah-hum. I remember Sybil."

James looked at his wife. Now he began to wonder about her. Maybe this was more than he'd bargained for. Sure, there had been other things in their marriage. He'd become accustomed to living with the unusual. But this? This was way out there. He looked at them in a new way. Strangers. They seemed like strangers.

Unsure of where to go from there, she looked from her mother to her father and back again to her mother.

"I don't know what to say next," Sybil's voice was quiet and unsteady. From the stony look on her dad's face, the set in his shoulders, her worst imaginings began to snake into her mind. She could see it. He was having a hard time believing her. "You don't believe me do you Dad?"

"Well, you must admit it is preposterous. I could believe you rode the water down into a cave and out, but this?"

"Now James," her mother began. "You don't know what Sybil has been through. Being caught in a lake during an earth-quake and going under…" her voice trailed off. The story she'd told was outrageous, that is for sure. But she had lived with the *gift*. She knew there was more, much more to life than current reality. That event in the summer had left even her a bit rattled. Didn't they always encourage Sybil to accept what she had been born with? Even James supported that. How dare he back out now when Sybil really needed them?

"James, I think Sybil has had enough for now. It's obvious this has been traumatic for her. We should let her get settled for a bit. We can talk again later. Okay?"

James could tell his wife was upset. Maybe he was being too hard, he thought, but this was too much. His rational mind was reeling from the onslaught of the—well, the absurd. There was no other way around it. It was absurd. Finally he mobilized.

"If you say so Franceska. Maybe we need some time to think about all this." He pushed his chair back and headed out to the backyard.

"Mom, I'm really scared. Dad doesn't believe me. He doesn't know what this is like. See! I told you! I never wanted this *gift!*"

She spat the word out like some rotten abomination had defiled her lips. She was fed up. Maybe she should have stayed in Hetopia. At least there, they loved her and accepted her the way she was. Then a terrible thought crossed her mind. Maybe she should stay here and forget about all that back there. Wouldn't it be much simpler? But Simon. She realized she did care for him like the brother he was. She had grown to love him. He was family. And he understood, had been through what she had been through. He lived in the Fifth, knew that other realm existed. She was torn.

And the *gift* would always be there haunting her. Never giving her any peace. It must be really strong in me, maybe because of Simon. They were a pair, born together, inheriting the *gift* at the same time. It was unheard of in her ancestry. But here it was and somehow it was more powerful in them.

She made up her mind. She would tell them about Simon in a few days. And if they didn't believe her? Well, she would have to live with that. She would return to Hetopia and they could have two missing children! So there!

James poked his head in the back door, "I'm going for a run."

He needed time and he did his best thinking when he was pushing his body hard on the trail. It cleared his mind and the Zen moment that always brought clarity would surely help him unravel his conflicting emotions. His fast pace brought him into the zone as he hit the riverside trail. The turmoil scathing his mind evened out and the turbulence that had hijacked him came sharply into focus.

Had he not always been supportive of his wife and Sybil? He knew when he married Franceska that she had this unusual side. He had always accepted it. Why was he changing now? Sybil's my daughter; how can *she* have this? Am I not part of her too?

Not that part, came the answer. But she did have his rational side. Of that he was sure. Maybe he was being too overbearing.

What about Simon, the child he had lost so long ago? Deep glacial grief, frozen solid with time, now exposed to the heat of anger, began to thaw. As he ran, a cascade of icy meltwater sluiced through his arteries, tumbling with force over the cataracts of his heart. Where was he? His face contorted and the dam of anguish broke, sending a torrent of pain through the valley of his soul. Tears now released the inconsolable sorrow he'd held in check all those years.

The rhythm of his stride stripped away the pain. Shreds and tatters lingered around his heart as he contemplated his son, the loss and emptiness, the gaping hole left behind. Why Simon? Why not Sybil? Did the fact that he had infinity rings play a part in this thing with her? She certainly seemed different than Franceska. Had Simon lived, taken his place in their family, would it have been different?

By the time he had reached their backyard he was prepared to listen more carefully. He conceded that things beyond their control did happen. He was slowly coming to terms with what lay before him. And he loved his family. Of that he was sure. That was enough for the moment.

A truce settled quietly in the corners of their relationship. The house held them cocooned in a lull of, if not contentment, at least one of quiet acceptance.

Finally, Franceska opened the subject with James one night as they lay in bed. She had allowed him the time needed to digest what he'd heard and she knew him well enough, was patient enough to give him the space to process.

"James, this isn't new to you. What has changed?"

"I don't know for sure. It's just that sometimes it feels like Sybil has become a total stranger. This story she has told us."

"I know honey. But she is our daughter, still the same Sybil we have always known. For some reason it seems the *gift* has come to her stronger than even I can understand. Do you think it was because of Simon?"

A stab of pain, still fresh from the riverside run, pierced him through. "Yes, I have thought about this. We always did wonder how that would have manifested."

Her sadness hung in the air. James could hear it, feel it in the darkness, as they relived the trauma of long ago.

He turned and wrapped his arms around her, holding her close. "Franceska, I am so sorry. Sorry for not being there for you, for Sybil. It's just that story is so hard to believe. But I think I can see. This has been very hard, something she never asked for. She deserves more than what I gave her. Please forgive me. Let's talk with her again tomorrow. Please, can you first let her know that I care and I'm ready to listen? She must be really frightened to think—I didn't react well. I'm so sorry."

"Oh James, I am sorry too. This hasn't been easy for you. Even I have had qualms. The *gift* has never manifested this strongly before. But I do know, that is what's behind Sybil's experiences. The story she told deserves to be listened to."

The following morning at the breakfast table James opened the subject, keeping his voice soft and his face tender. There was a look of acceptance and love washing away the reticence Sybil had seen before.

"Sybil, we need to talk."

"Okay, I'm listening," said Sybil, still wary of his emotions that could come crashing down upon her.

"Sybil. I've had time to think. I know I've behaved badly. I am so sorry. It's just hard for me, not knowing much about your mother's and your experiences. But she and I have been talking. Can you forgive me?"

Sybil's silence drifted between them, an obscure mist of mistrust that had crept in unbidden.

"Honey pie," her mom began. "Your dad and I think the *gift* has come out very strong in you. We've had time to think it through. Maybe now is not the right time to bring this up. But if we are to understand, we must."

James went on, stepping into the rift that had opened between them. "What your mother and I are trying to say is that— well, we think perhaps it had something to do with the fact that Simon…" He said the name softly unsure how to continue.

"We think that the *gift* is stronger because he was born with it too. At least he had the infinity rings. How that would have played out had we… " Franceska's voice broke in mid-sentence.

All three of them sat in silence. Sybil was processing this news in her own way, on her own time. They let her deal with it. She'd been called a freak so many times. If her parents didn't believe her, who would? Maybe she was a freak. But now she saw acceptance on their faces, even love and understanding.

They must believe me. Dad must know I'm serious. I am not lying or making things up. A tear trickled down her right cheek followed by another. Then she was weeping in relief as the flood of emotions gave way to the knowledge of their unconditional love and acceptance.

James was on his feet. He crossed the distance with one stride and scooped her up in his arms. She clung to him the way she had when he found her on the road after the earthquake.

"Oh honey, I am so sorry for causing you to think I doubted you."

Franceska softly touched her back, caressing her, willing her back to them, to hope and life. Their family had weathered another storm, a storm that had rocked them to the core. James carried her to the sunroom where they sat facing each other, his knees lightly brushing hers. Her mother sat beside her with her arm around her shoulders.

Sybil's face had brightened. The tension and worry of the past three days had passed. Joy and relief flooded through her as she sat with them, contemplating whether they were ready for the next thing she had to tell them. A trace of concern momentarily flickered in her eyes. Both her dad and her mom caught the change. Something was about to come forward. They braced themselves.

"What is it Sybil?" asked her mom.

"I'm afraid you won't believe the next thing I have to tell you."

"Go on Sybil," her father encouraged. He was prepared now for whatever she had to say.

"Please," said her mother.

Sybil drew a deep breath and took the plunge, "I found someone at Graenwolven Castle. It was scary. But I knew I must. I found a boy. A boy my age. Mom, Dad." She didn't know how to break this, except to say it. She had to tell them. "It was—Simon." The name escaped her lips in a low whisper, as though lowering her voice would lessen the shock.

The silence in the room was deafening. Her parents sat mute. Dumbstruck. Her father's face was blank. Then a baffled expression mobilized his features, growing to an alarming, almost grotesque stare. His chin worked incredulously and he stammered, "Si-Simon?"

The blood had drained from her mother's face. She sat with her elbows leaning on her knees for support. Her jaw hung slack, then gradually formed an, "Oh!" in dumbfounded surprise. A fine tremor developed in her fingertips, spread to her hands, up her arms and enveloped her whole body in an uncontrollable violent shaking.

"James," she croaked. Her throat had closed in spasm. She gasped for air.

"Mom! It's okay! Simon's okay!"

"Franceska!" James rushed to her side. "Breathe!"

He thumped her back and a rush of air escaped. She drew in a long breath and coughed.

She was used to unusual occurrences in her family, but this was not one she had been prepared for. It had knocked the wind out of her. The horror of all those years ago rolled over her like a rogue wave. It crashed upon her, drove her down, smothering her, drowning her in its depths.

James had thrown her a lifeline when he thumped her back. A feeble, tenuous lifeline. She surfaced.

"Si-si-mon?" her voice caught in her throat. "Simon?" she repeated, drawing in another deep breath. "Why? Who would do this? Where is he?"

"We brought him to Hetopia. He is safe, resting and growing strong."

"When can we see him?" The excitement rising in her, momentarily softened the tide of shock. Then she remembered all those other times when her hope had flown on the wind. So many false leads ending in the crash to earth in hopeless despair. Did they really want to do this another time? Why now? Why Sybil? What did Sybil getting trapped in an earthquake, have to do with this? Nothing she was sure! No, she would not let herself in for that kind of disappointment ever again. The brief freshet of hope slowed to a trickle and she rebuilt the dyke around her vulnerable heart. She listened to Sybil with reserve.

"We hope to come home soon Mom. I've been preparing him for the Third. Telling him stories of our family, what it's like here."

James too was grappling with this turn of events. He sank to his knees beside Franceska, holding her hand in a vice-like grip.

165

He thought he'd heard everything, he could not be surprised any further, now this? He was in a near apoplectic state while the news swirled and eddied through the backwaters of his mind.

"Simon," he whispered the name he had chosen so long ago, savoured it on his tongue, held it close, processing the surge of feelings coursing through him. "Simon…" He could hear Sybil speaking from far off.

"We've been in Hetopia for a while now. Shouldn't be much longer."

He lowered his head, allowing the blood to rush back to his brain, purging the blackness that had closed in on him. Taking some deep breaths, his mental clarity returned. Thoughts competed on the racetrack of his mind, tripping over themselves as he tried to come to grips with what needed to be done.

"Franceska. What do we do now?" came his feeble attempt at order.

"If, if this is for real? Well, it could get complicated," she replied half-heartedly. Her reservations still held her in check.

Catching the reserve in his wife's tone, James looked at his daughter, hope competing with doubt that so easily came to him.

"Are you sure?" After all he'd been through over the years; was he prepared to be let down again?

"Yes, I am sure! He has the infinity sign in the same place we—Mom and I have. I take that as proof positive!" She was indignant that he seemed to be questioning her once again.

"Oh Sybil, please don't take that the wrong way. It's just that…"

"What your father means is that we have had our hopes dashed so many times in the past."

"Well, you can believe me," she said, adamantly. She saw fear still haunted their eyes and softened her tone. "But I think I understand how you feel."

James found his voice and his logical thoughts came pouring out. "Wha-at are we going to tell the police, the press? After all these y-years?" he stammered.

Sybil shuddered. How would she explain to her friends? And school? The folly of this struck her with renewed force. Was she mad to think this would even work?

James finally allowed himself a small measure of hope. He dared, yes began to believe that maybe this could be true.

"We'll have to think more on this." It was his default when the way ahead was uncertain. He got to his feet and paced the room. Franceska nodded in agreement. Privately, her hesitancy remained.

Sybil took this as a sign that perhaps all might eventually work out. The main thing was, they had believed her. She sighed with relief, leaning back against the sofa as her parents took over the role of what to do about the shocking news she had given them.

Being home was abnormally strange. Alone in her room, Sybil was confronted by an unexpected culture shock that forced her to question her hold on reality. She touched her belongings. She studied her bulletin board; photos of herself crossing the finish line of a cross-country run, the first place ribbon hanging next to it, Explorers group standing beside Hamish and Marc, mountain views on hikes. Was that really her? It was another lifetime. She was a different person.

Hamish, and Marc? How would they react to Simon? What was she going to tell them? Would they understand if she told them the truth? No. Even they would think she was a freak.

She crossed to her bed and flipped the switch to her lamp on the bedside table. Opening the top drawer she pulled out her iPad. Familiar comfort washed over her. Lying back on her bed she rolled onto her stomach and powered up. The usual apps loaded. Games she played, lined up on the screen. Her eyes roved through them but none appealed to her. It all seemed so frivolous, after what she'd been through. Her eyes came to rest on the Google Earth app. An uncanny notion—a sudden dawning of genius forced its way into the crevices of her logical mind.

Hey! I wonder if it will work in the Fifth dimension! If I could get it to cross over, I could show Simon our home, our neighbourhood. A sneak preview! Her mind raced feverishly. This would speed Simon's transition. And what else could it do in the Fifth? The possibilities played across the film screen of her mind and she made a mental note to return as soon as possible.

Sybil spent less than a Third dimension month at home with her parents. She resumed her daily routines. School was a major adjustment. The talk in the halls, of how she had survived the Spoon Lake incident, was almost more than she could bear. The constant scrutiny was excruciating. Whispers and giggles, whether it was about her or not, made her cringe self-consciously. She was relieved when Thanksgiving week end arrived.

After the traditional turkey dinner was over, Sybil decided to break the news.

"Mom, Dad. I am going back to Hetopia. Don't know how long I'll be away. With this time travel thing, it could be only a blip."

"Oh honey pie! So soon?" Her mother's eyes grew round with fear.

"Mom. You may not even know I'm gone."

"How is that possible? Don't kid me Sybil."

"No, I wouldn't say that mom, if I didn't know. Longille and Maerwyn say that with time travel, I can choose to enter where I left off. I'm not very good at it yet, but I am improving."

Her mom looked at her skeptically. Remembering the gap that had opened between them, she thought better about voicing her objections. Sybil would just go ahead and do what she wanted anyway. She was growing up, flexing her independence.

"Oh, do be careful!" Her mom's anxiety level was going through the roof.

"I have to go. Simon is waiting for me. We'll be together," said Sybil, allaying much of her mom's fear. "Don't worry Mom. We have Longille and Maerwyn and all of Hetopia helping us!"

"Oh, I know. I just wish I could go with you, or at least meet these people. They do sound wonderful and caring. I suppose I can trust, even just a little."

Sybil spent the rest of the morning baking cookies with her mom and relaxing with her dad, all the while making plans to leave. After lunch she stuck her tablet in a backpack, added some freshly baked chocolate chip cookies and disappeared through the back door. The yard was lovely in the fall. Yellows, oranges and reds lit up the landscape.

"See you later mom, I'll be in the tree house."

She climbed the rope ladder. Settling comfortably on the floor, she focused on her breath, finding that small quiet space deep inside herself. Space and time flowed loosely, bending in a curve, then reversed on itself. A slight tingling sensation signified time and space dissolving as she held in her thoughts the exact place she would reappear in the past. She let go and rode the wave back in time.

*

"Hey, where'd you come from?" laughed Simon in surprise. "I thought you just left!"

"This time travel is just mind-boggling!"

"You haven't been gone more than a half hour."

"I'm getting better at timing. Maerwyn says eventually it becomes seamless. Don't even know you're gone!"

"Had my first lesson after you left," he grinned.

"Oh! I brought something back," she said, pulling a brown paper bag out of her backpack. "Have one!" She opened the bag and held it out to him.

He withdrew a cookie. "What is it?"

"Dad's favourite chocolate chip cookies. Go ahead, take a bite." She watched as he sank his teeth into the chewy goodness. His eyes opened in wonder and she knew he had just bit into a chocolate chip. She could feel how it was melting in his mouth.

"Yumm! I hope you brought more. They're delicious!"

"Sure, have another. Freshly baked, still warm."

"Ho, Sybil! There you are. Back so soon," laughed Longille.

Maerwyn heard the commotion and rounded the corner in the living area.

"Hi Maerwyn! Try these. You too Longille." She watched as the same heavenly expression appeared on their faces.

"Scrumptious! What're they called?"

"Chocolate chip cookies!" said Simon.

Sybil could hardly wait to show them her iPad, but the three of them couldn't resist the brown paper bag and made numerous visits to it until the contents were all gone. She turned the bag over. Not a crumb left.

"Now, if you think that was good. Wait 'til I show you what I brought next."

She sat on the floor in front of the brazier, powered up her tablet and crossed her fingers, hoping that with any luck, it might work here in the Fifth. They gaped at the screen when it lit up and the apps appeared.

Sybil's astonishment was greater than everyone's in the room. It was a long shot. She had no idea if it would work and now here it was, powered up! How did it still work in the Fifth? Did a time warp happen with electronics? Coming through time and space, did it not transition? Did it still receive the signals from Third? Or did the Plasma Energy Force convert the signals from Third for use in Fifth? If one could fly in Fifth's Energy Force, who knows what else that energy could do?

"What is it?" asked Maerwyn.

"It's called an iPad."

"What do you do with it?" Longille's eyes were glued to the screen.

"Play games, visit the internet, look up stuff."

"Internet?"

"Yeah, it's like a huge electronic library."

"Can I try?" Simon's curiosity was fully engaged.

"First I want to see if Google Earth still works."

"Google Earth?" asked Maerwyn.

"It's a program that has mapped out the whole earth's surface in 3D. Satellite technology is very useful."

"Satellite technology?"

"Yeah, pictures of earth are beamed back."

"Golly!" Simon was aghast. "Let me see!"

Adjusting the focus with her fingers, Sybil zoomed in on their home in the Third realm.

"This is where we live Simon," she let the fact drop with the precision of a seasoned stand-up comic. His jaw dropped in surprise. "How's that for spy technology!?" she giggled with satisfaction. She loved surprising him, loved the comfort of his presence and loved the way he appreciated her abilities.

"Wo-o-w-w!" he let out a long breath of wondering appreciation. "That is so cool! Show me more!" he begged.

"Here we go!" She slid her fingers across the screen and zoomed into the seclusion of their back yard, wondering how this technology was going to play out in the Fifth.

"This is where we relax in the summer. Mom and I grow most of our vegetables in the garden out back."

She swooped in over the rows of potatoes and carrots, past rows of spinach and lettuce, then along trellises where they usually grew green beans and peas.

"Here in the hot house, we grow tomatoes, peppers and cucumbers." She laughed at his eyebrows, which were standing at attention above his astonished eyes.

"Unreal!"

"You try it Simon."

"Can I?"

She showed him the gestures to navigate the screen. He scanned the back yard, focusing on a huge maple tree.

"Hey, what's in the tree?"

"Dad and I built a tree house."

"Wow! Ever spend a night in it?" asked Simon.

"Lots of times. Fun pulling up the rope ladder. No one can come up in the middle of the night. Well, I often wondered about raccoons. Pesky little critters."

"Can't wait to see it!" Simon's excitement grew as he eased the images back over the rooftop to their front yard. Then he zoomed in on the numbers beside the front door.

"That's our house number, 8480!" He zoomed back out, checking up and down the street. The street sign at the end read Lavendar Street. "I love it—8480 Lavendar Street!"

Longille and Maerwyn had been watching the interaction in silence, their eyebrows lifting with each exciting revelation.

At last Longille exploded, "Summer nights! This is incredible! And we thought we were advanced with flying the Plasmic Energy Force!"

"Well, you have time travel!" reminded Sybil. "This is nothing, compared to all that."

"Extraordinary," agreed Maerwyn. "I wonder. Might it work for the Fifth?"

Longille was halfway through the door. "Power up in the Wellness Sanctuary!"

Maerwyn's thought formed just as Longille said it. "Sybil! Bring that thing with you."

Longille was gone, heading through the forest shortcut with Maerwyn fast on his heels.

"Let's go Syb!" Simon raced after them.

Sybil turned off the tablet and tucked it safely in her backpack. She scrambled to catch up. "What's the big rush?"

But no one heard. They were far ahead. She could hear them crashing through the forest, the hounds baying in the distance and guessed they were on the trail to the sanctuary. She stepped up her pace. When she arrived at the Floe, Longille and Maerwyn stood grinning at her.

"Take that—what did you call it again?" Longille said.

"It's an iPad."

"Take the iPad through the Floe."

"Power on or off?" asked Sybil

"On, I guess."

She powered up the tablet and stood waiting. "Okay?"

"Go ahead. We'll follow you."

Sybil stepped through the Floe, wondering just what Longille had in mind. The iPad began to hum. A low frequency built, until the sound reached a high pitch. Then it settled into a steady mellow hum.

"Well? Let's see what happened," said Longille, emerging through the falls.

Maerwyn and Simon had gathered around. Even the dogs seemed interested. They hung nearby, curiously circling the group.

"Come over here," said Sybil, as she sat on a rock, balancing the tablet on her knees.

"Try that Google thing again," Longille's impatience had begun to show in the twitch of his fingers.

"Google Earth?"

"Yes, that's it. Try it again."

Sybil tapped on the Google Earth app.

"Try finding Hetopia!" Longille ordered.

"Hetopia? It won't show up in Fifth dimension."

"Go on, just try it."

"Okay, but I don't think…"

To her astonishment, the screen honed in on the blue crystal turrets, bringing the city of Hetopia sharply into focus.

"Oh!" cried Sybil.

"It worked!" Longille shouted excitedly.

This iPad thing could make his field missions a lot easier. Less travel. More time in Hetopia. I wonder if Sybil could get one of these things for me. He was about to ask when he noticed that she had panned west. Chemandor Tower came into view. Then she zoomed over the valley below. Spoon Lake winked back at her.

"How long before you think Simon is ready to make the trip?" There was urgency in her tone. She had become uneasy with the changes in her tablet and longed for the familiar comfort of home.

"Not long. Practice together," replied Maerwyn. "It's easier with two working in tandem."

Distracted by her own feverish thoughts, she noted his comment absent-mindedly. How come her iPad was behaving differently in the Fifth? She was stumped. Did the power source pick up signals from spy satellites and convert them. Did the Plasmic Energy Force have something to do with it? Did it somehow hack into classified information? She was horrified. It was as though her iPad had taken on a mind of its own. Maybe I shouldn't have taken it through the falls into the sanctuary. Creepy! She looked at her tablet in a new light.

Later that day, Longille found Sybil relaxing in the forest. It was a place to where she always went, when she was feeling anxious. He wasn't sure how to approach her.

"That iPad of yours is quite useful."

"I didn't realize how much I missed it."

It wasn't the answer he was expecting. Could he really ask her? He decided to plough ahead.

"You know I work field missions, Sybil. They can be long and far from home."

"An iPad would be useful wouldn't it?"

She was afraid to take it back to Third. Still, its enhanced ability might be of greater value in her world. She thought of the possibilities. But it might also get her into some serious trouble.

"You really think so?" Longille held his breath and dared to hope.

"Yes. Think of what we could have learned before we left for Leanoria."

"No doubt!"

"I've been thinking. Why don't you keep my tablet when Simon and I go back to Third? Try it out. See how you like it."

His eyes lit up. "Would you?"

"Of course."

"Very generous of you Sybil!" A grin lit up his face. "I never dreamed...er, I had hoped I could have one. Oh, thank you so much you darling girl!"

Sybil relaxed a little, having solved, at least temporarily, the problem of her iPad. She grinned, delighted by his reaction. "Let's find Simon and get down to work."

"Someone mention my name?" It was Simon swinging up the path, long sunlight casting dappled shadows on his face.

His dark hair had been cropped short. He looks quite handsome, thought Sybil. His warm smile revealed a sunny friendly nature.

"Yeah, let's work on time travel. Supposed to be easier when two work together."

"Ready you two," Longille instructed. "Slow down your breathing. Clear your mind. Breathe deeply. Find your centre. Stay there for a while. Now connect your thoughts. You are of one mind slowing down, totally present. Time is now."

They hovered in unison, lingering on the threshold of now.

"Relax even deeper. Fully alert, totally relaxed. Slower still…stopping. Find yourself in the moment before awareness, before the present. Breathe. Slow it even further…you find yourself stretching time…reach into the past. Let go and ride the time wave back. Stay here, hover in the past…at ease…comfortable in this state. When you are ready let yourselves come back to the present. Slowly, gently, until you are once again fully, completely in the moment."

"Amazing!" said Simon.

With daily practice, they soon became flexible enough to ride the time wave with relative ease. Within a short time, both Longille and Maerwyn were confident they could handle it well enough to get back to Third together.

There remained only the troubling alibi Simon needed to cover his long absence. Third dimension police forces were not ready for Fifth dimension reality.

Simon had been racking his brain. How was he to explain? "Come on Sybil. Think. We have to come up with a good story."

"What about this? You grew up south of the border. A childless couple desperate for a family."

"Nah, how would I know to leave?"

"And too complicated. Passports. Border crossings. How about this? A commune dabbling in the occult. It needs to be a juicy story."

"That might work. But again, how do I get away and know where to go?"

"Back to the first story? Only, on this side of the border. A childless couple. When the time is ripe. You. They strike, leave town and settle in the east somewhere or maybe northern British Columbia."

"That's it," cried Simon. "A couple who gives me a good home in spite of the kidnapping. Over the years I always had questions. Why I didn't look like them? They were blonde, I have dark hair. I have brown eyes, they have blue."

"You were always a bit of a snoop. You stumble across old news clippings, the Amber Alert, the Canada-wide search for Simon Huber, infant son of James Galowin and Franceska Huber."

"The birthdate. The same age. Why do they have the clippings? I begin to question. They are both killed in an accident. Any of those planes you mentioned go down recently?"

"Don't know. How about they disappear in the far north or on a fishing trip? Boat sank? They always lived in the back country. It has to be in the same province."

"Yeah? I still have to make it to civilization. Only been to civilization a few times but pretty good at finding my way around. Made my own maps on those trips."

"Yes, that's it!"

"I leave because they don't come back. I think they're missing on the fishing trip. Don't even know what lake."

"You are curious about those old newspaper articles. You decided to follow up. You make contact with James and Franceska. And there we have it. You think it might work?"

"Sure," said Simon. "Who's going to harass a poor kid when he's finally reunited with his long lost family?"

"It's the best we can come up with. Better than the truth! No one'd believe that!"

"A little rehearsal, get our facts straight and maybe we're ready."

"Maybe? We're good Simon! Born storytellers!" she laughed.

That evening at meal time they revealed the plan. Maerwyn and Longille were impressed by the story. Except for some questions that might come up, they thought it could work.

"What if they ask you to take them back to where you lived? Got to have an answer," said Longille.

"You lost the maps crossing a creek. Have to tie up the loose ends," said Maerwyn. "And what town do you show up in? How do you get there?"

"He doesn't get to a town. He hitches rides on the highway," suggested Sybil.

"You still need a map. How do you get to Chilliwack without a map?" asked Maerwyn.

Sybil shrugged her shoulders, "He asks the truck drivers who pick him up."

"Believable. Especially if you say you didn't want to tell anyone until you first checked out the Chilliwack angle—your family," replied Longille.

"What if they want proof?" asked Sybil.

"Blood tests? They do have such a thing in Third I presume," asked Longille.

"Yeah, needles!" Sybil cringed. "Hate 'em."

"I think you're ready!" Longille beamed.

"We're going to miss you!" said Maerwyn.

"What about time travel?" asked Sybil. "Can't we shorten it up so we don't miss you?"

"Pretty complicated business. Don't want to do that too often. It shortens telomeres," replied Maerwyn.

"Telomeres?"

Simon and Sybil looked baffled.

"They regulate aging. Do that too often, you grow old faster."

"We grow old when we time travel?" Sybil wasn't liking the sound of this.

"When you come back to Fifth, the Wellness Sanctuary will take care of that. But it needs to be done very soon after. If you stay in another time too long—could be a problem."

"Oh," Sybil said flatly. Why had they not mentioned that before? For sure she was not going to rely on time travel unless absolutely necessary.

"Don't look so worried," Longille offered some reassurance. "You haven't been gone long enough."

Sybil breathed a sigh of relief. There was always a catch to good things. *Lucky I asked that question.* She made a mental note to check things out more carefully. She thought of her friend Hamish. *I guess I can understand him better now.*

When Simon had heard more about time travel he began to have doubts. It made you older? Did he really want to do that? But he had to get to Third if he wanted to go with Sybil. It would be a strange new world. Sure, it looked exciting in a way. It certainly beat the Graenwolven scene. Still, it was a huge life changer. Did he really want to go? Could he come back if he didn't like it? Hetopia was not a bad place to live. At least it was in the Fifth. But so were the Graenwolven. And his family. Sybil had promised to help find them. Could he trust her? Then again, they might not even be alive. His doubts surfaced. That night he spoke to her about his fears. At least he could talk things over with her. She had always been a good listener when it came to how he felt.

"To be honest with you Simon. I'd rather not go back to the flatlands. It's one scary place. But I did make a promise and when the time is right I mean to keep it. We don't have to travel through time. I'd rather not. Only if absolutely necessary. There are too many unknowns, as far as I'm concerned. Maerwyn and Longille have assured us if we weren't away too long—but no, I think using portals between dimensions is safer. At least I hope so. They haven't warned us much about that."

"If we can find the portals," Simon's head bobbed in agreement.

"Well, we know of at least one. Spoon Lake. Not that I want to go through there again any time soon."

"Now that it has been activated, perhaps it will be easier."

"Let's find Maerwyn and Longille. Maybe they can tell us more about that."

Sybil rose from the floor where they'd been sitting in front of the brazier with the dogs. Simon and the hounds followed her down the hall to a lounge, where they found the two Hetopians.

Simon began with his concern about time travel, laying out their fears about age changes. "Do you think we should use a portal to go back to Third?"

"Certainly, that is possible. Now that Spoon Lake has opened, travel will be much easier. Each time a portal between realms is used, it opens more fully. It is easier to access," advised Maerwyn.

"Perhaps we should go through Spoon Lake," said Simon, having made peace with the thought of living in the Third. He did want to experience family life. He was afraid that nothing was left in the flatlands. His family there was gone forever. Sure, there was a slight chance, although he knew this was slim.

"It's still your choice," replied Longille. "But know this. Travelling via time is easy if you need to get back to preserve continuity. You needed to do this Sybil, when you went back the first time. You have been using the Wellness Sanctuary every day since and the risks are minimal, in this case. We think you should use time travel again so that Simon has a real life experience of it. It can't hurt to have that skill."

That settled it. They were using time travel to go back to Third. But Sybil was intrigued by the fact that she could use Spoon Lake if she ever needed to. It would have been heart-breaking to know she would never see Maerwyn and Longille again. Hetopia had become a very comfortable place to live, nearly a second home. She hoped they would not lose touch with them or Hetopia. There was no reason the Hetopians could not visit them in Third, was there?

"I don't want to leave, knowing we'd never see you again," Sybil made her feelings known.

"I feel the same way," said Simon. "Are you able to come to Third to see us?"

"Of course. We would be delighted to visit from time to time. But we must be extremely careful. Other Thirds would have difficulty understanding us or our presence," said Longille.

"That makes leaving more bearable," said Simon.

"Does that mean we're ready then? What do you think Simon? Tomorrow morning?"

"I'm ready if you are."

The following morning they said farewell to their Hetopian friends and arrived in Third as dawn was breaking. Sybil chose their backyard, a private setting, to make their entrance. Besides, Simon was most anxious to explore the tree house. She actually set them square in the middle of the floor of that intriguing structure.

"In my dreams!" cried Simon, looking through the small window into the backyard.

Sybil put her finger to her lips, "Shhhh! Careful," she whispered. "We don't want to wake the neighbours. It's the week end. Most people are at home. No work today."

"Sorry," Simon whispered back. "What now?"

"Dad should be back from his morning jog soon. He goes every morning, rain or shine."

Shortly, her dad rounded the corner of the house through the gate. He stood doubled over, panting, then walked around the yard cooling off.

"Hey Dad," Sybil whispered.

"Good morning honey. I didn't know you decided to spend the night in the tree house."

She had timed it just right. Neither her dad nor her mom would have missed her. Of that she was glad. Once they experienced this, they would be at ease. Or worse still, it might cause them to worry, not knowing when or where. She would have to alert them, to tell them if she had another trip planned. Though, now that she was home, she didn't think that was an issue. Did she really want to do more realm travel? Simon was home, what more could we want?

Sybil motioned for Simon to stay, while she climbed down to break the news of his arrival.

"Come on Dad, let's go make some hot chocolate."

"Your mother should be up. She'll have breakfast on by this time."

Sybil broke into a sprint. "Race you to the back porch."

"Not fair. I just finished a big run," he laughed, as he caught up with her.

They entered the house. Sybil's mom was sipping her morning coffee and reading the news.

"Morning Mom. What's for breakfast? I'm starved."

"Flapjacks, berries and maple syrup, her mom smiled. Better wash up first."

When they sat down to breakfast, Sybil began.

"Remember how I said, you might not even know I've been away?"

"Yes," replied her mom hesitantly.

"Well this is one of those times. And I have a surprise."

Her dad pushed back his chair and teetered crazily. "Don't tell me. You have Simon with you!" He had waited a long time, the splinter of hope was sealed over by the callus of denial.

"What? Are you sure?" Franceska's doubt was intransigently, stubbornly embedded. She jumped up and grabbed her arms. "Where? Where is he?"

"We came a few minutes ago. Just waiting for Dad to get back. We were in the tree house. He's still there."

James put his arm around Franceska to steady her. They were both numb, unsure what to do next. Finally, he looked to Sybil for a cue.

"Do you want to go out to meet him or should he come in?"

"Ask him what he wants to do," her mother said quietly.

Returning from the backyard, she knocked gently on the door and nudged it open. Her parents were standing in the middle of the kitchen, bracing themselves for the first glimpse. Simon walked shyly toward them. They stood facing each other, studying facial features; noticing the dimple in the chin, the dark hair and eyes, the same broad shoulders.

Simon's knees began to wobble. Now that he was here, after the excitement of preparing for, after all that Sybil had told him about Third, after the excitement of travelling in time—he was having second thoughts. A knot formed in his throat. His voice seemed stuck, unable to make its way past the lump. He was nervous. Would they like him? What if they didn't want him? Where would he go? The thought of rejection smouldered in his belly. A wave of nausea passed over him and he felt light-headed.

Sybil could feel the fine tremors of his fingers as he leaned on her arm for support. A sense of betrayal compounded his confusion. My family in Leanoria. Are they still alive? How will they feel? He was sinking. A hollow pit opened inside, threatening to swallow him.

Are these my real parents? The confusion deepened. What if they weren't his parents? Sure, even he could see the resemblance. But they were strangers. His parents were back there in the flatlands. He had a sister and two brothers. He stared. But I look like these people. His mind began to race. This is crazy. I shouldn't be here.

Floundering in emotions out of his depths, he took a deep breath, touched bottom and shoved off, surfacing once more. Sybil sensed the turmoil and squeezed his arm. Gratefully, he caught her eyes and found the reassuring trust he had come to know in Hetopia. He pulled himself together and stood prepared for what was to come.

Franceska, after studying his features, noting the resemblance, leapt the channel between them, allowing the flood waters to breach the rigid dyke surrounding her heart. She made the first move, by slowly extending her hands. Simon moved as in a dream, clasping her hands in his. His father closed the gap wrapping his wife and Simon in his arms. He drew them together in a long embrace. They opened the circle to draw Sybil in, clinging together in a tearful reunion.

Simon was overwhelmed by these two new people hugging him. When Sybil joined them in the circle, he felt a small measure of familiarity. This is going to take a while I guess, he thought, as he relinquished their embrace.

It was awkward. He had no recollection of them. As a baby? What did they expect? He glanced down at his shoes and scuffed his toe against the linoleum. He was hot, could feel the blush rising up his throat and spreading across his face. This was one quality he hated about his personality. Why can't I control that? It's embarrassing, he berated himself.

"Let me see you," Franceska held him at arm's length. She studied his beautiful brown eyes, his thick dark hair and his mouth that turned up at the corners. A smile came naturally to him. He was truly her Simon.

He shrunk under the close inspection, wishing this part of the meeting was over. Then she looked deeply into his eyes and whispered, "Welcome home honey pie."

Simon jolted at the sound of the endearment. He'd heard that before. But for the life of him, could not remember where. He felt reticent about having to hug these strangers. How can I feel this way? They are Sybil's parents. Since he had come to believe that she could be his sister, then they must be his parents too. Why don't I feel like I know them? Surely I would know if they were my parents. Something about them would tell me wouldn't it?

His confusion wreaked havoc with his imagination. A tempest of conflicting emotions played across his face, as he fought to reign in his uncertainty. He missed his other family. He felt disloyal, hated the fact that he had no control over this situation. The tenseness in the room was thick and he hated himself for feeling this way.

Then he remembered the softness when she had looked into his eyes and whispered, 'Welcome home honey pie.' There was something very appealing about that. He felt a slow kinship forming. Something familiar about it, made him feel warm inside.

"You must be hungry son," James eased the intense feelings in the room. "Come sit here by me. This is your place at the table."

"Thank you," his soft voice reflected good manners, as he sat down and pulled in his chair.

Franceska made up a plate of flapjacks topped with berries and maple syrup and placed it before him. She served Sybil and James and finally sat down with her family, together at the same table after all those years. Gazing across the table at her husband, their eyes locked in misty emotional relief.

Trying to break the ice that had settled between them at the table, Simon ventured a question. "What kind of berries are these? I know the raspberries. We had them on the farm..." He let that line of thought die.

"They are blackberries, Simon," answered Franceska. "They grow wild all over the Fraser Valley. We can pick as many as we like. They are free to everyone."

"And the others are blueberries. We grow them in our backyard," said Sybil. "Do you like them?"

"They are delicious," agreed Simon. "I haven't had anything as good as this, ever."

After clearing the breakfast table, they sat in the sunroom. The concern utmost on their minds, was introducing Simon into their world.

"Simon and I have been thinking about what we need to tell people. And Maerwyn and Longille had some good suggestions." They laid out the story that had been fabricated in Hetopia.

"Do you think it will work?" asked Simon, still very self-conscious. It was he who would have to tell the story. Assured of their support would make it easier.

"I believe it will. Not any better story we could think of," replied James.

"I'm sure it will be okay." Franceska was reliving the dreadful first day at home when the police arrived with support from Victims Services. It had all been for nothing. But now, now she had her dream fulfilled. Her long dark night was over.

"For the remainder of this coming week you will rest and we'll get to know each other a little. We will live as a family. Next Monday I will contact the local RCMP Detachment and have them attend the house. I am not taking you down there," said James.

There it was. He heard it. They would live as a family. How could he get used to that? All he wanted was to see his other family back in the Fifth. Yes. Now he had said it. His *other* family. He had two families. He had to learn to live with that. Maybe he could meld them into one somehow. Would they all get along? Would they like each other? He hoped they would. But how could he do that? Even if they were still alive, they were in Fifth. What was he thinking? How dumb, he rebuked himself.

"Would you like to see your room?" asked Franceska. "Ever since Sybil told us, we've been preparing it."

They followed her upstairs. She paused at the last door in the hall, then opened it, ushering Simon inside. It was a typical boy's room.

"We didn't know your favourite colour, so we went with the usual for boys. I hope that is all right."

"Actually, I do like blue. It reminds me of the open skies back home." Oh, oh. Shouldn't have said that, he thought. "Anything's okay really. Thanks."

"You can decide what you want in your room. Posters, music, sports, whatever. It's yours."

"Thank you. It's all so new."

Realizing the overwhelming information coming at him, Franceska decided to give him some space.

"Would you like us to leave you? Spend some time in here for a while?"

"That'd be nice, thanks. I think I'll rest." He needed time to process, to sort out the conflict he was feeling. A loneliness settled into the pit of his stomach. He was homesick. Now that he was in a family setting he missed those other people even more. He had called them Mom and Dad, just as his sister and brothers had. Were they really not his family? Yes they were! Nothing could take that away. Not these people. Not even Sybil. Still, these people were very nice. And he looked like them too.

Sybil sensed he was holding back. During their days in Hetopia she had begun to understand him better, could read the play on his face, the way he held his shoulders. His emotions were checked, held just below the surface on the verge of erupting. She sensed he needed time to sort things out.

"I'll be in my room down the hall. Give me a shout if you want company," she said.

Sgt. Stanton arrived at the doorstep the following Monday. He had been a corporal when he went to the hospital that morning. It was a perplexing case from the start. One that he'd been determined to solve. It still rankled him. He'd gone over and over the facts. Did he overlook something? Now, more than thirteen years later, to get a call out of the blue? Never expected that!

"Good morning. I'm Sgt. Stanton. Thank you for calling this morning."

"Yes, I remember," said James. "Never thought. After all these years."

"Extremely baffling case. None of the leads panned out. Now this? What has the boy been able to tell you? Are you sure he's your son?"

"Well, same age. And there's strong family resemblance."

"I will need to talk to him. Take a statement. You will be present of course."

"Sure. He's upstairs." He crossed the hall with the officer. "You can wait here in the study."

When Simon arrived, the Mountie stood and offered his hand. "Hi Simon, I am Sgt. Stanton. I am glad to see you. I hope you don't mind answering a few questions."

"No, I don't mind."

"Please have a seat," said James, leading them to the padded arm chairs.

"Simon," began Sgt. Stanton. "I will need you to start at the beginning. Please tell me everything you can remember."

James gave him a reassuring nod and Simon took a deep breath. Then he launched into his rehearsed story without embellishing the facts. As Maerwyn and Longille had predicted, there were the clarifying questions as to where he had been and could he lead them back to the place. But Simon was unprepared for the last question.

The only thing they'd forgotten were names! What were their names? How could I not think of that? He berated himself.

James stepped into the momentary silence. "Simon tells us his last name was Smith. He lived with John and Mary Smith."

Of course, thought Sgt. Stanton. The most common names in society. What else would they be?

"This must be very upsetting for you, Simon. But we need to establish for certain. I'm not sure how to say this. We need to make positive identification. We have to know beyond a doubt. The only way we can do that is to match DNA samples."

James drew in a deep breath. There it was. He too, needed to know, to be absolutely sure. Sgt. Stanton had provided the answer. He looked toward the boy.

"Are you okay with this Simon?"

"Sure. Why not?"

"Okay then. We'll make arrangements through our medical practitioner."

"I think that's all for now then," said the sergeant, as he stood to leave.

He walked to the front entrance, said goodbye and closed the door behind himself. This is really bizarre, even more so than thirteen years ago. Why couldn't we find any evidence then? I've rehashed it so often. Nothing to explain how he disappeared. Sure, there were those odd blips on the screen. Couldn't prove anything by that. He walked away muttering to himself. John and Mary Smith presumed drowned in some unknown lake. John and Mary Smith, an alias if he'd ever heard one. He shook his head. Another impossible task.

The DNA tests came back positive. They matched. Both Simon and the Hubers were assured beyond a doubt. They were blood kin. He was Simon Huber.

*

Transitioning to his life in the Third was not easy. Sybil broke the news privately first to Hamish, then Marc. Once she'd answered all the questions to their satisfaction, she invited them to her house to meet him. The McCrorys and Leesoms rallied in support, providing a buffer of protection where they could. The police released the break in the case to the media. Reporters flooded the street arriving at their door. Phone calls asking for interviews plagued the household.

News headlines read: 13-Year-Old Kidnap Victim Surfaces. It was a media frenzy. Television and radio carried the story, creating a national sensation. Offers for the exclusive right to their story came from journalists all over the country. A number of book offers came in. James and Franceska closed rank. Their story was not for sale. Simon would not to be sensationalized or traumatized any further. And Sybil by association, was as much in the news as he was. Certainly there were well-wishers out there, but Franceska and James remained fearful of the small percentage of the fringe population. They had already endured enough loss. No, their family was not for sale.

Eventually the media hype moved on and life on Lavendar Street began to settle. The Ministry for Children and Youth Development made numerous visits, offering counselling services and support, satisfying their legal obligations that Simon was receiving proper care. It was a delicate balance of support and family privacy. The subject of school enrolment was approached.

"We'll discuss this more fully, as a family," James assured the worker. "Certainly we have been concerned with the timing of this and how best to approach it."

After he closed the door on the worker he turned to Franceska. "Do you think we should homeschool?" asked James.

"I've been thinking about that a lot." She narrowed her eyes. "Sybil is back in school."

"It doesn't seem right. Her at school. Simon at home. They should be together."

"Either we homeschool both or they attend Vedder together."

"We ought to ask them."

Later at the dinner table, where most of the important decisions seemed to take place, James approached the subject.

191

"Your mother and I were thinking about schooling for you Simon."

"Sybil has gone back to class. Do you want to join her?" asked Franceska

"There is another option. You could do homeschooling. But your mother and I feel you and Sybil should be together."

Simon studied each face for a moment. What did they want him to say? He wanted to please them. He was grateful for the home they were providing. But there were times, when he still felt like an outsider. It happened less frequently now, but it was there in the back of his mind.

Sybil was the first to sense his hesitancy.

"Simon, I'd rather be with you. You decide if you want to come to school. If you want to be homeschooled, I will stay home with you."

As scary as this was, he didn't want to disrupt Sybil's life at school. Admittedly he was curious about it. After giving it some thought he nodded.

"I would like to try going to school with Sybil. I've looked at her text books and we've talked about some of it. It looks interesting."

"We'll make an appointment on Monday to speak with the principal. There may be assessments to establish where you should start?"

"Assessments?"

"Did you attend school where you lived before?"

"Not sure what you mean by school? We had instruction in numbers and language. I liked watching the seasons, the birds, animals, and how things grew. How everything fit together. The very best, was studying the night sky and watching the clouds, weather patterns."

"They will test you on knowledge. And aptitude."

"Aptitude?"

"Something that comes natural to you. Your talents. What you are good at," said James.

"Oh, that should be fun." He was feeling reassured and a little excited.

On Simon's first day, Hamish and Marc arrived at their door.

"Hey man. This is cool. Your first day at Vedder!" said Hamish. "Wanna walk together?"

A budding friendship had begun to grow, as the four companions hung out. Playing in their neighbourhood, Simon caught on to the rudiments of street hockey. He was introduced to some of their favourite hiking trails. Their best times were spent hanging out in the tree house, telling stories. With Hallowe'en just passed, ghosts and scary stories figured prominently in their conversations. Sybil's brother was a hit when it came to those tales. He had a whole different background that neither Hamish nor Marc could have guessed. It supplied fuel for his wild and fertile imagination.

Arriving at the schoolyard fifteen minutes ahead of the warning bell, gave them time to introduce Simon to some of their other friends. Soon a small crowd had gathered in the back field. Simon felt apprehensive. All the attention was a little overwhelming. Sybil was glad to see that many of the kids offered friendly welcomes and made him feel included. It was going well.

They went to first class together. It was science. Simon was alert and interested. He also proved to be adept in the subject of math, which was their last block. As soon as the dismissal bell sounded they packed up their belongings, shrugged into their backpacks and waited out front for Hamish and Marc.

"I think it went very well today Simon. How do you feel about it?"

"Awesome! I especially loved the first and last period."

Sybil grinned at his enthusiastic response. She could tell by his animated face and the broad smile, that he had had a good day.

"Oh no," she muttered under her breath. "Here come Wesley and Alex." She turned her back to them and looked the other way.

"Did you say something?" asked Simon.

Wesley's insulting voice interrupted before she could answer. "Lookie here. If it ain't the loser Sybil Huber. Who's the goofball you're talking to?"

They sidled up to them and nudged Simon's arm roughly, throwing him off-balance.

Startled by the rude voice, Simon looked to Sybil for clarification. He caught the look of disgust on her face.

"Go away Wesley."

"Your long-lost brother ain't it?"

He turned the harassment up a notch, "Lived in the boonies up north, eh?"

"With a couple of losers," Alex jeered.

"That makes you a loser too," laughed Wesley.

"Two losers! Hah. Better keep your head down and your eyes open."

Just then Hamish and Marc arrived on the scene.

"Back off," they warned.

"You back off. We don't take no orders from the likes o' you."

The teacher on bus supervision who was eyeing the fracas, casually walked over, listening to the altercation.

"What's the problem here?" he demanded. He was aware of the duo, Wesley and Alex. Trouble followed them.

Wesley gave Sybil a snarling look, warning her to beware.

"Nothing at all," she covered. It was her usual answer.

"It wasn't nothing," piped up Hamish. "Wesley and Alex are harassing Sybil and Simon. Calling them losers."

"Report to the office Wesley. You too Alex." He was determined to get this under control, before it got too far into the year. Those two needed some consequences.

"Now you've done it Hamish," said Sybil, as they were marched off by the duty teacher.

Hamish was fed up. "They can't keep doing this!" he said, resolutely.

"Have to stand up to 'em this year," added Marc. "Or it'll get worse."

"Right. You can talk. They never pick on you," Sybil retorted.

"When they pick on my friends, they pick on me."

"Yeah, no more," agreed Marc.

Simon was round-eyed by the altercation. He had gone pale and Sybil noticed a fine tremor in his hands. He was clearly having a flashback. There was fear there.

"Don't worry Simon. The school will figure it out," she reassured. Inwardly, she wasn't so sure.

"Come on Simon. Let's go," said Hamish, giving him a bolstering thump on his back. "That's taken care of 'em. They won't bother us anymore."

Simon relaxed a bit and stepped off the sidewalk, glad to be headed to the safety of home.

Sybil brought up the subject of Wesley and Alex at the dinner table, telling their parents of the confrontation and how they had been sent to the office.

"Those two have been up to no good since the first day of Kindergarten," sighed Franceska. "It's troubling."

She didn't know much about the family. She thought that Wesley's family had come from the east somewhere. Alex's background was even more of a mystery.

"I hope they get help for those two," she said. "I think there's still time to make some positive change."

"That's what I keep saying. But Hamish and Marc think there's little hope of that."

A reoccurring dream began to disturb Simon's sleep. The first time, he said nothing. When it came for the third night, he decided to tell Sybil about it. He found her in the kitchen, mixing up a batch of his favourite cookies. She stuck the last pan in the oven and set the timer.

"What's up Simon?"

He was lost in thought. By the way he walked, his head tipped forward, eyes downcast, she could tell something was bothering him.

"Let's go to the tree house, Syb."

"There's ten minutes left on the timer. Help me wash up the dishes. By that time the last batch will be out."

When the last of the cookies were cooling on the rack, she said, "Grab a cookie. Let's go."

Heading through the door, he munched thoughtfully, concern puckering his forehead.

"What is it Simon?"

"I had this dream. First time, I didn't know what to think. After the third time, I'm weirded out."

Sybil sat quietly. It was best to just listen with Simon. He had a way of thinking before he spoke. When he finally did speak, what he said was usually well organized and clear. She could see he was rattled.

"I am in front of an old cabin. Mist is everywhere. It's hard to see. I turn and walk into a graveyard and find myself standing by a headstone. The name is Huber."

He shivered uncontrollably, wrapping his arms around his shoulders, as though warding off a chill.

Sybil reacted with a swift intake of breath. It caught in her throat, rendering her speechless. She tried to swallow but her throat had closed up. Her heart plummeted into her stomach and the knot of anxiety gathering there began to churn. Several minutes passed before she could compose her thoughts to reply. "Can you remember the first name?"

"The mist. It's hazy. Begins with C maybe. Like Clara or Catherine."

"Was it Claire?"

"Yeah, could be Claire."

"What happened next?"

"I turn back to the cabin. A figure appears in the mist. A voice calling...find it...find it. Three times it calls out...find it. I woke up in a cold sweat. I was really scared."

"Simon! I've been there. You're dreaming about something that happened to me and mom this summer. The grave. It's her great-great-grandmother."

"What?" He was shocked. "It happened to you?"

Stunned by his revelation, she tried to make sense of it. Why would he be dreaming of that? He couldn't possibly know.

"I had a dream my first night in Hetopia, about falling into water. I remembered the graveyard and the voice from the summer. It's why I went searching at Lenore Lake, well Leanoria Basine I guess."

"And you found me. But the voice said, 'find it.' "

"Yes, same message? Do you think we should keep looking?"

"For what? Where?"

"I don't know. But I think we need to go back to Hetopia."

"When?" As soon as the question left his lips, he answered it. "As soon as possible!"

"Yes. And let's take our new iPad. Longille and Maerwyn can have it. Our gift to them."

"Great idea! Let's pack some of those fresh cookies too."

"Do you think we should tell Mom and Dad we're going?"

"Hmmm. They'll worry. If we don't tell them, we can slip out and come back in time."

"Doesn't seem quite right. Just to leave?"

"Yeah, but how do we explain our absence?" It was a dilemma. Spoon Lake was far away and they needed to get there fast. "Has to be timed right."

"Okay. It'll have to be time travel. I'll take my backpack again."

As soon as they were ready, they climbed into the tree house and left from there, hoping to use it as an anchor point for their return.

CHAPTER NINE
The Search

Back in Hetopia, Longille was mesmerized. After Sybil and Simon left, he had been playing on the iPad for much of the day.

"You still playing Angry Birds?" Maerwyn teased.

"It's addictive! Such fun," admitted Longille. *"But you're right. Should be doing other things."*

He turned his attention to Google Earth, which was why he had wanted the tablet in the first place. He was intrigued by Third dimension technology. Manufacturing played a low key in Fifth. Their methods utilized a more natural use of resources, that is, if you could call flying Plasmic Energy, natural.

To Sybil and Simon there was nothing natural about it. Fifth's use of solar power for light and heat they could understand, but the Wellness Floe? That was extremely foreign and exciting. Nothing in their experience had prepared them for anything like it. A cosmic energy source that could work out disease processes! Imagine that!

From what Sybil had told him, the Third had more mundane ways of dealing with disease. Cutting? That was a pretty invasive measure. And Sybil's description of those dreadful needles made his skin pucker! Granted, Third was making some very good progress with fancy gamma rays. What if Fifth and Third should team up? Wouldn't that be an accomplishment! Longille dreamed of making the world a better place.

"Cross-dimensional effort!" beamed Longille. *"Must remember to talk to Sybil and Simon about that!"* He brightened at the thought and turned his attention to the screen in front of him.

"Now how did she say to do this? Ah yes, touch on the app and there it is. Type in Hetopia. That's right."

The city loomed into view. He decided to check out Leanoria. Panning east, he followed the mountainous terrain until he came to the flatlands. The devastation was still plainly there to see.

"Try going north," urged Maerwyn.

As he panned over the area and zoomed in, further degradation was revealed. The land was dotted with ponds that flowed into streams. Tributaries merged into larger flows and new rivers had begun to form, making their way to the sea.

"Something's not right," Maerwyn's brow furrowed in concentration.

It was clear there were drastic changes taking place. They hurried to find Ebihinin, anxious to show her the evidence they found.

"What have you there?" Ebihinin's starry gaze lit upon the screen.

"It's Sybil's iPad. She left it for us to use. It's the coolest thing!" He was beginning to pick up the new expressions he was hearing.

"Coolest?"

"Yes, utterly fascinating," he corrected.

"Well? What does it do?"

"This Google Earth thing. Intriguing." He panned east across the Prominences, arrived at the flatlands, then showed her the northern country.

"Haven't spent much time that far north but I know enough about it. This isn't normal," said Longille.

Ebihinin's eyes filmed over. A fire appeared in each orb. There had been tumultuous times before. This did not bode well. She marshalled her thoughts, lining them up logically. A major upheaval was coming. She could feel it in her bones.

"Maybe Sybil isn't finished her mission," she ventured.

No sooner had she said that, Sybil and Simon came walking through the forest toward them. Thrilled to catch sight of the Hetopians, they broke into a run calling out joyfully.

"Hello Ebihinin! Hello Maerwyn, Longille!"

Surprised by the unexpected encounter, the Hetopians turned at the sound of their voices.

"You're right on cue," said Maerwyn, switching automatically to their language. "Couldn't have timed it better!"

"On cue?" asked Sybil.

"Yes," replied Ebihinin. "I just mentioned your name and now here you are!"

Longille intervened, "There's something we want to show you." He panned over the northern regions showing Sybil and Simon the changes. "Our weather patterns are off. Now this!"

"Hah! Maybe that explains why things are happening in the Third. Everyone's worried about climate change these days," said Sybil.

"But that's not why we came," added Simon.

He related the strange phenomenon of his dreams. It had started in Lenore Lake for Sybil. Maybe now it has more to do with Leanoria. Why would he dream about what happened to her?

"Maybe finding me was just the beginning."

His mind raced through the possibilities. Was there a chance to find people still living there? A ray of hope seeped through a crack in his armour. He shut it down. I can't allow myself to even think it. If it is in the stars, if it was his fate and theirs—he just had to accept it. No, hope would set him up for disappointment. He was coming to acceptance of what is. After all he'd been through, it was a painful fact he was beginning to under-stand. He would do his best, let go and accept fate.

"Finding you was just the beginning Simon? Sounds logical," replied Ebihinin. "If we follow that line of reasoning…"

"That means we have to return," said Sybil flatly.

She cringed, thinking of how happy she had been to escape the flatlands. To go back there? She glanced at Simon, could see the lift in the corners of his mouth, a bit of sparkle in his eyes. Was that a flicker of hope igniting within? As quickly as it flared, it was gone. She sensed it was up to her to keep that hope alive, if not in him, then in herself. This was the opportunity to keep the promise she had made. They would return.

Simon's eyes met hers. He acknowledged the resolve form-ing there and he met her on equal territory. Those dreams—they were meant to work together. Whatever they had to do, they would discover it together.

Sybil found the determination in his eyes equalling her own. They had to find each other, she knew that now. Sure, she found him at Graenwolven dungeon. But he found her too, helped her discover who she was in the Third, revealing parts of herself, even she had not known. The uniqueness of their kinship unlocked those possibilities. They were discovering themselves in new ways.

"Let's go to the palace. We need to plan our strategy," sug-gested Ebihinin. She was deeply troubled by events in the north and wanted to consult the ancient writings once more. Maybe they had missed something.

Arriving at the Great Hall, Simon was initiated through the six veils of colour. He emerged in wonder, as Sybil had done on her first day in Hetopia. Following Ebihinin, they descended to consult the Book of Wisdom once more. She riffled her hand over the surface of the water and found the passage she was looking for.

✧

Songs of Lament

Deep in the heartland, a force unknown
Gathers in power, all the world will moan.
A battle of the sea, a battle for the earth.
Gives rise to violence, and that of new birth.
Amidst weeping and sighs
Tales of sadness and woe,
One shall appear as guide
Above and in darkness below.
Powers of Ice prevail at last,
Crystal of the Dragon, danger's past.

"There must be something here. Powers of Ice prevail. What is this all about? The ice is disappearing."

"A recon field trip?" suggested Longille. "What do you think, Maerwyn?"

"Indeed, we need more close up intelligence. When do you want to leave?"

"When you go, Sybil and I are going with you," said Simon. He was determined to at least make an attempt to find his family.

"Is that wise? So soon after your return to Third?" replied Maerwyn.

"My strength is much better now. And those dreams. They're too coincidental. We need to follow up," replied Simon.

He did not believe in coincidence. Synchronicity had a purpose. And maybe he was right. Too many things lined up. Fate was fate. Hope always seemed to get in the way. It was useless. Living in Graenwolven prison, he had given up hope. Simon paled at the idea. Back to Graenwolven Territory? But then his rescue...maybe he needed to rethink that. A small spark flared to life unbidden, enkindling a flicker of hope. Fate and acceptance went out the window. Wasn't it better to have some hope? Maybe, just maybe, with a bit of luck, he could still find his other family.

"Please. Simon and I need to go back," Sybil reinforced Simon's request. "We can help."

Longille and Maerwyn looked at Ebihinin. She nodded her head.

"Those dreams are of portent. Something is yet to be discovered."

"All right. We'll stay together," replied Longille.

"Oh, we nearly forgot," said Simon, who was carrying the back pack.

He unzipped it and pulled out the new tablet. He handed it over to Sybil. It had been her idea to gift it. She should be the one who presented it to Longille.

"We brought you a new iPad. You can keep this one in Hetopia and we'll take back our other one."

Longille's eyes lit up with pleasure as he reached for it, eager to possess such a useful item.

"What can I say?" he spluttered. "To merely say thank you. How can we ever repay you?"

"We'll never get a day's work out of him now!" laughed Maerwyn. "Angry Birds will be taking over Hetopia!"

"You like those games?" Sybil was amused.

Then Simon remembered the other package and dug in the backpack. They watched with pleasure, as Maerwyn and Longille munched cookies.

"Ebihinin, you must try one. Delectable!" said Longille.

"Another addiction," sighed Maerwyn happily, savouring the sweet chocolate melting in his mouth.

"Yes, please, you must," said Simon, holding the bag open for her.

Ebihinin took one and bit into it delicately. They watched her expression change from surprise to pleasure at her first taste of chocolate.

"Heavenly! What is that melty bit?"

"That is chocolate!" said Maerwyn.

"Delightful indeed. Thank you!"

Longille clapped his forehead. "You haven't even seen the hounds yet. They will be very excited to see you. Come."

"See you later Ebihinin," they called, following Longille up the steps to the Great Hall above.

Lost in the pleasure of chocolate she gave them an absent-minded wave.

"We're still in the same apartments at the rear of the palace. The dogs seem comfortable there, so we've moved in permanently with them."

The hounds heard them coming and set up loud barking in the entrance hall. When they opened the door, they were bowled over by masses of writhing fur and wet tongues. Falling to their knees to meet them on equal turf, they tussled with them, the hounds cavorting in circles racing out and coming back for more. They couldn't get enough of the two young people who had befriended them.

"It's plain to see they belong to you!" sighed Maerwyn. He had hoped that at least one of them would remain in Hetopia, for he had grown very fond.

"Will you be taking them to Third when you go back?"

Sybil could hear the wistful tone. "We hadn't really thought about it. All three? Our home isn't big enough. Maybe one."

"Good guard dogs," said Simon. "Hard to decide which one to take."

"I think the dogs will make the choice." Sybil could see how each of them seemed to hang around their preferred person. For Simon and her, it was the big male who stayed close. The other two seemed to pair off; one with Maerwyn and the other with Longille.

"Can we take them back to Centralia with us?" asked Simon, hopefully.

"Excellent idea!"

It had occurred to both Maerwyn and Longille, for in truth they both enjoyed the hounds and felt immeasurable comfort around them. Besides, they had alerted them to danger on a number of occasions.

After lunch Simon and Sybil headed out into the forests of Hetopia, breathing in the sweet scent of the Pallid Elusive. It felt good to be back. How they had longed for the open meadows and deep lush woods.

"How do you feel about going back to the flatlands, Simon?"

"Scared. But I want to see if I can find my family. That doesn't mean to say you aren't my family," he quickly clarified, mindful of Sybil's feelings.

"Of course Simon. It is an adjustment for everyone. They are your family, the family that raised you as a child. That is the mark of family. We are very fortunate you had such a good family while you were away. You must tell me more about them. Please I really want to know."

Realizing that he wanted to share at least some of his childhood memories with her, he launched into life on the farm. How much fun it had been! He told her about their favourite games, building forts in the surrounding bushlands, swimming and rafting on ponds, playing in the hayloft, working the gardens and helping feed the livestock. It was a good wholesome upbringing. He lapsed into silence, afraid to share too much. There was an irrational fear that if he spoke their names out loud, he risked never seeing them again. They remained unspoken ghosts of his past. He could not explain it even to himself.

"That sounds like it was a lot of fun Simon." Sybil let the subject come to a natural close, thankful he was able to tell her that much.

Early the next morning, they had their gear packed and were ready. Bidding farewell to Ebihinin, they lifted off and entered the Plasmic Energy Force with the hounds safely on board the mind net.

"Are we going to Leanoria or heading straight north?" Simon asked.

While he wanted to go to Leanoria, a crushing melancholy increased the deep loss he felt for his family. He had hoped by visiting the area it would make him feel closer. He realized again, they were no longer there.

"North I think," answered Longille.

"Leanoria on our way back?" Maerwyn queried, keenly aware of how much it meant to Simon.

Powering to warp speed they were soon over settlements of deteriorating ice blocks. Below, the landscape was a desolate panorama of eroded ice, bare patches of earth and melt water, confirming what Sybil's tablet had revealed.

"Where is everyone?" wondered Sybil.

In a short while, they had reached the far northern regions, where the degradation of snow and ice was not as apparent.

"Haven't been this far north before. Not much is known about these people," said Longille. "If they're anything like the Graenwolven we've seen in the Leanorian area…" Longille's train of thought lapsed. A tall palatial ice structure loomed on the horizon.

"What's that?" asked Simon.

"Looks out of place," replied Longille.

Making a circular sweep of the area, they saw no signs of life.

"It's deserted," concluded Maerwyn.

"Extraordinary!" cried Sybil. Her curiosity got the best of her and she broke formation to check it out.

"Come back!" Simon called.

She kept going. Simon split off and sped after her.

"What are you doing?"

"It's so beautiful!"

They circled the façade, astounded by the intricate contours of the castle walls. Suddenly, they were confronted with evidence. They were not alone. This place was not deserted.

"Is that a light!?" asked Sybil.

"Where?"

"The last small parapet. See? A faint glimmer."

"Yeah, I see."

"Should we check it out?"

Simon's curiosity was now fully aroused, "Try and stop me."

As they neared the level of the window they heard a plaintive strain of music, a lamenting lyric of clipped throaty sounds accompanied by soft drums. The suffering in the voice gripped the two onlookers, as they drifted closer to the dormer window.

Inside, a figure knelt in front of a brazier fanning a small fire. Smoke from the twisted grass plumed upward as she gathered handfuls, scooping it in a circular motion, smudging herself in a reverent manner. The plaintive song stopped abruptly and the figure slowly turned to face them. Her peaceful stare held them in place while they appraised each other.

Abruptly, the g-force of re-entry hit Sybil and Simon full on. They were pulled through the atmospheric change, landing inside the room with a thump.

"Beg your pardon! Please, so sorry to disturb you!" apologized Sybil, dismayed by her intrusion.

Simon quickly spluttered an introduction, hoping to lessen the impact of their sudden arrival.

"I'm Simon. This is my sister Sybil."

The figure looked startled. Her face moved from puzzlement to concentration, ending in a slow dawning of recognition. Then a wide smile lit up her face.

"You have come at last!"

They were left speechless, shocked by what they'd just heard. Finally Simon managed a reply.

"At last?"

"I am the Ice Empress Icelandia. My family has known of you," she said, excitement lighting her face. "As predicted, the stars have aligned. The Aurora Borealis has had exceptional displays this season; all indicators that your time was drawing near."

The Hetopians. Now Icelandia? The realization that she and Simon were part of something mysterious, beyond understanding, struck Sybil forcefully. Simon acknowledged the sudden shift in her, coming to a fuller awareness himself, as they processed the unexpected comment.

Not knowing how to respond, Sybil blurted out the only thing she could think to say.

"Where is everyone? What has happened?"

"Invasion from the north we think. The Seventh dimension is involved. There are forces beyond my control," lamented Icelandia.

"Your Highness. Can we help?" asked Simon.

"Please, call me Icelandia. I put no store in titles. It has been a long time since the invasion. Most of our citizenry have been carried off into slavery I believe, to the great land barons in Centralia. I don't know." She became lost in thought, visibly distraught.

"That's why it's so deserted!" Sybil replied.

Coming back to the present, Icelandia asked. "Do you know how things are in the south? The plight of my people lays heavy on my heart."

"Very bad when I was there," replied Simon. "I was held captive in the castle dungeon at Leanoria Your Highness...er, I mean Icelandia." A sudden chill juddered through him in a flashback of the fearful time he had spent there. "Sybil and her two friends rescued me."

"Oh!" At the mention of their friends he remembered. "Maerwyn and Longille will be worried."

"Who?" asked Icelandia.

"We came with friends from the west."

"Ah, the western force. Please bring them here. I wish to make them welcome."

Abruptly, Simon accelerated to warp speed, leaving Sybil and Icelandia staring at the empty space where he had been. In a nanosecond, he reappeared with Maerwyn and Longille at his side. The three hounds capered about the room, happy to stretch their legs after the confines of the mind net.

Simon began the introductions, "Maerwyn, Longille this is the Ice Empress Icelandia; this is Maerwyn and Longille from Hetopia in the west."

Icelandia spread her arms wide, greeting the Hetopians enthusiastically.

"Wonderful to meet you! Welcome to Graenwolven Territory. It is foretold that the western force would play a great part in these troubling times."

"Graenwolven Territory?" asked Sybil, now confused.

"Yes, you are in Graenwolven Territory."

"Then who is in control of Centralia?"

"I don't know for sure. Can you tell me more? What is happening out there?"

Sybil quickly related the story of her arrival in the Fifth dimension, their trip east to Centralia, the encounter with the Leanorian lake dwellers, the Namors Guardia and the discovery of Simon.

"That's shocking!" said Icelandia, clearly disturbed by these events. Where were her people? And where were the Centralians? Were any of them still alive? Extremely upset, she began pacing the room, until Longille intervened.

"Please, come sit with us Icelandia. Tell us what has happened here."

He led her to the chair in front of the brazier while the big male, sensing her distress, settled at her feet and laid his muzzle across her boot. She leaned down to stroke his soft fur, missing the comfort of her own dogs. Sybil and Simon sat on cushions near her while Maerwyn and Longille relaxed on chairs, stretching their long legs toward the brazier. Longille caressed the velvety head of one of the hounds nuzzling his knee. Four sets of eyes turned their attention to the Ice Empress.

"I have been imprisoned here many years. Although I am comfortable enough, an invisible energy force keeps me in place. Fortunately, not all of our people have been subdued. There are partisans in outlying areas who keep me supplied with food and fuel by way of a secret passage."

"Why would anyone do this?" asked Sybil.

"Not sure. We know Seventh is involved. According to our partisans, we think there's a faction in the Leanoria Truids that has taken control of Centralia. They've reported a race of hideous looking sentries in the Leanorian area."

"Namors Guardia," confirmed Simon. Security at Graenwolven castle—er, I suppose we can no longer call it that. They hunted us down at Leanoria Basine."

"We thought they were Graenwolven," said Sybil.

"If this is Graenwolven Territory, who are they? You thought invaders from the north?" asked Longille.

"Can you find out?" asked Icelandia.

"Should we check out the far north before returning to Leanoria?" asked Maerwyn.

"Haven't been this far north before. If the Seventh is involved there will be risks," Longille replied.

A moist sheen had developed, collecting in the crevices of his craggy brow. Sybil had learned to pick up their distress. A definite uneasiness had come over the Hetopians. They were unsettled and unsure.

"If we go, I think it would be unwise to bring the dogs," said Longille, definitely unnerved.

Scratching the big male behind his ear Sybil hesitated. She didn't want to leave them behind but the apprehension in her Hetopian friends, set off warning bells. No one knew what lay ahead for them. She turned to the woman in the lounge chair.

"Could the hounds stay with you Icelandia?"

Simon felt the unease of the Hetopians and could see that Sybil too had become alarmed by the change in them. "We can pick them up on our way back," he said, trying to sound assured and encouraging, but the sober faces before him defeated his purpose. A long silence ensued.

Finally, Longille turned to Icelandia, "It would be very kind if you would allow the dogs refuge." A resolve had settled in his bones. There was a determined set to his shoulders, as he steeled himself for the task ahead.

"Of course. I am grateful you are taking this on—going north I mean. Besides, it's lonely here. I miss our own dogs. I will enjoy having them around." Icelandia felt hope for the first time in a long while. Crossing to a desk, she produced a stylus and parchment and began to write.

"I will give you an introductory missive to explain your presence, should you encounter our partisans." She stamped the enclosure with her thumbprint, using the burnt ash from her smudge and handed it to Simon. He tucked it safely inside his chest pocket, patting it reassuringly.

S.S. Huber – The Dragon's Eye Crystal

They bid Icelandia farewell promising to return at the earliest opportunity. She bowed, wishing them a safe journey. With a last comforting pat to the hounds the foursome re-entered the Plasmic Force and were outside the ice palace.

"Icelandia told us the most extraordinary thing!" Sybil couldn't hold back any longer. "She said her family has known of Simon!"

"Simon? How!?" asked Maerwyn.

"She didn't say," replied Simon. "Just that her family was aware of me. Strange! What have I got to do with any of this?"

Longille was subdued. His usual aplomb had taken a dive. Who invaded the North Country and took over Centralia? He knew almost nothing of what lay north, and yet they had to check it out. Trying not to reveal the apprehension that lay rooted in his gut, he turned to Sybil and Simon.

"We use extreme caution. No more flying off on our own without warning."

"Neither Longille nor I have been this far north," added Maerwyn. The dread he felt in the core of his bones echoed a reinforcement of Longille's admonishment. "It's important we stay together and watch each other's back."

"If the Seventh is involved, there is reason to be concerned. The Fifth cannot enter," Longille continued.

"It would be total annihilation," Maerwyn confirmed.

"What about Third?" asked Simon, his eyes contracting in fear, as he considered the consequences.

"Unknown," replied Longille. "As far as we know, Third has never encountered Seventh."

Duly forewarned and chastened by the reproach, Sybil apologized. "Sorry Longille. It was so beautiful."

Simon came to her defence. "We all thought it was deserted."

"It is partly our fault," conceded Maerwyn.

"We should have been more careful. But it turned out well," said Longille.

"Lesson learned," concluded Maerwyn.

Sybil made a mental promise to herself. She *would* be more careful. Simon sensed the resolve by the stiffening in her attitude.

"It's okay Sybil. We'll work together."

"Thank you Simon. Sorry."

Flying in close formation, they headed deeper into northern territory, each responsible for watching one of the four directions. Longille was in the lead when he drew up short, stopping abruptly. The others shot past him.

"Stop!" he called out harshly.

"What is it?" Maerwyn wheeled about in his direction.

"Something is ahead. I can feel it." His sensitive intuition was born out of many years of field missions, something learned only through experience and rigorous training.

They regrouped. This time Longille cautioned everyone to stay close behind him. His flaring nostrils and alert eyes alarmed Maerwyn. "What do you see?"

"I don't see anything. I feel it."

Flying slowly, they became aware of a mass of swirling mist. The atmosphere grew dense, until the pressure began to draw them forward.

"I don't like this," said Longille. He grabbed Sybil's hand. "Hold on everyone!"

"Pull back!" warned Maerwyn. He back-peddled furiously, throwing his might against the magnetic force that was sucking them in. "Hard!"

They strained fiercely, resisting with every muscle fibre.

Suddenly Sybil and Simon were wrenched away. The Hetopians rebounded like a slingshot, hurtling south at warp speed.

"Thank the stars!" Longille's breath rushed out in a long gasp.

"That was close!" shouted Maerwyn.

"Where are Sybil and Simon!?" Longille's frantic voice rang out.

"I-I couldn't hold on!" Maerwyn said, fearfully.

"They're gone! By Fifth Dimension Oaths! What have we done!?"

"We've lost them!" wailed Maerwyn. His Hetopian heart wrenched violently in his chest.

"We can't follow into Seventh! What should we do?"

"We must return to Icelandia. Warn her, then alert Hetopia."

"It's my fault!" cried Longille. "I should have pulled back sooner. When I felt the first drag."

"Don't Longille. We decided together."

"Still, I was in the lead. Oh why did I not pay heed?"

"Longille. Listen. There's nothing we can do here. We need to go back."

"We can't just leave!"

Maerwyn's patient voice did nothing to alleviate Longille's desperate remorse.

"We must go! Find help or—we'll find a way." Maerwyn's determined steel broke through Longille's wall of regret.

"Yes, Maerwyn. I know."

Longille conceded defeat, turned and sped off, ripping through the Plasmic Force with a ferocious anger that left Maerwyn gasping in his tailwind. Then he too, tore through the ragged edges left in the wake of his friend.

CHAPTER TEN
The Seventh Dimension

The churning mist morphed into a high speed vortex. Sybil and Simon were wrenched away abruptly, caught in the turbulent magnetic energy force that swept them into the abyss.

"Help!" shouted Sybil. "Simon! Where are you?"

Her cry of distress was swallowed by the deafening roar of the magnetic tempest.

"Sybil!" Simon's frantic voice rose above the din.

She turned to her left. Was that Simon?

"Sybil, where are you?"

She leaned toward the faint call. Her weight shifted and she gained momentum.

"Sybil!" Again she heard him, this time more clearly. She fought hard, throwing her full weight into the struggle.

"Simon! Over here!"

"Sybil we're close. I can hear you."

He shifted his weight, pressing hard against the turbulence and fought his way toward her.

They caught a fleeting glimpse of each other. Frantically maneuvering, they battled until at last they were near enough to touch. She reached out and felt his fingertips graze her hand. Again and again they tried. It was no use. The speed was too great.

"Hang on. Stay close!"

"I'm trying Simon!"

The momentum began to ease and the velocity slowed incrementally. Trying again, their hands met, clasping frantically. They held fast, tightening their grip as they started to move in the same direction.

"Thank the Fifth! I thought I lost you!" cried Simon.

"Me too!" she shuddered. "W-where are we?"

"Déjà vu! Sounds crazy, eh?"

"How could you?"

"Don't know. This is really creepy."

The vortex slowed and they drifted gently to the canyon floor, landing softly in an oceanic trench. Gel water walls towered around them on both sides.

"Now *I'm* having déjà vu! Lake bottom settlement? But this is humungous. Ginormous!

As they walked, a gentle grade led them deeper. The darkness gathering around them was frightening. Further ahead, the way seemed to be illuminated. As they approached, they saw it was lit by a myriad of glow fish, swimming on the other side of the gel walls.

"Ingenious," said Sybil, brightening at the prospect of no longer walking in darkness.

"Look up!" gulped Simon. "An octopus?"

"Two heads, all those eyes? That's no octopus!" Sybil quickly counted, "Four pairs of eyes, more than eight tentacles—maybe a mutant."

"Move faster!" urged Simon. "It's giving me the heebie-jeebies."

Stepping up the pace, they were aware that the creature was now beside them on the other side of the wall. They increased their stride but soon others joined the cavalcade.

"What do they want?" whispered Sybil.

He reached out to a tentacle with his right hand. A jolting current of electricity leapt through the gel wall, to his out-stretched fingers.

"Ouch!"

The creature seemed to shrink in size and wither away into the background. Another took its place. Again Simon reached out and was zapped. This creature too cringed and slithered away.

"They're just curious. I don't think they mean any harm. Nasty shock though!" he admitted, rubbing the tips of his fingers.

"Right, this *is* creepy!" said Sybil, as the procession multiplied in number.

Maybe they were just curious, but it felt more like they were being herded. Looming before them, the gaping mouth of a huge cavern drew them into the sheltered space. The gel walls receded. Standing dumbstruck, Sybil glanced back. Outside the entrance, the multitude of eyes glittered, then faded into the seascape leaving them alone.

"Where are we?" Sybil whispered, turning in circles to check out the enormous cave.

"We're not in the Fifth dimension anymore Sybil."

"Do you think it's the Seventh?"

"Don't know, but I have a strange feeling."

"I don't like this." There was danger here, she could sense it. It was beyond anything she had ever known, maybe even odder than the Fifth, if that was possible.

A rushing sound, at first a low hum, grew to an intense deafening roar. The thunderous sound of flapping wings beat overhead. Winged creatures swarmed them, their beaks gawping hideously. Sybil and Simon ducked for cover, leaning into overhead ledges as the wings beat against them. Their gaping bills pecked at them mercilessly. These weren't birds in the normal sense. Slime oozing off the wing tips slathered their hair, dripping down their foreheads.

"Eeeugh!" shrieked Sybil, flapping her arms about her. "Get off me!"

As they tried to fend off the marauders, Sybil, remembering the beautiful birds who had showered her with feathers in the Hetopian sanctuary, began to sing. Her clear soprano echoed through the cavern. The onslaught of wings slowly subsided as the creatures found roosts on the rock ledges. Mesmerized by the hypnotic melody reverberating off the limestone walls they cocked their heads first one way, then another. Simon joined her, adding his tenor voice, sending beautiful harmony resounding throughout the cave. They crept forward, gradually fading to melodic humming, as they entered a passageway near the back. The winged horde sat transfixed, frozen in time until they were out of sight.

"Hideous! Hurry, before they wake up," Sybil urged.

Entering deeper, an unworldly glow emanated from the rock faces ahead. They edged forward hugging the walls.

"O-w-w!" Stifling a yelp, Sybil sprang toward the center of the cave. "The wall is hot!" Steam began hissing from fissures on either side of them.

"Get down Sybil!" yelled Simon, grabbing her shoulders and forcing her to the floor. A hot cloud of pink steam scorched the air overhead.

"It's volcanic!"

They slithered ahead on their bellies avoiding the walls.

"Can't stand this much longer," Sybil shrieked as she squatted on the floor of the cave. "It's too hot!" She held out her hands and watched as blisters began to form on her palms.

"Run for it!" shouted Simon. He was on his feet, pulling her up by the elbow. "Run Sybil!"

A low rumble issued from deep below the canyon floor. The ground shook and rocks cascaded from above, rolling in behind them. When the tremor subsided, the cave brightened and the luminous walls gained intensity. The way back was barred, for a wall of rocky debris had sealed up the entrance.

"We're trapped here!" wailed Sybil.

"Could be. No choice but forward now."

"Maybe we should have stayed in Hetopia. This is crazy. If we thought the Fifth was bad!"

"Steady Sybil. If there's another way out, we'll find it. Let's keep going."

Buoyed by Simon's encouragement, she shook off the dread and followed him. Hurrying on, the temperature receded as they made their way out of the volcanic area.

"Your burns. Let me see your hands Sybil."

He opened the first aid bag he was carrying around his waist and applied soothing ointment. Then he covered them with a light dressing.

"You don't have any burns on your hands?"

"It's my forearms," he answered, rolling up his sleeves. "My hands are okay." He gingerly applied salve to his own burns.

"Let me try to wrap them," she said, slowly unravelling the long gauze and awkwardly binding his scorched arms.

After a brief rest and a refreshing cold drink they continued. Descending into the subterranean world, a waft of cool air sifting through the passageway renewed their energy.

When the way divided, they chose to keep to the left, moving steadily toward a bright glow in the far distance. Approaching cautiously, they hid behind a pillar of limestone extending from floor to ceiling, where stalactite and stalagmite met.

"Would you look at that!" said Sybil.

Peering around the edge they were amazed to see a vast panorama opening before them. A metropolis of sky scrapers, buildings of every imaginable shape, extended as far as the horizon.

The feeling Simon had had earlier, intensified. A wet blanket of dread rolled over him, weighing him down, cutting off his breath. He stopped in mid-stride, petrified.

"What's wrong Simon?" She thumped his back, kick-starting his lungs. Hauling in a deep breath he turned to her, fear brimming his eyes.

"We won't find many friends here. I feel it. Let's take shelter. Over there Syb. A stand of trees?"

Sybil followed Simon's questioning finger.

"They're upside down!"

The tops of the trees were scraggly-like roots and the lower portion sprouted fuzzy green fronds. It was a perfect place to hide. Moving rapidly, they made their way through the safety of the lacy green undergrowth. Periodically they approached the perimeter of the forest to look out at the strange buildings. Impossibly tall skyscrapers emerged from the marine floor. The bases of the buildings were huge and circular. Each floor above it became smaller until the top seemed to end in a sharp point.

"Where are the windows?" asked Sybil.

The only breaks in the walls were street level entries. The tall doorways were adorned with decorative curlicues, shells and swags of calcified seaweed fronds.

Looking about, Simon searched the seabed forest for a safe spot. "We better lay low for a while until we figure this out."

"Up there, on the hillside," suggested Sybil. "That big tree."

"Good idea."

She squeezed forward through the dense underbrush. Edging their way slowly up the slope they gained the summit where the imposing tree branched out. Its aerial roots, tall and scraggly, swept the sky as wafts of oceanic breezes sifted through the valley. A lacy skirt of green fronds grew over halfway up the trunk.

"You first, Sybil." Reaching through the fronds, he parted the way for her. When they reached the interior of the greenery, he saw that the branches began close to the ground. Folding his arms into a step, he winced, as Sybil climbed up.

She reached the first branch, then turned, extending a hand to her brother.

"Sorry, your arms!" she said realizing her hands were basically useless. "Maybe you should go first." Extending her bent forearm, he grabbed hold and gained altitude, as his feet edged up the trunk. Her strong pull leveraged him onto the limb beside her.

"Seems to be a safe place for the night, Sybil."

"Yeah, but I think we should climb higher."

"This time I'll go first."

Simon hoisted himself to the limbs above. Each time he gained another branch, he pulled Sybil up to his level. It was slow, painful progress to the top.

"We're a long way up, Simon," said Sybil, peering out of the foliage at the forest floor below.

"Not much further before the fronds thin out." He settled into a comfortable crotch in the tree.

Sybil crouched next to him and leaned back against the sturdy trunk. She looked up in wonder through the thin green haze at the waving root system overhead. Feeling safe for the moment, they sprawled out, resting their weary legs.

"We could build a tree house!" said Sybil

"Yeah. Our vacation spot!"

She grinned, "Some vacation!"

"Bon Voyage!" He grinned back. The comic relief amidst the sheltering fronds temporarily eased their dread.

Sybil tried to reach into the BanquoeBag, but her bandages got in the way.

"Let me help," Simon reached over and took it from her. He pulled out a salmon sandwich, unwrapping it for her and leaned back again to rest.

"Thank you."

He retrieved another for himself. Peering through the fronds surrounding them, Simon drew her attention to the bird's-eye view of the distant city below.

"Check that out! This place is—how did you say? Ginormous?"

The skyscrapers towered above the landscape and lower buildings sprawled toward the horizon, a marine-like replica of suburban splendor.

"Can't see where it ends," she agreed. "What are we going to do? Can't stay up here forever."

"Let's decide in the morning."

Glow fish swimming above the gel canopy that held back the tidal waters, lit the night sky. As the bustle of the city slowed, lights dimmed and streets grew dark. Their first night in the Seventh dimension, was spent in a comfortable bough of a tree in an old-growth marine forest.

In the morning, scores of water sprites circled overhead, replacing the glow fish as they settled into their daytime naps.

"Aren't they cute? They look like tiny elves with their turned-up noses and pointy ears," laughed Sybil.

"Or curly-tailed squid."

"Too curious, if you ask me. Could be spies."

"We better get out of here," Simon rolled over quickly and dangled his legs to the first branch. They climbed down from the night's resting place, relieved to be concealed in the undergrowth once more.

"Hey, I don't need these bandages anymore," said Sybil, undoing the end flap with her teeth and ripping them off.

Simon unwrapped his forearms and ran his forefinger over the smooth surface of his arms.

"That ointment has done wonders!"

"Ointment? What about our gift for healing?"

"Oh yeah, I keep forgetting. Still, it shouldn't be that fast!"

Making their way farther into the dense vegetation, weaving past occasional outcroppings of limestone, they came upon a brook that meandered through a clearing.

"Let's stop for a rest," suggested Simon.

He pulled a muffin out of the BanquoeBag, offered it to Sybil and reached for another, biting into it eagerly. Sitting at the edge of the stream, Sybil ran her fingers through the cool water, scooped up a handful and splashed her perspiring forehead.

"I'm so hot. We've been walking for hours," she moaned, exhausted by the long trek.

"Yeah, I'm beat too."

He sat beside her on a rock, scooped up the cool liquid and was about to take a sip from his cupped hand, before Sybil reached out and stopped him.

"Should you drink that Simon? We still don't know enough about this place."

"You're right," he said. Reaching into the BanquoeBag, he pulled forth two globes of pure water.

"Here, have one."

"Thanks," said Sybil, between gulps of the cold liquid.

"Do you think the water sprites are spies, Simon? Like spy satellite technology in the Third realm?"

"Maybe they have iPads and Google Earth," Simon joked. He swung his feet over the rock he was sitting on and dangled them above the water rushing by.

"Hey, this water is running faster. I think it's deeper!" he called out to Sybil, who had picked up the BanquoeBag readying to leave.

She turned back just in time to see a wall of water rushing toward them. "Run!" she hollered, grabbing his collar and yanking him off the rock. His feet flew out from under him. She dragged him along the rocks, his legs scrambling to gain foothold. Sybil eased up a bit, let him find his legs and pulled him alongside her, as they raced up the embankment. The water eddied around their ankles and rose to their knees as they pushed up the hillside.

"Hurry, Sybil!" Simon's desperate cry was barely heard above the roar of the rushing water.

"Help! Simon! I can't touch bottom!" Memories of that moonlight swim reverberated in her head. Reaching into the water he found her hand, yanked her up against him and held her close, until her panic subsided. Fighting the current, they looked up the slope ahead.

"See that ledge Sybil? Swim for it. You okay if I let go now?"

"Think I can make it."

He let go hesitantly, keeping her in arm's reach. She began to swim. Soon her strokes matched his powerful swimming style. They swam the distance and gained the solid platform of rock. Clinging to the edge, they rested until their strength returned, then hoisted themselves onto the safety of dry rock. Their lungs heaved laboriously while they lay prostrate for several minutes.

When their heartbeats slowed, Simon gasped, "That was a close call!"

"Where did all that water come from? And so fast!"

Resting, with their backs propped against boulders, they nervously watched the water level slowly recede. By evening, it had returned to the size of the meandering brook they had relaxed beside earlier in the day.

"Is it safe to go on or should we stay on this ledge for the night?" asked Sybil. "It'll be dark soon. Don't know what's up ahead."

"Maybe safer here. We can make a fresh start at first light."

"Not much shelter though. Maybe we should look for some shrubs."

"Makes sense. Let's climb a little higher."

Drenched and shivering they made their way up a narrow draw above the ledge, the exertion soon warming them. Approaching a huge bluff of rock, Simon warily peeked around the edge.

"What do you see?" whispered Sybil.

"There's a thicket of small shrubs and it looks like it opens into the forest again."

"Let's shelter in those shrubs for the night."

Sprinting across a field of porous lava rock, they dove for cover amid the foliage. Discovering a heap of fronds in the undergrowth, they burrowed into it, covering themselves with boughs plucked from tree branches overhead. It was a cramped, uncomfortable night. Surprisingly, despite the drenching swim, they were warm enough.

When the first faint light seeped through their nest, Simon nudged Sybil's back. "Are you awake?"

"I'm awake. I didn't want to disturb you," replied Sybil. "Did you sleep well?"

"No, I kept dreaming about all that water. And every time I turned over, I felt something sharp digging into my back."

"Roll over. Let's see what it is."

He turned onto his side carefully, exposing the curved surface of a bright blue rock. Poking with his fingertip, he dislodged it from the soil.

"Doesn't look much like a rock," he remarked, curiously.

Intrigued by the discovery, Sybil reached for the blue oval that covered the palm of his hand. Cradling it gently she turned it over. It was still warm. Suddenly, a crack appeared in the surface, then the tip of a red beak enlarged it into a small jagged hole.

"It's an egg!" she shouted. "And it's hatching!"

"Be careful! Who knows what's coming out of that thing," he switched to Telepath, as was their custom when confronted with the unknown. Thankful to have this second useful language, he and Sybil had been practicing ever since he went through the blue veil in Hetopia.

He took it from her and gently laid it back in the soil. They watched it with fascination. The jagged hole widened and a shiny blue head emerged. Two half-closed eyes protruded from the front of the head. It swivelled in the direction of Simon's voice.

"Ohhh my! There's another eye on the back of the head!"

The creature turned toward Sybil's voice.

"Ho-o-o-l-y! You're right! Do you think it can see us?"

Again the head turned toward Simon.

"I don't know for sure, but I think it can hear us!" said Sybil. *"And that would mean it, it must understand Telepath!"*

Just then the shell cracked further and one long red skinny leg popped out. The three-toed foot was webbed, with shiny red suction cups that gripped the rocks to steady its foothold. Another foot emerged as the shell fell away. A plump little body, shiny and blue, supported the three-eyed head on a long neck. It stretched its legs awkwardly, then wobbled into standing position. The creature gained strength as it took its first faltering steps, the suction cups making little popping noises while it pranced in a circle. Slowly, the two eyes at the front opened fully to reveal bright green orbs. Next the third eye blinked open.

"It's purple!" exclaimed Simon, switching languages again.

"Purple? You're joking!"

The purple eye glared at her. *"Don't be so rude! What's the problem? Haven't you seen a purple eye before?"* demanded a squawky voice.

"Oh! Dreadfully sorry," apologized Sybil. "To tell the truth—we haven't. Haven't seen anything as beautiful as you."

"You think I'm beautiful? You haven't seen anything like me?" asked the creature, switching to their language, very pleased by the revelation.

"We certainly haven't. You are very beautiful!" agreed Simon. "Tell us, please. What are you?"

The creature fixed its purple eye on Simon and its two green eyes on Sybil. "I am what is known as an Opeggee."

"A what?" Sybil asked.

"You know—a one purple eye, two green-eyed people eater. But don't worry, I don't eat people," it added hastily. "I am strictly an herbivore."

"Then why do they call you a people eater?"

"Misconception? Prejudice? Who knows? Things get distorted," said the precocious little fellow.

"Do you have a name?" asked Simon.

"I think I'd like to be called Roark," replied the Opeggee.

"Okay, Roark it is!" smiled Simon. This was the first friendly face they'd met and he wanted to believe something good lived here.

"Pleased to make your acquaintance, Roark," said Sybil. "My name is Sarah and this is Dominic," Sybil replied cautiously.

Simon eyed her with renewed appreciation. Sybil was always thinking ahead. If this creature understood Telepath, who knows what else it was capable of. They would have to guard their conversation.

"Are there many more of you around here?" asked Sybil.

"Oh yes, lots of us. We hatch singly," he replied. His two green eyes looked toward the cliff top. "You see those structures? I must be there before I am discovered out here in the open."

"How do you know all that?" asked Simon. "And how do you know two languages?"

"Instinct. Innate intelligence."

"We're going that way, right under the cliff. Can we help? We can keep you safe that far," suggested Sybil.

"Don't want to impose," Roark demurred politely. "But it would be helpful. Very kind of you."

Simon responded with eager pleasure to be of service.

"No problem at all Roark. You can ride on my shoulder if you think it safe enough. Do you want a hand up?"

Simon knelt down and proffered his hand, gesturing for the creature to hop on. The two green orbs eyed him curiously, then he stepped lightly into his palm.

"Steady Roark, I'll bring you up slowly," he reassured the Opeggee. "Here we are. Over you go," he said, gently transferring him to his broad steady shoulder.

"Oh! Comfortable. And so high off the ground! S'pose I'd best get used to it," he gestured skyward with his little wing. "I'll have to live up there soon."

"You sure you're okay there?" asked Sybil.

"Yes indeed, this is just dandy."

"Then we're off," said Simon, delighted by the intriguing little hitch-hiker. Sybil slung the BanquoeBag over her shoulder and the trio set forth.

They trudged along the gorge path gaining altitude all the while. Soon, they were directly under the rookery where tiny squawks could be heard from overhead. Adult Opeggees were soaring to and fro with stringy bits of seaweed dangling from their beaks. Eager red bills gaped widely, receiving the food offered to them.

"How will you get way up there?" Sybil asked the Opeggee, eyeing the cliff doubtfully.

"Haven't the foggiest idea," conceded Roark. "Never thought much about it. Just knew I had to go up."

"Perhaps we should have left you at the nest. Maybe an adult must carry you up top," Simon ventured an explanation.

"Drat and blast!" said the little creature. "I don't 'spect you'd care to make the climb, would you? Your shoulder's so comfortable, so warm. Please," he added appealingly.

Simon acknowledged Sybil's nod, then offered, "If we can find a safe way, we'll try."

Pressing forward along the trail, they soon found that the slope gave way to a rocky incline, allowing them to climb further with relative ease. Shortly, they were within reach of the homing nests. An adult Opeggee swooped treacherously close.

"Careful there, no need to get all riled up," Roark squawked. "I hatched early. Thanks to Sarah here and Dominic, I have found safe passage. If one of you doesn't mind, would you please show me where my home is?"

A large blue bird sailed in and landed on a boulder, shoulder-level with Simon. Red, webbed feet clung to the rock surface with suction cup grips. She eyed Roark anxiously.

"Welcome, young one. The sensors on your shell alerted your mother of your imminent hatch. She has flown off to guide you back. She'll be frantic if she doesn't find you. Wait here while I send out a signal."

She flew to the uppermost prominence on the cliff and sent a message by Telepath. Then she soared back to accept Roark into the rookery. "Your mother was terribly worried when she found your broken shell and no sign of you! I assured her you have arrived safely, thanks to these two good Samaritans. What did you say your names were?"

"Sorry, I am Dominic and this is Sarah."

Just then, Roark's mother swooped in and landed beside her offspring.

"You gave me such a fright young man!" she squawked.

"I have chosen the name Roark," he announced. "No need to worry mother."

He flapped one tiny wing, which had begun to sprout pin feathers. "I have been well taken care of by my friends here." He gestured toward them, explaining how they had spent the night.

"Dominic and Sarah, this is my mother, Meerak."

"How can I ever repay you? Did Roark ride all the way on your shoulder Dominic?"

"Yes, afraid so," chuckled Simon, tweaking Roark's tail feathers. "What's this, you have grown feathers?"

He gawked, open-mouthed at the little bird who now seemed double in size.

Roark's mother cocked her pretty head, turning her green-eyed charm on Simon.

"Oh yes, we Opeggees waste no time. We must be airborne as quickly as possible. Those Aquadrian beasts are always on the hunt for fledglings to plop into their kitchen stockpots."

Hearing this, Simon and Sybil felt a measure of reassurance. Allies in this strange and wild country were a welcome turn of events. Still, they did not want to tip their hand, so they held their tongues, waiting for the opportune time to disclose their real identities, if needed.

"I am curious though. Why do you lay your eggs way down there in the shrubs? Wouldn't it be safer up here?" asked Sybil.

"Our eggs are thick-shelled, as you may have noticed. We use thermal heat sources from the soil for incubation. And there really isn't enough space up top to accommodate the nursery nests. We already have so many chicks to look after."

Her wings opened wide to sweep lovingly over the adoring brood that had come out to meet the newest member of her flock.

"No, we've evolved over generations. This works best for us."

"Yes, I can see that! It's very original," conceded Sybil.

Simon caught Sybil's eye, then nudged her gently.

"What do you say Sarah? Think we had best be moving on?" Simon reluctantly relinquished the Opeggee chick, setting him gently on the rock surface next to his mother.

"Must you leave so soon?" asked Roark, looking imploringly at his new friends.

"Afraid so. Have a long way to go," replied Simon, wiping his brow with the back of his hand.

Sybil watched the little Opeggee's face brighten, when she suggested they stay for a bit. "It is a long way down and we need a rest."

Roark's mother unfolded her brightly coloured plumage and gave them a small curtsy.

"It's my pleasure to show you around our home," she offered. Beckoning them to follow with a flourish of her feathered wing, they fell in behind her and Roark, watching her purple eye light up in delight.

"This is the trail to our communal nesting ground," she indicated with her other wing. "Not far, just up ahead around this bend in the cliff wall."

Easing her plump form around the projecting rock face, she admonished, "Do be careful dears."

Simon followed her glance over the edge to the trail far below. Flattening himself against the rock, he inched around to safety.

"Okay Sarah, your turn. Face outward and keep your back tight against the wall."

Extending his hand in reassurance, he beckoned her forward. Sybil looked back at Roark who had fallen behind to see her safely across.

"Look at all your feathers Roark!" she beamed, admiring his downy blue fluff.

"Yes, it is growing in rather nicely," he acknowledged, ruffling his new feathers with pride.

Turning to the task at hand, Sybil began the treacherous crossing. The precipice yawned below her as she inched forward. Unexpectedly, an overhead rock loosened and careened down the cliff face, bouncing off an outcropping near her head. Spinning in mid-air, it ricocheted off the cliff wall and rolled onto the trail below.

"That was a close one!" shouted a voice far beneath them.

Meerak peered cautiously over the edge, "Hurry, Sarah. It's a contingent of Aquadrians! Don't let them see you!"

Sybil moved forward quickly, gaining the safety of the wider trail.

"Those scoundrels are up to no good," Meerak blustered. "They plan on flooding this whole valley one day. Our brethren have overheard their talk as they traipse about. They think they own the countryside."

"Flood the whole valley?" asked Sybil.

"Yes, it's true. Emperor Aquadorus wants to expand his empire. So many Aquadrians. Population has about tripled in the last year!"

"Wow! They're multiplying fast!" cried Simon.

"Come my lovelies," Meerak, ushered them ahead of her. "Over there on the left is our humble abode." Her wing tip brushed the air with feather-lightness, indicating the way.

In the distance, Sybil and Simon saw an ornately decorated structure, consisting of a hutch with four or five large rooms. Meerak took the lead, guiding them past weathered rock bluffs. She stopped abruptly in front of her home, beaming with satisfaction.

"It may not look like much, but it is our home and you are welcome to share it for as long as you need," she offered generously.

"Thank you for your kindness," Sybil and Simon said in unison. Instinctively the trust had grown of its own volition. They were amongst friends.

"Come Roark, come friends. Please enter," said Meerak, extending a warm welcome.

Roark's delightful caper led them through an open entry that turned at a ninety-degree angle. It provided shelter from the formidable cliff-top winds that sometimes buffeted them at speeds up to eighty kilometres per hour. The three of them scanned the brightly lit interior with incredible wonder.

"Sweet!" said Roark. "This is where I live?"

He scampered about, delighted by his good fortune. The ceiling vaulted high above them. Trees of noble bearing grew from the earthen floor. Overhead branches provided comfortable roosts where a number of offspring lounged lazily, preening their brightly-hued feathers.

"Children, come at once and make our guests welcome," Meerak called, her voice rising to her brood overhead.

A flurry of obedient wings rustled in unison, as her family settled around her in a glistening array. Their glossy feathers caught sunbeams flooding in through rooftop skylights.

"Please sing the welcome song, my darlings. On the count. One, two, three…" A chorus of exquisite beauty echoed throughout their acoustically sound abode.

"That was lovely! Thank you for making us feel so welcome!" The unique combination of the Opeggees' sound ended in a peace that could only be described as reverent.

"Please, come sit," she patted the low roost beside her. A thick branch, heavily padded with downy feathers, extended along the back wall. Sybil and Simon hopped up onto the lounge, settling comfortably against the soft back cushions.

"Loreeak, my dear. Would you be so kind as to bring our guests some refreshments please," Meerak asked one of her eldest children.

Chatting amiably over cups of cool nettle tea, Meerak explained, "The advantage of the cliff offers us safe refuge. More importantly, we have learned to stay out of their way."

"We need to find out more about the Aquadrians," Simon confided, biting into a crisp wafer made of sea lettuce. "M-m-m-m, these are good!"

"You don't mean to go down into the city?" asked Meerak. Her voice, edged with panic, squeaked thinly. "Stay clear of that den of iniquity!"

"Just close enough to see what's happening," said Sybil.

"Well, if you must. But I rather you didn't."

"We'll be very careful," they reassured her, touched by her concern.

"If you run into any trouble, please come back here straight away," Meerak's motherly voice advised them. "This cliff is the only safe place. They can't negotiate the footholds with those long flippers of theirs."

"Thank you so much for your hospitality Meerak," said Simon, as he stood to go.

"Pleasure to meet all of you," added Sybil.

"I am very grateful to you for seeing Roark safely home."

"And Roark, look at you now, fully feathered! More beautiful than ever!" said Sybil, amazed at his size, which had tripled since his hatch.

"Look how much you've grown!" He was now standing knee high to Simon. "It's incredible how tall you have become in such a short time!"

"Will Roark grow to be taller than you?" Sybil asked, looking at Meerak, who came to shoulder height beside her.

"Oh yes, I believe he will. His father is the lanky one in our colony. He should be home soon, out hunting for the young ones, he is."

Roark beamed. He hadn't met his father, but already he liked what he heard, tall and a good hunter.

"Goodbye Meerak, everyone," said Sybil and Simon, turning to the crowd of blue gathered around them. "And Roark, we'll see you again."

At the mention of his name, Roark plumped his feathers, and bowed gently to say goodbye. A single tear slid from his purple eye, rolled down the wrinkle in his scalp and re-emerged on his forehead. It continued its downward journey, until it dripped off the end of his red beak.

"Sniff, I will miss you both," he cried, then turned to hug them, his soft blue wings curving gently around their legs.

"Don't worry little buddy," Simon soothed. He set him on the roost and stroked his feathered back, noticing it was getting harder to lift him. "We'll be back before you know it. If we can, we'll try to get word to you."

They were reluctant to leave the delightful family of Opeggees and the safety of the cliff top. But, if they were to accomplish what they had set out to do, they must deny their own comforts.

CHAPTER ELEVEN
Aquadorus

After making their way down the cliff, they regained the trail. "The Opeggees warned us about routine Aquadrian patrols on the main forest paths. Do you think it is safer to stick to the undergrowth?" asked Sybil.

"It'll slow us up, but you're right. Let's get off this trail."

They entered the thick vegetation to their left and skirted the metropolis, slogging their way through dense growth. Alternating point, they navigated their way through thickets; first Simon breaking trail with Sybil spelling him off.

"Ouch!" yelled Simon, sucking the tip of his thumb. "Man this stuff is nasty."

Up until then, they had not encountered the deadly brambles that seemed to have come out of nowhere. Thorny branches raked their bodies, clinging to their clothes and ripping deep gouges in their flesh. They were stopped in their tracks, struggling to work the tangled vines loose, one by one. They tried holding them back and allowing each other through, but it was next to impossible to make any progress.

"Ow! Get off me!" Sybil yelled, smacking the red bloom that had sunk its teeth into her forearm. She covered the bite mark with her hand, staunching the flow of blood.

"This plant just bit me! Simon!" she called back, afraid to take her eyes off the blooms rearing up before her. "They have teeth!"

"Teeth! Where?"

"The red blooms! At the top of the bushes. Look at those fangs!" gasped Sybil, as the yawning jaws towered over her.

"This is crazy! How do we get out of here?"

"I don't know!" Sybil sunk to the ground in despair. "It's impossible to get past them."

She thought about the dogs, thankful they'd had the good sense to leave them with Icelandia. They would be lucky to get themselves out of this pickle. It would have been impossible for the hounds, maybe even more dangerous. They would have tried to defend themselves against those snapping jaws.

Resting a moment, she maneuvered her body into a prone position. The way seemed clearer underneath and she began to wriggle forward on her stomach making better headway.

"Hey, where are you Sybil?" How could she have disappeared in this mess?

"I'm down here, Simon. Lay on your stomach and crawl through. Those jaws can't reach us at the bottom. It's much easier." Sybil stopped to wait for him.

"Way to go Syb! Man eating plants? This is some messed up place!"

They continued their painstaking progress, cringing at the snapping sounds overhead. Before long, the vegetation thinned out and they left the deadly brambles behind.

"I thought we were done for," said Simon, breathing a sigh of relief.

"That was nasty!" moaned Sybil, stopping to inspect her injuries. "Better wash these wounds before they get infected. Who knows what kind of plants they are." She pulled a globe of water from the BanquoeBag.

"Let me see that bite first." Simon flushed the two puncture wounds on her right forearm with large amounts of water. He smeared them with salve from the Hetopian first aid kit, applied a bandage and attended to her other abrasions.

"Thanks Simon, that feels so much better."

She began to pull barbs from Simon's gouged skin, flushing any toxic residue that may have been left in the lesions. After applying salve, she followed up with a liquid protective bandage that dried in place.

"Hey Syb, I've had enough of this. Let's head to the edge of the forest to see where we are? The city should still be on our left."

"Good plan. I'm fed up with this too." She handed the first aid kit to Simon and slung the BanquoeBag over her shoulder. "Ready? You lead the way."

They headed out, keeping to the left, wondering how much further to the clearing that surrounded the city. From the cliff top rookery, they had spotted some very tall towers and decided to see if they could locate them. Abruptly, the forest ended and they ducked for cover in the fronds. The bustle of the city noise could be heard clearly.

"Simon!" she whispered. "Look! To the right, by the wall of the city. There, near the gate."

Two strange humanoids, a pair of sentries, were posted on watch. One leaned against the limestone wall, chatting with the other who was standing alertly at attention, his nostrils flaring into the wind.

"Can you hear what they are saying?" asked Simon.

"Shhh, hang on. Listen," cautioned Sybil. Slowly their ragged breathing returned to normal. The buzz of the city became more distinct.

"Our Intelligence informs us there are two of them," rasped a sharp voice. Sybil raised her head to get a better look.

The one lounging on the wall waved his long fingers at him dismissively. "Hearsay, that's what I think," he drawled lazily, yawning into his long thin palm.

"Quiet, you fool," barked the other one, clearly annoyed. "You want someone to hear you?"

Discipline in the city under Aquadorus was strict. He didn't want to be associated with the likes of this guy. Suddenly, he stiffened. His head swung up and his nostrils quivered, catching a whiff of a foreign scent. He shifted a long spear to his other shoulder, scanned the tree line and caught the smallest detail of a form hidden in the underbrush.

The other sentry continued to babble on, while the alert one paid close attention. As the form shifted slowly, and sank out of sight, he formulated a plan. He was the best on the squad he gloated to himself. The inept ninny he was saddled with as a partner today was useless.

"Say, Rinaldo," he slyly suggested. "Can you hold the fort here by yourself? I sure am getting hungry. I'm going to pop into the city and bring us back a bite to eat. Some of those fish balls from that diner on the corner of Cliff View and Urchin St. A couple of grande orders should do us nicely, my treat," he said expansively.

"Gee, thanks Dimondus, awfully nice of you. I can hold this gate. No problem," Rinaldo blathered.

Dimondus turned, disappeared through the gate and set off on a quick trot. He veered left on the first street, running double time, parallel to the city wall. At the next gate he greeted the sentries and said, "Can't stop to chat. I am on an important mission."

They let him pass unimpeded. Once he entered the forest, he turned left, stealing softly through the sheltering greens. Growing up playing in these forests, he knew them well and could have found his way in the dark. He knew precisely where this form lay hidden.

Just as Sybil and Simon were about to slide back into the thick of the forest, the crackle of brush under the approaching slap of finned feet sent a cold tremor of fear up their spines. The sucking noise of his gills automatically pulsing warned them he was close. Sinking to their bellies in the thicket, they flattened themselves against the forest floor. All went silent.

"Don't breathe!" telepathed Simon.

"No kidding! I can't even move!" A cold slimy flipper placed firmly on her back, trapped her, as she squirmed to get away.

A frigid voice slithered into her brain, "Get up you two!"

Simon was now held by the neck of his tunic. Cold sweat oozed down his back as he fought to stand, for he had gone weak in the knees. A vice-like grip grabbed Sybil's arm, wrenching her abruptly to her feet.

"What are you doing here?" commanded a steely voice.

"Sorry sir, w-we've lost our way," stuttered Sybil. "W-where is this place? We'll be on our w-way, if you just show us how to get out of here."

"Not so fast! You aren't leaving here until we find out more about you." The humanoid shoved them forward. "You're coming with me!" he barked.

Dimondus propelled them ahead, marching swiftly out of the forest, heading toward where Rinaldo continued to sprawl against the wall of the city. They were nearly on top of him before he straightened up to take notice.

"Dimondus, what are you doing? I thought you were in the city getting us something to eat," he drawled, gaping at Simon and Sybil. "What do we have here?" he said, eyeing the two strangers.

"Quiet you imbecile," smirked Dimondus. "It is I who noticed them in the bush over yonder. Stand up straight when you're spoken to Rinaldo. Now do your job and keep watch here, while I march these two into the city."

He glared at Sybil and Simon who stood woodenly, petrified with fear.

"Move, you two!" he snapped, forcing them on a swift march. Sybil was in the lead, Simon was next, with Dimondus pressing them onward at an exhausting pace.

Fearful as she was, she managed to stare in wonder at the buildings. A variety of limestone towers rose to dizzying heights. Other humanoids were rushing about, in and out of buildings, slapping each other on their backs and merrily skipping along the limestone pavers, their flippers slapping a staccato rhythm.

A soft, "Ohhhh!" escaped Sybil's lips, her eyes growing round at the sight confounding her senses. Except for flippers and gills and the green cast to their skin, they resembled humans.

"They must be amphibious! They seem to be okay on land. But those gills, their webbed hands and feet—maybe they like water better!"

"Oh-h-h-mmm," Simon moaned.

A fragment of memory niggled its way into his brain. Although he had been very young at the time, his recollection of the years he had spent with this civilization was sharpened by the distinct fishy odour permeating the air. His mind raced. How many years had it been—maybe four? He was with the Leanorians for at least seven years. Maybe he had been four when he left here.

More memories surfaced as they were marched through the streets. The beautiful architecture had struck him then, as it did now. Spending his boyhood here had been rather fanciful. True, he was always made to feel very different but usually he was left to come and go as he pleased, for the most part, especially toward the end of his time here. Recalling Sybil's story, he decided that he must have been brought here after he was kidnapped from the hospital in the Third realm.

"Hey Syb. Guess what!"

"What Simon?"

"I remember!" He was eager to share his recovered memories. *"This is where I spent those first four years. Here with the Aquadrians."*

"No way! How did you get here?"

Simon sought his sister's questioning eyes, *"That—I don't remember."*

"Huh! Well, how? How did you get to the Fifth dimension at Leanoria?" asked Sybil.

"I don't think it was easy," replied Simon. *"It was so long ago. I have a feeling it was not pleasant."* Then he added, *"I might be able to find a way out again. I'll have to think about it."*

"That's encouraging," replied Sybil. *"We could always try time travel out of here. But I think we need to know more about this place before we try to escape."*

"Time travel? Nah, don't want to risk that too often. Telomeres and all. Best save that for emergencies."

"You don't count this as an emergency?" Sybil's annoyed look caught him off guard.

"Could be Sybil, but as you said, we have to learn more about this place." Something in his bones told him they needed to check it out. Besides, he really wanted to recover more of his memories.

"Catfish got your tongues?" interrupted the harsh voice of the humanoid. "What have you got to say for yourselves?"

"Beg your pardon sir," replied Sybil. "Don't mean to be rude. Just admiring your buildings. I've never seen anything like them."

"Yeah, fantastic," agreed Simon hoping the guy wouldn't remember him. He'd seen this one before at the court of the emperor Aquadorus Oceanus.

"So, you like this place do ya?" replied the sentry. "We'll see how you feel when you're locked in the palace dungeon!" he threatened menacingly.

Sybil tried to swallow, forcing down a knot of dread rising up her throat. They trudged on in silence, fearful of raising his ire further.

"Do you know the palace?"

"Yeah, I think I've been there. We'll be taken for questioning first I think. We'd better get our story straight."

"Can't we say that we fell overboard off an ocean liner and found ourselves in this strange place—that we just want to get back?"

"What if they figure out you're from the Third dimension?" replied Simon. *"And someone might recognize me."*

"Let's hope you've changed enough in nine years. Do you remember much about your life here?"

"Not too much. When other kids started teasing me—that's when I first knew I was different. They called me Nogillers. Yeah sure, my feet and hands were different but then I saw my reflection in a pool. Whoaaa, I didn't look like anyone around here!"

"Must have been a shock!"

"It was. I learned to stay quiet and pretend I was invisible. It's funny, in all those years I was with the Leanorians I couldn't remember this place. Wonder if they used mind control."

"Possible. You were so young. Could be something was so scary that you didn't want to remember."

"I'm terrified now," Simon shuddered, working the knot in his throat. *"I remember this guy. The other one called him Dimondus. He was as creepy then as he is now."*

"He's scary all right."

As they approached a pool, a group of sentries coming in the opposite direction came to a halt. "Everyone stop for refreshment," ordered the leader.

"I remember these pools. Used to play in them."

Dimondus stopped, clearly fatigued. They could see his energy was flagging. His pace had slowed and his gills pulsed laboriously.

"Sir, I have a request. I am in need of refreshment. Would you do the honour of standing guard over these two, while I partake?"

"The name is Herclan." He glared at Dimondus. "Of course. Go ahead. Enter with my troop. I'll go last."

He stood erect, eyeing Sybil and Simon curiously. Who were these two strangers and why were they here? Usually well informed of current events, this was surprising. He always kept his ear to the ground and was well aware of the discontent brewing. Couldn't blame people, he thought. He didn't like the way things were going in the city either. Something was up and he was determined to look into it.

The entire party dropped their shell shields and spears, then plunged into the pool. After a few minutes, their grey faces turned bright green. Reinvigorated, they hopped out of the pool with verve, donned their equipment and fell in line. They stood at attention, waiting for their commander to conduct his ablutions.

"That feels grand!" chortled Dimondus, hopping out of the pool. "Thank you sir for your assistance, I'll take it from here," he said, readjusting his equipment self-importantly.

"They need to top up their oxygen levels!" Simon cried. *"I always thought everyone just played in the pools."*

Dimondus waited for the other commander to finish his refreshment, unable to resist the opportunity to brag about his capture of the two strangers.

"Sir, thank you once again. I'm on my way to the palace, reporting directly to the emperor. Found these two near the west gate. Pretty impressive wouldn't you say?"

"Is that so? Huhmm," the commander shrugged. "Platoon, fall in!" ordered the officer, and they marched away in the opposite direction.

Suddenly a warning blast from a fog horn sounded. Up and down the streets, everyone clambered out of the pools. A swoosh of water swilled down the drains, making empty slurping noises. Fresh water eddied into the pools, refilling them to the brim.

"The flood!" Simon connected the dots. *"That's where the water came from! The stale pool water!"*

"No doubt!" Sybil gaped, trying to makes sense of it all.

A thought slowly began to form in Simon's mind as Dimondus lined them up. *"Hmmm…do you think this has anything to do with Leanoria?"*

"Yeah, maybe. I've been thinking about that."

Once more they set off, this time at a faster pace.

"I don't know if I can keep up much longer," groaned Sybil, nearing exhaustion. *"Dimondus seems to have gained super strength after the pool."*

When they thought they couldn't take another step, Dimondus's shrill command stopped them in their tracks. "Halt!" he hollered.

Panting hard, they stood in front of an imposing structure. Dimondus rang the gong at the gate and was admitted to the outer courtyard by the sentry standing guard.

Sybil, who was bent over gasping for air, pleaded, "Can we rest a minute please?"

His malevolent glare, seared her to the core. "What's wrong? Can't keep up?" he taunted, determined to show her who was boss. "Look smart and follow me," he ordered and set off toward the palace.

They fell in behind him this time. He slowed up and their breathing returned to a more comfortable rate. Sybil's fear settled into a manageable lump in the pit of her stomach. She kept pace, counting her steps to keep her mind from reeling. Eventually she calmed enough to lift her eyes, admiring the coral gardens ablaze with colour. Seaweed trained on trellises cascaded elegantly overhead. Tall trees, their roots sprawled festively in mid-air, grew in large planters. Sybil ran her hand through the lush green foliage trailing from trunks.

"So grand," she murmured, awestruck by the opulent gardens. Statuesque limestone obelisks and ornately carved statues adorned the alcoves along the garden walkways.

Simon, watching from behind, saw her shoulders begin to relax, as she came to appreciate the wonder of the courtyard. She appeared to be far away, zoned out. When facing threat Sybil seemed to recover quickly. He liked that about her. Remembering his time in the dungeon at Leanoria, he wasn't looking forward to the end of this march. But then Sybil had not been held captive for two years and wouldn't know what was to come. He wished he could protect her from what lay ahead. What could he say or do? Finally, words tumbled out.

"Have to admit, it is pretty grand." Useless words, not what he had intended. But there was nothing he could offer, to change the situation. She came back to reality with a thud, when they halted in front of a large arched doorway.

Dimondus pulled the latch and shoved them through the portal into the vestibule. They proceeded through a hallway, turned right, and entered a narrow shaft of stairs that spiralled to the left. As they climbed, Sybil caught sight of the streets below. The walls were transparent!

"That's why there are no windows!" Sybil noted. *"One way glass. Ingenious!"*

Very nearly winded and out of breath, they were approaching the top floor when Dimondus barked, "Halt! We're here. Pay attention and don't speak until you are spoken to."

The door swung open to reveal a reception area inhabited by an attendant seated at a desk. "We have them in hand and the Emperor Aquadorus is expecting us."

"Emperor Aquadorus! Oh, bollywocks! The highest command in all of Aquadria! Not good!" cried Simon.

They were ushered into a large oval room furnished lavishly with sea-sponge chairs, scallop shell lamps and sculptures. Trophies; various mounted sea creatures, serpents and what appeared to be small dragon heads, hung on the walls. Clearly, Aquadorus was a warrior hunter. Spears, crossbows, arrows and knives were displayed prominently in polished glass cases. Shields of lustrous material reflecting rainbow hues, hung interspersed between the mounted trophies. Behind the desk of polished coral, a stony face scowled at them.

"Who are you? What are you doing in my kingdom?" shouted the emperor. He fixed baleful eyes on Sybil, then turned to Simon. "Explain yourselves!" he boomed.

Fighting back fear, Sybil squared her shoulders, lifted her chin and forced a smile, "I'm Sarah, and this is Dominic. Excuse us sir. We don't mean any harm."

Simon drew himself up tall beside her. "There was a dreadful storm and we were swept overboard. No idea where we have landed or how we got here. We hope you'll help us to return, if you could find it in your generosity."

"Generosity? My flippers!" bellowed Aquadorus. "You have no right being here!"

Then he narrowed his eyes sharply, peering intently at Simon. "Do I know you?" he glared. "There's something about your eyes."

"No sir, not possible. We have only just arrived," he said, crossing his fingers and holding his breath. It was a half-truth.

The fierce scowl fell on Sybil. "And you! What manner of life form are you?" he glowered.

If he was intending to intimidate, he was succeeding. "No gills or flippers." His probing eyes came back to Simon. "Hmm…" Then his face roared to life as he shouted, "You're that baby we had here from the Third dimension!"

Simon fought to conceal his emotions. "Oh no! Sorry sir, you are mistaken. We are castaways from an ocean liner while on holiday. We met on board ship." The blood in his veins turned to ice water.

"There is no need to shout so," Sybil covered her ears, hoping to divert his attention.

"Silence!" blustered the emperor. "Don't be impertinent. I will decide!" he thundered, glaring at her ominously. Turning his back on them, he paced, considering his options. She has spunk, he thought. No one had ever dared to contradict him before. Turning around to face them again, he growled, "Be off with you! Throw them in the brig!"

Dimondus sneered, "Move you two!" Out in the hall, he snorted loudly. "Ha, I told you. You should 'a held your tongues!"

"We had to answer his questions," replied Sybil.

"You don't tell the emperor, not to shout!"

"But…"

"Silence!" shouted Dimondus, imitating the emperor. He liked the sound of his voice giving orders and dreamed one day of ascending to the lofty title himself.

He marched them away. Back down the spiral steps they plodded, past the entry level floor until they descended into the bowels of the building. The way grew dimmer, illuminated only by glow fish lanterns set in wall sconces.

"I don't feel so well," moaned Sybil.

"It was a long walk. All these stairs," said Simon.

"No, it's more than that," said Sybil. *"My head is aching. I feel really hot all of a sudden,"* she gasped for air. She was wheezing, and coughing.

Simon looked at Sybil in alarm. Her face was ashen and there was a bluish tinge around her lips. *"What is it Syb?"*

"Simon, I think that bite—from the red flower…"

"Sybil!" Simon was frantic. "Dimondus! Ss-sy…" Very nearly blurting out her name, he caught himself. "Sarah is sick! Help her please!"

Extremely annoyed, Dimondus snarled, "What's the trouble now?"

"It's Sarah! We ran into some horrible bramble bushes. Red blossoms with fangs. One bit her! What are they?" Simon was becoming panicky.

"Red blossoms with fangs? Oh no! She'll need treatment fast! Stay here. I'll get help."

Dimondus hastily turned a key in the lock and shoved a sliding door aside. He pushed them into a musty cell, sparsely furnished with a clam shell basin, a bucket, and a dried sea kelp mat.

"Lay on that mat," he ordered, then rushed out, clanging the cell door shut behind him.

"Be right back," Dimondus called over his shoulder in a panic. If something happened to these two before the Emperor could deal with them, he would surely be held responsible.

Sybil was weakening fast. "Hurry up Dimodus!" Simon called after him.

Why? Oh why did we ever come back to the flatlands? A dread deeper than any he had known chilled him to the bone. It's my fault. I made her promise. My other family. They can't possibly still be alive anymore and now—the thought of losing Sybil was overwhelming. Guilt washed over him. He bottomed out, sitting stunned in a pool of remorse. How much more can I take? What will become of me?

"Sybil! You can't go too!" Tears sprang from his eyes as he contemplated his bleak future. *"Sybil don't leave. You don't deserve this!"*

Waiting in the cell, a heavy despair set in, weighing him down, anchoring him to the mat. He was unable to move, frozen immobile for what seemed a desperately long time.

But Dimondus, in fact, returned in a few minutes with the palace physician in tow. "She's in here!" he motioned breathlessly, quickly sliding back the cell door.

The physician, who seemed a kindly old humanoid with greying gill whiskers, rushed to her side. He propped Sybil up in a semi-reclining position to alleviate her laboured breathing and checked her pulse. She was barely conscious.

"Classic case of Crimson Snakebush poisoning." He pulled the plunger back on a hypodermic syringe, filling it with green fluid from a vial. "The antidote needs to be administered within the hour. How long ago was she bitten?"

"Close to that time now," replied Simon, terrified.

They had just found each other. To lose her now would be the worst thing imaginable. His emotions, shredded and raw, lay exposed on the mat beside her. A suffocating mask of misery settled across his face, sucking the breath out of him. Stifling despondency pulled him under, as hope, always so tenuous in him, faded to darkness.

"Please, please." A plea of paralysing regret fought its way to the surface. "Please let her live."

"I'll do my best," soothed the kindly old physician, tapping the air bubbles out and spraying a tiny squirt into the air.

Gill Whiskers expertly raised a vein and administered the antidote directly into her blood stream. He popped a cap over the needle and set the syringe on the mat beside Sybil.

"Intravenous is the best in a case like this. If we are in time it should work very quickly." He looked at his time piece. "Should see some changes shortly."

Simon sat on the mat, anxiously gripping Sybil's hand. *"Hang in there Syb. Please."*

His words of encouragement reached her through the stupor. She moaned in feverish delirium. Simon squeezed her hand. A barely perceptible movement of her fingers gave him…what? Dare he permit even a sliver of hope? He tried to reason with his irrational fear. That fear of allowing hope in, only to be dashed yet again. For her sake he must. He must give her that. Could he reach her? He must try.

"You'll be all right Sybil. The doctor has given you something. Shouldn't be long." Simon watched but there didn't seem to be much change.

He switched languages. "Come on! You can do this!" He willed her to live.

"We're not out of the woods yet," said Gill Whiskers with a worried frown. He checked her vital signs again. "She should be further along by now. Humph! I think she needs more." He reloaded his syringe and gave her another half dose. "It's going to be close."

"You can do this Sybil! Come on! Live!"

"Harrumph!" the doctor wheezed. "It'll be a close one." He arched an eyebrow at Simon. Sybil? "Hummph! She's a fighter though."

Simon's insistent voice aroused a feeble response. *"We're a team. I need you. Remember. We have to get back to Third. Fight Sybil!"*

Gradually, the toxic haze began to lift and Sybil's eyelids quivered. Her colour began to improve as her breathing eased. There was no longer a bluish cast to her lips. He gave her hand another squeeze. This time she acknowledged it with a stronger response. Her eyelids fluttered open, then closed again. The physician repositioned her on her side and she rested on the mat.

"I think you'll be all right young lady. I will stay until we see what gives." He peered over his half glasses in concern.

Within a half hour, Sybil sat propped up against the cell wall. Her eyes had cleared. The hint of a sparkle gave Simon the reassurance he so badly needed.

"How are you feeling?" he said, realizing he hadn't said much to anyone since the physician had asked him the first question.

"I'm much better, thank you." She gave the doctor a grateful smile.

"I'm Dr. Teselwode," he acknowledged. "You gave us a very bad fright young lady. Lucky I was not out on a house call. Got here just in time."

"Thank you," said Sybil. "How can I ever repay you? I have nothing."

"Now don't you worry none about that. We'll find something," he patted her hand gently. "Rest and get better. I think it is safe to leave you now. Drink lots of water. It'll flush any residual toxins. I'll check in on you later this evening."

Dimondus, who had been hovering in the background, stepped forward. His hide was on the line. If anything went sideways with these two, he'd suffer the full wrath of Aquadorus. The emperor was not one to show mercy to subordinates. His voice floated thickly on the air, as he muttered a strangled cry of relief.

"Thank you doctor. I'll take it from here." He ushered him out and bid good afternoon. If this had turned out badly, he would have had a lot of explaining to do. He might even end up demoted or worse still, here in the brig! He paled at the idea.

Simon sat on the mat beside his sister, offering her sips of water and speaking in hushed tones. "I don't know what I would do if something happens to you Sarah." His concerned frown, touched her.

"Don't worry Dominic. I'm strong. I feel much better now."

Dimondus interrupted, "Good thing too," he shivered. Aquadorus, what might he have done? "You two have caused quite enough trouble."

Simon turned to him, "Sorry Dimondus. Thank you."

"Don't thank me. Just doing my duty," replied Dimondus with a disgusted tone. "I'll be standing guard outside. If she has any more problems let me know." He turned and stalked across the room, slid the door shut and turned the key in the lock.

"Dimondus is just outside and the walls might be bugged. Telepath only," warned Sybil. *"This was bad, Simon. Have to be more careful."*

"Who knows what we'll run into next. Looks like we're back at square one. Stuck in a prison cell."

She shuddered, *"I'm afraid of tomorrow. We have to come up with a plan before morning."*

"Yeah, me too." Then he added a cheerier reply.

"Well, Sarah, I wonder what they'll serve for dinner. You getting hungry?"

Catching the ruse, she answered, "It'll be seafood supper!" They chuckled loudly hoping to mislead listening ears, if you could call them ears. One could hardly refer to skull openings designed with flaps to keep out water, as ears.

Shortly after a light dinner, the doctor came back to check on Sybil. He was very pleased to see her pacing about the cell. "Well, you look much improved!" he said. "Good to see you up. Did you manage to eat something?"

"Yes, thank you. I enjoyed the steamed cod and seafood salad," she answered gratefully.

Dimondus stood in the background eyeing her with contempt. "So doctor. Is she in good health?" he inquired, hoping he wouldn't have to spend the night on duty in the cell block.

After doing a thorough check up, Dr. Teselwode announced, "Looks like you've made a full recovery. Keep drinking lots of water and get a good sleep tonight. You may feel a bit off, but by morning you'll be your old self."

"Good!" said Dimondus with relief. He would be glad to be above ground again. The dungeon always gave him the creeps. He led the doctor out and slid the door shut with a resounding bang.

Sybil stifled a yawn. "I'm pretty tired Simon. We've had a lo-ong day." She nodded off, curled up on the mat in the far corner, while Simon slumped against the wall.

Upstairs, Dimondus gave a sparing report to Aquadorus, minimizing the dangerous episode. "She's fine. Had a minor brush with the Crimson Snakebush, but nothing the palace physician couldn't handle."

Aquadorous leaned close to his head tribune. "I am holding you responsible for these two Dimondus. Keep an eye on them. I want to know everything that is said. If they are legitimate refugees, we'll soon sort out what to do with them. Now that we are so close to achieving our goals, I want no trouble stirred up."

"No doubt, my lord. You'll get to the bottom of it," replied Dimondus, making a mental note to scurry back and assign a guard to do the night duty he so hated. The thought of a whole night in the dungeon made him squeamish. Should 'a known to do that myself, he rebuked himself for his lapse in judgement.

Aquadorus nodded with approval. "Still, there's something about that boy. What was his name, Dominic? His bearing seems familiar. It might be good to let them have a little freedom."

He paced the length of the room, his head lowered in thought. Then he turned abruptly and returned to Dimondus. "I've decided to put them on work detail. They can live at the palace work quarters. I want them under heavy surveillance. Put a tail on them tomorrow and see what those two are up to."

"Brilliant tactic," Dimondus agreed, hoping to win favour in the emperor's court. He had worked long and hard to rise to his position. His ruthless treatment of staff, exacting work out of them with demonical precision, had everyone cowering in obedience.

Simon rolled over and cracked an eye slit open. *"You awake?"*
A mumbled reply told him she was listening.
"Maerwyn and Longille must be worried sick about us."
"Ah hmmm," she nodded. *"They'll go back to Hetopia to make a report."* Her quiet voice revealed the effects of the near disaster that had felled her. It left her a bit hazy and vulnerable.

"Probably right. Guess we really are on our own now. No hope of rescue this time."

There it was again. Hope! It always boiled down to that. He had dared to hope for Sybil, when all seemed lost. It came through for him this time. Then he reasoned, hope had nothing to do with it. It was Dr. Teselwode. He reproached himself. If they were to get out of this, they would have to rely on themselves, they had to work hard at it. His resolve solidified into a determined will to do all he could to get them back to Fifth. When the time came, he knew he could rely on Sybil to do her part.

Sybil lay on the mat shaken by her ordeal. The nightmare was real. She had not been dreaming. A wispy fragment of memory surfaced. The squeeze of Simon's hand had left a subtle mist of remembrance. His cry of anguish willing her to live had floated hazily through space, a faint plea for her life that warmed her. It fanned the smouldering fire, igniting her own will to live. The misadventure with the Snakebush poisoning had left her exhausted and depleted. Simon was her mainstay in this dangerous land of greed and suffering. She had come to rely on him, felt his strength and compassionate nature. She was left stunned and deeply grateful by the depth of his caring.

Exhausted from the day's trials, they fell into a deep dreamless slumber, awakening refreshed in the early morning light.

"Rise and shine sleeping beauty!" called Simon from across the mat.

"You're certainly chipper this morning," replied Sybil. "Have a good sleep?"

"Best sleep, since the storm. How are you feeling this morning?"

"Good as new. My old self, just like the doctor said."

"Still don't believe the size of those waves! It's a wonder the ship held together that long!" said Simon, alluding to the story they had given. Then he added, *"I wonder when they'll come for us."*

"Soon I suppose," answered Sybil. *"We want to be up, moving about. Show them we aren't afraid."*

"No guilty conscience, right?"

"That's the plan!"

She rose and stretched her tall slender frame, extended her arms to the ceiling and did a swan dive to the floor, then stepped back into a down dog yoga pose, working the kinks out of her aching muscles. Flowing smoothly into plank pose she held the position, then lowered to the floor rising into cobra. Repeating the sequence, inhaling and exhaling deeply with each flowing movement, the oxygen-rich blood cleared the last vestiges of her ordeal.

"Try this Dominic. Even two or three of these will make you feel so much better. Releases tension and warms your muscles."

"Hey, this is nice. Very relaxing, yet wakes you up," said Simon, staightening up on the last round.

They barely had time to splash their faces with water in the shell basin, before a key turned in the lock. The door slid open, revealing Dimondus clad in a shiny mother-of-pearl doublet. Long fishnet-style sleeves extended to his wrists where his arms terminated in long finger-like projections.

"His hands are morphing," telepathed Sybil. *"They look even longer today!"*

Green leggings, ending at the ankles, fitted tightly against his long muscular legs. His flippers were polished to perfection, emitting a lustrous verdant glow.

"His flippers are already complete," Simon observed. *"Are they becoming fully aquatic?"*

"Meerak says they will flood the valley. What if the Seventh is not big enough? What if Aquadorus wants more?"

They shuddered at the thought of what may lay ahead.

CHAPTER TWELVE
Aquadria

Dimondus poked his head in. "Get ready to move you two!" he snapped. "Emperor Aquadorus is expecting you first thing this morning."

"You ready for this Syb?"

"Not much choice, is there?" She walked to the cell door and stood calmly. Simon joined her.

"Move out," ordered Dimondus. They set off at a brisk pace, climbing the stairs to the main level.

"At least we're getting our morning exercise," said Simon. *"Feels good after a night in that cramped cell."*

Shortly, they were standing before Aquadorus. "Well what has the night done for you? Still claim to be lost overboard?" His cold eyes landed on Simon. "So you think I should let you go, do you? How and where do you expect to go?" his harsh voice needled.

Simon thought carefully, then answered as calmly as he could. "I'm not sure how we came to be here, but we'd appreciate your assistance to return."

"Tell you what," said Aquadorus. "If there is a way back, as you seem to think, maybe we can discover it."

He scrutinized them with an icy glare. "I have decided. You will be allowed to stay. Out of my divine benevolence, I am giving you your own compartments. But at the first sign of trouble you will find yourselves back in the brig," he blustered. "And don't think you'll have it easy. You will work while you're here."

"Get a load of this guy! Divine!?" Simon's ears were ringing. It was clear by this comment that Aquadorus elevated himself beyond the status of a mere mortal.

"Third realm has had enough despots like him. He's dangerous," agreed Sybil.

Turning to Dimondus, he ordered, "Outfit these two with the necessary gear. I am assigning them to polishing detail. See that they are properly trained."

With a flourish of his hand, he dismissed Dimondus. "Take them away."

Simon and Sybil were placed in comfortable rooms across the hall from each other in a building that housed palace staff.

"You are to report to me every day at the mess hall. I expect you there at first light when the water sprites change watch with the glow fish. Breakfast first, followed by work detail," ordered Dimondus.

Life in Aquadria soon became a routine of rising early, reporting in as ordered and daily chores. They were assigned to flipper polishing in the street. Aquadrian town folk who came by, hopped up on the comfortable sea-sponge cushions, extended each flipper dutifully and expected to leave with a high gloss shine. They became so proficient at their trade that Sarah and Dominic were soon well known for their dazzling finishes. They were in popular demand and required to work all areas of the city.

During the first week, Sybil noticed a familiar figure dawdling in the alley.

"Simon, we're being followed!"

"No wonder he isn't keeping us locked up. He thinks we're up to something."

"Guess we could expect that. Doesn't leave much scope for us to explore."

"And they don't seem to care if we know they're watching."

"Doesn't make much difference. We're all over the city anyway."

One day while they were plying their trade, an old woman appeared on the street across from where they were working. "Who is that?" asked Sybil, astonished to see another human form in the city.

Simon stared at the woman making her way through the throng of people. "Wonder why she's here." He scanned the streets. "Doesn't look like she's being watched."

"Perhaps she knows a way out of here."

"She may look like us, but I wouldn't trust her," cautioned Simon. "Seems too much at ease here."

"Maybe we can ask Rinaldo. He's rather dull. Wouldn't think much of it if we did."

"Excellent idea, Sybil."

The following morning at breakfast they casually approached the table where Rinaldo sat alone. *"Good thing the other sentries avoid him,"* Simon said, helping himself to the mound of seaweed salad and shrimp.

Placing his bowl on the table beside Rinaldo, he asked, "Mind if we sit with you this morning?"

Rinaldo's face lit up with unexpected pleasure. "Why sure, I'd be much obliged," he said, moving over to make room. Simon slid onto the bench beside him and Sybil set her bowl down across from them.

"How are things going at the gates these days?" Simon chatted amiably.

"Oh, you know, same old thing. Hasn't been much of note. Nothing as exciting as the day you first arrived."

"Quite a day all right," agreed Simon.

"I hear you two do a great job on flippers. Like to come by one day and have mine done."

"Would be a pleasure. Stop by next week after your first day of gate duty. What time are you finished?"

"Doing an eight bells shift. It ends one bell before dinner."

"Great, we'll set up near your gate and shine you up. Maybe we can have dinner together. See you then." Simon stood up, picked up his plate and turned to leave. He hesitated a moment then sat back down.

"Just remembered something, Rinaldo. Been meaning to ask you."

"Sure, go ahead."

"Sarah and I saw someone on the street yesterday near our work area. Older woman, looks different than everyone else in the city. Just curious, is all. Do you know who she is?"

"Yeah, I've seen her around," Rinaldo grinned. "Been here a number of years. Lives over on Abalone Way," he grunted with self-satisfaction.

"Do you know her name, Rinaldo?" asked Simon.

"Not off hand," Rinaldo replied. "But I can find out for you. I can find out anything in town," he boasted with pleasure. It wasn't often anyone asked his opinion.

"Thanks Rinaldo," Sybil gulped down the rest of her breakfast and stood up.

"Yeah, thanks Rinaldo," said Simon with an easy smile. "Pleasure having breakfast with you. See you after work next week." They bid him good day, collected their gear, exited the building and broke into an easy trot heading toward the eastern part of the city.

"If we set up where we saw her, with any luck we'll find out which building she lives in," said Simon.

Sybil's caution surfaced. "Maybe so, but I don't think we should be seen by her."

"Right Syb." He stopped near an alcove adjoining Abalone Way. "What do you think? Safe enough?"

"Excellent. We can duck into the shop behind us if we need to."

Sybil started unpacking her polishing kit and set up her work station. Later that morning they were rewarded by the sight of the old woman emerging from a building halfway down the street. She looked about curiously and headed off in the opposite direction, carrying a basket toward the open air markets.

"Simon, you hold the fort. I'm going to sneak through the side street. Maybe we can find out what she's up to."

"Our tail will see you go," warned Simon.

"Just look at him Simon. He's not very alert. He needs refreshment soon." The drooping head and sucking gills indicated he was near depletion. His eyes were beginning to glaze over.

"He seems in a bad way. Okay, you go and I'll watch this guy. Hurry before they change watch."

Sybil ducked into the shop behind her and emerged through the back entrance into the alley. Plying her way swiftly through the masses, she caught up to the old woman, just as she entered the fish market. She watched her browse through the stalls making her purchases. When she was about to leave, the woman casually turned to the person beside her, greeting him with a nod.

"Oh no!" Sybil gasped, *"It's Rinaldo!"*

"Sybil get out of there before they spot you!"

"Wait, I want to see what he does. He chatted with the old woman briefly. Now he's talking with the street vendor working at the food market. He's ordering some food. The old woman seems at ease and is going on with her errands. I don't think he has betrayed us."

"Okay, but come back right now! There's a sentry coming up the street to relieve the first one."

"On my way!" She turned and fled through the alley. Arriving at her post, she took up her position and accepted the next customer in line.

The fresh sentry called out.

"Calazone, you look spent. I'm here. Hurry man, get to the pool."

He stood alert and poised, watching the fatigue overcome Calazone, as he hobbled off in the direction of the nearest pool. The old woman re-emerged up the street and entered the building she had come out of earlier that morning.

"Come on, let's find a new corner," suggested Sybil. She began packing up their belongings.

"Let's go farther east," agreed Simon, preparing to head off in the direction Calazone had gone. "He can't be too far ahead."

They pulled up shop and casually sauntered off. The sentry on duty trailed them until they came to the pool where Calazone was submerged.

"Wow, would you look at the size of that pool!" said Simon. "Bigger than any we've seen in the city!"

Calazone's head lifted out of the water, his strength slowly flooding back into his fatigued limbs. Ducking under for a second time, he thrashed around making great splashing noises. Suddenly, the alarm sounded. Heedless, Calazone kept on swimming, oblivious to the warning.

"He's so far gone, it's affected his hearing," yelled Simon. He rushed forward, reached over the side of the pool, grabbing Calazone's arm just as the fresh sentry arrived at poolside.

"Get out of there man!" shouted the sentry, yanking on his other arm. The water level was sinking fast making great slurping noises as it eddied, disappearing down a large drain in the bottom. Simon and the sentry held fast, their feet skidding into the side of the pool, bracing against the force of the suction. Calazone's shocked face surfaced. Immobilized with panic, his eyes bulged in terror.

"Come on man, get a hold of yourself. Kick your flippers," shouted his friend.

With a final swoosh the water disappeared and the pool was empty. The gaping hole of the drain yawned ominously, then slowly closed. Calazone regained his senses and scrambled over the edge onto the city square dripping water everywhere.

"That was a close one, Hermaine!" he breathed a sigh of relief. "Never again will I wait that long. Thank you!"

"Sorry man! It was my fault. I got held up on the way over. I just couldn't make it any sooner," apologized Hermaine, beside himself with regret. "You know Dimondus and his inspections!"

"All too well," Calazone grimaced. "Don't worry." He placed his morphing hand on Hermaine's shoulder, absolving his friend with an understanding nod.

"And this fellow here, if he hadn't grabbed you. You'd have been a goner!"

Calazone turned and appraised Simon with appreciation. Although he was on surveillance, he hadn't expected to meet these strangers to the city face-to-face, let alone be saved by one. "Your name is Dominic, I hear?"

"Yes sir. I am Dominic," he answered. "And this is Sarah," he motioned to Sybil, who had appeared beside them.

"Are you okay?" Sybil's concern touched his heart and his eyes softened.

"It was frightful! I think I'm all right. My name is Calazone and this is Hermaine."

"Pleased to meet you. Glad we could help."

"Thank you most kindly," answered Calazone, making a deep bow of appreciation.

"And I, Hermaine, am very thankful you came along or my best friend here would be gone to the other side!"

Simon's ears perked up. Before he could react Sybil asked, "The other side? Other side of what?"

"Don't know. Heard a lot 'a tall tales. A conduit to other realms, crossover to great divide, portals, alternate realties. You name it," Hermaine offered. They peered over the edge of the pool they were leaning against. Fresh sparkling water was filtering in, replenishing the bath. "Probably all drivel really, but I doubt anything good would come of disappearing down that abyss!"

"Yeah, people like to gossip. There's always a lot of nonsense," said Simon, downplaying their interest. "And stories get wilder each time you hear 'em," he laughed.

"Well, Dominic," said Sybil. "We'd better get back to work."

"Sorry to leave you guys," apologized Simon.

"Let's head back west," Sybil suggested, then added, "Are you sure you're okay Calazone?"

"Ah, I think so. Haven't finished my refreshment," he said, eyeing the pool. "Safe now I guess." A tremor of fear crept into his voice.

"Go on Calazone," urged Hermaine. "I'll stand by until you're finished."

"Thanks once again," he nodded to Simon. Then he spun around and climbed back into the pool, hovering near the edge.

Sybil and Simon packed up their gear and made their way across the street before realizing Hermaine had actually stayed with Calazone.

"Looks like we've earned a measure of trust," observed Simon. "I hope he doesn't get into any trouble with Dimondus."

Sybil stood watching Hermaine encouraging his friend. "Let's hang around to make sure. We need all the friends we can find in this city."

"Good call Sybil," replied Simon, leaning against the wall of a shop. They watched Calazone emerge from the pool, while his friend slapped him on the back reassuringly.

"Poor fellow," said Sybil. "Must have been real scary. I wonder if this has happened before. Surely this isn't the only time."

"Maybe we're on to something here Syb," replied Simon, stooping to pick up their gear.

"Another portal?"

"Yes. I got out of here somehow. Could be how I left this place."

"I'm all about avoiding time travel if possible. A portal sure would be nice."

"I wonder if Fifth has more portals."

"And Third! Spoon Lake for sure. Could be more."

Looking over their shoulders, they gave a friendly wave and hurried back the way they had come, avoiding Abalone Way, lest they encounter the old woman. Hermaine followed leisurely, thankful for the lad who was walking on ahead.

Back in their rooms after dinner, they took account of what they had learned of Aquadria.

"What do we know so far, Simon?"

"The humanoids living here need water to survive. Soon they'll be fully aquatic," he responded.

"The Opeggees said Aquadorus is intending to flood the valley."

"And the most important discovery? That large pool in the east may be our way out," said Simon, excitedly.

"If the flood happens soon, we have to get out of here, especially if the water rises above the cliffs."

"That means the Opeggees won't survive either!"

"What if it isn't the way out?" asked Sybil, her voice quavering at the thought.

"Have to take that chance. If we get cold feet, we can always fall back on time travel if needed. But how do we warn the Opeggees before we go?" Simon's worried face betrayed how much he cared for Roark, his family and the welcoming brood nesting on the cliff top.

"There has to be a way. Send a telepath? How close can we get?"

"If we can make it to the eastern city limits—scale the highest building—maybe it'll work," reasoned Simon.

"Then we must do it tonight! When the alarm sounds at noon tomorrow, we have to be ready to go! Fifth needs to be warned as soon as possible."

As soon as darkness settled over the city, Simon and Sybil stuffed their blankets with pillows to disguise their sleeping platforms. When the sentry outside the building pivoted to make his way west along the street, they disappeared into the shadows. Fleeing into the night they gained access to the eastern part of the city, passing the pool where Calazone nearly met his end. Further on, they approached one of the tallest trees within city limits.

"Hey, that tree! Better than a building!" He offered his clasped hands as a step. "Hop up Syb."

After gaining access to the first level of branches the climbing got easier. When they climbed as high as they dared, Sybil said, "Okay, try it!"

"Roark, are you there? It's me Simon. Roark, please answer." A deathly pall of silence settled around them.

"You try, Sybil."

"Roark. It's Sybil. Wake up! Please, wake up!" There was no answer.

"Let's try together," suggested Simon. "Ready, go… *"Roark! Wake up! Can you hear us? It's Simon and Sybil. We must talk to you!"* There was no response.

"Okay, once more Simon."

This time they leaned together, concentrating all their power into one point. *"ROARK! WAKE UP!"*

That did it. Roark's sleepy squawk filtered through the cool night air.

"Wh-wh-a-at? Wh-wh-who is calling m-me? Can't a guy get any sleep?" he mumbled groggily.

"Roark it's us, Simon and Sybil."

"W-who did you say? I don't know any Simon or Sybil," he squawked grumpily.

"Oh sorry! It is Dominic and Sarah," Simon apologized, realizing they had forgotten about the earlier deception. *"Sorry to bother you so late at night. Our real names are Simon and Sybil."*

"We couldn't trust anyone. Can you forgive us?" Sybil asked, hope-fully.

Roark's voice brightened at the realization he was speaking with the two friends who had carried him to the cliff top. *"Non-sense. One can never be too careful. Simon, you say and Sybil? Grand to hear from you. Mother Meerak saw you being led into the city by that beast. We Opeggees have been deathly worried about you."*

"And we are very concerned for you Roark and the whole Opeggee rookery. We think Aquadorus will carry out his plans very soon."

"We're leaving tomorrow at noon if all goes well," said Sybil. *"Your lives are in danger."*

"Dirgeful darkness!" cried Roark, frantically. *"This bodes ill for all of us. I will alert our people. Go now. Be careful and may the Universe protect you. Trust to the fates. We will meet again."*

"Good bye Roark. We'll try to find help. Will be back somehow."

"Farewell, my dear friends. We wait in hope!" Roark's fretful squawk was the last they heard as they climbed down the tree.

Sybil smacked her forehead.

"I nearly forgot! The BanquoeBag. I hid it under the shrubs when Dimondus stepped on my back. We have to go back for it."

"We have to leave the city?" Simon's voice was grave with concern.

"Can't leave the bag. With any luck Rinaldo will be on duty tonight at the gate."

"Well, no use stalling," answered Simon, setting off at a brisk pace. They stuck to back lanes, stealthily working their way to the distant gate.

"Can you see who's on duty?"

Simon edged his way around the corner for a better look.

"It's Rinaldo, but he's wide awake!" They slunk back into the shadows and waited patiently. As the night wore on Rinaldo remained alert, standing at attention.

"Dimondus probably wrote him up on report, so he's being extra careful," said Simon.

"Don't give up yet, we still have a few hours left." Sybil's encouragement checked his impatience.

It was nearing third bell of the night watch when Rinaldo's head began to dip and sway.

"Luck is with us," said Simon. "His head's down. He's asleep. Go now!"

Stealthily, they fled through the city gate, running softly over the open area toward the woods and ducked into the under-growth.

"I think we're very near the place," said Sybil.

"You're right Syb," he said, parting the branches and looking back across the open space. "I can see Rinaldo. Looks about the same angle."

Scrambling on all fours, they felt under the shrubs searching frantically.

"It's impossible. We'll never find it," groaned Sybil.

"Listen. What's that noise?" A munching sound coming from the left, caught Simon's attention. The sound stopped. He held up his hand in warning. They crouched together, waiting. After a few minutes the crunching resumed.

"Something is eating from the BanquoeBag," whispered Sybil. "Now what do we do?"

"Can't leave without it. I'll go around the other side. Wait until I give the signal."

"Simon, be careful." Feeling in the underbrush, she found a rock. "Here, take this with you."

Simon eased his way toward the right, angling in a curve, which put him directly opposite Sybil. She armed herself with a stick and waited patiently.

"Okay, all set," he telepathed.

"What is it? Can you see?"

Narrowing their vision acutely in the direction of the sound, an image began to take form. First the outline of a furry body came into view. Two floppy ears dangled from a massive head. A curved tail stood erect, then began to wag. A contented whimper came from deep in its throat.

"Sybil! It's one of the dogs!" Simon cried in disbelief.

"You can't be serious!" Sybil was dubious.

"Here boy, come," she called in a hoarse whisper. Sure enough, the big male bounded over, jumped up, placing his forepaws on her shoulders and began to lick her face, his whole body writhing in ecstasy.

"Where did you come from boy?" asked Simon, joining the happy reunion. The hound turned to greet him, wriggling with joy. He scampered in circles around Simon's legs, emitting happy throaty sounds.

"Down boy. Sit," commanded Sybil quietly. She calmed him by running her hands over his back and scratching his ears.

"Too much noise. Rinaldo will hear us," admonished Sybil.

"This sure throws a curve in our plans for tomorrow!" Simon groaned.

"Can't be helped. Unless we figure out how to get him into that pool at noon tomorrow…" The thought of abandoning him, shook her up. She walked over to the BanquoeBag, picked it up and came back to Simon and the hound.

"He must have tracked the scent of food," said Sybil. "I thought he'd be safe at the castle."

"Or tracked our scent. Maybe he missed us." The thought of this made a huge impression on Simon. He loved this dog. Could it be the dog loved them too?

"How did he get so far north?"

"Escaped and followed the hunter's trails? He must have got sucked into the portal."

"Now we have a whole new problem. How do we get him through the gate and into the pool tomorrow?" asked Sybil.

"I don't see how it can be done," Simon scratched his chin thoughtfully, a plan beginning to take shape. The notion of leaving the dog behind did not sit well. He hated the thought, but he couldn't see any other way to solve the problem. "Do you think the Opeggees would take him?"

"If we leave the dog with them we'll have to act fast." Sybil's reluctance to part with him again, weighed heavily on her conscience. "Morning's not far off."

"Roark would take good care of him and maybe he can help the Opeggees," reasoned Simon.

"And maybe we can come back for him," added Sybil hopefully.

"We'll do our best," Simon tried to reassure her, knowing the odds were against them.

"I suppose we must," agreed Sybil, unsure of the decision and hating how little time they had to make it. "Guess we better get moving."

Once they came to an agreement Simon leapt into action. "You stay here Sybil, I'll run across country. I can get to the rookery and back if I leave now."

"Wait!" Sybil buried her face in the dog's soft fur. "Hey boy. I'll miss you. Promise. We'll come back for you if we can." Her voice broke as she choked back a sob. "Go now Simon. This is too hard!"

"Come on boy. Let's go," Simon turned away.

"Watch for the Crimson Snakebush. Don't need that again! Here take this," she said, handing him the illuminator.

"No problem. Back in no time." He disappeared into the undergrowth running with the hound.

Sybil settled down in the thicket to wait, fretful about their decision and worrying Simon wouldn't be back on time.

Simon bushed his way through the undergrowth and soon found the path that led him to the Opeggee cliff. He began to climb, calling out to Roark.

"Sorry little buddy. Need your help. Can you meet me at the top?"

"Where are you?" croaked Roark.

"I'm coming up the cliff."

"What? You're here? Thought you were in the city!"

"Sorry to keep waking you," apologized Simon.

"No problem. Been awake since you last called. Such frightful news! I'm on my way." Roark's agitated tone revealed the tension he felt.

Rounding the bend in the trail, Simon met up with Roark.

"Boy, am I glad to see you! We have a problem. Look who followed us to Aquadria! Don't ask me how. Bloodhounds are great trackers."

"Cool! Never seen anything like it! What did you call it? A bloodhound?" asked Roark, fascinated by the new creature.

"Yeah, he's a bloodhound all right. Come here boy. Meet my buddy Roark."

The hound warily edged closer to Roark and sniffed his wing feathers. Roark giggled.

273

"Hey that tickles. You sure are cute!" He laughed and brushed his wing along the dog's head. The hound responded to him by sidling closer and giving him a lick on his red beak.

"He's awesome!" chortled Roark. "Love his soft pink tongue!"

"Glad you feel that way, because I'm going to ask if you will keep him here," said Simon hopefully. "We can't take him with us tomorrow."

"You mean I get to keep him?" he asked excitedly, hopping up and down, his suction cups popping in delight. The dog scampered around Roark, enchanted by the enthusiastic little creature.

"Yes. Until we can come back for him." His heart sank at the thought. What if they couldn't get back? What if the flood… He shut out the thought as quickly as it formed. "Do you think Meerak will mind?"

"Of course not!" replied Roark.

Simon knelt beside the dog and ruffled his neck fur. He buried his face in the soft mat, nuzzling him tenderly. The hound's body tensed slightly. He seemed to sense that he had to stay and began to whine. His soft whimpers tugged at Simon's heart.

"It's okay boy. You will love my friend Roark. Be a good lad and stay. I will come back for you."

He rose to his feet and commanded, "Stay now," signalling him with the flat of his hand. It was one of the hardest things he'd ever done. The hound settled at Roark's feet, while Simon said goodbye once again.

"Come boy," signalled Roark with his wing tip, turning toward the hilltop rookery. "You will be safe with us. We'll have such fun!" The hound followed obediently.

Simon fled down the cliff trail leaving behind the memory of his furry companion. Knowing he was with Roark, gave him little comfort. He grieved silently as he veered onto the path leading toward the city running at high speed. When he ducked into the undergrowth, his thoughts turned to the task ahead. The route was more familiar and he made good time.

Breathlessly approaching the thicket where he left Sybil, he alerted her, "I'm back. You there Syb?"

"Thank the stars! I was beginning to worry you got lost or something bad happened. We have to get moving." She readjusted the BanquoeBag and leapt to her feet. "How was the hound? Was he okay? Any trouble making him stay?"

"No. He and Roark are getting along famously. You know Roark, easy kind of guy. Loved the dog instantly."

"Good! It was the only thing we could do," Sybil's remorse escaped as a sigh of relief.

"Now let's see if we can get back through the gate!" said Simon, ducking under the branches into the clearing.

"Wait!" cautioned Sybil. "Is Rinaldo still on duty? Is he asleep?"

Simon stopped abruptly and hastily retreated under cover.

"Sorry Syb, I wanted to get back." He checked his impatience, folded back the fronds and scanned the area. Rinaldo's still figure had shifted forward and his head was now lolling to one side.

"Still asleep, I think."

"Okay, careful now," she said. They left the sheltering greenery and stole across the open space. Just as they were nearing Rinaldo, his weight shifted and his head fell to the other side.

"Stop," said Simon, blocking her way with his arm. Rinaldo settled and the soft soughing sounds of sleep deepened into heavy snores. Simon inched forward with Sybil creeping along beside him.

"Slowly. Careful now. Okay we're nearly there." He held his breath as they edged through the gate and slipped into the nearest shadows. They stopped to let their heart rates slow to normal.

Up the street a fresh sentry appeared, marching swiftly toward them. He approached the gate and sidled through.

"Rinaldo, you oaf, asleep on duty again. Dimondus will hear of this!"

Startled, Rinaldo jerked awake and straightened up.

"S-s-sorry sir, I just nodded off briefly," he spluttered, drool seeping down his chin. "Didn't get much sleep yesterday. Too much noise in the streets. Please," he begged. "It won't happen again."

"You're right. It won't. I'll see you are relieved of your duties Rinaldo. You are a disgrace to Aquadria!" he yelled.

Taking advantage of the commotion at the gate, Sybil and Simon slipped into the back streets and raced through the city to their lodgings. A fresh sentry on duty marched dutifully back and forth in front of their building.

"What do we do now?" Simon, who had just finished the run with the hound, was visibly flustered.

Knowing he was nearly spent, Sybil offered, "I'll keep watch. You rest a little."

He slumped against a tree trunk in the park across the street where they waited. It was very near morning when the sentry wandered farther than intended.

"Good to go," whispered Sybil. She grabbed Simon's wrist and he woke with a start. "Now!"

Simon, still half asleep, let himself be guided across the street. They scuttled through the entry and found their way safely to their rooms.

CHAPTER THIRTEEN
Re-entry

The remainder of the night was spent planning their escape before reporting in at breakfast. They were still dressed in their clothes when the first shafts of light hit the cobbled streets. Sybil's hands fidgeted nervously as she clasped the BanquoeBag tightly, a knot of anxiety twisting her innards.

"I'll hide this under my cloak when we leave."

"Leave it here for now. We can come back for it after breakfast." Simon's focus was intent on getting them out of Aquadria. He'd had his fill of the place and couldn't leave fast enough.

At breakfast they sat across from Dimondus, who wolfed down his meal at an alarming speed. Sybil pushed the food around on her plate, her stomach churning with apprehension.

"Not hungry this morning?" he sneered.

She picked up a morsel of food and made a pretense of eating, quieting her free hand in her lap by clutching her knee. She forced down the food, finished most of it and pushed back from the table.

A commotion at the entrance attracted their attention. It was Rinaldo being led in by another guard.

"Oh, oh," Sybil sighed. She hated to see someone berated in front of others. *"Poor Rinaldo. In trouble again."*

He was marched over to their table to stand in front of Dimondus. The mess hall fell silent, while everyone stopped eating to watch the spectacle unfold.

"Rinaldo was asleep on sentry duty again last night," reported the guard. "His relief made him turn himself in."

Dimondus stood up and glared at Rinaldo who was standing inert, his head lowered in shame.

"This is the third time in two weeks. I don't tolerate laziness. Look at me when I'm talking to you!"

Rinaldo slowly raised his eyes to the dark anger scathing his face.

"You will spend a week in solitary confinement. After that, you are demoted to polish detail. You can join these two here on the streets." He gave Sybil and Simon a withering look.

They winced at the thought of the disgrace heaped upon Rinaldo. He wasn't a bad sort. He just had trouble staying awake. They rather liked his easygoing nature.

Sybil got to her feet, her anger at boiling point.

"Yes, Rinaldo can work with us. We'll teach him what we know."

Simon reinforced Sybil's proposal. "Maybe he's just not cut out for sentry duty sir. Sarah's right, he'll do a good job with us."

Dimondus scowled at Simon then turned his scornful eyes on Sybil.

"Oh, you'll see to it all right. If he doesn't measure up to expectations, I'll hold you two responsible."

"No problem sir. We can handle it," Sybil retorted abruptly. "Now excuse me, I must wash my hands," she said and pivoted to leave.

Rinaldo, who was still standing in front of them, shot a fleeting grateful glance their way.

"Be quick about it!" snapped Dimondus. "Time to work!"

Turning back to Rinaldo, he boomed, "I'll see you later. Throw this lout in the brig!" He turned on his heels and loped across the floor, disappearing into the street.

"Nasty bully!" Sybil's indignation erupted. "One day he'll pay for this. It's appalling."

"Makes you want to stay around to see it," added Simon.

"Wouldn't go so far as to say that!" snapped Sybil. "See it all right—better yet, to see Rinaldo do well."

"Well, we can't help that," sighed Simon. "Hurry Sybil, let's get the bag and we're out of here!"

When they finally made their way to the street, Dimondus had disappeared.

"I'll be glad to see the last of that guy!" said Sybil, still fuming.

"Ah-huh, won't miss him one bit," agreed Simon, as they threaded their way through the thronging streets.

When they approached the pool where Simon had rescued Calazone, they saw Dimondus inspecting the scene.

"Heard you had a little excitement here yesterday," he laughed. "That dumb Calazone needs to pay attention. Maybe next time he won't be so careless."

"What a jerk!" Simon clenched his fists spasmodically. *"Can't stand the guy."*

"Big ego, that one!" replied Sybil. *"I hope he moves on pretty soon. If he hangs around, he might get suspicious."* Her brows knit together in worry. *"What if he decides to stand guard here himself?"*

"Who's on duty?" asked Simon. His eyes scanned the area.

"Over there, Simon. It's Hermaine. He followed us from the mess hall."

Simon followed her gaze down the street and saw Hermaine standing alertly on watch. Then he marched toward them and greeted Dimondus.

"Good morning sir. Fine day."

"Hummph!" replied Dimondus. He grudgingly added, "I hear the emperor has commended you for your role here yesterday."

"All in a day's work," replied Hermaine. "I have been assigned Calazone's watch today. There won't be any problems."

"See to it then," replied Dimondus and marched off.

Sybil let out a sigh of relief, as she watched him tramp west and disappear into the crowds. Hermaine worked his way back to his post down the street, weaving through the masses that jostled to get by.

"I'm having second thoughts about this," said Sybil. "Maybe we should use time travel instead."

"Yeah, but that age thing really shakes me up. I think I'd rather find out where this pool goes."

"Not sure which is worse," she said, frowning doubtfully over the edge of the pool.

"Come on Sybil, we have to make a decision one way or the other."

"I guess," she replied hesitantly. "Maybe the pool."

"We have 'til noon at least."

"So many people on the street today!" Sybil looked about in bewilderment. "Has the population doubled over night?"

"Can hardly walk today. Have to turn sideways to get by," answered Simon.

"Well, whatever we decide, in this crowd no one will notice if two disappear," said Sybil, her nervous tension easing at the thought. "Let's set up shop right here. Can't get through this mob anyway."

She cracked open her polishing kit and threw down the sponge seats. Her first customer hopped onto the sponge and extended his flippers.

"Shine 'em up!" he laughed, lounging against the pool wall. He glanced at Simon beside her. "Ain't you the guy who helped rescue Calazone yesterday? Boy! Lucky y'all fellers didn't git pulled down!"

"I guess," replied Simon, hoping to change the subject.

"Ta last accident was 'bout nine year ago. Some little kid distappeared! Course, can't be sure. No witnesses. Never been found." He scratched his head, looking puzzled. "Ta kid was a foundlin'. Not like us. Well, that's what you git fer tryin' ta convert people," he sighed. "Little duffer had no gills. Shouldn'ta been allowed in ta pools in ta first place."

Simon glanced sideways at Sybil.

"That must have been me!"

"At least we know you survived the ride!" Sybil's audible sigh of relief caused the guy on her chair to sit up and take notice.

"Looks like you just won ta sea horse races," chuckled the old one, watching her flush with embarrassment. "Oh, c'mon now. Just teasin'. No need ta colour up so."

Sybil managed to laugh and spluttered, "I'd love to win!" Then she settled down to the job of shining his old flippers to a dazzling finish.

"By gar'. Tank ya lass. Best'est spit polish ever!" He grinned, hopped off the sponge and gave her a little nod. "I'll be back a'gin lass." He disappeared in the throng of bodies.

"Now that makes our decision easier," Simon's reassurance calmed her nerves. "It's the best option, don't you think?"

"Must admit hearing that, makes me feel a whole lot better. So yes, we'll use the pool. But I wish the time would go faster!" She plopped down against the wall for a break.

Simon sat beside her and pulled out a snack. "Here, have one," he offered, holding out some fish fillets the kitchen had packed for them. Gratefully, she took one and bit into it.

"I'll miss the seafood," she said. "No matter where you are, I guess there's always something to be thankful for."

"Have to admit, I will too," agreed Simon, munching on the last of the crisp fish strips. "Okay, back to work!" He picked up his cloth and began polishing in earnest.

"Last day Syb!" He grinned at her in anticipation as he greeted his next client.

The sun had risen high above the city, when the alarm began to sound. Everyone in the pool scurried over the side to safety.

Just as the last of the water was disappearing through the drain in the pool floor, Sybil and Simon hopped nimbly over the wall and dove into the gaping hole. The tiles closed behind them leaving no trace.

"Hold on, stay together," Simon warned, as they cleared the opening. Clinging to each other, they picked up speed, twisting and turning through a maze of light filled tubes.

"Don't know where we'll end up. Maybe we can think our way through! Where do we need to go Sybil?"

"Third dimension?" suggested Sybil hesitantly. Whoosh, they picked up speed, entering a vast void. Then they were out the other side. Landing on their feet, they shook themselves off.

"That was a wild ride!" Simon's hands trembled, as he helped Sybil step off the dock on which they had landed.

"Say! This looks familiar!" said Sybil. She turned a full 360 degree circle and let out a gasp. "It's Lenore Lake! But the water level is high! No dried mud flats!"

"And look Syb, the meadows are green. The fields! The crops are golden—heavy. Bumper crops!"

"It's the Third dimension for sure Simon, but see that!"

Simon followed her outstretched finger and gawped at a team of horses pulling a plough working the summer fallow.

"Yeah, we're in the Third dimension. But what time period?"

Sybil remembered her mother telling stories about her great-great-grandparents arriving in Canada. What year was that? About the turn of the last century, maybe 1903. The land had been raw and unbroken then, so it must be a few years later. "I think we're in the early 20th century around 1910, maybe earlier."

"Oh oh! I think we got time travel mixed up somehow with that last portal we used!" Sybil was a little shaken by the idea. "We might need more instruction on this."

"I hope we can get back!" Simon's concern about using time travel resurfaced. "Maybe we shouldn't have tried to think our way through."

"Maybe—or you never know, perhaps we are supposed to be here. What did the Hetopians always say? Trust in the Universe?"

As they contemplated what to do, the beauty of the landscape drew them in. They were immersed in the deep peace of the countryside.

"The land is stunning! Look at the sky!"

The penetrating blue stretched into eternity. Fleecy white clouds drifted lazily on the western horizon. It was high noon and the sun's brilliance washed the fields in dazzling golden hues. Simon's nostrils flared, taking in the robust fragrance on the autumn breeze.

"Smell the ripening wheat!"

"Let's head to the village," suggested Sybil.

They set off through the sun-bronzed wheat field, their outstretched hands brushing the spikey heads. The grain undulated in waves under the westerly breeze. Ahead, they saw a family of harvesters, backs bent to the task of reaping their crops. A man wearing blue denim overalls wielded a long-handled scythe, its sharp blade cutting the stalks at ground level. A woman gathered the cut stalks into a bunch, bound the sheaf with twine and dropped it on the ground. A young boy of about ten followed her, stacking the sheaves into groups of eight to form stooks that stood upright across the harvested field. The woman straightened up, rubbing her aching back with her right hand.

"Gut gemacht! Good work Georgie. Stooks look good. Keep 'em dry in rain. Dry out gut," she beamed with satisfaction.

Her son, who was bent to his work, stood up and gave her a smile. "Danke Mutter," his boyish grin broadened with pleasure.

"English," reminded his mother. "New country, learn English," she reinforced.

"Ja! Okay! Thank you Mama," he replied, his grin growing wider.

Claire beamed, as she watched her family. She had four boys. George, who was turning ten, stooked the sheaves she bound. Joseph, at eight years old was responsible for cutting the twine for her. Bernhard, a toddler of three years was sleeping in the field down the row of stooks. Her newborn, Anthony, was bundled on her back. There was a gap between Joey and Bernhard where sadness dwelled. A painful stab pierced her heart when she thought about the set of twins she had lost. The little girl had died at birth. The male infant followed three days later.

"All in the past," she sighed. Pulling a rag from her apron pocket, she loosened her bonnet and mopped sweat from her brow.

"Hard vork! Georgie be gut boy. Bring mir bitte Wasser, ah—water please."

George stacked the last bundle he held and ambled over to the earthen jug, glad to stretch his aching back muscles.

"Hier, trink das Wasser Mama." Then he corrected, "Drink water Mama," smiling shyly at his strange new language. The baby on her back stirred and began to fuss.

"Feed kinder—ah, kids. Joseph help. Vee have dinner. Setz dich hier hin—come sit here," she motioned, sinking to her knees upon the stubble field. "Pa, komm essen—come eat."

She unpacked the bundle Joseph had carried over; pork sandwiches, fried chicken, carrots from her garden and pickles. They passed the water jug and drank freely, slaking their parched throats. Then she settled down to nurse her newborn, attending to his cries of hunger. She laid him over her shoulder and patted his back until he burped contentedly.

"Schmeckt gut, Claire! Lecher!" her husband Friederich laughed and stuffed a sandwich in his mouth.

"Yes, tastes good! Pa. Delicious. English, ja?"

"Ja," he chuckled and picked up a drum stick. He devoured it and picked the bone clean with his pocket knife. "Ich versuche es. I try!"

He was very happy to own land in his new country. Back where he came from, most land was held by overlords. He worked on freeholds for other people. Now he could say he was a farmer. His chest swelled with pride, as he surveyed the bountiful crops. He sucked on his tooth, trying to dislodge a morsel of food. Annoyed, he picked up a wheat stock, broke off a piece and began to pick at the offending lump.

"Ach, besser," he grinned, as it came free. He chewed it up and swallowed.

He reached for a whetstone and applied it to the cutting edge of his scythe, sharpening it with skillful ease. When he was satisfied, he ran his thumb along the edge and yelped. A tiny bead of blood welled up.

"Whew! Scharf!" he whistled, popping his thumb in his mouth. He packed his whetstone away, picked up his scythe and resumed the rhythmic swing, gathering the crop before winter settled upon the land. His smile conveyed a deep satisfaction while he worked. Claire packed up the dinner and sat down to change the baby's undergarments. She tucked him in the sling on her back and once more began the tedious work of tying sheaves.

Sybil and Simon drew nearer. The man doffed his straw hat. Beads of sweat on his brow trickled into his eyes. His callused hands retrieved an old blue handkerchief from his back pocket and proceeded to mop his brow. When they stopped to call out, there was no response. They approached the man and tried to get his attention, but he paid them no heed.

"He doesn't see us," said Sybil. She turned to the woman.

"Hello. How long have you been in the fields today?" There was no response. She walked over to one of the boys and waved her hand in front of his face. He looked right through her.

"Simon, they don't see us!"

"Hey, we're invisible. This could work for us!" replied Simon, pondering the situation. "Let's stay with this family. We'll tag along and find out where they live."

They walked through the wheat, watching the changing glory of the sky and settled down alongside the family through a long hot day of sweat and toil. It was quite late when the family packed up their tools and gathered the children for the long trek home. They approached the village perimeter, a small settlement of about a dozen dwellings. Following respectfully, they watched the family approach a two-storey log cabin on the very edge of the village. A small log barn out back, housed a pen holding a few pigs. A chicken coop stood open and the hens and roosters had settled on the roost for the evening. Pa walked over to close the door against marauding foxes and coyotes. Two cows stood near the barn in a fenced pasture bawling insistently to be milked, their udders engorged and leaking creamy white fluid.

"Georgie, Joey, milk cows, bitte—please," said Pa.

"Ja, right away," replied the boys. Sauntering to the barn, they herded the cows into the barn stalls. Perching on three-legged milking stools, they leaned against the heifers, their foreheads resting on the soft brown sides, as they began to pull on the teats. The spray of milk hitting the empty bucket set up a melodic pinging. As the pails filled, the sound turned to a gentle frothy song. Three barn cats sat expectantly waiting for a stream of milk to come their way.

"Hier Katzen. Wollt ihr etwas trinken?"

"No! Speak English Joey! Here cats. Want something to drink?"

The boys laughed as the cats' pink tongues lapped at the white stream in mid-air. Their furry whiskers frothed into white mustaches. When he finished milking, Georgie stood up and rubbed the cow's flanks.

"Gut girl, Gertie." He walked around behind her and approached Joey who was stripping the last of the milk from his cow's teats.

"Gut, Bess is dry too. You good milker, Joey," he encouraged his younger brother.

The boys set their milk pails aside and scratched the cows behind their ears, murmuring endearments. They gave them a little tap on their rumps and herded them out the back barn door into the pasture. The two milk cows pulled grass with their tongues and set to chewing, lowing contentedly, as they settled in a soft straw pile near the barn for the night.

Carrying two full pails of milk into the kitchen, the boys related the story of the cats to young Bernhard, who giggled with delight. Mama was frying up pork chops and pan potatoes. Corn on the cob boiled in a pot on the wood stove.

"Vash up," she ordered. Everyone stood in line at the well outside, while Pa drew a pail of cold water and poured it into a basin. In turn, they each lathered up with mama's home-made lye soap, scrubbing away the grime and sweat of their labour.

Mama called from the doorstep, "Joey, brink tomatoes please."

He obeyed, skipping across the yard to the garden. He returned with four juicy, red globes, the pungent odour of tomato on his green-stained fingers.

"Here Mama," he grinned up at her.

"Georgie, cut bitte," she directed. The vegetable garden was her pride and joy. It kept her family well fed over the winter months. Sauerkraut, weighted down by a large round rock on top of overturned dinner plates, was fermenting in a 25 gallon crock. It stood in the kitchen corner near the wood stove. Another crock held bacon and hams that were curing in brine. Soon they would be ready for the smoke house.

Pa stood at the sink straining the milk. He skimmed off the heavy cream that floated to the top and Mama saved some for their coffee. After supper she and the boys would take turns at the handle on the butter churn to make the remainder into butter. There was nothing better than a thick slather of fresh butter on her home-baked bread. The boys drank fresh milk with their supper. Sometimes mama made cottage cheese with it.

Storage of perishable items was a priority. To keep milk products cold, they were sealed in large earthen jugs, tied to ropes and lowered deep into the well. Pa had built a root cellar, dug deep into the black prairie soil, where they stored root vegetables. During the harsh cold of the winter months, frozen fresh meat products were placed in a large stock tank behind the house. Pa made sure the cover was secured against predators looking for an easy meal.

Sybil and Simon settled into a corner of the kitchen, feeling like intruders. After supper was cleared away, the family sat at the table. Pa trimmed the wick and lit the kerosene lamp. He opened the family bible, smoothed the first page and gazed lovingly at the names of his family. He had inscribed it himself with nib and ink, in fine calligraphic penmanship. Friederich Wessel and Claire Huber, followed by the entries of each child and their birthdates.

Sybil sidled closer, then gasped. Claire Huber!

"Si-Simon," she spluttered. "You won't believe it! Guess where we are!"

"Come on, no games Sybil. Tell me."

"This is Friedrich and Claire! Mom's great-great-grandparents!"

"No-o-o way! You're joking!"

He turned to the family seated peacefully at the table. Their dark eyes and hair, which framed evenly proportioned features, confirmed the facts. Yes, they did have a familial resemblance to these good folks.

"Monumental!" he cried, a huge grin spreading across his face. "Wish we could talk to them!"

"Me too! I feel like an interloper, eavesdropping on their conversation." Sybil's respectful caring nagged at her conscience. "Oh, I wish they could hear us!"

"If we weren't meant to be here, we would be elsewhere," reasoned Simon. "We are here because we need to be," was his simple explanation. "Isn't that what you said earlier?"

"Perhaps you're right."

After reading passages from the family bible, Pa closed the book and yawned. "Wir gehen schlafen mein Sohn," said Pa, as he tousled Bernhard's dark hair. "Morgen come soon."

"Ja, we go to sleep now," confirmed Mama. "Long day!"

The family climbed the narrow stairway leading to the upper floor, where two bedrooms provided sleeping arrangements. Home-made straw mattresses and goose-down pillows covered in feather ticking comforted their aching bodies, as they turned in for the night.

Sybil settled in the corner near the stove, her conscience still bothering her.

"If they knew we were here, I don't think they'd mind. Do you?" She sought Simon's warm brown eyes, still wrestling with her sense of right and wrong.

"Of course not. We're family Sybil!" replied Simon.

"I'd feel better if we could explain," her wistful voice revealed how much she cared about family tradition, especially knowing about the women in her family—and now Simon.

Morning came quickly. Sybil was glad to stretch her limbs and massage the pressure points on her hips. Lying on a hard wooden floor all night was extremely uncomfortable.

"I think I'd rather sleep out in the straw pile with the cows tonight," she grumbled.

"Hey, that's a great idea!" agreed Simon, rubbing his tailbone. "I think I have bedsores!" he chuckled, delighted with his own quirky humour.

In short order, bacon and eggs were frying in the pan and Mama had buttermilk biscuits baking in the oven. The wood stove gave off comforting warmth. The nights already had a nip in the air, a harbinger of the long, cold winter to come. The older boys and papa came in from chores, having finished milking, collecting eggs and feeding the animals. The family gathered around the breakfast table.

Simon's nose twitched. "Mmmm bacon! I haven't had that since living on the farm in Leanoria." His stomach rumbled and his mouth began to water. He didn't dare snitch a piece off the platter Claire set on the table. Instead he reached into the BanquoeBag and produced the standard rations.

"Do you think she'd notice if we had a piece?" asked Sybil, yearning for the taste of bacon.

"See how it goes. Might be a chance to grab a slice if there's any left."

"I don't want to take their food though. They work so hard for it."

Simon eyed her with appreciation. "Your right Sybil. It wouldn't be right." He liked that about her. She was mindful of other's feelings. She had a good sense of right and wrong.

"Guten Morgen Mama. Hast du gut geschlafen?" Pa hugged her from behind.

"Okay. I sleep okay. But you snore Pa, saw logs all night!" she bantered.

Coffee brewed the old-fashioned way and strained through a sieve, steamed out of the mugs she poured. Pa, grabbed a jug of cream and splashed some into his coffee, then stirred it round and round. The tinkle of the spoon against the cup set up a rhythmic musical tune. Looking into the depths, he watched the shade turn from deep mahogany to warm caramel, just the way he liked it. He missed the sweetness though. Sugar was expensive and reserved for special occasions. A sudden look of delight crossed his face.

"Hey, Mama. Biene!" his excited voice rang out in the warm kitchen.

"Vas? Du what? You vant bees now!"

"Ja, Mama. Bees!" He cackled at his clever idea. "Ja!" He would set up bee keeping to satisfy his sweet tooth.

"Vas ist next?" His proud wife beamed at her husband's smiling face.

Friederich's grin split his face from ear to ear. She was easy to please and he loved her for it.

The family settled to their morning meal, eating thought-fully. The only sound came from the clink of forks scraping against plates while they savoured their food.

Mama stared off into the distance. She wasn't sure why she felt so unsettled this morning. When these feelings came over her there was no rest. Sometimes she worked it out. Other times she knew in hindsight what she should have done.

"Papa," she began hesitantly.

"Ja Mama?"

"I haf dis feeling. Like vee not alone. Like vee are vatched." She felt foolish saying it, but there were many times before, when she didn't heed these feelings and she wished she'd had.

"Look around Mama. Only us," said Friederich, sweeping the kitchen with his arm.

"Ja, I see dat," she replied. "But…" she shook her head. "Tings not right."

"Did you hear that?" Sybil's eyes grew wide. "Do you think she is beginning to sense that we're here?"

"I don't know, Sybil. They can't hear us. That's for sure."

"Claire has the gift. Maybe we're just under her threshold."

"Komm on Mama. Sunday today, vee rest," said Pa, hoping to take her mind off what troubled her.

Claire had the gift of foresight and Friederich had been through this before. He tried to accommodate her many moods and usually succeeded by changing the subject.

"Sunday, keine Arbeiten—no work. Vee go lake," he dropped the suggestion casually. The boys looked up in surprise, a cheer forming on their lips. Pa silenced them with a look.

"First vee pray. Den vee go picnic," he said in halting English.

Mama shook off the feeling that was weighing on her and smiled in agreement. "Gut! Dee lake is gut!"

There was plenty to do to get the picnic organized. She scrambled to her feet, wiped little Bernhard's face clear of rhubarb jam and began giving orders.

"Joey, put eggs in pot. Vee haf hart boilt eggs. Georgie, peel potatoes. I make Kartoffelsalat. Ah, ah…potato salad. Ei yie yie! Dis English!" she scolded herself. "Ich lerne langsam—I learn slow."

She cut thick slices of ham and wrapped them in greased brown paper. In a short time, all was nearly ready. Georgie covered the prepared salad with a clean dish towel and tied it in place with string. Then Mama packed plates, forks and knives, mugs for cold tea and finished up with tomatoes and pickles.

"Georgie, pull carrots from garten. Vash at vell and vee go!"

"Can we bring Benjamin Peters?" Georgie asked hopefully.

"Ja, Benni!" Joey's excited voice pleaded, hopping from one foot to the other.

"Pa, vas denkst du? What you think? Boys brink friend?"

"Ja, sure. Dey vork hart all veek. Today dey haf fun."

The boys ran off down the path to the nearest neighbour, the Peters, a half mile distant. Soon they were back with Benni in tow, laughing and talking.

"We go fishing Pa?" asked Georgie.

"Brink dee poles," agreed Pa. Joey ran to the garden and dug worms, storing them in an old canning jar.

Pa hitched the horses. In those days, the family could not afford a proper buggy. Pa had built a deep-sided wagon with a seat and foot rest for the driver. The wagon had a tongue to which he hitched their two horses, Nellie and Schwarzie. A yoke attached to each horse collar, ensured the team worked together. Papa always rode up front driving the horses and Mama, usually holding a newborn, sat beside him. The boys piled in the back.

When all was ready, Mama and the boys packed the picnic into the wagon. They scrambled aboard and set off, following the rutted old wagon trail leading to the lake.

"So! Vas denkst du, Mama? Vee happy, huh!"

"Ja! I think vee happy!" she beamed, her eyes twinkling with love.

The water was clear and sparkling blue in the fresh breeze. Sun-spangled diamonds danced off its surface.

"Raus. Wir sind da. All out, vee here," corrected Pa in a merry voice.

The boys piled out of the wagon, grabbed their fishing poles and ran to the dock.

"Nein, nein kommt Jungs. Come boys, pick berries first."

Slowly they returned to collect their bowls, then headed east along the lake to find wild cranberry patches. When the bowls were full, they ran back along the shore to give them to their ma. She would serve them later with thick cream and a little sugar as a treat. Their favourite juneberries, which grew plenti-fully in the area, had long since been picked and made into pies, cakes and preserves.

"Haselnuss—er hazelnuts ready soon Mama," Georgie re-ported.

"Gut, vee pick before squirrels," she confirmed.

"Vee go now Mama?" asked Georgie.

"Ja, off mit you! Go fish," she laughed at their impatience. They were good boys, hard-working and respectful. She watched proudly as they ran to the dock. They scrambled aboard a row boat that was left tied there for community use and shoved off eagerly for a few hours of fishing. Pike, perch and walleye were some of the best eating, especially the way Mama pan-fried them up nice and crisp. Pa always liked the perch pickled with onions best.

Sybil and Simon had been watching the family fun and were amazed at how much the land had to offer. There was plenty of wild game. Rabbits, ducks, geese, grouse and deer supple-mented their farm-raised animals. In the winter they went trap-ping for muskrats, rabbits, and weasels. The tanned fur hides made warm mittens and trimmed their parka hoods to shield their faces against the biting sting of the prairie winter. The hides they could not use, were sold on the fur market.

Watching the boat carve through the waves moving far out on the lake, Sybil's eyes widened in awe.

"I just thought of something."

"What? What are you thinking?"

"One of those boys could be our great-great-grandfather! I don't know why I didn't think of it before."

"Well, what was his name?"

"Hmmm, let me see. I think it was Jacob."

"So, he hasn't been born yet," confirmed Simon. "Too bad. It would have been fun to see what he was like as a boy."

"Ah, but those boys are our great-great-uncles!" Sybil's satisfied look of pleasure grew into a smile. "Pretty interesting. But seeing Claire and Friederich is the best!" said Sybil.

The wind picked up and a dark thunderhead rose in the west. They looked out over the choppy water and saw the boat turn. The boys were rowing furiously, knowing they must beat the approaching thunderstorm. As they neared the shore, a flash of lightning tore through the sky, followed by a loud boom that echoed across the water. The heavens opened and a deluge drenched them in a cloudburst of water. The boys pulled hard on the oars, bobbing up and down on the rough surface.

Finally reaching the safety of the dock, Georgie and Joey hopped out. They pulled the boat even with the post, attempting to tie up in the madness of lashing waves. A sudden flash of white-hot light seared the sky. There was a dreadful sizzle, followed immediately by a horrific thunderclap. It shook the ground, laying them prostrate. Sybil and Simon covered their heads under the deafening chaos, cowering close to the ground. Shouts of alarm filtered through the uproar. Sybil lifted her head to see Mama and Papa dashing frantically to the dock.

She pulled herself to her feet, trembling on confused legs. "What happened Simon?"

Simon looked up at her, stunned, his eyes bulging in horrified alarm. Turning to the boat where the boys had docked, they saw Georgie and Joey, lying face down, unmoving on the dock. Mama was screaming uncontrollably.

"Georgie, Joey! Mein Jungs!"

Papa, reaching the scene first, lifted Joey and laid him on the grass near Simon. He was breathing, but rendered unconscious. He went back for Georgie and deposited him beside his brother. Georgie lay on the grass moaning softly, his arms and hands badly burned.

Simon looked at the shattered mess of the boat. The lifeless body of Benni Peters lay crumpled in the splintered hull. He watched Friederich approach the boat with horror. Kneeling on the dock, slivered shards digging into his knees, he gently cradled the scorched body of his neighbour's child in his arms. He rose with tears streaming down his face and carried him to shore.

Mama was screaming into the rain, her eyes lifted to the heavens.

"Vhy Gott, vhy? Mein kleiner Junge! My little boy! Our boys!"

Her wails reached Sybil's ears and she slowly turned her head, afraid to look. The horrendous scene before her, thrust a dagger of terror through her heart. She closed her eyes against the horror and took a deep breath.

"Okay, breathe," she willed herself. "Are you all right Simon?"

"Yes, I think so," he said, checking himself for damage. "I don't think lightning can strike people from the future. But those poor boys. And Claire and Friederich!"

The smell of burnt flesh assaulted Sybil's senses, as she tried to come to grips with the carnage left by the storm. She began to sob softly, "Poor Benjamin! His family!"

As the storm front moved through, the rain slowed to a fine drizzle. A brief ray of sunshine poked through the clouds forming a half rainbow in the north-east. It disappeared again when the canopy of clouds closed over the desolate scene below.

They watched helplessly, as Friederich packed the wagon. Claire stayed with the boys comforting them with soft words of encouragement. Friederich drove the wagon to dockside and lifted his boys gently into the back, covering them with Claire's cloak and his coat. Lastly, he lifted the lifeless body of Benni, placed him near the end of the wagon box and covered him with the picnic blanket. Considering the task ahead—how to tell Henry and Adelaide Peters their beloved son was gone, his heart plummeted; a cold wet stone in his stomach.

Sybil and Simon clung white-knuckled, leaning on the insides of the wagon box for, the jostling ride back to the village, their faces numb with shock. Mama sat in the back beside her boys. Bernhard leaned against her, crying hysterically, his terrified eyes darting from his mother to his brothers lying next to them.

"S'okay Bernhard. Mama ist here, shhhh." She wrapped one arm around him and did her best to console him while the baby wailed in her other arm, squirming and kicking. She felt overwhelmed and helpless, her attention divided between four children. She broke under the strain and wept uncontrollably.

"Whoaa!" Pa stopped the team and reached back to her. He laid his hand on her shoulder. "Komm Mama. Bernhard hier." He lifted the frightened boy onto his lap.

"Sit mit Papa. Gut boy." He stroked his back and gently kissed the top of his head. "Help Papa mit horses."

Bernhard sat on his lap and clutched the reins under Pa's big warm hands. A tug on the reins sent a wave of leather, slapping the horse's rumps. He clucked the side of his cheek and cried, "Giddyap!"

297

The team moved out at a swift trot. The safety of his father's arms and the rhythmic sway of the horse's backs soothed his crying to a subdued fretful hiccough.

Friedrich pulled up in front of their home.

"Stay hier Bernhard." He hopped off the wagon and carried Georgie and Joey into the kitchen. Claire prepared a comfortable pallet near the stove to keep her boys warm, until they recovered from the first shock. She rummaged in her bag of herbs and found what she needed to prepare a soothing ointment for Georgie's burns. She wrapped his hands and arms in clean, torn bed sheets. Joey had regained consciousness and was mumbling incoherently.

In her busy worry, she had lost all thought of Bernhard.

"Bernhard! Wo bist du? Bernhard! Where are you?" She ran out the kitchen door. "Pa, habt ihr Bernhard gesehen?"

"Ja Claire, er ist bei mir," replied Friederich.

"Komm Bernhard. Your Papa must go now." She lifted the little boy down from the wagon seat and he clung to her when she hugged him to her breast.

"S'okay Bernhard, you stay mit Mama."

"I go. See Henry Peters, Mama."

Mama nodded silently.

Sybil and Simon could only stand by silently, watching the scene unfold. When the wagon began to roll, Sybil ran after it. "Let's go with him. Maybe in some way he will feel we are there beside him."

"Can't hurt any," replied Simon. They hopped over the tailgate, scrambled to the front and clambered onto the wagon seat, one on either side of Friederich. This was no easy task. Sybil and Simon laid their hands on his shoulders trying to help him, hoping that a bit of comfort would seep through the barrier.

Friederich gave his wife a small wave, and grim-faced, he left the yard heading north-west toward the Peters' homestead. His mind wandered in circles of ifs and shoulds. If only he'd noticed the storm sooner, or if we'd let them go berry picking later. We should have told them to stay closer to shore. On and on his mind whirled. They would have been off the lake if any of these things were changed.

By the time he pulled into the Peters' yard the storm had passed and the sun was beginning to show through the last of the clouds.

"Whoa." He brought the horses to a stop and climbed down from the wagon, his knees buckling. Sybil and Simon jumped off and tried to steady him by his elbows. He seemed to gain some composure. Crossing the short distance to the front door, he stood for a minute steadying his nerves. He tapped lightly. There was a stirring from within and Henry appeared at the door.

"Hello Friederich. Some storm we had! Hope you folks found shelter and…" His voice stuck in his throat. Friederich's stricken face told him something had gone wrong. "What is it man? What's happened?"

Friederich drew a deep breath and his shoulders sagged. "Sturm—ein grosser Sturm! Big storm Henry! Dein Sohn—your son." He broke under the weight of grief and his failure to keep the boys safe.

"Es tout mir leid!" He dissolved into great wracking sobs, shaking uncontrollably. "Sorry, I sorry!"

Adelaide came to the door when she heard the commotion. "What is it, Henry? What's going on?"

Henry pulled her to the rocking chair on the porch.

"Sit Adelaide. It is Benni—the storm—he's gone." His voice cracked. Adelaide's face contorted. She let out a deep low wail. The blood drained from her face and she sagged against him in a faint.

"Help me Friederich," he pleaded.

They lifted her together, brought her inside and laid her on the bed. He called their daughter Anna.

"Stay with your Mama."

Anna came obediently and sat in the chair beside the bed. Her brother was dead. She trembled, frightened, and her mother was not there for her. She laid her hand on her mother's arm.

"Come on, Mama. I need you. Please wake up."

There was no response. Anna sobbed into her hands. This was not fair. How was she going to live without her little brother Benni? And now Mama...she hoped she would wake up soon. An emptiness, lonelier than the vast uninhabited spaces of the prairie, settled in her heart, squeezing it until she thought it would break.

"Let me see him," Henry's voice had gained some strength.

"Ist bad," warned Friederich.

"Still, I need to see him."

"Ja, I know. Lightning hit boat. Mein boys down on dock. Benjamin in boat."

He stopped, wondering if they would ever forgive him. Tears brimmed his eyes.

"Forgif, bitte. Forgif...please." He wiped his tears and blew his nose with his handkerchief.

Henry followed him to the wagon box and gently lifted the blanket from his son's face. At the sight of his boy lying inert and burnt, he crumpled and fell to his knees, clutching Friederich's outstretched hand. Deep anguished sobs rolled out, the grief bearing down on him with all the force of the storm that had taken his son.

"Come Henry," Friederich lifted him to standing position and gently guided him to the porch. "I bring Benni in for you."

Returning to the wagon, he lifted Benni in the blanket and brought him to the door where Henry stood holding it open.

"Bring him into the bedroom."

Friederich crossed the room and placed him on a cot where Benni usually slept. Henry pulled up a chair and sat with his son, resting his hand on the form hidden under the blanket. Friederich was at a loss. There were no words to bring comfort. He placed his hand on Henry's shoulder.

"I go now. Be mit my boys. Claire waiting. You be okay?"

Henry nodded slowly, "You go please."

Friederich gave his friend's shoulder one last squeeze and left the room.

The rest of the day passed slowly, dragging on toward supper. Except for Bernhard and the newborn, no one else felt hungry. The picnic they had prepared went uneaten. Claire and Friederich sat at the kitchen table, trying to take comfort in the scriptures and each other.

At the Peters' house, Adelaide came around and began to wail anew. Henry tried his best to comfort her. He had washed Benjamin's body, dressed him in his Sunday best suit and laid him back on his bed. Adelaide finally rose to her feet that evening.

"I need to see him," she whimpered. Henry steadied her and walked her to the bedroom where Benni lay peacefully.

"He didn't suffer. With lightning strikes no one knows what's hit them," he tried to comfort his wife.

"No? Well he shouldn't have been on the lake in that boat!" she spat, her anger boiling over. "They have their boys. We have lost all. Our only son!" she screamed.

"It wasn't their fault, it was an accident. No one can control the weather," he tried his best to persuade her. "Friederich and Claire are in a lot of pain over this."

"That doesn't concern me," she hissed. "It is we who have lost. They lost nothing!"

The funeral was held two days later. Benjamin's body was laid to rest in the family plot inside the little graveyard next to the log church. Claire and Friederich tried to comfort her in the best way they could but she seemed indifferent. It would take time.

Sybil and Simon stood next to the children, reliving the horrible scene over and over.

"This is so sad. I wish we could do something to help," said Sybil.

"We can," replied Simon. "If we help with the chores; that would be something."

"Sure, that would help out. We could collect the eggs and leave them in the basket on the table."

"We could weed the garden too!" Simon was warming to the idea. "We could bring in a fresh pail of water every morning. We just have to be up before everyone else."

"Milking and feeding animals won't work. For one, we don't know how to milk, and two, the animals would get spooked. But the other chores I think we can manage, without raising concern."

"Won't they wonder who did the chores?"

"Nah, they'll think someone else in the family has already done it. That's what I think."

"If they notice things were moved, it would alarm them. We'd have to be very careful not to let them see that!"

"It'll be a challenge all right. But we can't sit idle while they are going through this terrible time."

Over the following days Mama was happy with the way her boys were healing. "Boys better now. You vorking hart."

Her skill as a healer was gaining a reputation in the area and many of their neighbours appeared at her door when they needed treatment.

Mama and Papa praised them as they regained their strength, thinking they were responsible for the chores that always seemed to be done. Still, Claire could not shake the strange feeling that hovered around her. The house seemed full. It had a presence somehow.

As time passed, Sybil grew concerned. "Simon, I'm worried. We've been here too long."

"Yeah, the age thing is starting to bother me," replied Simon. "But we couldn't just leave after all that's happened."

"I know, but I think it's time."

"Why did we come here? I've wondered so often. Do you think it was because they needed some help?"

"Don't know. I suppose we did help a little," said Sybil. "For sure we understand a lot more."

"I wouldn't have missed this chance for the world," replied Simon. "Seeing family from the past? Pretty special experience." As soon as he said it, he realized that this family was now woven into the fabric of his life. If there had been a last vestige of doubt, it no longer existed.

At the Peters' home, a suffocating blanket of despair settled over the household, infiltrating the corners of every room. Adelaide spoke little, grieving the loss of her son. Numbness set in and she languished in bed.

"Get up Adelaide, please. You must try," encouraged her husband. "Anna can't do all the work by herself."

"I don't care!" she hissed.

This state of inertia went on for weeks, until one day Henry noticed a resolve settle upon her face, as though she had come to terms with the loss. That morning she got up, dressed, washed her face and began to make flapjacks at the wood stove.

"It is nice to see you up Mama," said Anna, relieved that her mother was returning to her usual routines.

"Yes, it is good to be up. I must go over to see Claire and Friederich one day soon." She hesitated, then turned to her daughter. "Would you like to come with me?"

"Sure Mama, I can walk over with you. We can bring some flowers from the garden. I am sure it has been hard on them too."

"They still have their sons." She could not let go of that bitter thought.

"They were injured too," Anna tried explaining.

"Not dead though!" she retorted. Anna left the conversation drift. No use getting her mother riled up. She was still pretty fragile. It would take time to find a way to go on living without her son. Her brother. Anna's breath caught in her throat, as she tried to clear the lump forming there.

The next morning Adelaide and Anna pulled their cloaks around their shoulders and set off on the path between their farms, carrying a bunch of mums from the garden and a freshly cured ham. The trail was well-worn, for they had been good friends since the move to this country and visited as often as time allowed, trading recipes and preserves.

Sybil and Simon were working in the garden when they saw the visitors approaching.

"Never expected to see Adelaide here!" said Sybil. "I wonder how this visit will go."

"Let's follow them in. Maybe we can help ease the situation."

When the door opened, Sybil and Simon hurried inside and stood beside Claire. Placing their hands on her back, they watched the scene unfold.

"Willkommen! Come in Adelaide, Anna. Gut to see you. I misst you, old friend."

"Yes, me too. Anna has cut a bunch of mums for you. The garden is blazing with them."

"Thank you, Adelaide. Und danke. Thank you for de ham. Vee haf you ofer soon. Come eat ham with us."

"You're welcome Claire. Thank you. Be nice to have a meal with you again."

"So far, so good," said Sybil. Then she felt a small tremor pass through Claire, as she stood there wondering what to say next. An awkward moment of silence ensued. Sybil gave her grandmother's back a gentle rub. When Claire did not respond Simon reinforced the comforting gesture.

Claire relaxed and smiled, "You gut neighbor. Close friend, Adelaide. Gut you are here. Ich—I feel so bad, guilty. Vee try, so sorry. You and Henry. So sad. Forgif, forgif us, please."

Tears welled in Claire's eyes, as she tried to make amends and comfort her old friend. Her new language skills could not express the terrible hollow ache, the remorse, the guilt she felt in the pit of her stomach.

"Of course Claire, how can anyone change what happened?" replied Adelaide. "Life must go on."

It had taken awhile for her friend to get on her feet, to recover from the terrible blow. Claire tried to help out the best she could, when Anna had to carry the weight of the household. The fact that Adelaide was here, gave her a small measure of comfort. This first visit was a beginning. It seemed their old friendship had weathered that terrible storm. "Poor Adelaide," she whispered under her breath. Her heart grieved for her old friend.

CHAPTER FOURTEEN
The Ninth Dimension

Rubbing her hands excitedly, Claire chuckled, "There are two Adelaide. We must act quickly! She has given birth to twins and never before has a male child been born with the sign! This bodes well for the universe."

Riffling the atmosphere with her fingers, the images settled into place. "Here, in the great Book of Wisdom, it is foretold." She smiled in anticipation.

"Wonderful news Claire!" Adelaide responded. "Has she named them?"

"Yes. Sybil and Simon. The connection between the Third and Fifth dimensions needs to be established. There's no choice. They must be separated before enemy forces intervene."

"Separate them? The parents! Are you sure?" Adelaide questioned her course of action.

"Positive. It's the best way. The only way. Hard for the family, I know. But they're strong. They will weather it. We'll place Simon with a loyal family I know in the Fifth. Humble people, they shouldn't attract attention."

"Isn't that a bit drastic?" cautioned Adelaide, again questioning her intentions.

"He'll be safe there. Sybil will stay with her mother. Once they come into their birthright and reunite, their powers will be strong. It's our only hope for the future!"

"I suppose," Adelaide nodded her head doubtfully.

"Once the dust has settled, I'll find a way to make myself known to Franceska. She's a clever one. She'll understand."

Gesturing toward the holographic image in front of them, Adelaide conceded, "We don't have much time Claire. You see the build-up of Aquadrian forces here in the Seventh dimension," she stabbed her boney finger at points on the map. "It won't be long before they are ready to strike."

"Where do you think the invasion will begin?" Claire asked, staring at the map.

"From the north," replied Adelaide, running her hand over the hologram. "At least, that is my best prediction."

Claire Huber nodded, "I agree. We must act quickly. A full moon is an opportune time to enter the Third. This is our first time back. I've missed it," she said wistfully.

"I miss it too. Third realm has such beauties," sighed Adelaide.

Claire smiled, savouring the memories, "Eternal blue skies, wide open spaces, sparkling streams, haunting lakes. Hard to say what I miss most. All of it really."

Her mind drifted in nostalgic reverie. "And the wildlife. Absolutely stunning! The variety of animals and birds defies imagination."

She was about to say, raising her family there with Friederich was the happiest time of her life, but she thought better of it when she recalled the tragic storm. Instead, she added, "I'm so happy we're returning together. We spent many lovely days there on the plains."

"Wide open spaces. I miss that the most," replied Adelaide. "There's something freeing about gazing across miles of prairie. Hmmph, now it's all kilometres," she grumped. "The country roads are still the same. Still a mile between crossroads. Confusing. Makes no sense."

"We've seen many changes," agreed Claire. "Some are confusing. Still I'm so glad we're going back."

"I wouldn't miss this opportunity," replied Adelaide. Then thinking more pragmatically she asked, "What do we need to bring with us?"

"We'll travel lightly. All we need is a haversack to keep Simon safe and warm." Claire lowered her head in concentration and in a moment produced a length of lightweight fabric.

"This will do," she said, compacting it and tucking it in the folds of her gown. "I don't anticipate any problems. The Third dimension doesn't have the powers of concealment we have," she explained. "I could go by myself, but I'd much rather have you with me. Besides, I want us to revisit all our old haunts together. If we leave early we can spend a bit of time there."

"Wonderful Claire!" agreed her friend. They stood together in silence, gathering their conscious thoughts. In a moment they found themselves transported to the Third realm, standing before the homestead Claire and her husband had farmed in the District of Lenore Lake. The sun was already setting, painting a rich, fiery hue across the western horizon.

"Wonderful days!" reminisced Claire, but was stunned to see the condition of the buildings. The barn sagged. The log house stood empty, boarded up. The chicken coop had been demolished altogether.

"It's deserted. I suppose after my last son left there was no one to take it over," she said plaintively, then turned away. "Well, that's all in the past. Only memories. Can't expect things to be unchanged. Adelaide, do you want to see your old place?"

"We're here. Shame not to," replied Adelaide.

Crossing the yard to the back field, Claire suggested, "Let's find the old path we used." Coming to a barbed wire fence, she stepped on the bottom wire and stretched the next one upward to make an opening for her friend to pass, then crawled through herself.

"Now where is it?" They searched in vain.

"Gone too," Adelaide sighed, forlornly. A field of grain obliterated all signs of the once well-trodden trail. Instead, they waded into the standing wheat and followed an approximate trajectory toward the Peters' old place. Side by side they wandered, remembering family picnics, ball games, and days spent at the lake. On Sunday afternoons, people from miles around gathered there to visit.

"Remember the old-time dances out at the pavilion Adelaide? No such thing as a babysitter in those days."

"Bundled up our kids and took them along. Danced until they couldn't keep their eyes open!"

"Fell asleep in the back rooms under coats. And slept soundly all the way home in the wagons."

"I miss those horse and buggy days. But travel now is much more convenient."

"Can't beat realm travel!" laughed Claire.

By the time they arrived at the Peters' farm, the moon had travelled across the sky, casting a ghostly aura over the rundown log house that stood in the corner of the yard. It had been converted to a storage shed by the present owner.

"The house is unloved. It looks so lonely and broken-down. Seems the whole countryside is empty, not as many folks living hereabouts now," Adelaide's voice choked with emotion.

"Sad. Life changes and we move on," Claire said, trying to sound encouraging. Maybe it wasn't prudent to bring Adelaide back here, stirring up those painful memories. Changing the subject, Claire drew her arm around Adelaide's back and they turned to leave.

"Let's head back to the village and see what's happening."

Wandering through the field toward town, their long skirts grew wet with dew. A chorus of frogs sent chills of longing for those peaceful bygone days. Arriving at the outskirts of town, it was evident that a lot of expansion had taken place. They strolled past many houses lining the streets, past the community hall and the shops in the downtown core. A few lights were still on but the majority of the town folk had turned in for the night.

There was one more thing she had meant to do—visit the cemetery where her body lay buried beside Friederich. But something held her back. Adelaide is not ready for that, she decided. Funny how everyone fears the end. Really, there's nothing to it. Just another consciousness raising plateau. Letting go is the simplest thing to do. So why am I here? Was there some unsettled business? This insight clouded her vision for a moment. Then she shook her head and pushed the nagging thought below the surface.

"Nice to see it again, but we are more in tune with the Ninth dimension now," remarked Adelaide. Shaking her head, she turned away sadly.

Glancing up at the sky, Claire was shocked.

"Adelaide! Where did the time go? It's very late. Time to get on with the task."

In a brief moment the scene changed. Claire and her companion were on the street in front of the Chilliwack hospital.

"I think it is best you stay here Adelaide, while I collect Simon. Two disturbances in the energy field might attract attention indoors."

She drew her brows together in concentration and found herself outside the elevators on the third floor. Crossing the space to the double doors leading to the maternity ward, she resigned herself to her course of action and entered. Proceeding swiftly through the hall, she stopped before the neonate nursery, then swept into the room. The nurse sitting at the desk, shivered. Rubbing her arms, she grabbed the cardigan off the back of her chair and pulled it on. She turned in Claire's direction, concentrating on the buttons as she bundled herself against the coldness in the room. Returning to her tasks she sat down in front of the computer to finish her reports.

Claire hurried across the room and checked the names on the bassinets, where the infants lay sleeping. Simon was curled up on his left side swaddled in a flannelette wrap, his eyes closed to the world. She turned to look at Sybil in the bassinet next to him. The newborn squirmed, whimpering momentarily. Her downy eyelashes fluttered open seeking the love she suddenly sensed and came to rest in Claire's warm gaze.

"What a beautiful child!" Claire whispered. "Forgive me Sybil. One day you'll understand. What I am about to do is absolutely necessary. Go back to sleep wee one," she soothed reassuringly.

Turning to Simon, she gently lifted him into her arms and wrapped him in the fabric stowed in the folds of her robe. She snugged him against her warm chest, tying the sling securely over her shoulders and drew her cloak around herself, concealing the precious cargo within.

As swiftly as she entered the room, she left, retraced her route to the elevator and found herself outside on the street standing beside her friend.

"Sybil is a divine beauty, Adelaide. It took all my will-power not to bring her too. But we must choose this path for the higher good."

"While I was waiting, I had a bit of tea. Would you like some?" Adelaide handed her a flask. "It has been a draining trip and the journey ahead will be hard."

"Thank you Adelaide. You're right. We have to return through the ozone portal. It will take more energy."

She accepted the drink gratefully and handed back the half-empty flask.

"There's still a little left Claire. Finish it if you like. I've already had my share."

"Oh, no thanks. That was lovely and refreshing but I couldn't. I've had plenty." She was anxious to be on her way. The less time spent en route, the better.

She secured Simon closer to her bosom. He would rest near her heart on the journey. Concentrating their collective wills into one focused effort, they prepared for the transition, leaving Third dimension behind and in time landing safely in Fifth.

"We've done it Adelaide!" cried Claire in triumph, as they approached the ice palace in Graenwolven Territory. "Empress Frestoria has agreed to provide shelter until it is safe to move Simon. I am ever so grateful for your support."

"No, don't thank me Claire, I was glad to have done it for you old friend," assured Adelaide. "I cherish those days of old. You were my only friend in those desolate early times in Canada. I felt great sorrow when you went on ahead of me. Had no idea whether I would ever see you again."

"Life in Third wasn't always easy," Claire agreed.

"When it was my turn, you were there to ease my transition into Ninth. It is I who must thank you."

Feeling suddenly drained, Claire heaved a sigh of relief, "Finally! So good to stop." She lifted the knocker and let it drop.

A resounding gong rang out from deep within the palatial structure. She leaned against the door post wearily, cradling Simon close to her breast, his soft breaths sending vaporous puffs into the cold air.

"This has been quite an adventure my wee one," she cooed. Simon made contented little grunts, squirming in the safety of the confined space of her wrap. His little fist escaped from the folds as hunger began to nag the pit of his tummy. A tiny cry alerted Claire to his need.

"Shhh, honey pie. I will feed you soon," she soothed, as the door opened.

A pleasant face appeared at the door. "Come in Claire, you've made good time!"

"Yes, well, we couldn't travel by our usual route because of the wee one. Had to use the ozone portal."

"It was rather an arduous trip," confirmed Adelaide. "Claire here has a lot of stamina."

"That part, I could not have done without you Adelaide," Claire's voice was ragged at the edges. "So grateful…" The trip had taken a lot of her energy. "Need to feed Simon. Then I'll rest a little."

"Go on Claire, I can see to Simon's needs," suggested Adelaide. "I'll take him to the lower kitchens to find some musk ox milk for him."

"Would you? If you don't mind. Thank you Adelaide. I have no idea why I feel so spent…" Her voice drifted in space, as she made her way to a settee in the foyer.

Adelaide crossed the room and bent to take Simon from Claire's weary arms.

"I have him now, Claire. Don't worry. I'll see to him," she reassured, then left the room in search of the stairs leading to the lower kitchens. Locating the way, she quickly descended to the lower floor, muttering to herself.

"We lost everything in that storm." She fingered the pouch of wolfsbane under her cloak. "Took a long time Claire, but now you're gonna' pay for it!" she seethed under her breath.

On the floor above, Antonia approached Claire. Taking her by the arm, she urged, "Come with me, Claire. We have a room prepared. You must rest."

Claire reluctantly let herself be ushered up a flight of stairs into a comfortable room. Although she trusted Adelaide with her own life, she still had qualms about letting Simon out of her sight. She had come this far, but her plans were not complete.

Two levels below, Adelaide prepared milk for the tiny bundle wriggling in her arms. His cries grew to lusty wails, while his little legs thrashed against the swaddling that bound him.

"Be still now. We'll get you fed, then we're off," Adelaide's shrill voice sliced through the kitchen. Simon's insistent wails were stifled by the nipple Adelaide stuck in his mouth. The urgent sucking noises subsided to gentle tugs as the hunger pangs were satiated. A bubble of gas escaped his lips and he snuggled against her contentedly.

"They won't expect me back this soon," she whispered triumphantly. Wrapping Simon tightly, she secured him in the length of fabric again, tying it snuggly around her shoulders. She turned abruptly and fled through the door at the back of the kitchen.

"So far, so good," she said, sending billows of frost into the frozen atmosphere. She chuckled and took to the air flying due north. In a short while the ozone vortex opened before her. She approached with precise caution, then the magnetic force pulled her in. Circling downward she veered right, entering a deep canyon—the oceanic trench into the Seventh dimension.

Arriving moments later at the perimeter of the city, she hurried through the shell-paved paths toward the palace. Throngs of Aquadrians bustled along the street or lay bathing in the many pools she passed.

"Living amongst such strange folk might be harder than I imagined," she mumbled to herself. "But it's worth it. I'd like to see the look on Claire's face when she wakes up! Hah! She never had to live with what I endured. Benni, my poor boy."

314

She'd made her choice, there was no going back now. "Better living here than with those who don't appreciate me. I am of little importance in the Ninth realm." Her addled thoughts escaped into the atmosphere as jumbled words. She smiled slyly. Aquadorus would be most pleased with her. She rang the gong at the palace gate.

A sentry peered through the porthole. "Who goes there," he demanded.

"It is Adelaide of the Ninth. Please announce me to the court. I have something of grave importance. Aquadorus is expecting me."

The sentry closed the porthole and slid back the bar allowing the gate to swing wide enough to permit her entry. He let it clang shut behind them.

"Follow me," he said briskly, his flippers beating out a rhythmic slap, slap along the cobblestones.

Looking about the courtyard in fascination she had to admit the Seventh had advanced far beyond the rumours she'd heard.

"They certainly have adapted well," thought Adelaide. "It's been nearly five decades since the Seventh began its transformation."

"What did you say?" barked the guard.

"Oh, nothing of importance," she lied. Admonishing her carelessness, she closed her lips tightly. Better watch myself. Always had a habit of thinking out loud.

They arrived at the ornately decorated entrance of the palace. The sentry swung the door open, stepped to one side and motioned for her to enter. He closed the door behind them and proceeded across the foyer to the staircase. Curving left, they ascended the spiral steps. Simon wriggled, one little heel thudding sharply against her rib cage.

"Be still you little beggar," she muttered.

Arriving at the Emperor's office he swung open the door, stepped inside, presented Adelaide of the Ninth and stood silently awaiting further orders. The office attendant pressed a button, announced the visitor and showed her into the chamber where the Emperor lolled lazily on a chaise lounge.

"So, Adelaide of the Ninth, back so soon," he raised one eyebrow in disbelief. "What is it this time? What can you possible need?" he scowled.

"I beg your pardon, sir, but I have carried out the task to which we agreed."

She unfolded her cloak, exposing Simon's pink face. The cool air awakened his slumber. His feathery lashes quivered and he slowly opened his eyes.

"Hideous little brute, ain't he?" laughed Aquadorous, sitting up straight on the lounge and leaning over to get a better look. "PINK! What a wormy color. And look at those floppy ears! Nothing like the elegant flaps we carry. How can they keep out water? Hah! Vermin," he snorted.

He stood up, rubbed his hands with pleasure and exclaimed, "Unbelievable! You did this in such a short time? I am most impressed with you, Adelaide of the Ninth. Even my own spies couldn't have done better."

"Thank you, your highness!" beamed Adelaide with obvious pride. "I have kept my part of the bargain your majesty."

In return for her help, he had offered her refuge and safety once his kingdom was established. It was imperative he gain control of the Third and Fifth realms. After all, the insight for those who could understand, was there in the Book of Wisdom, was it not? These births were of significant portent. These two stood in his way, yet he dare not offend the powers of the Universe, lest it unleash cataclysmic forces against him. He was content to keep this one in his care until he was in a position to repel them.

"Very well Adelaide of the Ninth. I will keep my word. A set of compartments has been made ready for you."

Addressing the sentry, he spewed out orders. "Take this woman to the apartments we have prepared. The address is 2313 Abalone Way. See that she is comfortable. She is to remain there until I send for her."

Then he called for a page.

"Take this child to the Aquadrian nursery beds. I have assigned him to Anemone. She has strict orders. No one else is to interfere with this child's care."

He paced the length of the room, hands behind his back, gloating triumphantly over the coup he had masterminded.

*

Back in Graenwolven Territory, Frestoria decided to check on her friend. It wasn't like Claire to be so low on energy. When there was no answer to her knock, she gently opened the door.

Claire had been vomiting. She crossed swiftly to her bedside.

"Claire! What's wrong?"

"I don't know. My mouth is burning." She spit into a bucket beside her bed. "I can't feel my lips," she gasped.

She tried to rise. Dizziness overcame her and she fell back on the bed cushions.

Shaken by the state of her friend, she called for Antonia. "Please go find Adelaide. Maybe she can tell us what's happened on the trip. This doesn't look good at all."

Claire was perspiring and finding it difficult to breathe. Frestoria propped her up on pillows, trying to alleviate her discomfort. She felt for her carotid pulse. Alarmed by the irregular slow rhythm, she called out.

"Antonia! Where are you? Come here quickly."

After anxious moments, Antonia bounded into the room.

"Adelaide is nowhere to be found. She's not in the palace and we can't find Simon anywhere. Last we knew she was headed to the kitchen right? We checked, not there. But a set of footprints left by way of the back door."

"What? Adelaide has gone? Has she taken Simon?" She couldn't believe her ears. Slowly, the realization that Adelaide may have given something to Claire niggled its way into her thoughts.

"The treachery of it all!" she thundered. Her friend was slipping away. "Claire, Claire! Can you hear me? Wake up, wake up!" She tapped her friend's cheek trying to evoke some kind of response.

"What did that wretched Adelaide give you?" she bellowed, seething with frustration. "Simon is gone. Claire, I am so, so sorry. I should have had more security in place."

Her cry of anguish roused her friend momentarily.

"We've failed, Claire. Claire can you hear me?" She grabbed her shoulders and shook her desperately. Claire's eyes fluttered briefly. "Claire, wake up!"

"Wwwh-a, hmmm," an incoherent moan escaped her cyanotic lips.

"Quick Antonia, fetch me some charcoal."

She reached for her mortar and pestle, added the charcoal and beat it furiously, pulverizing it into a fine powder. She poured a small amount of water into a flask and added the charcoal, stirring it quickly.

"Antonia, help me." Propping her shoulders up, she shook her violently. "Wake up Claire. Claire do you hear me? Open your eyes. Wake up!"

Claire moaned again. Her eyelids quivered.

"Open your lips Claire. Drink this." She poured a bit of the concoction into her mouth. "Swallow Claire!" Claire gulped and again she poured more into her friend, coaxing her until the flask was drained. She eased her back on the soft hide pillow.

"Rest easy there Claire." Frestoria kept watch at her friend's bedside, while the hours dragged on. Each time she repeated the charcoal treatment, Claire was able to take more of it in. Gradually her pulse grew stronger and her breathing began to return to normal.

"We aren't out of danger yet," whispered Frestoria. "Come on Claire, fight. You'll get through this!"

By mid-afternoon she grew hopeful. Claire's colour was beginning to return and she was moaning softly. Holding her hand, she squeezed her fingers occasionally.

"Claire, look at me. Squeeze my hand," she ordered. Sluggishly, Claire's weakened grip closed over her fingertips. "That's it my friend. Come back to the land of the living. Open your eyes."

Claire looked out from under drowsy eyelids. "Wh-where am I?" she moaned softly, trying to raise herself on one elbow.

"Easy now. Sit up dear and drink this," she coaxed, offering her a flagon of water. "Take as much as you can. We need to dilute whatever it was Adelaide gave you."

Claire drank freely while Frestoria supported her. "Rest back, we have you now," Frestoria reassured her soothingly. "You'll be right as rain in no time."

"Wh-a-a ha-p-pen?" Claire's voice was slurred. Saliva drooled from the corner of her mouth.

Frestoria gently wiped it away. "All in good time, my dear. Right now you need to rest and get well."

Claire slipped into a deep healing sleep, her body repairing itself from the onslaught of the poisonous herb Adelaide had given to her before they left for the Fifth.

"Her dosage must have been off," murmured Frestoria. "Did she mean to drug Claire or was it an attempt on her life?"

"Lucky for Claire, you found her when you did," replied Antonia. "Who knows what Adelaide had in mind!"

"Well, she has a head start on us. It will be some time before Claire's ready to travel again, let alone confront that wretch."

Claire stayed in bed for a number of days, while her body recovered. Slowly she eased her way to standing position with Frestoria's help. The cook's rich meat broths and vegetable stews restored some of her old vigor. Gradually regaining her strength, she was soon able to walk a few steps in her room. With her attendant's assistance, she ventured out into the hallways. Eventually she was able to go down to the dining room for meals.

"She was a trusted friend. How could she do this to me?" Claire's anguish at the loss of her beloved Simon, the hope they'd had for the future, lay heavily on her heart. "Surely she doesn't still hold a grudge for what happened in that storm. After all these years?"

"Very likely," said Frestoria.

"What are we to do? Where should we begin the search?" Claire's voice trembled in despair.

"We'll figure it out," Frestoria replied. "I have my people scouring the countryside. Something will turn up. You're not well enough to travel Claire. You must stay here with me."

Claire acknowledged the wisdom of this and heeded her friend's advice, rebuilding her health until she was fully recovered.

"It's beyond me how I could've been so deceived," lamented Claire. "I've been such a fool. To think we nearly had Simon safe with us. Now what?"

"My people in the outlying areas have been searching all the while Claire. There's no sign of her. Someone should have seen or heard by now. It's a mystery."

"She's had help. That's my guess. She's no longer in this country, I can feel it in my bones," declared Claire. "I'll return to the Ninth to see if I can uncover any leads there."

"Perhaps you're right," agreed Frestoria. "But you must make this your home base. Promise me Claire, you will check in with us often. We must work together if we are to find him again."

"Yes, of course. I will go to the ends of the universe if I need to. Simon disappeared from the Fifth." Claire's resolve and determination steeled her to the task ahead. "I will always come back to the Fifth."

Years passed. Nothing was heard of Adelaide or Simon. The Graenwolven remained vigilant, pursuing every angle, to no avail. Claire had investigated all leads she'd uncovered in the Ninth but she came up empty-handed. Returning many times to Graenwolven Territory, Claire and Frestoria commiserated, speculating wildly about why Adelaide had carried out such a treacherous act.

"This is the worst catastrophe I could ever have imagined. I haven't even tried to contact Franceska," Claire said, wretchedly. "My family will never forgive me for what I've done."

"There, there, don't give up hope," Frestoria's comforting voice bolstered her flagging spirits. "We must remain positive. Remember after all, it is foretold in the Book of Wisdom."

"You're right of course. It's just that, well, it is I who am to blame," she said, shaking her head sadly. "To tell you the truth, my patience is at breaking point. What has it been now, nearly four years?"

"Blame or no blame, we had no recourse, Claire. You know that. It was the only logical action we could take." Frestoria's sensible line of thought strengthened Claire's resolve.

"Yes, I do know. Thank you," Claire replied. "But something must happen soon if we are ever to see this thing through!"

CHAPTER FIFTEEN
Good News!

Greeting Claire at the threshold of her drawing room, Frestoria's excited voice echoed through the hall.

"We have good news! As soon as our messenger arrived, I sent a plea into the energy force hoping you would contact me."

"Yes, I sensed something," replied Claire. "I left immediately. What is it Frestoria?"

"Come in quickly! Let me take your cloak." Claire entered the room breathlessly, handing her outer garment to her friend.

"Please tell me you have word of Simon!"

"Slow down Claire, catch your breath. At this point there's no way of knowing. A boy of about four has been found in the far regions."

"Must be him!" shouted Claire jubilantly.

"Our hunting parties maintained constant watchfulness. We never gave up. One of these expeditions noticed an atmospheric disturbance in the polar region. When the ozone portal was activated, they set out immediately. Arrived just as the ozone entry was recovering. Wasn't completely restored before our people heard wailing beyond a ridge they had been following. When they climbed to the top, they were astounded to find a small boy wandering about. Appeared to be in shock. And my goodness why wouldn't he be, after coming through that maelstrom of activity."

"How far away are they?" Claire asked, her eagerness rising to match Frestoria's.

Remembering her manners Frestoria made introductions. "Gabrion, this is my friend Claire from the Ninth. Gabrion brought the news. One of our best runners."

"Thank you Gabrion!" exclaimed Claire.

He nodded in acknowledgement, "I arrived not long ago, just enough time to give the details..."

"Yes, and then I put the message out and here you are," interrupted Frestoria, excitedly. "How long would that take? Five or ten minutes?"

"Been on the trail for three days," continued Gabrion. "They shouldn't be far behind."

"I'm indebted to you," Claire said gratefully.

"Not at all. I'll put together an advance party to meet up with them." He turned and left.

Claire paced the length of the room in nervous anticipation, sighing impatiently. Finally, she sat down in front of the brazier to reflect on the flames. Frestoria handed her a mug of hot chamomile tea to calm her frayed nerves.

"After all this time! Just think Frestoria! We may be able to salvage this operation yet." Claire's voice stilled, as she heard the baying of hounds in the distance.

"That's the hunting party Claire!"

Rising to their feet they rushed simultaneously into the hall careening into one another, as they scrambled toward the palace foyer. When they opened the front door, a strong hunter lifted a small form wrapped in hides and entered the doorway into the warmth of the palace. Frestoria directed him to the drawing room.

"Lay him here before the fire, Androsium."

He did as he was directed, then backed away, waiting.

Claire approached the small boy who was sleeping under the fur coverlet. She had to know but was reluctant to disturb his peaceful slumber. Checking her impatience, she stepped back and turned to Androsium.

"Can you tell me more about this child? Did he say anything when he was found? How was he dressed?"

Androsium looked at Frestoria, who nodded.

"We found him wandering, crying incoherently. Wasn't dressed for the northern climate. Odd looking apparel. Never saw anything of the sort before."

"Odd apparel?" Again Claire stifled her impatience. "Go on," she encouraged.

"We approached him gently. Didn't want to frighten the poor little fellow. He was so glad to see someone. Didn't object when I lifted him. He was suffering from exposure, so I undid my cloak and tucked him inside against my warmth. Once he revived, I wrapped him in fur hides. We placed two of our hounds next to him on the sleigh and headed south."

Claire contemplated what she had just been told. Strange clothing? Her curiosity got the better of her. She approached the sleeping child and gently unwrapped the upper part of the hide. Underneath, she saw a peculiar tunic made of an iridescent substance. It seemed to glow with rainbow hues. She reached out gingerly, rubbing her fingertips along the surface. It was smooth and cool, certainly no protection against the ice and snow of the north. Folding the hide back further, she saw the green fishnet fabric which covered his two small arms. No protection there either. The child stirred under the hide, arched his back and stretched his arms. He yawned widely, rubbed his eyes and slowly became aware of his surroundings. A look of fright clouded his features.

The old woman before him smiled encouragingly.

"Don't be frightened child. We mean you no harm. These good people here," she turned and gestured to Androsium and Gabrion. "Found you about half-frozen."

The boy's features relaxed a little, but a residual wariness remained in his eyes. It was warm here and the woman kneeling beside him at the hearth had a kind face. This was better than the dreadful cold. One minute he had been playing in the city pools and the next he was lost in a strange wasteland of ice and snow.

Frestoria intervened, "My good people you must be famished after that long run. Please go to the kitchens and ask cook for some leftovers. There's a lovely meat stew in the larder, just the thing to warm your insides."

"Thank you," replied Androsium, gratefully. "We didn't stop to eat."

"Just gnawed on dried provisions while on the trail," explained Gabrion. "That hot stew will taste good!"

"Will you please ask the cook to prepare some for this child? I'll be along in a moment to fetch it," Frestoria called out, as they disappeared through the door.

She turned to Claire, "I'll be back shortly with some warmer clothing for this wee one."

"What is you name child?" asked Claire gently.

Looking shyly at the kind face before him, he answered hesitantly. "Called me Nogillers."

What sort of name was that, Claire wondered. And what manner of people had he been living with?

"You can call me Claire," she suggested, hoping to relieve some of his tenseness.

"Cla-ire?"

"Yes, that's right, Claire," she reaffirmed. "Can you tell me son, where do you come from?"

"Don't know. They look different. Not like me."

Frestoria returned with the clothing and a bowl of food.

"Come child, we must get you into these warm clothes," Claire suggested, for she sensed she had gained a measure of trust. "These are no longer useful in this weather."

The child obediently rolled back the remainder of the hide. Claire studied the green leggings that clung tightly to his well-muscled little legs. The stockings extended past his ankles to cover his feet. One foot was clad in an odd flipper-like slipper, the other was bare except for the legging. Odd clothing, she thought.

"This won't give you any protection against the snow, dear. Please take it off," Claire instructed pointing to the flipper-slipper.

"Now let's get these clothes off, honey pie," whispered Claire gently. "Don't worry, we'll have you dressed in no time."

She took off the leggings and replaced them with warm hide pantaloons. Holding out fur-lined slippers, he shoved his feet into them, giggling, as she rubbed the bottoms of his feet.

"So soft!" he cooed. "Warm!"

"Yes honeybun, now for your shirt." She helped him out of the stiff iridescent tunic and set it aside. Pulling up the fishnet undershirt she said, "Lift your arms now, oops-a-daisy, up and over your head."

"Tickle you under your arm?" she laughed, making a game of it.

The child giggled. "No, no tickles," he replied shyly.

The shirt peeled off inside out. Claire held her breath, waiting… Astonished at the two intersecting rings on his left upper chest, she closed her lips tightly, lest her reaction alarm the boy. This was too much to hope for. It was Simon!

"There's a good lad, we'll have you snug in no time," she chuckled, drawing the downy fur shirt over his upper body. The boy clasped his arms around his torso and hugged the shirt to himself.

"Soft and cosy."

"Come here now honey pie," laughed Claire. "You must be hungry. Have some food. Sit at this small table beside the fire."

She uncovered the bowl of meat stew. The child looked into the bowl and sniffed the delectable aroma. "What's this?"

Smiling at his curiosity, Frestoria answered. "It is musk ox stew. The best this land has to offer. The hunters who found you keep us supplied all year round."

Claire rested her hand over his small one. "The place where you lived before, was it very different?"

The child looked at her between bites of stew. "Not much fun. I like it better here." No one had been as kind or paid him much attention.

"The name they gave you. Nogillers. Do you like it?"

"Not much. They teased me."

"Would you like a new name, now that you live here?"

The boy thought awhile. "Might be nice." Then he put his spoon down. "What name should I have?"

"Well, what do you think of the name Simon?" Claire asked, kindly.

"Simon." He rolled the name around on his tongue, liking the sound. "Simon," he repeated. "Yes, I like Simon."

During the days that followed, Claire played with the child while Frestoria showed him around the castle. He began to feel very much at home. Claire's intention was to carry through with her original plan, to place Simon safely with the Leanori Truid family in the south. She had made contact with them and they were willing to shelter him, as earlier agreed. Claire knew, very soon, before he became too comfortable with his present surroundings, she must break that news. He was far too young to let him know his true identity. He must live with a minimum of concern until the time was right.

The next day, Claire broached the subject. "You know son, we can't stay here forever. I've come from a very long distance. I must return soon."

"Where from?" he asked, curiously.

"Long way from here. If I could take you with me honey pie, I would," sighed Claire, grieved to the heart.

"I don't want you to go," Simon said in a small voice.

"I know son. But it is impossible. You can't stay here in the north either."

Simon watched the conflicting emotions flitting across Claire's face. He sensed she was struggling with the news she was about to tell him.

"I've thought long and hard about this," she hesitated, drawing in a deep breath, then continued. "I have some dear friends who live in the south. There are other children in the family. You'll have fun there. This family would like you to live with them."

"I don't know them," objected the child.

"They are lovely, kind people. I will stay with you until you feel at home. I promise. You will be quite happy there," she reassured.

"Not fair. I want to stay with you," Simon's little voice echoed the pain in her own heart.

"I'm sorry Simon. I don't like this either. It is the best I can do. Please try to understand," Claire's stricken tone touched him. He could tell she was unhappy.

He thought over what she had told him.

"You promise to stay?" asked the child, doubtfully.

"Of course I will," assured Claire. "Now what do you say? Shall we leave tomorrow?"

"If I have to," he answered, looking about forlornly.

Early the next morning Claire prepared her young charge. She decided to travel south overland. A Graenwolven escort took them as far as the Leanorian village. Setting out on foot, they walked the final four kilometres to the farm. Halfway there, she hoisted him on her back. Resting his chin on her left shoulder, Simon watched a grove of evergreens come into view.

"Are we going there?" he pointed.

"Yes, dear. It is a lovely home, lots of open space to run, trees to climb and best of all, other children. They are waiting to see you."

They turned into the yard on a dirt track, walked through the grove of pines and stood in front of a screened front porch. Claire took the boy's small hand in hers, climbed two steps and knocked on the door. A scurry of footsteps approached from the other side and the door was flung open.

"They're here!" shouted a young girl of eight years, her eyes twinkling with excitement. Two other children raced to the door and stood behind her beaming.

"Come in Claire," called a woman at the table shelling peas. She stood up from her work, wiped her hands on her apron and crossed the kitchen floor to embrace her in a warm bear hug. "So glad to see you! Come in," she repeated. "You must be tired after your journey."

"Thank you, Josie. It has been a long trek. An overdue one at that."

"Yes, four years overdue," said Josie. She turned and knelt down to greet Simon.

"Well young man, let's have a look at you. Simon is your name. My, aren't you a bonnie one!"

Simon smiled shyly and stuck out his little hand. "Nice to meet you…" He didn't know what to call her.

The woman, realizing his confusion said, "You can call me Josie." She chucked him under his chin in a fond welcoming gesture. The kids bobbing up and down around him were anxious to get acquainted.

"Take Simon's coat," she instructed her eldest child.

"I'm Elsie," she said, smiling widely, as she helped Simon with his coat. "And this here is Peter," she added, pointing to her six-year-old brother, who had stopped bouncing and was watching Simon curiously. "Over there is our Davie. He's almost four."

"Claire, please give me your wrap and we'll sit at the table here. Don't mind the mess," she said, clearing pea pods into the slop bucket. Nothing was wasted. The pigs in the sty would squeal loudly, jostling for position when it was swilled into the trough.

"Will you have a cup of tea? I have some scones baking in the oven. They'll be ready in a few minutes. Children, bring Simon over." She placed a plump cushion on the chair to boost him to table level. "He can sit here."

"That would be lovely, thank you. I am so glad to finally see this day Josie. I promised Simon I would stay until he is settled, if that agrees with you and Karl."

"Of course Claire! No need to ask. You know how we stand on things. Our home is always open to you."

Josie poured a large glass of goat's milk for each of the children and offered Simon a warm scone with raspberry jam. He took a bite, grinning with pleasure at the delicious berry spread. He'd never tasted anything like it. The cold milk left a pleasant after taste on his tongue. Elsie sat on one side of Simon and her brother Peter on the other, engaging him in their banter. Davie sat next to his mother, smiling bashfully at Simon. Claire's mind was eased by the relationship developing between them. Simon would be well cared for and happy with the Dugalls.

The children began telling him a story about the goats that roamed freely in the yard.

"You should have seen it," giggled Elsie. "We were all playing outside and Mama left the front door open. It was so funny!

Nanny Goat came running out of the house with a gingersnap hanging out of her mouth!"

"Yeah," laughed Peter. "Stole it right off this kitchen table! Good thing they weren't still hot!"

"You'll love Nanny Goat! And wait 'til you see the kids she has. Two of the cutest little goats ever!" Elsie was beside herself with excitement.

"Now Billy Goat! You got 'a be a little careful around him," continued Peter. "He likes to butt you with his head. Mostly he's protecting his family I think. He doesn't butt too hard. Just gives us a warning look most times."

"Come on Simon, finish your milk. Let's go see them," said Elsie. Simon gulped down his last swallow, eyeing the plate of scones and raspberry jam. He would have to wait to be offered another.

"Thank you Josie. It's the best!"

Claire gave him a nod of approval. He jumped down from the chair and followed Elsie, Peter and Davie who had already disappeared through the screen door, their happy voices calling back, "Thank you Mama!"

Josie and Claire were laughing hysterically at the story, or rather the way Elsie and Peter had told it. For Claire, it was reassuring to see the amusement of the small, shining faces around the table. Tears were running down her cheeks. She wasn't sure if it was from joy or sorrow, for the thought of leaving Simon weighed heavily on her heart.

*

Having witnessed the catastrophic storm at the lake, Sybil and Simon were loath to leave. Many weeks had passed and they grew anxious to complete their mission. Concern about shortened telomeres and aging had been momentarily trumped by the storm. As time passed they grew restless and the nagging worry resurfaced.

"We have to move on," Sybil motioned to Simon, with a wave of her hand. "Our best chance is to return to the dock. Let's try re-entry there." They set off walking across country.

"But where to?" Simon's perplexed scowl mirrored Sybil's uncertainty.

"Not sure. We couldn't communicate in the past with Third dimension Claire. Maybe in the Fifth? We need to try."

Arriving dockside, Sybil wistfully scanned the remnants of the stricken boat still scattered along the shoreline.

"What a tragedy," she sighed.

"This dock has a lot of history," replied Simon. "Let's hold Claire in our thoughts and see where it takes us," he suggested, as they walked to the end of the wharf.

"Dare we risk another? What if we're off again?" asked Sybil.

"We weren't off. I really think we were meant to be here with Claire and Friedrich. It's no coincidence."

"Let's try then. It seems the best option."

Looking across the expanse of lake, now a calm mirror of glass, the images began to shift. Fluid shapes wavered in and out, grew more distinct, and began to take form. Claire's magnetic image standing before a hologram, shimmered, transcended space-time and came sharply into focus. She turned and waved a greeting. Crossing the distance with arms extended, she folded them in a warm embrace.

"Simon! Sybil! At last! I have waited a long time for this moment!"

"Grandmother?"

"No, please call me Claire. Here in the Ninth we are equals. No hierarchy." Welcomed in this way, she affirmed their role. "We need to confer," she said, drawing them close to her.

"We're in the Ninth?" asked Sybil. "Is that what you said? The Ninth dimension?"

"Yes," confirmed Claire. "There is so much to tell you! So little time. Take a look at developments." She swept the air, her arm arcing the hologram from top to bottom.

"See here," she indicated, running her hand over the north. "At the pole, a vortex has developed directly below the ozone portal. It is penetrating the earth's crust." She shuddered, as though a sudden chill raked her body.

"How long has the vortex been there?" Simon asked.

"A fairly recent development in Earth time, perhaps a half-century or so. More recently it has begun to enlarge," replied Claire.

"What does that mean?" asked Simon.

"It means that the invasion force from Seventh will sweep into Fifth from there. And the Third could be next to fall."

"We spent time in the Seventh dimension. Aquadorus is a ruthless tyrant," declared Sybil.

"I haven't much knowledge of the Seventh," replied Claire. "I know they are Aquadrians, beyond that…what manner of race inhabits it?"

"It seems they are hybrid humanoids. Mutating from am-phibious to aquatic. Won't be able to survive out of water much longer," advised Simon.

"And multiplying rapidly!" added Sybil. "Before long they won't have enough land base—er water base, that is. From what we have learned, Aquadorus means to flood the Seventh com-pletely," said Sybil."

"So! Flood the Seventh, then access the Fifth through the vortex. We must stop him!" cried Claire, realizing the implica-tions.

"How can this be happening?" asked Sybil.

"A half-century ago there was a terrible battle. Aquadorus fought the Dragon of the Universe. In this battle the dragon lost its eye crystal. It was hurled through space-time and is commonly believed to have landed somewhere in the Third dimension."

"The Dragon of the Universe? Never heard of it! And the crystal is in the Third dimension?" asked Simon.

"Yes. The Dragon of the Universe. Universal power—energy some call it. Without the eye crystal the quantum field remains unbalanced. The universe is thrown off. That's where you come in. Do you think you can find the crystal in Third?"

"Where is the dragon now?" Sybil tensed. Fear distorted her face and leapt across the space between them, sending shivers up Simon's spine. He grabbed her hand and held it tightly.

"No need to be frightened," Claire quickly reassured. "Dragons have been given a bad reputation in Third. The Dragon of the Universe is nothing like that!"

"Yeah, fire breathing and all that. You sure?"

"Yes, of course Sybil. I wouldn't ask you and Simon if that was the case. The Dragon of the North is a gentle creature."

They visibly relaxed and Simon released Sybil's hand. He rubbed his palms against his tunic, wiping away the film of moisture that had collected.

Claire continued, "We fear that the dragon is in Seventh. In captivity."

"You mean the dragon was there all along? While we lived there?" asked Simon.

"The eye crystal must be restored. It will be up to you and Sybil. We're counting on you."

"Us? We can try to find the crystal. But you want us to go to Seventh? To find the dragon and restore the crystal?" Sybil's jaw dropped when she realized the full impact of what they were being asked to do.

"Yes, I hope you will. There is no one else who can do this. You know the Third. You're coming to full power, now that you are reunited. And you have been to Seventh. Familiarity with the lay of the land goes well in your favour."

Seeking to reassure them, she consulted the writings of long ago, riffling the air with her long fingers. Here in the Book of Wisdom, what does it say? The script settled into place.

Days of Reckoning

Gathered forces, balances shift,
Earth in peril, mantle's rift.
Seek the gemstone of long ago,
Hurled to Third amidst snow.
Return to Third, retrieve anew,
Balance restore, Earth renew.

A sudden inspiration escaped Sybil's lips, "Simon! Back where I started!" Her hands clasped his arm with excitement and all thoughts of danger vanished.

The hologram snapped shut and the page from the Book of Wisdom faded.

"We must go!"

"Where are we going Sybil?"

"Back to where I started!"

"Sorry Sybil. Where did you start?"

"You know. The field trip!" Sybil's fevered pitch conveyed a sense of urgency he had not seen before.

"I'll explain on the way. We have to leave now!"

"Goodbye Claire. We'll meet again soon." They enfolded her in their arms for one last embrace. Simon gave her a long hug. The warmth of the strong shoulder was familiar. The sudden realization that this was the same one on which he had rested his chin when he first saw the evergreen grove, struck him with tremendous force. This was the lovely woman with whom he

335

had travelled south to Leanoria! He disengaged, holding her at arm's length.

"Claire! It was you who brought me to the Fifth!" His face distorted with disbelief. An uncontrollable wave of anger exploded in his brain. "How could you!?"

His warm brown eyes now held a cold glint of steel. Claire could see the turmoil, a seething well of fury tightening his features.

Turning to Sybil, she asked beseechingly, "You both do know the seriousness of what you have discovered and what needs to be done?"

She studied his tightly drawn features, then began hesitantly in a calm voice.

"Simon. Do you believe in what you are doing?"

"But to take me from my family? Wasn't there any other way?" replied Simon, fighting his rage. His mind was reeling from the knowledge.

"It was the only thing I could think to do at the time," said Claire, her voice wavering from the weight of her decision. "If enemy forces had discovered you…" She looked imploringly from one to the other. "If you had been taken together, this chance for survival…" She sagged with weariness.

Simon studied her a long moment, recalling their encounter with her in Third dimension. She was that joyful, happy woman, that proud, hard-working woman, the woman who cared deeply for her family. He recalled the terrible storm, the suffering of unimaginable tragedy. Claire was a strong woman, one who had known joy and loss. The decision she had made, the sacrifice that impacted on their lives—did it not reveal her strength, her will to do what needed to be done? The repercussion on her own life was enormous. Who was he to judge? He was flesh of her flesh, bone of her bone. He reigned in the turbulence that was consuming him.

Sybil could feel his thought processes. "Simon," she began gently. "Claire has made the right decision."

"Yes," he said, hesitating. "I am beginning to understand that."

Drawing a deep breath, his arms relaxed, as he came full circle. He realized that he loved her. She was counting on them. He turned to Claire. Gently placing his hands on her shoulders, he lifted her chin so he could look into her eyes, the same warm brown eyes he and Sybil had inherited.

"You are a remarkable woman." He drew her into his arms. "I am proud to be family."

He turned to include Sybil and they stood together in a long warm embrace, letting the strength of their bond cement the course of action she had set them on, all those long years ago.

Sybil released them both. "We must go."

Simon hesitated. Turning back to Claire, he asked, "What happened? After you took me from the hospital?"

"I was betrayed by an old friend. You were gone for four years, but we never gave up hope."

Claire turned away, misty-eyed. "You must hurry. No time to explain all that. Remember, I am only a thought away now."

"Grandmother, thank you!" Hierarchy or not, at heart she would always be grandmother to them. "Claire, thank you." They turned to leave and waved farewell.

CHAPTER SIXTEEN
Dragon of the Universe

Streaking across the flatlands, over the Roccocian range, desperately hoping her theories were correct, they neared the coastal area.

"Not much further now. We need to head directly to Spoon Lake below Mount Cheam!"

"What are we looking for?" asked Simon.

"Something very shiny," replied Sybil. "Pray it is still there!"

Realizing she had not told him the full story of how she came to the Fifth, she began to tell him about the moonlight swim in Spoon Lake, the earthquake, the terror of her wild ride and her first encounter with Maerwyn.

"That's some story!" said Simon. "After hearing that, I'd say we're getting better at realm travel! Don't always need a portal anymore!"

"For sure! Time travel helps but what did the Hetopians tell us? Once a portal has been opened, it enlarges each time it is used. And of course the age thing with time travel—still very troubling."

"Yes, that's what they said." Suddenly he understood. "You're going to try the Spoon Lake portal!"

"Should work! We can enter from the top. If it is larger, I think we can miss the water. Don't really want to get wet if I can help it."

"I hope you're right." Then another thought occurred to him. "Did the Hetopians say if it ever stops enlarging?"

"Nothing said about that. Crickey, there's a thought! And does is ever close up again?"

"Sheesh! Let's not talk about that now!"

The thought of getting stuck and having to search for another way out—best left alone for the time being. They made a mental note to ask Longille and Maerwyn.

After sunset, the first stars glimmered feebly in the pale sky when they swooped into the basin below Mount Cheam. The full moon rising in the eastern horizon, cast elongated shadows below Lady Peak.

"I can feel it drawing us in already Simon."

"Yes, it's getting stronger. We'd better hang on to each other."

Linking up, they maneuvered closer. They were pulled in suddenly, moving at warp speed, twisting, turning and gliding through space-time, first through darkness, then drifting through a space alight with a myriad of stars. Then darkness again at top speed through a tunnel of dazzling colours. They were thrust out at the edge of Spoon Lake.

"If the portal was the lake, then it's larger now. By about three metres," said Sybil, estimating the perimeter. "That makes it a whole lot easier."

"The northern portal in the Fifth must be gigantic. Is that why the rift is developing in the earth's mantle?"

"Very likely. I wonder how wise this is. To enlarge portals?"

"Well, we're here now, we'll go back the same way. Either way has its disadvantages."

Sybil had already moved on. She scoured the terrain, searching for the unworldly glitter she had seen, when she was caught in the churning pandemonium. The earthquake that rocked the region had uncovered something. She was certain. It sparkled in the light of the moon that night. How long ago was that? It couldn't be more than four or five months. Maybe less? Time travel was confusingly fluid.

"Hamish called to me and Marc from that bank over there. He wanted us to see something. Marc got out of the water. That's when the earthquake struck."

They sharpened their concentration, focusing together on the south bank where the pile of debris had been thrown upon impact.

Just below the surface, lay a large crystal reburied by the tremors of the quake. As the moon emerged from behind a cloud, a tiny sparkle danced off the tip, that lay partially exposed.

"There! Help me dig!" shouted Sybil.

"I see it!"

They knelt to the job, clawing at the loose soil.

Two Hetopians accelerating over the tip of Lady Peak, glided into the valley floor. They accessed the portal and landed in Third, beside Spoon Lake. Still digging, Simon and Sybil were unaware of their arrival.

A shout of jubilation rang out, "Sybil, Simon! You're safe! Wonderful to see you!"

Startled by the sudden voices behind them, they gasped, leapt from their knees and spun around.

"Maerwyn! Longille! Give us some warning before you sneak up on us like that!"

"Sorry Sybil. Simon. Didn't mean to startle you. Never thought! Sorry, so sorry!" They dipped their heads slightly, beaming with pleasure, both overjoyed to see them again. "We were terribly worried. Had no idea what happened after you were pulled into the ozone portal," said Maerwyn.

"We've kept watch every day. Delighted to see you!" Longille's pearly grin flashed in the moonlight.

"Great to be back, but we haven't much time," Simon replied.

"I think we've found something we need!" Sybil's excitement punctuated the night air.

Simon knelt to finish the task and unearthed the brilliant stone.

"Found what?" asked Maerwyn.

"The dragon's eye crystal!" cried Simon, holding it up to the night sky. Moonbeams scattered dancing points of light off the crystal's facets, as Simon turned it, admiring the unworldly beauty.

Sybil caressed the surface. "The dragon's eye crystal. It has to be!"

"You mean the Dragon of the Universe? But what is the crystal doing here in the Third dimension?" asked Longille, looking dumbfounded.

"Claire told us about the terrible battle, in which the dragon lost its eye crystal. It was Aquadorus who fought the Dragon of the Universe and is now holding it captive. The eye crystal was hurled through space-time," said Simon. "You know of the dragon?"

"Yes. The Fifth knows. But we had no idea about the battle and the crystal! And who is Aquadorus?"

"He's the ruler of Seventh. A nasty one. He means to take over the Fifth and who knows from there, maybe even the Third."

Longille and Maerwyn paled in the moonlight. Sybil noticed a moist sheen developing on their faces. The news had rattled them.

"What's to be done?" asked Maerwyn, his voice betraying the uncertainty their news had brought.

"The impact of the crystal created Spoon Lake! That's why I could enter the Fifth through it! We have to find the dragon and restore crystal power," said Sybil.

"Who is this Claire, you mentioned?" Longille asked.

"Our great-great-great-grandmother—that's three greats if you lost count. Claire of the Ninth dimension," Sybil explained.

"It was Claire who brought me to Fifth, but her plans did not work as she had hoped. She was betrayed by an old friend."

The thought of it still jarred him. But he was caught up in the turbulent times unfolding and decided not to dwell on it. There would be time enough to sort it through later.

"The old woman!" Sybil's face lit up with sudden revelation. "The one who lives in Aquadria!"

"Claire's friend from Third? Adelaide?" Simon's surprise nearly toppled him. "Her son Benni died in the storm! It must've been Adelaide! We were that close!"

"She won't survive the flood! Aquadorus will double-cross her." Sybil's anger flared. "Serves her right!"

Then she remembered the storm and poor Benni lying in the splintered boat. It was hard to include Adelaide and Benni in the same thought. The treachery. What she had put Simon through—what they were going through now. She needed to talk to Claire, but when that would happen, she did not know. The task at hand was immediate.

Rotating the crystal in his hands, Simon turned his attention to what needed to be done.

"If the dragon is still in Seventh..." He groaned, realizing the enormous undertaking that lay ahead of them.

"No other way around it," concluded Sybil.

Simon handed her the crystal. "Here, hide it under your cloak Sybil."

She accepted the crystal, tucked it safely inside and they lifted off. After exiting the portal the four friends sped eastward to the flatlands and entered the Plasmic Energy Force streaking northward to the pole. The Aurora Borealis danced brightly across the northern hemisphere.

Hovering at the edge of the magnetic force, the Hetopians wished them well. "We'll wait for you with Empress Icelandia. Meet us there."

Zooming across the Aurora display, they entered the ozone rift hurtling through a maze of space-time. Guiding their travel, they kept the Opeggees in mind. They came out at the base of the cliff and started to climb, calling out to Roark as they gained elevation.

"Roark! It's Sybil and Simon. We're on our way up!"

When they neared the top, Roark, who had come out to meet them, let out a surprised squawk of welcome.

"Simon, Sybil! Thank the Universal Stars! You're back! Things are bad in the Seventh."

Sybil came straight to the point, "Roark, we need your help! Aquadorus has captured the Dragon of the Universe and is holding it in captivity. Have the Opeggees seen or heard anything?"

"The Dragon of the Universe! Here in Seventh? Had no idea. Nothing's been heard."

"We'll need to search then."

"Oh good, good, good! A scouting mission! At last, something we Opeggees can do!" He sent a telepath to Meerak. She would alert the rookery and get things organized.

Upon reaching the cliff top, they were greeted by loud barking. The big male hurtled toward them.

"Here boy, good dog!" shouted Sybil. The hound leapt around them in frenzied circles, jumping up to lick their cheeks, dashing away and circling back. Excited guttural sounds came from deep in the back of his throat.

"He's one very smart hound, all right!" laughed Roark. "Watch this!"

"*Sit!*" Roark commanded. Obediently the dog sat in front of Roark.

"*Down!*" he signalled with his wing tip, and immediately he sank to his belly.

"*Roll over!*" Roark twirled his wing tip in a circular motion. The hound did a complete rotation and sat up panting excitedly.

"*Fetch!*" he shouted, as he threw a stick across the clearing.

The hound bounded over, grabbed the stick, ran back and dropped it at Roark's two red feet.

"How did you get him to do all that?" cried Simon.

"Didn't take long," Roark chortled. "And have you noticed? It's all in Telepath!" he said, gleefully.

"Are you serious?" cried Simon.

"Hey, perfect name!" said Sybil, astonished by the performance. "Sirius! We'll call him Sirius! Sirius the Dog Star!"

Roark bobbed up and down excitedly. "Awesome name! And a star he certainly is!"

"*Sirius come!*" he called, and the hound pranced over to the Opeggee, his tongue lolling out happily.

"*Come Sirius!*" called Sybil. The hound pivoted and raced over to Sybil, brushing against her legs. "*Sit Sirius!*" she ordered and Sirius sat beside her, happy to have her back.

"He certainly is excited!" laughed Simon. "This time when we leave, you can come," Simon reassured him. He slapped his thigh, encouraging the dog to his side. "*Come Sirius.*"

He knelt down, caught the furry jowls between his hands and looked into the hound's huge brown eyes. "What do you think boy? Sirius. Good name for you?" Sirius gave an excited woof and licked Simon's nose.

Sybil laughed, "Sirius it is! No doubt about that." She squatted beside Simon, encircled the dog's torso with her arms and hugged him close.

"Smart dog! Hey Sirius?" Simon reinforced the behaviour by giving his massive head a playful tussle. "It's this big brain of yours!"

"Not so surprising. He understood the mind net and got himself to the Seventh!" laughed Sybil.

"We're taking him back to Third when we go," said Simon adamantly.

"No quarrel from me on that. Sirius needs a home and we can give it to him."

Roark looked a little downcast. "I'll miss him. He's a great companion."

"Sorry Roark. Thank you so much for looking after him for us."

"Sirius is your dog. Rightfully," agreed Roark. "Maybe one day we will have one. The rookery could use a good watch dog."

Meerak came out to greet them. "Sybil! Simon! Welcome back! Good to see you both safe and well."

"Hello Meerak. Nice to be back with you. Thank you for allowing Roark to take Sirius for us."

"Oh, he has a name?" she asked, delighted by the choice.

"Yes, just now. Simon and I have decide to give him a permanent home."

"Wonderful news! He is a lovable sort. Very clever too!"

Turning to other concerns, she added, "We have organized a search throughout the whole of Aquadria. Our squadrons left immediately."

The group climbed to the lookout at the top most part of the cliff to watch for the search parties. Flying the breadth of Aquadria, they regrouped and set out time and again as they worked their way across the land conducting a thorough search of the region.

"This is time consuming!" lamented Sybil. "We need to step up the search. Let's join them Simon."

Meerak intervened, "No, Sybil. Leave it to us. Let them make one more pass toward the north. If they spot you, we're done."

Sybil hesitated, then acquiesced. "Of course, you're right. But if that fails, Simon and I will have to try." The flock, which had returned, set off once more flying swiftly to the northern most regions of the territory.

"I can't sit here and wait Simon," Sybil's impatience got the best of her. "If we don't find the dragon soon, it'll be too late."

"Just a bit longer, Sybil," replied Simon. His steady voice held her in check but her exasperation threatened to spill over onto him. How can he be so cool and collected at a time like this?

They were scanning the horizon for signs of the returning Opeggees, when suddenly Sybil let out a whoop.

"There to the right!"

A lone Opeggee was hurtling toward them, flying at breakneck speed. He back flapped frantically to slow himself and slid onto the rock face beside them.

"Think we found the dragon!" he gasped, struggling to catch his breath. "Large contingent! Far! Edge of Aquadria. Farther than we've ever flown!"

Meerak looked shocked, "How far is this?"

"More than three times the distance we thought before!" replied Fergak, the Opeggee scout.

"Surprising!" Meerak's worried voice revealed the strain she was under. "Had no idea!"

"Let's go Simon!" Sybil shouted. "We have to find the dragon! We'll take Sirius with us. That keen bloodhound nose of his will help."

346

They formed the mind net and Sirius hopped aboard. The contentment he felt was complete. While the rookery and Roark had been great fun he knew his place was with Sybil and Simon. He loved Roark, had learned a lot from him and there would always be a special place in his heart for him. And Mother Meerak had been so kind. They were Sybil's and Simon's friends. He owed them a lot and would always feel protective of them.

Meerak nodded, "I will stay with the young ones. Roark, fetch the vulcan sacs please. It is our only defense against them."

Roark flew off and returned shortly with small sacs slung around his neck. Closing in behind him, a large rank of youthful Opeggees bearing sacs, fell into place.

"Roark, you are in charge of this. Go with them. Follow Fergak. You can explain on the way."

"Right Mama!" Roark, excited at the prospect of his first mission, puffed up his chest feathers.

The large force lifted off the rock cliff. "Stay safe my dears!" Meerak's tender voice blessed them as they flew out of sight.

"The vulcan sacs!" Roark's excited voice peppered the air as they flew north. "Every year we collect volcanic pellets."

Fergak interjected, "Most extraordinary things!"

"Let me tell!" Roark's disappointed cry cut him short.

"Of course Roark, so sorry, go ahead," said Fergak, recalling the thrill of his own first mission.

"As I said, the pellets. After our initiation flights we become young commanders. It is our duty to return to the volcanic hatching fields. We gather astonishing amounts of pellets."

Fergak interrupted again, "Yes, these young ones have great responsibility. Roark here is one of our most dedicated."

This time Roark didn't mind the interruption so much. He swelled with pride at Fergak's praise. He carried on, "We'll distribute them to all our people when we link up. If the Aquadrians want a fight, a fight they will get."

"How do the pellets work?" Simon asked.

"As Fergak said, most extraordinary things. Drop one of those—KABOOM! Instant lava flow!"

Approaching the frontier, they gained altitude to survey the larger scene. The Opeggees, who had been in holding formation waiting for Fergak's return, flew to greet them.

"Glad you're back!" cried a senior Opeggee named Profrak. "We haven't been spotted."

"Mama sent reinforcements with vulcan sacs," reported Roark, his strong blue wings sweeping over the force of young Opeggees behind him.

"Good work son. Your Mama is a capable woman!" Profrak responded. "Young Opeggees, job well done! See to it that everyone gets a sac," he ordered. "Now Opeggees, you know the routine. We only use these when necessary. If you hear my order to drop, you will do so. Then, and only then. We will back Sybil and Simon if it comes to a fight."

Roark was a little disappointed. He was anxious to test his nerve in battle. Being asked to show restraint in such desperate times was frustrating. He held his tongue and accepted his orders, respectful of his rank. He realized he had much to learn.

"Now my friends," said Profrak, turning to Sybil and Simon. "Tell us what you have in mind."

Sybil addressed the crowd first. "We think the Dragon of the Universe may be held in this compound. Our purpose, we believe, is to restore the dragon's eye crystal. The Book of Wisdom supports this theory."

Simon resumed, as Sybil paused for breath. "It will be safer to hunt for the dragon after dark. Once we find it, we must restore the eye crystal and get out. We have faith the dragon will take it from there."

Profrak acknowledged their plan with a spread of his wings, indicating his agreement.

"Okay folks, we have a few hours of daylight left. Maintain holding pattern for now," suggested Profrak. The entire force flipped over on their backs, their wings sculling air in leisurely strokes. Some of them nodded off, content to let updrafts arising from the south buoy them while they rested.

"Amazing people aren't they?" said Sybil.

"Yes, they may look like birds, but I've come to regard them as people. And good people they are. Profrak will not use force unless absolutely necessary. He's a wise guide."

"We'll do our best to avoid it, but I have no doubt he will have our backs if there's trouble. With any luck we should be out of there in ten minutes."

Night fell and shadows deepened. There was very little light from the glow fish this far north. "I hadn't counted on it being so dark," Sybil confided. Her nervous fidgeting was making Simon edgy.

"Breathe Sybil. Together," he prompted, taking a long slow inhalation. She had taught him this, now he reminded her. After a few minutes, her hands stilled, but she remained apprehensive.

"It's just so dark," she repeated.

"With our eyesight? No problem!"

"Yes, of course! I'm still not used to all that." At least they had something in their favour.

"And we have the greatest bloodhound ever!" Simon tousled the dog's scruff. "Hey Sirius? You are the best. Aren't you?"

Sirius woofed softly and licked his hand. "We'll need you to help us find the dragon. Use that sensitive nose of yours, okay bud?"

A soft high-pitched whine told them he was anxious to get started. His tail wagged and he wriggled with anticipation.

"Not long now Sirius." Sybil restrained him, laying her hand on his head.

She watched the Opeggees sculling the air. They seemed at ease. Why was she so nervous? She thought of the search ahead and wondered. The unknown was always hard. It'll be okay once we begin, she promised herself.

After advising Profrak that they were leaving in five minutes, he sent out an all points telepathic message to his people.

"Everyone look alive! Mustering in five minutes." The Opeggees became alert, flipped over onto their stomachs and readied themselves.

"May the Universe be with you!" Profrak's steady voice strengthened their resolve.

"Thank you Profrak. Listen for the all clear signal."

Shifting into stealth mode, Sybil and Simon sped towards the encampment looking for the compound. Focusing carefully on the scene below, they came directly over the command centre. Two sentries were on guard at the entrance. All was quiet. Cruising high over the gatehouse they surveyed the area.

"There, over to the right. Looks promising," Simon switched to Telepath.

"Gently now, lower, lower. It's an open pit! We'll have to go into it…" Sybil's alarm stretched her nerves to breaking point. They were bow-string tight. There could be a guard posted. Or some unknown threat could be lingering inside.

Simon's trepidation grew, as they approached the black pit yawning before them. His determination shriveled. *"We have to? What should we do?"*

"Yes, we have to!"

She hesitated, looking to Simon for some sort of sign. Was he as scared as she was?

"Woof!" Sirius wriggled with excitement.

"Quiet Sirius," warned Simon. Realizing the danger of being discovered, he stilled him with his hand. *"You need to be quiet, Sirius."*

It won't take him long to catch on thought Simon. He was glad to have Sirius with them but realized he would need further training in this. Then he grabbed Sybil's hand, gripping it tightly. *"Yes, we have to!"*

They forged ahead, flying cautiously through the dark opening. Just inside the pit a sentry jumped forth, blocking their way.

"Who goes there?"

Sybil and Simon came to an abrupt stop. With explosive force, Sirius leapt off the mind net throwing himself at the figure. He latched onto the sentry's leg and yanked. With a mighty tug he felled the sentry, pulling his legs out from under him. He pounced on his chest with his front paws and clamped onto his throat pinning him to the ground.

Simon and Sybil gasped at the speed of Sirius's assault.

"Good boy! Hold him!" The Hetopians had prepared them well with a field kit. Simon felt in the bag and came up with a rope. He bound the sentry's wrists and secured them to his ankles, effectively hobbling him. Sirius stood alert, body tense, ready for action.

"Do you think we should bring him aboard with Sirius?" asked Sybil.

"Don't know how that would go. Maybe Sirius won't let him. Nah, leave him here. He's not going anywhere. Come on Sirius."

They slowly accelerated, skimming low to search the hollows cut into the side walls. Deep inside, their eyes adjusted. Pitch black darkness faded to gloom. They stopped, listening for sound.

Gentle snoring came from a black area near the back of the pit. Hovering closer, they peered into the darkness. Lying at the back of the depression they discovered a large form curled up sleeping peacefully. Softly they approached the slumbering figure and studied the outline. The body was very large with two wings folded neatly along the upper back. Its long neck stretched out across the floor in front of them. In the dimness they could see a comely head with elegant ears resting along the sides of it. The skin appeared soft as velvet in the low light.

"Now what do we do?" asked Simon, reluctant to disturb the peaceful atmosphere.

"Claire says it's a gentle dragon. Why don't we try to wake it?" replied Sybil hesitantly, unsure if this was the right course of action.

"All right, let's get this over with. You with me?" asked Simon. He dropped to the soft sand on the floor of the pit.

"Of course I'm with you," replied Sybil, landing beside him.

A low rumble issued from Sirius's throat. *"Easy boy. Stay Sirius,"* commanded Simon. The hound settled reluctantly. He wasn't sure what this was. The scent was foreign, though it did not smell of danger. Simon and Sybil didn't seem to be alarmed so maybe it was nothing to fear.

Suddenly the dragon's ears twitched and slowly rose to attention.

"Who's there?" a soft voice chimed. *"Is anyone there?"* repeated the dragon. There was an undercurrent of anxiety brimming the surface. The dragon had been vanquished for many years and the loneliness of its exile weighed heavily. It perceived the presence of three forms, somewhere to the side of its long neck.

"Who's there? Please." The inquiry conveyed an undertow of fearfulness, as it turned its head toward the unknown figures. It sniffed the air trying to discern the foreign entities. *"You aren't Aquadrian."*

The uncertainty of its plea aroused a tender compassion that swelled inside Simon. He sensed the dragon's apprehension, could feel the long lonely years of frustration endured in solitary confinement, as surely as if he had been in the pit himself. The icy fear he had flown in with was replaced by a caring so deep, it flowed out of him toward the gentle creature in distress. He understood all too well the bonds of captivity.

"You speak Telepath?" asked Simon, awed by the knowledge. Then quickly added, *"Have no fear. We mean no harm."*

The dragon relaxed visibly but remained cautious. *"I do speak Telepath. It is the language of mystics."*

"We come in peace Dragon of the Universe," reassured Sybil, keeping her voice soft and gentle.

"You have the gift too, I see," replied the dragon, turning in her direction, somewhat reassured.

"We have been sent by Claire of the Ninth," added Sybil.

"Ah, that good woman," said the dragon, trust and hope beginning to seep into the chasm of loneliness. *"Why has she sent you?"*

"Your lost eye crystal. We have come to restore it to you," replied Sybil.

"You found it!?" said the astounded dragon, the beginnings of trust now turning to joy. *"Where? I have been waiting a very long time for this."*

"It was discovered in the Third realm. A place called Spoon Lake," replied Sybil. *"Near where I live."*

"What are your names dear ones?" asked the dragon, switching languages, when it realized she was from Third dimension.

"I am Sybil. Claire is our grandmother from long ago. Many generations past."

"And I am Simon. We are brother and sister."

"You must be the ones!" cried the dragon, overjoyed. "At last. The writings in the Book of Wisdom! It makes sense!"

"Do you have a name?" Sybil asked. "What shall we call you? Dragon of the Universe?"

"No. I *am* the Dragon of the Universe, but you can call me DOU—like the word NOW. It's much easier, less formal."

"That wouldn't be respectful," replied Sybil.

"Nonsense, it has the same meaning," reassured the dragon. "The Ninth maintains no hierarchy. A name is just a name. It conveys neither respect nor disrespect. It just is."

"That's what Claire told us. She insisted we call her Claire, not grandmother."

"It's neither here nor there," replied the dragon. "If you'd rather call me Dragon of the Universe you may, but DOU is much simpler. I take no offense. I like DOU myself—it conveys the energy of friendship."

"Then DOU it is." Sybil and Simon were so at ease, they wondered why they had feared to come.

"But there are three of you. There is someone else beside you."

The years spent in blind captivity had heightened the dragon's awareness. It could feel another presence.

"Sirius is a little hard to explain," replied Simon. "Why don't you replace your crystal and you can see for yourself."

"This is indeed a fortuitous moment in Ninth history. Oh how I have yearned for this," said the dragon, excitement mounting in its chest. "Let us proceed."

Sybil brought forth the crystal and held it aloft. It sparkled in the depths of the pit. Simon reached over to caress the surface. The soft coolness began to glow, as the dragon sensed its nearness. The hollow cavity where it had sat in the centre of its forehead quivered and the flap of its eyelid retracted. The crystal came to life of its own accord. It left Sybil's hand and floated gently into place.

A resounding pop echoed in the cave as the crystal connected. The energy force surged and the quantum field generated flow, beginning the transformational balance. The dragon, now fully engaged, blinked the sleep from its eye. Sharpening its focus, it shone glorious DOU radiance on Sybil and Simon. Bathed in the brilliance of universal energy, deep peace resonated within. Gazing star-struck into the depths of the restored crystal, stunning vistas opened before them. The vast expanding universe resonated at a profound level, as they were drawn into the mysteries of deep space, intensifying the encounter. What they were experiencing in the outer realm was replicated within, as a manifold revelation of inter-connectedness. Time floated on a haze of ecstasy drawing them into the mysterious realm of the dragon. They were at one with the whole of the universe. They were held spell-bound, resting in the security of presence, as full and abiding as the moment of now. There was no past and no future, only the safety of the present moment. DOU was the present moment.

"Magnificent!" breathed Simon and Sybil, as one voice.

"Magnificent!" replied the dragon. "Now you see all there is to behold, what it can mean for our world—across all dimensions. This universal energy flows through all, connects all. Not one part can stand alone. We are One."

Sybil's thoughts drifted on the solar winds, wavering, then slowly re-emerged in the pit. The experience left her with a deep and enduring sense of harmony. She felt Simon's presence next to her, encompassed by the totality of all that is. They exchanged glances, knowing that each had had the same experience. The abundance of the universe held them in the palm of its hand. Memories of the pool in the Wellness Sanctuary resurfaced and she realized the Hetopian civilization was evolved to a high degree.

"And now, who is this with you?" the dragon indicated, bathing Sirius in the glow of the crystal beam. Sirius who instinctively understood the meaning of the dragon, responded to the magnificence flowing around and through him. He felt his own goodness affirmed by the gentleness before him.

"This is Sirius, our bloodhound."

"You are very special. I can see that," replied the dragon. The crystal flashed a brilliant sparkle affirming the comment in the depths of Sirius's soul.

The hound wriggled closer, yearning for the gentle nature that touched his being. He was a creature of the universe deserving of love and affection. Sirius didn't dare lick the dragon but he wanted to. Instead, he gave a soft, "Woof!" He wriggled forward again to within inches of the dragon's feet. He inhaled the scent of the dragon, letting it fill him to overflowing, as his love flowed off the wag of his tail. It was very much like the memories of that day in the mountain top meadow playing with Simon and Sybil. It was the same glorious smell coming from the meadow!

The dragon reached out with its wingtip and caressed his head. Sirius gave a soft yap. Happiness spilled over and he began to run in circles around Sybil and Simon leaping with joy, his love binding them together, his unconditional loyalty pledged forever.

"You have restored the Power of the Universe! The crystal aligns all energy with the quantum force field. Thank you!" The dragon's jubilant voice resonated deep peace.

A commotion at the far side of the pit raised alarm. The force of the re-engaged crystal had awakened slumbering guards. A group of them had arrived at the pit and released their bound up comrade. It sounded like a whole army running across the shadowy depths, the slap of flippers resounding off the walls.

"DOU!" cried Sybil and Simon. The peace of the moment was shattered by the reality of the danger rushing toward them.

"I am free!" cried the dragon. The power welled up inside, breaking the bonds holding it in place. DOU rose out of the pit, and beckoned them to follow. Sirius leapt onto the mind net and they swept into the air. The dragon shone a beam of light into the open pit, bathing the confused sentries in a warm glow of understanding. They dropped their weapons and stood inert, a fleeting look of awe washing over them. They had caught a glimpse of what the dragon could mean for them.

"Rally!" cried one of the leaders. "Pick up your weapons you fools!" In swift obedience they leapt into action.

The dragon slowly circled with Sybil and Simon. The view from above showed a pathetic group of confused individuals amassed as a fighting force, oblivious to anything but blind obedience. The dragon felt a deep sense of pity, which emanated from the crystal in its forehead. It suffused Sybil and Simon with a clear understanding of what it means to be Dragon of the Universe. Sirius gave a loud bark of warning and an irresistible peace swept over him. He settled in the mind net ready for the flight to freedom. DOU nodded and they rose as one and flew off.

Once they gained safe altitude, a profound sense of awe held Sybil and Simon spell-bound. What they had just experienced was so far beyond any reality they had ever known, they were speechless. As the distance between them and the pit grew, they slowly roused, gaining their equilibrium.

"Simon, what did we just see?" asked Sybil, trembling with excitement.

"Beyond anything I have ever known!" Simon's voice betrayed the quivering mass of emotion in his chest.

"What this could mean for humanity, for everyone! In all dimensions!" Sybil was beside herself with the simplicity of it all.

"Compassion, the root of love..." Simon's feelings overflowed as he wept at the realization.

"In the here and now..." added Sybil.

A profound understanding passed between them. They reached out and placed their hands on Sirius's head, allowing a tranquil sense of peace to meld them as one.

"Profrak! We must give him the all clear!" Simon suddenly came to his senses.

"Oh! How could we forget?" cried Sybil, still in a daze. Then she collected her thoughts and sent the pre-arranged signal. *"All clear!"*

The answer came back swiftly. *"Splendid! Waiting and ready to leave!"*

With her spirits flying high on the winds of success, Sybil grabbed Simon's hand in mid-flight and gave it a congratulatory squeeze. "Now we can go home! You too Sirius!"

Together, they flew high into the night to join the Opeggees, then headed southward to the rookery.

Meerak, who had kept watch throughout the night gave a jubilant cheer. "Thank the Universe! You are all safe!"

The dragon alighted gently beside her and beamed, its crystal eye emitting a dazzling glow of gratitude.

"We have no time to stay dear lady, but I do want to say..." The dragon turned to address the crowd.

"My dear friends, the Opeggee nation. This is a momentous turning point in history! All of life in the universe will be gathered as One. We make this transition together. From fierce warriors to Beings of Light, led by compassion for one another. Compassion for all. It is up to you! All of you gathered here! You must work together, strive in your daily lives with the certainty of all that is within you. The goodness that dwells there deep inside, the magnificence you were endowed with from the moment you were formed, that my dear friends is your strength!"

"A half-century ago Aquadorus began his invasion. A terrible battle! The power of the crystal was lost, hurled to Third dimension. My captivity in Aquadria endured. Sybil and Simon were called by the Ninth realm. They have completed the arduous task of restoring the crystal, reclaiming the power of DOU, the Dragon of the Universe." The dragon paused a moment overcome with emotion.

"All here before me have risked their lives! That is the testimony of your love. The universe is deeply grateful! It is hope that sees us through. One must never give up! It is the steadfast faith and courage you have exhibited, it is your willingness to take on the most difficult of tasks, this is what brings hope to fruition! With special gratitude, I thank Sybil and Simon, and Sirius of course!" said the dragon. A sparkle of gratitude landed on the hound sitting quietly between Sybil and Simon. Sirius responded with a soft, "Woof!" and a ripple of laughter passed through the crowd.

"I salute all of you standing here before me. Thank you!"

The dragon bowed with deep humility, reaffirming its undying commitment to the source of life permeating the universe. "It is time for me to leave," said the dragon.

As the brilliance of the crystal swept the crowd, all present were drawn into the overwhelming kindness. For a fleeting moment the way ahead was clear to all. That glimpse would be strength enough to carry them through the turbulent times that lay ahead.

Hope, thought Simon. Maybe there was something to that after all. It was as he had always felt, always believed. It takes hard work and much of that requires courage and perseverance. And sometimes things just fall into place of their own accord.

Sybil and Simon turned to the dragon. "The Fifth played a huge part in this. We must return there before we go home.

"Then I shall come to Fifth with you. Shall we travel together?"

"Delighted!" they grinned broadly.

"Come, let us say our goodbyes," replied DOU.

Sybil and Simon embraced their friends, thanking Profrak and the Opeggees for their generous support. With heavy sadness they bid farewell to Meerak who had welcomed them so openly into her home. Roark approached them gently weeping.

"Don't forget me," he whispered, caressing Simon's shoulder and reaching up to brush Sybil's cheek with his soft blue wing tip.

They couldn't help but exclaim, "Roark! My how you have grown!" He was standing chest high to them.

Roark beamed, then he bent down to Sirius. "You are the best friend an Opeggee kid could ever ask for." He buried his red beak in the hound's ruff and breathed in the scent, committing it to memory.

"We will never forget you and we shall meet again. Friendship like this lasts forever," Sybil and Simon reassured, patting his wings softly. "Until then."

"Come Sirius," they signalled. Bringing him aboard the mind net they lifted off, waving goodbye.

A great cheer went up from the Opeggee crowd. The dragon turned and bathed the crowd in the warm glow of its crystal. "I leave you now my dear friends. Remember, be present. Together we shall prevail!"

Veering north, the four figures disappeared into the sooty darkness. This time the dragon led the way through the continuum of space-time, landing them outside the palace of the Empress Icelandia. A stunning transformation was taking place. Snow was falling, the temperature had dropped and the palace was invitingly open. The force that held the Empress in place, had been broken. Icelandia arrived at the palace entrance and greeted them with a cheer.

"Welcome Dragon of the North, Dragon of the Universe! Welcome to Fifth!"

"Empress Icelandia! All is well!" replied the dragon.

"Sybil, Simon! You've done it!" said Icelandia. "Our most grateful thanks! Please come in. Maerwyn and Longille are waiting for you."

Hearing the commotion outside, Maerwyn and Longille rushed through the door joining the crowd. Their two hounds raced out to greet Sirius, cavorting in circles around Sybil and Simon in joyful reunion.

"Sybil, Simon!" they shouted. The Hetopians hurried forward, enveloping them in a warm embrace.

Turning to the dragon, they dipped a low bow and smiled widely. "Greetings Dragon of the Universe!"

The dragon bowed deeply, acknowledging them with a brilliant sparkle.

Quietly entering the scene, Claire Huber stood silently beside Sybil and Simon. Gradually, they became aware of her presence.

"Claire! You're here!"

Opening her arms wide, she embraced them lovingly.

"Well done," she whispered. "Wouldn't miss this for anything in the world." She smiled warmly.

Her attention was drawn to the dragon who acknowledged them with a brilliant sparkle, its eye casting a warm glow upon the small group gathering outside the palace.

"I am DOU, Dragon of the Universe. To all assembled, I thank you for your bravery."

The Dragon of the Universe launched into the speech given at the Opeggee rookery, while everyone stood rapt in the wonder that lay open before them. The united bond of all those gathered, sent a hush of silence over them as the dragon spoke, drawing them into the beauty of all that is. Presence beyond knowing stilled each heartbeat, as deep ecstasy drew them into the crystal horizons of deep space and time—into the now of DOU the dragon.

"To the Fifth and Third, I commend you for your stalwart faith and courage. The Ninth sought your help and you gave freely. Thank you for the perseverance you have shown all these years in bringing me home."

A hushed murmur swept through the crowd. This is what they had waited for. They had kept hope alive, had endured the ravages of oppression over those long frightful years.

"Remember dear friends," DOU reinforced. "It is you! You have the strength! Beings of Light. Compassion for all! Look within! Take heart. Presence is upon us, we shall prevail."

Looking to Claire, DOU bowed gently. She was largely responsible. It was in her demeanour. The humility, the way she held her head, the softness about her shoulders, it was all there. It was she who had mustered the Ninth, led the thrust; had coordinated the realms.

"Claire of the Ninth. We owe you a huge debt of gratitude. We shall never forget."

Claire smiled and nodded imperceptibly. She was all too aware of the near failure. Then she bowed deeply, accepting the dragon's tribute.

The Dragon of the Universe looked to the north, lifting its head to the sky.

"I must return to the Ninth where I belong. There is much to be done. Stand fast dear friends!"

Looking from Sybil to Simon and back to Sybil, DOU said, "You are just beginning. Much still remains."

"What do you mean?" Simon asked.

"It is *yours* to discover." DOU flashed them a brilliant sparkle. "The Universe is within!"

The dragon lifted off, pivoted in mid-air and said, "Remember, I am as near as your heartbeat. Think of me when you look to the North Star." They watched as the dragon waved a final salute and was gone.

Ω

Group Discussion Questions

1. What does the Dragon of the Universe represent to you?
2. Do you think the characters of Sybil and Simon are symbolic in any way?
3. How do you think Sybil's mother Franceska would feel if she knew who was behind Simon's disappearance?
4. Was Claire Huber right to do what she did? Why or why not?
5. Do you think Adelaide is deranged or is she at the mercy of her basest feelings for another reason? Why?
6. What role do you think Ninth dimension plays? Why are Adelaide and Claire in the Ninth?
7. Why doesn't Adelaide meet her son in the Ninth dimension?
8. Do you think there are other dimensions?
9. What do you think has happened to the Graenwolven citizenry? What has happened to the Leanorians?
10. Do you think Simon's family are still alive in the Fifth? If so, what do you think has happened to them?
11. How would you feel if you had two families? What constitutes a family?
12. What makes Wesley act the way he does? Why do some people bully others?
13. Do you think they are born that way or do things happen to make them bullies?
14. Could they choose not to bully and what would it take in order for them to change?
15. Would you like to live in Hetopia? Why or why not?
16. Would you like to live in any of the other dimensions? Why or why not?

S. S. Huber – Rise of the Dragon

CHAPTER ONE
Chaos in Seventh

✫

Sybil patted her thigh, "Come Sirius. Time to leave." The large hound capered to her side, licked her fingertips and whimpered. He turned and scuttled away, then came back and whined again.

"What's wrong big fella?" She knelt and tussled his ruff. Letting her hands slide to the dog's ears, she turned his head toward her. The intelligent brown eyes reflected concern. There was tension in the depths.

Simon knelt beside her and stroked his back. "Something isn't right Sybil. Sirius is trying to tell us."

The dog whined again, broke free, cantered off and stopped to look back.

"What's wrong boy?" Simon asked. Sirius returned and nuzzled his leg, then ran off again.

"He wants us to follow," Sybil said. "Go on boy, show us."

Setting off on a fast trot, Sirius headed north. Simon and Sybil jogged after him. "Where is he going?" asked Sybil.

"Beats me," Simon responded. "Let's follow him for a while and see where he's headed."

They'd been running behind the dog without let up for a good half hour, when Sybil stopped. "He's making a beeline due north. You don't think he's headed toward the ozone portal do you?"

"Sirius! Come back!" Simon shouted.

The dog kept running. "Sirius, stop!" commanded Sybil.

The big hound slowed, came to a halt and turned to look at them. Then he began to run again, barking loudly.

"Sirius where are you going? Stop!" shouted Simon. This time Sirius came back and began running circles around them, whining and barking wildly.

"Something is definitely wrong," concluded Simon.

Catching hold of his thick neck, Sybil calmed him. "All right, all right. We understand. Lead the way Sirius."

"Hold on Sybil. We need to move faster than this. Let's use the mind net."

"But how do we know where he's taking us?" asked Sybil. "If it's back to Seventh dimension, I don't think that's such a good idea."

"Sirius is pretty wound up. I think we need to check this out. He won't come with us and we can't leave him," reasoned Simon.

"Okay, I see your point, but I don't like this," said Sybil. She joined Simon in creating the net. "Hop on Sirius."

The big male climbed aboard and they sped away. "You have full control Sirius. Take us where you want to go."

Streaking north, they soon encountered the aurora. Sirius knew the way. He'd found it before when he had followed them and was pulled into the abyss. The ozone hole loomed before them. Before they could change their minds, they were drawn into it and were hurtling down through the void. Veering right, they entered the oceanic trench.

"This is different than the first time we came!" Sybil whispered anxiously. "Where do you suppose he's taking us?"

"Trust him. He knows."

In a short time they landed on high ground near the sea forest. Sybil gasped, "The flooding has started!"

All low-lying areas were covered in sea water. The aerial tree roots of the old growth forest, just visible, dangled above the surface. Tops of buildings protruded from the water. Higher areas of the city remained dry.

"How long do you think we have?"

"Don't know. We'd better find Roark."

"But we're on the opposite side. The rookery is across the city."

"Can't get there on foot. We'll have to risk flying over."

Zooming high above the flooded areas, they headed directly to the cliff top rookery in the distance. "Look at that! Many have completed full transformation!" whispered Sybil, peering into the depths.

"The unflooded parts still have amphibious people," observed Simon. "Should we have a closer look?"

"First we need to see the Opeggees. Find out what's happening there. Maybe they can tell us more."

"Right. This time we can land on the cliff top."

Soon they were hovering over the settlement. There was a flurry of activity below. The Opeggees were in crisis mode.

"Roark!" Simon sent out a distress call. *"Where are you? Are you okay?"*

"Simon?" Roark's panicky voice could be heard above the frantic chaos.

"Roark. We're landing right now. Meet you at your place!"

They set down safely in front of Meerak's home. Sirius leapt off the net before it could dissolve and headed off toward the cliff trail.

"Sirius wait!" Simon and Sybil bounded after him.

As he neared the trail head, Roark's distraught face appeared around the bend in the cliff wall. The big hound slid to a halt in front of him, mindful not to bowl him over. He had learned that Opeggees were rather precarious on their feet. Their suction cups could let loose if he was too exuberant with his greetings. He gently nudged Roark's round blue form. It was all he could do to control himself. He began to lick his new friend all over.

"Sirius! Stop that," laughed Roark, giggling with mixed delight. "You sure know how to make a guy feel better!"

When the canine greeting was over, Roark ran to meet Sybil and Simon.

"Boy am I glad to see you guys! What are you doing back here?"

"We got to the Fifth and we saw Icelandia. DOU has returned to Ninth. We were about to leave for Hetopia and home to Third but Sirius was acting so strange. He took off and wouldn't come back to us. We knew something was wrong. He wouldn't stop, so here we are."

"Looks like Aquadorus has started to flood the valley. What's happened Roark?" Simon asked.

"It began shortly after you left. But it stopped for some reason. It has only flooded part way."

"Do you know why?" asked Sybil.

"That's where I've been. I went down the trail to check the high water mark. Our nursery grounds are underwater. But not deep. I can still see the shrubs where I hatched."

"There must be something we can do!" cried Sybil.

"What's to become of you and the Opeggees?" Simon was thinking hard. "Can we evacuate you to the Fifth?"

"The Fifth!?" cried Roark. "I don't think that's possible!"

"Why not?" Sybil's frantic voice made him reconsider.

"Last resort, maybe. Seventh is our home. I don't see why we have to leave."

"Aquadorus is a tyrant. Who can stop him?" asked Simon.

"There are a few people in Aquadria who have nothing to lose by opposing him," said Sybil. "Maybe we can find some allies."

"Too risky," replied Simon. "It would be a long shot."

"What about Calazone and Hermaine? And poor old Rinaldo. No one cares about him. He doesn't seem to have one friend in all of Aquadria." Sybil's heart went out to him. She knew what it was like to be different.

"I wonder what happened to that woman, Adelaide. She must be in big trouble with all this water—if she even survived the flooding," said Simon.

"And I'd like to know more about the far north, where DOU was. What else is up there?" asked Sybil.

"Hey! Maybe you have something there. Let's scope it out."

"What are we waiting for? Let's go north!" cried Roark.

He wanted to do all he could to save his colony. His mind wandered into visions of glory. The accolades he would have— if only he could do this!

"I'm all for that!" agreed Sybil.

They hurriedly made their way toward Roark's home to advise Mother Meerak of their plans. Her worried frown indicated that she was anything but pleased by the prospect.

"Very well," she said, hesitantly. "Get word to me if you can. Roark, Sybil, Simon, please be careful!" She gave them her farewell blessing.

Sirius let out a long mournful howl. He was troubled by the distress he could smell on those around him. The people he loved; they were his responsibility. He was a guard dog after all. Fitfully, he settled on the mind net and they sped away.

"Easy Sirius. You must be quiet if you come with us," said Sybil, stroking his back gently. She glanced back at the Opeggee settlement far below, wondering if they would ever see it again.

"Let's go high," suggested Roark. "Better chance of getting there undetected."

"You know the way best," replied Sybil. "Lead us in."

They left the flooded areas behind and were soon over the compound where they had discovered DOU the dragon. There was a heavy concentration of Aquadrian personnel on the ground.

"Still amphibious!" observed Sybil. "Maybe some of them are not able to change!"

"That might account for the dissension among the Aquadrian folk. Dimondus is obviously hated by a lot of people in Aquadria," said Simon. "Maybe they don't like Aquadorus much either."

"Yeah, he does Aquadorus's dirty work. Thinks he's earned favours there. Maybe he has. Perhaps they need to cut the head off the snake. But how do we make contact? Who can we trust?" asked Sybil.

Checking for clues from the air, they flew on hoping to gather more information. Further along, they came to a conglomeration of halls set up in long neat rows. The appearance of the buildings had a familiar contour.

"Simon! Look at those buildings! They look like the duplicating hall, the one at the lake bottom settlement!"

"Is that why the population seems to be doubling overnight?" cried Simon.

"Surely not! You think? This is all connected?"

"We've had our suspicions all along, haven't we?"

"We did. But this?"

"Beginning to make sense. If Aquadorus is planning on flooding the Fifth—but how do the Aquadrians fit in with Leanoria?"

"I don't think all of them agree with this. At least I hope not," replied Sybil, her thoughts racing ahead.

What about those who have already morphed? Were they being forced through the duplicator and set free outside the gel walls? Is Aquadorus amassing a huge army of Aquatics to do his bidding when the time comes? Are we too late? Can we still stop it? Should we try to destroy the duplicating halls?

She voiced all these fears to Simon and Roark. Roark hopped up and down with excitement.

"I can destroy those halls. You bet. Vulcan sacs. Poof!" he shouted eagerly.

"But first we have to know who is with us and who is not," cautioned Simon. "And exactly what is happening."

"We need to find Rinaldo first I think. He has nothing to lose and he seemed very grateful to us that morning he was hauled in," replied Sybil.

Her compassion for the underdog ran deep. She would love to see Rinaldo succeed for once in his life. Dimondus was a bully, and she was painfully aware, knew firsthand how that felt.

"How do we make contact?" asked Simon. His bafflement struck a chord in both Sybil and Roark. It was very risky.

"Now that we know what's up here maybe we need to bring Profrak on board," suggested Sybil.

"No. We can handle this. The fewer involved, the less chance of being discovered." Roark's adamant reasoning made sense.

"Okay, but do you have enough vulcan sacs on hand?"

"Do I? I'm in charge of the stockpile. I can get in and out for as much as it takes to do the job."

"Good!" said Sybil. "Now all we need to do is make contact in the south if we can."

"Not so fast. I don't think we should destroy those halls until we know what we're up against," said Simon. "And we don't even know what the halls really are."

"He's right," said Roark. "Guess I'm a little trigger happy. Can't help it. All this water!"

"We certainly have our work cut out for us," replied Sybil. "How about we split up?"

"What? Go in different directions? You think that's wise?" asked Simon.

"We don't have much time. Lots to do. Check the halls, organize the vulcan sacs, see if we can find any allies. What do you suggest?"

"All valid points," replied Simon.

"Okay then. I know about the duplicating chamber. It makes sense that job is mine."

"And I can handle the vulcan sacs," said Roark.

"So that leaves me with finding friends in the south," agreed Simon.

Sybil grimaced. The tasks seemed equally onerous.

Roark piped up, "With you two out of the picture, I'll need my two best buddies to help me. I can trust them."

"Give ourselves until mid-afternoon, say third bell and meet back here?" suggested Simon.

"Long enough, I hope," she said, turning toward the halls. "You'd better take Sirius with you. I can't take him into those halls with me. Be careful Simon, Roark."

"You too Syb."

She watched as they sped southward, then decided to hover from a distance and watch for clues. The crowds below were scurrying about frantically. A wedge of recognition slowly pried its way into her awareness. A familiar figure? She'd seen him before. Who was that? Slowly it dawned on her. It was that squadron leader she'd seen the first day when Dimondus marched them into the city. He had stood guard over them while Dimondus refreshed.

"Oh boy," she muttered, scratching her head. What was his name? Helpin? Halcron? Herclan! That was it! She continued to watch. People were approaching Herclan who was set up at a field desk. He seemed to be consulting charts and giving directions.

I wonder if I can get into one of those halls. Maybe at night but that's too far off and they'd be heavily guarded. Crumbs! This was going to be a tough job. Well, who said life was easy? Then—another familiar figure! It was Rinaldo! What was he doing here?

Think fast Sybil. This might be your chance! She watched as he spoke with Herclan. His shoulders squared in an official way and he gave a sharp salute. Then he marched off smartly along the rows of halls, until he reached the last of them. What was he doing?

Sybil watched him unlock the double doors and enter. This is it. I can get in now! She accelerated, widely skirting the compound and swooped in from the opposite direction, landing in front of the open doors. She entered stealthily and proceeded through the echo chamber, willing her feet to tread lightly. It was the same so far! Sybil's excitement rose. Next should come the business section with office spaces, then the mirrored maze.

She crept forward until she entered the narrow hallway in the business area. Someone was rummaging around in one of the offices. Stealing closer, she saw Rinaldo, as expected. He was sorting through files and going through documents.

She was about to turn away, when something scuttled across the floor in front of her. It was tiny and quick. Out of the corner of her eye, she caught the form disappearing around the doorway into the room where Rinaldo continued to work. It launched itself at him and latched onto his ear.

Ears? Since when did Aquadrians have ears? Did he have them all along? Had she missed them? Sybil was flummoxed.

"Ow, ow, ow!" yelled Rinaldo, trying to pry it off. But it held fast.

Unthinking, Sybil leapt into action. She rushed into the room and grabbed the tiny critter by the tail and squeezed. It was hard and crusty, some kind of shelled creature. It made a high-pitched shriek as its jaws let loose. It fell to the floor and Rinaldo stepped on it with his flipper. An ugly cracking sound and a final squeal signified the end.

"Sarah! What are you doing here?" cried Rinaldo, recovering from fright. "Where did you come from?"

He gaped at her, hardly believing his eyes. Then a gleam of satisfaction broke the tension on his face and he laughed and slapped his thigh with glee.

"Dimondus was fit to be tied! What an uproar when you didn't show up for work report at breakfast that morning! Hah!

Old Dimondus got hauled up before Aquadorus. Serves that coward right!"

Remembering their deception, Sybil was unsure of what to say but decided to play it safe for a little longer. She was enjoying his story about Dimondus. And she remembered how much she liked Rinaldo.

"What is happening Rinaldo? Where is everyone? And what was that thing?" she pointed to the crushed lifeless body on the floor.

"It's a rat crab. Vicious little beggars. But the least of our worries. It's Aquadorus. He's flooding the valley, taking over the whole of the Aquatic kingdom. His Aquatic clones govern the high seas. It's only a matter of time before they destroy the gel walls and we're all lost. Aquadorus means to turn us all into Aquamatons. Many are unable to change or don't want to. We've formed an underground. I've been leading a double life."

"Oh Rinaldo!" Sybil's voice held a deep regard for his plight. "That's why you couldn't stay awake on duty."

"Yes. This is nasty business. I played the fool to maintain my cover."

Sybil saw Rinaldo for what he was. A resourceful sort who would do what must be done for the cause. Her regard for him grew with each revelation.

Sizing him up, she decided on a course of action. Whether it was wise or not she did not know, but she made one of those leaps of faith and decided to reveal her true identity.

"I have a confession to make Rinaldo."

"Oh? What's that?"

"You aren't the only one who has been leading a double life!"

Rinaldo perked up. This was an intriguing bit of news. "How so?"

"My real name is Sybil. We didn't fall overboard off a boat. We came through the ozone portal."

"You and Dominic?"

"Yes, but his real name is Simon."

Rinaldo's surprised look was replaced by a grin that was growing wider with each disclosure.

"Say now! This is some new information—might be useful to northern forces! Came from where?"

"Now that's a long story. We entered from the Fifth," she replied, deciding to leave Third out of it for now. "Fifth is in dire straits."

"Yes, we know about Aquadorus's expansion into Fifth. He means to take over everything!"

"I've seen this type of hall in the Fifth Dimension Rinaldo. Aquadorus may not stop there. Could want more."

"No doubt! He's ruthless and power hungry."

"What do these halls actually do?"

"Some of them produce clones, some new prototypes. They use existing life forms and transform them."

Sybil was shocked. Her heart dropped into her stomach, fluttering like an injured bird. What if she and Simon had been sent through? Why weren't they? She thought about the Leanorians the Namors Guardia and the Graenwolven. Her jaw fell open, as she contemplated the implications. Maybe they would have been, if they had not escaped from the Leanorians!

Afraid to ask the next question, she let an uncomfortable silence lapse between them. Rinaldo studied her face, saw the fear, the hopelessness slowly shutting her down. He rummaged his heart for something to say that would stem the tide of loss registering on her face.

Finally he offered a feeble, "Sorry Sybil, I wish I had better news."

Stunned by this information, she fought to get back on even ground. Her equilibrium had taken a dreadful hit. After several moments of horrified silence, she managed to revive enough to stammer, "Ca-can they be changed back to what they were before?"

"We're working on it. That's what I'm doing right now. Going through files. Everyone who has been through this is registered. So many!" His voice cracked with emotion.

"They will change back to their former selves?" she repeated, willing the answer.

From a distance she heard Rinaldo's voice. "Our scientists have been working on that. Right now it is not possible. But we are very close."

It wasn't what she wanted to hear. Very close. Too far, when so much was at stake.

"What is happening right now?"

"It's civil war. We're divided into two camps. Aquadorus in the south and us in the north. We hold the balance right now because we have control of the halls. Once we make the breakthrough, the Universe willing..." His thoughts stalled. The outlook was bleak.

"Simon has gone south to look for reinforcements. We had hoped to make contact with allies down there."

"Bad move Sybil. Don't know how safe that is now. Most who have chosen northern forces have already fled and have linked up with us. Still, he may find a few. I can send help to him if you think..."

"Oh no. Thank you," Sybil interrupted. "I think Simon will turn back when he sees the situation. I will try to find him myself. You have enough to do. Who is in charge up here?"

"Herclan has assumed general responsibility. Hermaine, Calazone and I lead contingents reporting to him. We plan strategy as a united command, operating as a unified force. It works."

"Where are your scientists?" she asked. "How close are they to finding the solution? Can Fifth do anything to help? What can I do?" Her questions bubbled forth like hot lava. "What about the Opeggees?"

The blood left her face as she remembered Roark readying for battle. She must get to him and warn him to hold off on the vulcan sacs. He wouldn't go ahead without conferring would he? No, she didn't think so, but his two friends?

"Rinaldo, I have an urgent matter to see to. I must also find Simon. I'll leave you now, but we'll be back soon. Watch for us. If we aren't back by nightfall please send reinforcements. I'm heading to the cliffs near the Opeggee rookery. I think Simon will go there first. It's familiar territory."

"Most of the area below that is already under water, Sybil. Still it won't hurt to scout it out. Good luck. May the Universe be with you! Hurry back."

Sybil left the hall and headed south immediately. Soon the rookery cliffs were in sight.

"Where are you Roark?" she said under her breath. She scanned the area. Where would they keep the vulcan armaments? She veered toward the back side of the cliffs. Below, she saw Roark struggling to load supplies on his own.

She dropped down swiftly, landing beside him. Sirius, who was left with Roark, gave a happy woof and bounded over to her. "Hi boy," she said ruffling his fur.

"What are you doing Roark? Where are your friends?"

"Couldn't find them, so I decided to get started on my own. I'll go back in a bit and recruit them."

"That won't be necessary right now Roark. We have time." She told him about her meeting with Rinaldo and what she had learned.

"Lucky wing feathers! That is some good news for a change!" Roark did a skip-hop dance, popping his suction cups in a tap dance rhythm. "Where is Simon? Has he returned?"

"No. I'm on my way to find him. He may run into trouble in the south. Come with me Roark."

"You bet! I'm your wing man." He laughed at his pun and Sybil couldn't help but grin too. They were under a lot of pressure and a bit of humour lightened the mood.

"Oh Roark. You truly are one of a kind!"

"Yep, that's me. Only one Roark in all of the rookery!"

"Where do you think Simon would go first?"

"I don't know, maybe the nesting grounds? But they're under water. Still, I think he would begin near there and follow the trail as far as he can."

"Okay then, we'll begin our search there. We can put out telepathic bulletins. Maybe he'll hear us."

Deciding a ground search was best, they set off down the path. Sirius, favouring Sybil, brushed against her left leg every now and then, reassured by her nearness. There was no guarantee that Aquadrian forces weren't still patrolling but they had to take that chance. If they flew over the area Sybil's presence might become known. How had Simon chosen to travel? Was he still out there or had he been captured? Her heart rate increased.

"We have to find Simon fast. All this water. Flooding could resume at any time!"

Made in the USA
Columbia, SC
24 July 2017